A Freeway
In My Back Yard
(a collection of short works)

Daniel Keys Moran

Dedication

THIS IS FOR Richard Kevin Stout Moran. I love you forever.

Acknowledgments

THIS BOOK EXISTS because Steve Perry kept sneering at me for not writing, because Kevin J. Anderson asked me to write four of the stories in it, and because JJ Sutherland at NPR asked me to write most of the essays.

Notices

This edition of "A Freeway In My Back Yard" is copyright © 2010 by Daniel Keys Moran. Individual pieces are copyright in their initial years of publication.

Star Wars: Empire Blues originally appeared in "Tales From Mos Eisley Cantina" and is copyright © 1995 by Lucasfilm Ltd.

Star Wars: A Barve Like That originally appeared in "Tales From Jabba's Palace" and is copyright © 1995 by Lucasfilm Ltd.

Star Wars: The Last One Standing originally appeared in "Tales of the Bounty Hunters" and is copyright © 1996 by Lucasfilm Ltd.

The right of Daniel Keys Moran to be identified as the author of this collection has been asserted in accordance with the Copyright, Designs and Patents Act 1988.

Note

This is FSAnd Version 1.1 of this text.

If this is a pirated copy of the fsand.com edition of Daniel Keys Moran's "A Freeway In My Back Yard," you can do the right thing and support the author of this book by going to fsand.com and buying a copy for yourself. Once you've purchased it, you can refer it to your friends and fellow readers and make ongoing referral fees from their purchases. For more information about the fsand referral program, and how it can actually help you to make money from your reading, go to fsand.com/faq.

If you've purchased this book, you are forever entitled to a new download of the book, whenever a new edition is issued for the sole purpose of correcting errors. If you've noticed errors yourself, you can come to fsand.com/text to suggest copy editing corrections, and if the author approves we'll roll them into the next edition of the book.

Contents

Dedication...................vi

Acknowledgments...................viii

Notices...................x

Essays...................1

A Freeway In My Back Yard...................3

The Road Goes Everywhere...................5

The Vast and Endless Sea...................7

It's Great to Be Me...................9

Motorcycles...................11

Two Guys Talking about Cars...................13

The Conduct of a Gentleman...................17

Freedom Highway...................19

For My Father...................23

Queen Of the Angels...................25

Total Information Awareness...................27

Nonfiction...................29

Speech to the Coalition for
Networked Information (1995)...................31

A Faster Darkness (1995)...................53

Driving to San Antonio (1997)...................63

Infinite Methods (2007)...................75

Fiction...................81

A Day in the Life of a Telephone Pole (1974)...................83

In Cool Blood...................89

STAR WARS: Empire Blues...................119

STAR WARS: A Barve Like That......................145

STAR WARS: The Last One Standing......................171

Roughing It During the Martian Invasion......................235

On Sequoia Time......................257

Spiderman Kevin Stout Moran......................277

Everywhere You Want To Go......................279

Scripts......................283

5-Minute Brick......................285

Pasty D......................293

Dream On: Another One Bites The Dust......................307

A Moment in Time......................341

Essays

*The essays in this section were mostly written for
J.J. Sutherland at National Public Radio. They're
short because they had to be; they only ran three
minutes when recorded.*

A Freeway In My Back Yard

WHEN I WAS a little boy they built a freeway in my back yard.

It's one of my earliest memories – climbing up the hill in my back yard and standing at the edge of the freeway, watching the cars blow by me at 70, 80, 100 miles an hour, sometimes faster than that. I can still see the shocked expressions on those driver's faces ... zooming along from here to there, *making time,* when abruptly a five year old, blue-eyed blond-haired boy appears at the edge of the freeway, sitting on the railing, watching ... imagining the places he would go.

That freeway was the 60 Freeway, the Pomona Freeway, in Southern California. When I was seven years old my parents moved – to a nicer house, yes, but in the new house there was no freeway outside my bedroom window. In the new house, I didn't hear cars rushing by in the darkness when I went to bed at night. I couldn't climb the hill after sunset and watch the rivers of red and white lights go streaming by me.

When I was in my early thirties I moved to Greenwich Village, New York. My first night in the Village was a Friday, in an apartment that overlooked West Third Street near Sixth Avenue, a little stretch of road with two jazz clubs at either end, with an astonishing cacophony of noise from all the people come to party – horns honking, engines rumbling, people yelling, music blasting from twenty competing sets of speakers: the sounds of traffic. I went to bed at ten o'clock that night, completely exhausted, with the window open and the sound pouring in, and slept like a dead man ... until at three o'clock in the morning I sat bolt upright in bed and said *"What the hell was that?"*

A horse had neighed outside my window. In Greenwich Village there are still mounted police. Plainly in my brain, traffic does not include the sounds of horses … .

Today I live in Woodland Hills, California, and I sleep fifty yards from the edge of the 101 freeway. You can hear the traffic blasting by, at rush hour, at midnight, at two in the morning on Sunday, a never-ending river of traffic. It's a comforting sound, a sound I know in my bones, and with it as the backdrop to my nights, I sleep very well indeed.

In a novel I wrote many years ago I said that freeways were America's only native art form. Maybe that's an exaggeration, but only maybe. My will specifies that when I die my ashes will be spread at the intersection of the 10 and 710 freeways, one of the most beautiful places in Los Angeles, or indeed the world. And there are days when I picture the cars lifting up my ashes and carry-ing them off down the freeway … and I imagine all the places that I will go.

The Road Goes Everywhere

ONCE THERE WERE Engineers in this country. They built sky-scrapers, highways and spaceships.

Years ago I had a long argument with a conservative friend about the role of the federal government, and from that argument we agreed that America's greatest accomplishments during the 20th Century were, first, victory in World Wars I and II; and second, construction of the Interstate Highway System. Many years before that argument I had a Jesuit history teacher who felt it was a tragedy the Greeks got conquered by the Romans, because the Greeks were so much more civilized, the Greeks were *artists*.

Screw art[1]. The Romans built *roads*. They were the first ones. They didn't build roads to service the empire; they *had* an empire because they leveled and graded and cambered, laid gravel and then volcanic stone atop the gravel. And the roads made it possible for people to go places, to meet other people and other *kinds* of people. It fostered the exchange of information and led directly to the very idea of personal freedom.

Construction on the Appian Way, the world's first highway, began in 312 B.C. Over the next 700 years, Romans built 55,000 miles of road. Before there were paved roads, any substantial traffic would turn even a good dirt road into a muddy, rutted, impassable mess. Someone traveling hard might make only a few miles a day. But on Roman roads, a courier could make 60 miles a day; and that ability to travel and communicate made the Roman Empire pos-sible.

Within living memory *we* were the Romans. The generation that fought and won World War II next built 43,000 miles of the Inter-state Highway System, built the space program that sent men to the moon ... but since then we have turned inward, we've hunkered down to live small lives in the world they built. We have not lost the

---

[1]   It seems quite possible I am the only person to ever say "screw art" on NPR.

ability to build highways and spaceships, merely the desire; perhaps we can still change that.

We are so accustomed to our freedom that we have forgotten its source. Before the ballot box there was the road. The road gave us the ability to go somewhere else, try something new, become something better. That freedom – to vote with your feet – may be more important than the ability to cast a ballot. In the U.S. a vote is usually a binary action, for this, against that ... but the road has endless choices: the road goes everywhere.

The Vast and Endless Sea

IT'S THE YEAR 2000, but where are the flying cars? I was promised flying cars. I don't see any flying cars? Why? Why? Why?

– Avery Brooks, IBM Ad

And where's my damned future shock? Alvin Toffler promised us we'd have future shock, but I don't have future shock, no, *I* have the fucking[2] Internet. Where are the rocket cars, and where the hell is the space program I was promised? When I was six years old I sat on my father's lap while men walked on the Moon; it's my first memory of the outside world. I still remember my father telling me how important it was, how it gave us hope of escaping the planet of our birth and going elsewhere. And yet ... science fiction writer Jerry Pournelle wrote once that he always knew that he would live to see the first man on the Moon; but that he'd never dreamed he'd live to see the last.

We were supposed to go places. That was the essence of the optimistic future we were promised; we'd get off this ball of rock and see the universe. But that future was a lie, because it cost too much, to afford it we'd have had to cut back on our professional sports or makeup or cruise missiles, so here we are living in the future and we don't have rocket cars or double-decker freeways or jet backpacks or real spaceships or a mission to Mars that isn't a dreadful joke of a movie, we don't have a Moonbase or orbital hotels, small bonus on the hotels because I feel really sorry for the first newlyweds who actually try to lose their virginity in zero gravity, but for the rest of us, *please*: the only reason the space program still exists is that people need to put up satellites so that they can beam radio shows at you for $9.95 a month, and here we are, instead of the future we were promised we have this gyp, this horrible Internet, and as pathetic as it is, just how stupid would you feel *without* it? Because if you squint, if you rub your eyes hard, you can at least pre-

---

[2]   I'm sure NPR didn't let me say "fucking" on the air. But I probably did write it like that.

tend this is the future, even if it really is just 1975 with better ergo-nomics.

The ad we ran at the beginning is from IBM, and it goes on to ar-gue that you don't need flying cars, because the Internet cuts down on your need to travel, and this is true, I don't need to travel as much because the Internet gives me a substitute for travel. I don't need a flying car ... I just want one. I want one, I want one, *I want one*. The Internet is the booby prize, what we got *instead of* the fu-ture we were promised. We wanted better ways to travel, rather than a way to numb the pain of staying home. If you had to choose between the Internet and the feel of Tahitian sand between your toes, or the sight of the Earth rising over the mountains of the Moon, would you really have picked the Internet? I wouldn't ... and I wish I'd been given the choice.

Antoine de Saint-Exupery wrote, *If you want to build a ship, don't drum up the workers to gather wood, divide the work, and give orders. Instead, teach them to yearn for the vast and endless sea.*

The next chance you get, on some dark clear night, go outside and take a look at the Moon. Men walked on that thing, when I was a little boy.

It's Great to Be Me

THERE ARE AT least three flavors of the anthropic principle: the weak anthropic principle, which says the universe was created to sustain life; the strong anthropic principle, which says the universe was created to produce human beings; and the very strong anthropic principle, which says this is my universe, buddy, and you're just renting.

This actually has something to do with your car. The first real powered vehicle, a steam-powered tricycle capable of a speedy two-and-a-quarter miles per hour, was built in 1769. The reciprocating four-stroke gasoline engine – basically the engine in your car today – came in 1876. After that automobile construction took off. There were 50 car builders in the U.S. in 1898; there were 241 in 1908, when Henry Ford perfected the assembly line and built the first Model T. The worldwide automobile industry hasn't changed in any major particulars since then, over ninety years ago.

On Christmas Eve, 1906, the first known radio broadcast took place in the United States. Fourteen years later, in Pittsburgh in 1920, the first commercial broadcast took place, on radio station KDKA. Less than two years later there were over 500 licensed radio stations in the U.S.

The 1920s were unique in American history. Household electricity became common, as did the automobile and radio. The average American's world expanded in a way that was never seen before and has not been seen since. Suddenly you could hear people talking across the country, or around the world; if you owned a car, you could get on the road and go see those people and find out how on Earth they got those outlandish opinions.

Who put the first radio in a car is in some doubt. Motorola claims to have done it in 1930; Blaupunkt claims the Blaupunkt Autosuper in 1932; and Delphi claims the first radio actually installed on the instrument panel, in 1936. Whoever did it, the next major improvement in your car radio took until the 1950s, when

FM debuted – but something interesting happened first. In 1945, Arthur C. Clarke proposed what he called the communications satellite; a satellite that orbited the Earth in geosynchronous orbit, beaming content down from orbit. For five decades this insanely great idea was wasted by people who used it to broadcast foolishness like ... television ... until, on June 30, 2000, the world's first satellite designed to deliver radio broadcasts was launched by Sirius Satellite Radio.

This is a remarkable chain of events ... and boy, it's great to be me. Because by the Very Strong Anthropic Principle, the entire purpose of all of this has been to produce this moment we're now sharing ... you, sitting in your car, listening to me, Daniel Keys Moran, on the Sirius Satellite Radio Network. Don't think I don't appreciate it.

Motorcycles

FASTER, FASTER, FASTER, until the thrill of speed overcomes the fear of death.

I'm chasing 140 mph down the 10 freeway, 4 A.M. on my Honda Magna. I'm crouched over the bike, lying on it, and I've passed 130 but now I can feel odd harmonics working their way through the bike as I hit 136, 137. I never do reach 140, the needle hovers just under the mark as I blast through San Bernardino and out into the desert, and finally I ease back on the throttle and come back to the world, and I know this: *I need a faster bike.*

I never bought it. In August of 1995 I leave work at three and it's psycho hot outside, I'm wearing my helmet and a backpack, no leathers for fear of passing out in the furnace heat, traffic is bunched up tight with people trying to beat the rush, I'm in the left lane and Bruce Springsteen is, I swear, running through my head:

I got a bad desire

Oh oh oh I'm on fire

The guy in front of me swerves, brakes, I touch his bumper with my front tire, and I hit the ground at 55 miles an hour, a van behind me, a semi to my right. I hit the ground on my back, on my backpack, I feel the big bone in my right calf pop the moment my right foot touches the ground, and then I'm swimming on concrete as the backpack shreds beneath me, slapping at the pavement to try and push myself out of the way of the van coming up fast behind me, of the semi that's breaking hard to my right, the bike slid under the semi and vanishes and I swim between the machines until I've slowed enough to come to my feet ... and there I was, there I was, *there I was* ... on the 101 with the top of my right knee ripped off, my right tibia broken, that tough canvas backpack and its contents shredded straight down to the shirt, a quarter inch from the precious spinal column it ended up protecting ... and I looked so good, because I'd been immortal again.

I remarried after that, and now I have four children, three from my wife's previous marriage, two older girls and two young boys, and most mornings my boys and I have a boy-hug before I go to work, sitting together with our arms around each other. I'm never going to break 140 now. Dying didn't scare me when I was young, but that was a long, long time ago ... five years and then some.

*

> *This piece didn't work and JJ Sutherland knew it; I don't think we even recorded it. Most new parents[3], those who aren't stupid or broken, have that moment of, "Oh, my, children really are the most important thing in the world!" This is normal and commendable, but it's not of great interest to anyone except the person having the moment. In further news, sex is great!*

---

[3] I, as my wife Amy was fond of saying, got the zero-to-sixty version of it, marrying a woman with three children and then having a fourth child almost immediately

Two Guys Talking about Cars

                    DAN
    Welcome to Two Guys Talking About Cars.
    Your hosts today are me, Daniel Keys
    Moran, and Richard Kevin Moran, age 2.

                  RICHARD
    Two guys talk about cars. Daddy and
    Richard.

                    DAN
    Right. We're here today to talk about
    important matters. Orange Lamborghinis.
    The Batmobile. The 1987 Buick Grand
    National. And Hot Wheels. Recently
    Richard and I went to the L.A. Car Show
    together. Richard, what was the best
    thing at the car show?

                    RICHARD
My orange! Zoom!

                    DAN
The orange Lamborghini?

                    RICHARD
My orange. Zoom! I'm driving!

                    DAN
I'd never been to a car show with a
two-year old boy before. Richard was
completely infatuated with the cars,
and it led me again to the not too
surprising observation that boys and
girls are different. No little girl
I've known, and I've known several, had
that slack-jawed stupid car love, not
at the age of two ... and the
fascinating thing is that at 2 years
and 4 months Richard could *tell the
difference* between cars that were cool,
and stuff not to bother with.

                    RICHARD
Volvo is *yucky*.

                    DAN
The yucky stuff didn't get a second
glance; but we had to drag him away
from the Ferraris and Porsches and
Formula One cars - usually by promising
him the car for his birthday. I
promised Richard well over a million
dollars worth of cars for his birthday.
Fortunately eight months will have
passed by then, and he'll have
forgotten. I hope ... Are you getting
cars for your birthday, Richard?

                    RICHARD
Yeeeeessssss.

                    DAN
Umm ... Okay. How many?

                    RICHARD
Lots of cars. Batmobile and my orange.

                    DAN
You're getting the orange Lamborghini?

                    RICHARD
My orange.

                    DAN
How about some Hot Wheels instead?

                    RICHARD
Otay. Hot Wheels. And a motorcycle.

                    DAN
That's a deal. A little motorcycle for
Richard.

                    RICHARD
No no no no no. Big motorcycle. *My big*
motorcycle. I'm riding!

                    DAN
Uhm. Okay. Mama might have something to
say about that.

                    RICHARD
Mama can ride too.

                    DAN
Well ... that's going to take some
negotiation. How about ... a Grand
National for Daddy? A low-mileage 1987
Buick Grand National? And you get a big
motorcycle and take Mama for a ride.

                    RICHARD
Otay.

                    DAN
You back me up, I'll back you up. Is
that a deal?

                    RICHARD
It's a deal.

                    DAN
Say "Grand National."

                    RICHARD
"Grannal!"

                    DAN
Close enough. I love you, Richard.

```
          RICHARD
I love you, Daddy.


          DAN
This has been two guys, talking about
cars.
```

The Conduct of a Gentleman

THE AD IN a California newspaper read: "Wanted. Young, skinny, wiry fellows. Not over 18. Must be expert riders. Willing to risk death daily. Orphans preferred. Wages $25 a week. Apply Central Overland Express."

T.K. Whipple wrote: "Our forefathers had civilization inside themselves, the wild outside. We live in the civilization they created, but within us the wilderness still lingers. What they dreamed, we live, and what they lived, we dream."[4]

One of our dreams is about the job those young men applied for, a job riding for the first overland mail service connecting the East with the West – the Pony Express. The young riders, at least one as young as 11, also took an oath "not to use profane language, not to get drunk, not to gamble, not to treat animals cruelly and not to do anything else that is incompatible with the conduct of a gentleman."

The first rider left St. Joseph, Missouri, on April 3, 1860. The riders took a brutal route to Sacramento, California; west across the Rockies to Salt Lake City, west across the desert to the Sierra Nevada, up the Sierra Nevadas and back down them into California, then, as now, the most beautiful land on Earth; crossing Kansas, Nebraska, Colorado, Wyoming, Utah, and Nevada in between. During its operation the Pony Express delivered to California both news of Lincoln's inauguration, and the outbreak of the Civil War. The last run was completed on November 21, 1861.

The Pony Express was a dismal failure as a business. It lost $200,000, a large fortune by the standards of that time, in its 19 months of operation. Its founders died broke and broken.

And yet ... in a time before telephones, before radio and television, before the telegraph, the 183 men who rode for the Pony Ex-

---

4   I lifted this straight out of the opening of *Lonesome Dove*. It's the quote with which McMurtry starts the book; I wouldn't be familiar with Whipple otherwise.

press covered 650,000 miles and carried 34,753 pieces of mail; and lost only one rider and one bag of mail along the way.

Technology killed the Pony Express. I say "before the telegraph," and it was … by 19 months. The Pacific Telegraph Company opened a line to San Francisco on October 24, 1861, and the Pony Express faded into history.

But that image – a young man riding out of the East, in his bright red shirt and blue pants, trailing a cloud of dust, crossing two thousand miles on horseback – that image has not faded. It's been burned into our cultural memory, and we're fortunate for that. The promise not to do anything "incompatible with the conduct of a gentleman" – the brave and faithful completion of a job, in difficult and dangerous circumstances – has fallen out of favor as an ideal in our culture. This shouldn't have happened, but it did; and perhaps the only encouragement we can take is that somewhere, in our hearts if not our heads, we all of us know better: because every one of you knew, before I even started talking, what the Pony Express was.

Freedom Highway

WOODY GUTHRIE WAS born on July 14, 1912, in Okemah, Oklahoma. At 15 he left home to ride the freights. Guthrie is still important today because of the experiences he had and the songs he wrote in the years that followed.

He wrote a national anthem for those of us who wanted one that didn't involve bombs, a national anthem for the poor and the forgotten. *This Land is Your Land* is, aside from being one of the most beautiful songs ever written, an angry song that had two of its stanzas censored by society at large. You probably learned the opening stanzas of the song in school, but you've probably never heard the lyrics *"By the relief office I seen my people/As they stood there hungry, I stood there asking/Is this land made for you and me?"*

To this day there are conservatives who despise Woody Guthrie, in part because they suspect him of being a communist, but in part because he dared to write a song as strongly patriotic and strongly critical as "This Land is Your Land."

It's hard to overstate how important Woody Guthrie was to the music and literature of the road. Without Guthrie, Bob Dylan would not have existed and could not have written *Highway 61*. Without Guthrie, Bruce Springsteen could not have written *Born to Run* or *The Ghost of Tom Joad*.

If Dylan and Springsteen would not have existed without Guthrie, Guthrie as we know him would not have existed without the Dust Bowl. In 1935, during the depths of the Depression, the Great Dust Storm tore across the flatlands of Oklahoma, wind-burnt the topsoil into dust and literally blew away the farmland. As Guthrie wrote in *So Long, It's Been Good to Know You*, the Okies "loaded their jalopies and piled their families in" and took off westward down Route 66, looking for a life in California. Guthrie himself didn't even own a car; he hitchhiked and rode freight trains to get to California.

During the course of his life Guthrie wrote 10,000 songs. I only know a few dozen of them. But the ones I do know, though filled with the rage of a man who had lived in poverty and seen people he loved destroyed by it, are also touched by the hope of the road, by the relentless belief that it's not just possible but noble to pick up and try again somewhere else.

Woody Guthrie died in New York on October 3, 1967. Twenty-five years later Texas Governor Ann Richards proclaimed October 3 "Woody Guthrie Day" – and they renamed U.S. Highway 60, which crosses the Panhandle, the Woody Guthrie Memorial Highway.

I was hired to do these commentaries because NPR thought I had something worth saying, and the skill to say it. But when you're in the presence of the master sometimes the best you can do is shut up and get out of the way. The last stanza of "This Land Is Your Land" is:

> *Nobody living can ever stop me,*
> *As I go walking that freedom highway;*
> *Nobody living can ever make me turn back,*
> *this land was made for you and me.*

The preceding essays were done for the show The Way In. *The motorcycle essay was never recorded, and I'm not sure that all the essays that were recorded were ever broadcast. (Also, I never got paid for them – a check showed up once for fifty-odd dollars, which was a fraction of the $300 or so each one was supposed to go for, but that was it. I was working 90 hour weeks at the time at an internet startup[5] where I had 100,000 shares of stock, so I ignored it rather than try to track it down. Given what the stock ended up being worth, I'd have done better to chase down the NPR money ....)*

The Way In was NPR's first new newsmagazine in 30 years. It was an interesting idea, but it didn't pan out: it was going to be broadcast over the Sirius Satellite Radio Network. Unfortunately, the Sirius network had problems getting off the ground – the satellite receivers that were supposed to go into the car were not ready to ship, even though NPR was already in production with the show – and as a result NPR ended up producing a show with no means to deliver it. They canceled "The Way In," and I stopped writing essays ... which may have been just as well: I was the "transportation" guy on this show, the car guy – and as you can see toward the end there, I was already stretching the subject matter by my tenth essay.*

A couple years later, JJ Sutherland, producer of The Way In, *got a chance to produce another show,* Day to Day. *It was a bigger sandbox, and the following essays were written for it.*

---

5   VideoGreetings.com. Long since gone into the archives of the internet way-back machine....

For My Father

Intro by JJ Sutherland:

If you're a boy growing up without a father, how do you learn to be a man? Some take their cue from the macho men in movies. Clint Eastwood as Dirty Harry or John Wayne as ... well, John Wayne. Writer Dan Moran was luckier. He had a model right there at home.

MY FATHER WAS no film hero. He was better than that. If he had tangled with John Wayne, the Duke would have had his clock cleaned. If he'd taken on Clint Eastwood, he'd have made Dirty Harry's day ... miserable.

When my dad was 70, two punks mugged him. They hit him in the face several times before he knew what was going on, bruised him dreadfully ... and then he settled down and destroyed them. He knocked one attacker out with a single punch. He got the other one in a headlock and started pounding him in the face. The first guy stirred slightly so my old man stomped on his hand and broke it and stood grinding that broken hand into the sidewalk until the police arrived. When my sister called me at work to tell me, I yelled loud enough to be heard in the next building: "My Daddy is Bad!"

He *was* Bad. He was also a liberal and a feminist, at least after he had daughters, but he had no patience with people who didn't think that being a man meant something, something tied up with violence, with courage, with never, ever, ever quitting. When my parents got divorced, the last thing Dad said to me before leaving was, "You have to be a man now: take care of your sisters." The last thing he said to me before he died was "Take care of your sisters." He never did quit himself. He fathered us to the end. He had cancer for three years before he died – and told no one, I think for fear that they would treat him like he was dying. He could handle dying: he couldn't handle being treated like something less than a man.

My father's sister wanted me to speak at his funeral, and I couldn't ... so this essay will have to do. My father's name was Richard Joseph Moran and, thanks to him, I have never had to wonder what it meant to be a man; I just had to look.

Queen Of the Angels

Intro by JJ Sutherland:
Of course, many writers toiling in Los Angeles do
try to create a fictional version of the City of Angels,
and here's one of them, Dan Moran.

THE WHOLE WORLD thinks Los Angeles is shallow. It's not. It's just warm, and dry ... it hasn't rained on the New Year's Day Rose Parade since 1955! Lord knows, we Angelenos *could* be deep. And depressed. And wet. I'm sure everyone in Seattle is deep, because they can't do anything except read and watch old, meaningful movies of the sort they don't make anymore, since they can't go outside for nine months of the year.

Let me tell you something about Los Angeles, anyway. I don't merely live in Los Angeles: I live in La Ciudad de Nuestra Senora la Reina de los Angeles – the City of Our Lady, the Queen of the Angels. Where do *you* live? In New York? Dallas? Chicago? Unless you're very lucky, you don't live in the City of Our Lady the Queen of the Angels.

Alas, there are more of us lucky people every year. I've done my bit in this area: for years I sent the same Christmas card to everyone I knew around the country. It said: "Greetings from L.A.! Things are a bit whiff at the moment, from all the dead fish caused by the radioactive sludge that regularly washes up in Santa Monica Bay, but fortunately, the incense we burn in our Satanic rituals helps mask the odor."

The card showed a picture of what I suspect was New Jersey, but was certainly not any part of L.A.

So listen up ... the truth is Los Angeles really is a lousy place. Don't visit us. You wouldn't like it here. We hate tourists and we have nasty traffic and we *shoot* people who don't merge correctly. We got homeless mimes and homicidal inline rollerbladers and racist cops who worship Jack Webb and will drag you from your rent-al car and beat you bloody for wearing Sacramento Kings gear. We got women with bad, exploding boob jobs who are liable to ruin your lunch at any moment; since cheeseburgers do not taste better with silicon, you'll need to carry a barometer with you at all times, and stay indoors when the air pressure gets low. We got skin cancer that travels like the common cold. All those low-budget zombie movies? They shoot them on location in Santa Monica. Folks, Hollywood is the original Matrix … and the things they show you on television are not true. It rains *all the time* out here. Those sunny dry Rose Parades I mentioned? Special effects, baby.

Hey, you ever been to the Excalibur, in Las Vegas? They got a dragon in that joint!

*

> *I wanted to work in a line about the lonely mating call of the independent producer, echoing across the city's canyons: "Hey, baby, wanna be a star?" – but couldn't manage it in the space allotted.*

Total Information Awareness

IN MAY OF 2002, I participated in a Space Command mailing list on next-generation weapons systems. I've been a database designer over 20 years; one of the things I proposed was a monstrous world-spanning Database Of All Things ... highly automated, with humans involved only at the endpoints, feeding the system with data, and consuming the system's output. This database emphasized military applications, including the tracking of terrorists. Here's the conclusion of my recommendations:

> *This work could begin today. It's not something that needs to wait for better storage or more computing power, though it will benefit immensely from the inevitable advances in those areas.*

Seven months after I wrote that, in December of 2002, the Pentagon announced the creation of TIA, Total Information Awareness ... and put John Poindexter in charge. He was an astonishing choice: a former National Security Adviser who had been convicted of conspiracy, perjury, defrauding the government, and destroying evidence. These convictions were later vacated because the testimony he was convicted on was immunized by Congress – one of those "technicalities" the law and order crowd find outrageous when it's not one of their own.

Here are some of the things this convicted perjurer's database is supposed to track, as eloquently summarized by William Safire: "Every purchase you make with a credit card, every magazine subscription you buy and medical prescription you fill, every Web site you visit and e-mail you send or receive, every academic grade you receive, every bank deposit you make, every trip you book and every event you attend." But it's even worse than Safire realized: TIA aimed to take all that information, and tie it into your biometric profile – that's your face, your fingerprints, your retinal patterns, your DNA.

Even the logo was creepy: an all-seeing eye atop a pyramid, beaming a death ray across the Earth, with the logo *Scienta est Potentia* – "Knowledge is Power."

There are things in this everyone will hate. Because it will track all purchases, it'll know who's buying guns – the national gun registry the NRA has long feared. Because it will track your reading habits, your phone and internet use, it'll know who you're talking to, and about what, which'll freak out the liberals. It'll know what your finances are like, and your health – we have damn little real privacy today: if TIA is implemented, even the illusion will vanish. Government officials will have access to every meaningful detail of your lives outside of those tucked safely away inside your skull. Orwellian? We need a new word: Orwell never imagined anything this thorough.

Since December of 2002, there's been a lot of complaint about TIA. In May of 2003 the Department of Defense addressed the concerns people had about Total Information Awareness. They renamed it: "Terrorist Information Awareness" – and they got rid of the creepy logo.

Nonfiction

Note: I gave this speech to the "Coalition for Networked Information," on Tuesday, April 11, 1995. It went over well – lots of applause and laughter.

Interesting crowd; older executive types, probably an average age somewhere upward of forty. Also the largest crowd I'd ever spoken to; about four hundred people, or a bit more.

The speech as follows is neither exactly as written nor exactly as delivered; after delivering it I went back in and, listening to the tape of the speech, added some off-the-cuff stuff that either struck me as nicely phrased, or funny. One of them was "the deadliness of our abstractions."

Speech to the Coalition for Networked Information (1995)

OKAY. THE HUMAN race is doomed, everyone in this audience has a real shot at personal immortality[6], and our grandchildren are going to be gods – but we'll come back to that in a bit.

About two months ago I received the following mail from Paul Evan Peters. It was:

"The theme for this meeting is 'Digital Library Research and Development.' I hope you will take this opportunity to present your views on the Clinton Administration's National Information Infrastructure (NII) initiative, the public fascination with the "information highway" concept, and, as Speaker of the US House of Representatives Newt Gingrich puts it, 'Toffler third-wave information revolutions,' whatever they may be. Your works of fiction provide both serious insights to and humorous commentary on matters of

---

[6] Not so much. Paul Evan Peters, the individual who invited me to give this speech, died less than a year after I gave it. Fifteen years later, I still think that personal immortality is a real likelihood – for my children. It's going to be touch and go for people my age.

this general sort, and I am intrigued at the prospect of you addressing them head-on in this talk."

Now, these are pretty broad guidelines ... and I interpreted them
to mean that I could talk about pretty much whatever the hell I
wanted to as long as I touched the bases. So yes, we're going to talk
about the information superhighway, we're going to talk about
Toffler third-wave information revolutions, whatever they may be –
but mostly we're going to talk about truth, fairness, and Michelle
Pfeiffer.

I want to start by introducing myself. I'm a thirty-two year old
science fiction writer, and my life has been defined by two events.
The first event is my earliest memory of the outside world; in the
summer of 1969 I was six years old and I sat on my father's lap and
listened, along with half the world, as Tranquility Base told us that
the Eagle had landed. Surely one of the proud moments, not just in
the history of the United States of America, but in the history of the
human race. It is perhaps worth noting, in today's political climate,
that this amazing feat came not from private industry, but from the
(in recent years) thoroughly despised federal government of the
United States. We're going to come back to that later.

Also late in the 1960s, a book was published, and if anyone here
has ever heard of it I'll be pleasantly surprised. It was called *Philosophy and Cybernetics*[7], and I ran into it when I was about twelve
years old. That book had a profound impact on me. Early in the
book it talked about the difference between data and information.
Data is merely bandwidth; a thousand zeros is exactly as much data
as a thousand characters of text – but a thousand characters of text
can carry a message of considerable complexity and significance.
When we talk about bandwidth, then, we're simply talking about
the ability to carry raw data, regardless of the information content
of that data.

---

[7]   Not only had someone in the audience heard of it, he had a copy and mailed
      it to me. Academics are Not My People, but they are an interesting bunch.

At the age of twelve I learned that information was an abstraction of data. You can have data without information, but you cannot have information without data. To put it another way – to put it, in fact, in the immortal words of Frank Zappa and the Mothers of Invention: "Information is not knowledge. Knowledge is not understanding. Understanding is not wisdom. Wisdom is not truth. Truth is not beauty and beauty is not love and love is not music. Music is the *best*."

This will, it seems to me, be the central issue of the upcoming century – we're drowning in data, inundated by the very tools we designed to help us, networks and the personal computer. Drowning in data, swimming in information, and we need a way to bridge the chasm between data and knowledge – you're on your own with the most of the rest of Zappa's observation – understanding, wisdom, truth, love, that's all your job. Beauty and music I can help you on – Michelle Pfeiffer, Melissa Etheridge and Counting Crows, and you can trust me on this one.

So here's where I came from, and you can all apply your filters to what I say from this point forward, because I'm identifying my biases pretty clearly: one of the greatest accomplishments in human history came at the hands of a federal government that current political wisdom says isn't very good for much of anything; and in the history of Unintended Consequences, there is probably nothing since the invention of writing that comes anywhere close to rivaling the chaos that has been, and will be, caused by the development of the personal computer, and the internetwork that has come to tie us all together.

BERTRAND RUSSELL SAID, "Men fear thought as they fear nothing else on earth – more than death. Thought is subversive, and revolutionary, destructive and terrible; thought is merciless to privilege, established institutions, and comfortable habits; thought is anarchic and lawless, indifferent to authority, careless to the well-tried wisdom of the ages. Thought looks into the pit of hell and is not afraid … Thought is great and swift and free, the light of the world, and the chief glory of man."

All true – unfortunately, thought is limited by the relatively clumsy tools we have available to communicate with one another, speech and writing. Of the two, speech is less accurate and usually more honest. Honest writing is very hard, because we get to edit ourselves before someone else sees it –

I made a decision when I set out to be a writer that I was going to be as honest in my writing as I could force myself to be. Now, telling the truth, this is where it gets tough for writers. Writers, all the good ones, are Natural Born Liars. Actors, good actors, are also good liars; but actors only need to be able to lie for short bursts, while the cameras are on them. A writer who's doing his job has to build up a long lie, an extended lie over an extended period. Actors are good liars; writers are good liars with good memories.

Now, to be a good writer – I won't talk about greatness, the word is overused and there would be the implication that I consider my-self a great writer, when that's something no writer can ever really know about his own work – in my heart I think I am a great writer, but there is every possibility that I could be wrong about that. Any-way, *good* writers, ones who move people, who make a lasting im-pression on their readers, tell the truth about the human condition.

Some of the truths about being human are embarrassing. We can be petty beyond belief. Our bodies are imperfect; our minds are imperfect; our lives are imperfect. (I'm thirty-two years old, my knees are shot, Michael Jordan is four months younger than I am and can still dunk from the free throw line. I'm losing my hair and I have a pimple on my forehead today – you wouldn't think it'd be too much to ask for, to stop breaking out *sometime* before you go bald.)

There are people who will kill other people, or themselves, rather than be embarrassed. Usually the expressions of our embarrassment are less violent than that – the way it expresses itself, in written communications, when you sit down to read a story, what you get as often as not is a writer who's trying to look good. We're all guilty of it, I am. Not just writers, all of us – people we love, or would like to, don't return our love because we don't meet their standards; people who would like to love us, or simply to be our friends, we turn away because we're ashamed to associate with them, to be seen with them. We want to look good – even if that means behaving with no style.

I'm not saying that everybody actually does this or behaves this way – I am saying that impulse to do that, and worse, is there, in all of us. I've never killed anybody, but I've damn sure wanted to, I mean put a bullet in 'em.

I don't act on that desire because it's uncivilized, because the animal nature that's in all of us is so scary and so primal and damned nasty sometimes that we lie about its very existence – to other people, sure, but to ourselves as well, I think mostly as a way of keeping ourselves from acting on it. And any lie that you tell over and over and over again, becomes, through transmutation, a kind of truth – for you. Believing a lie is often easier than living with the truth that as a species we're violent, we're selfish, we're lazy, we're either barely civilized – or uncivilized and sometimes we fake it good.

That's what I mean by the desire to look good. Most "looking good" is a lie. Not all of it – sometimes you just look hot – but most of it, I think.

That desire to *look good* is amazingly common – and it's fatal to writing stories about human beings in all their variety. To write well you must be willing to go naked into the world. To tell people by the hundreds of thousands, or by the millions if you're fortunate, that *you* are flawed. There are only two ways to characterize – to describe somebody from the outside in, and to write about yourself from the inside out. The second approach is almost always better because it's principally where resonance comes from. If you really want to know what somebody thinks about himself, look at how that person treats the people around himself – because there's no one else out there except you. I don't know what goes on inside you folks – I *assume* that it's the same sort of thing that goes on inside me. There's no way for me to know, but my best guess, as it must be for everyone, is that other people are pretty much like me. In fiction, one of the things this means is that villains never *think* they're villains.

Telling the truth is important *because it's dangerous.* Because it's rare. Because by God the power structure not just today but through all time will nail your ass to a tree, or gun you down in the streets – for saying the wrong things, things that endanger the ability of the current power structure, whatever it may be, to stay in power. And by power structure, I don't mean Congress and the President; every one of them was bought and sold a dozen times before they ever reached office. I mean the liberalmediaelites *Time Magazine*, and *Newsweek*, and *ABC*, and I do mean Rush Limbaugh and the stations that carry Rush Limbaugh, and General Motors and IBM and Microsoft and the oil companies for whose sake we sent our children to die in the Persian Gulf, for whom we blew apart thousands or perhaps tens of thousands of Iraqi children, for no better reason than that the United States of America doesn't have a sane energy policy because it's cheaper not to – when people are dying before their times, it's almost always because money is involved.

What the power structure is afraid of is that we're going to learn to recognize the truth when we hear it.

Before Watergate and Viet Nam, the American public, as a whole, believed everything it was told, and since then it doesn't believe anything, and both of those extremes hurt us because they prevent us from recognizing the truth. The very words we use have been debased almost beyond recognition – "truth" and "lie" become Orwellian Newspeak, interchangeable words, because what the power structure has done is tell us to be honest with each other, but really what they *want* is for us to lie, to them, sure, but most particularly to each other, because when you get lied to all the time you lose the ability to recognize the truth when it does show up. But the problem they have is, they can't tell us that they want us to lie, because that would be telling the truth, which is the *last* thing they want. So instead what they're forced to do is tell us to tell the truth, but do it in such a way that *we know they're lying.* So this is the social equation we're dealing with – we're supposed to lie and we're supposed to lie about the fact that we lie and then everything will be fine.

That's "hypocrisy" and it's among the more distinguishing feature of American life.

As an exercise, if you're wondering how valuable telling the truth is in this society, tomorrow I want you all to go to work and try telling the truth to your boss. Go to him, say just for today, sir, I'd like you to try, try really hard, to not be more of an jerk than is in your nature. Now ... your nature is that you're a pretty big freakin' jerkoff. But you're worse when you try, and *I can tell the difference.*"

Make sure your resume is up to date before you try this experiment.

Probably the single most useful thing the American public could stand to be taught is that the mass media, all of them, exist to sell advertising, to convince you that you're driving the wrong car, you smell bad, and your girlfriend is ugly.

How does this tie in?

My favorite President, Thomas Jefferson, said, "Shake off all fears of servile prejudices, under which weak minds are servilely crouched. Fix reason firmly in her seat, and call on her tribunal for every fact, every opinion. Question with boldness even the existence of a God, because, if there be one, he must more approve of the homage of reason than that of blind faith."

Question everything, Jefferson said; and whenever you run into an answer that translates to "Do it my way because I'll hurt you if you don't," you know you've found an enemy who is not civilized and whom you need not treat as though he were; whenever you run into someone who says, "This is the answer because I/We Say So," you know you're dealing with a fool, and an authoritarian one, too.

This is from *The AI War*. It's set in the year 2080 – it's a history lesson buried about midway in. My hero, Trent the Uncatchable, has been off Earth for about ten years, and he's just returned – and he's just about to go across the Interface.

EVOLUTION OF THE Machine:

In 1945, the computer ENIAC is designed to calculate ballistic trajectories. It can do in twenty seconds calculations that takes humans three days.

In 1958, Jack St. Clair Kilby creates the monolithic integrated circuit at Texas Instruments. A year later, Robert Noyce, working at Fairchild Semiconductor, creates monolithic integrated circuits based on aluminum traces laid on a silicon oxide surface, laid on a silicon substrate.

Doped sand has become the basis of computing: slightly more than a decade later, in 1971, the first microprocessor is invented, the Intel 4004.

In this, the dawn of the Information Age, Gordon Moore formulates Moore's Law: silicon density, he predicts, will double every two years. The implications of this are profound. As density improves, so does power. As power improves, so does usefulness. As usefulness improves, so does cash flow —

By the end of the twentieth century, chip fabrication plants are a multi-billion dollar proposition; chip production, a hundred billion dollar industry.

And this was before nanotechnology and optical engines.

EVOLUTION OF THE Interface:

In the Beginning is the Card.

The Hollerith card is a piece of stiff paper. It holds room for eighty rows of punched holes. Each hole holds a single binary: punched or non-punched. Keypunch operators program them by punching holes in the paper.

This is the mid-twentieth century. Well into the twenty-first century, the bulk of all computer systems will still default into an eighty-column text display. Most users of those systems do not know that their screens display eighty columns worth of characters because they were originally designed to replace teletype machines — which were designed to print eighty column Hollerith cards ... .

Hollerith cards are fed into the mainframes they service, in sequential order. Complex programs — "complex" by the standards of the day; they rarely reach eight kilobytes worth of instructions – are given to the computer in a sequence of Hollerith cards, a "batch."

Well into the next century, computer users will still perform basic programming of their computers by listing series of commands in "batch" files. Functions change: language persists.

Hollerith cards are, with the passage of time, replaced by magnetic storage: "core" memory. Core memory consists of small, circular electromagnets, cored out, which are switched on and off to store binary information. Keypunches are replaced by keyboards whose keystrokes are stored directly into random access storage, and from there to magnetic storage – tape and spinning magnetic media. Teletype printers evolve into monochrome cathode ray tubes: the green cyclops.

A seminal event is the creation of the Xerox Alto. It has what macho purists of the time call a "WIMP" interface – Windows, Icons, Mice, and Pull-down menus. A company called Apple licenses it from Xerox; a company called Microsoft steals it from Apple.

But the key innovation here is not the interface: it's the use of bitmaps to display data. Bitmaps are capable of presenting information more densely than the traditional text-based interfaces prevalent at the time. Monochrome bitmaps interfaces are surpassed by eight-bit color bitmap interfaces, which are surpassed by true color bitmap interfaces, which are surpassed by true color three-dimensional interfaces.

Screens and keyboards and voice. Rich data types proliferate – all designed to mimic reality. Screens are replaced by goggles, and later by holos; speakers are replaced by earphones. Keyboards are supplemented and sometimes replaced by verbal input.

Early in the game, it's still possible for unaided humans to navigate the Net manually. The hardware is faster than they are, but the software is dumber.

But hardware gets faster; Moore's Law. And the software gets smarter –

Tracesets appear. Humans, webdancers, sink into a meditative state. Complex biofeedback, and sometimes drugs, helps them to interpret the signals those early tracesets pump directly into their forebrains. It enables them to continue to function in the InfoNet, even as the Net gets faster and the first replicant AIs appear. But they're chasing a moving target –

Since the dawn of the Information Age, webdancers have used programs to help them navigate the Net. The programs get smarter with the passage of time; they become agents. They interact with the Net as their owners have instructed them. The agents evolve into Images.

The Images help. For a while –

The target moves.

Inskins appear. The skin is breached. Neurons marry silicon.

It's a stopgap, but it works, briefly. Humans become second class citizens in the InfoNet that they built; only the greatest of the webdancers, the Players, dancing the InfoNet through their Images, are able to compete with the AIs who increasingly dominate the

Net. Images themselves become more and more like AIs, are invested with more processing power, more ability to make independent decisions without recourse to the far-too-slow-wetware sitting on the other side of Interface.

By the time Trent the Uncatchable is born in 2053, there is two hundred times as much computing power built into his optical Image coprocessor, as can be found in the entire world in the year 2000. Most of that power is inaccessible to human beings: AIs and expert systems, Datawatch and a rare few Players, make most of the use of that capacity.

In 2069, Trent the Uncatchable is married to an inskin neural coprocessor. It models the way he thinks, and then it tries to think like him. Usually it succeeds.

In 2080, Trent the Uncatchable has been away from Earth for over a decade. He has been away from the Wind – away from the "unreal" world that Players call the Inside – the world on the other side of the Interface.

In the experiential world of humans, time is measured not by the passage of seconds, but by the passage of events. Reality is measured by its complexity.

By 2080, cyberspace, the Inside, the Crystal Wind, is over a hundred years removed from the hardware and software on which it was born.

Early in the year 2080, a milestone is passed.

More events are occurring in the Wind than in Realtime:

The Inside has become larger than the Outside.

YOU ASKED ME to talk about the Internet, about the future of the Information Superhighway. Well, the future of the Internet is ... Reality.

There are two principal kinds of reality. The first one is trivial and obvious – water is wet, stones are hard, don't step in front of the truck. The second kind of reality, and unless you're a mathematician or engineer, probably the more interesting one, is internal, and it consists of our thoughts as influenced by our perceptions. And our perceptions, the information of our senses, is – bandwidth. Yes, there is an external reality – but that's not the world you and I live in. We live in a world defined for us by the data we receive from senses that are amazingly crude. We can see only a tiny part of the electromagnetic spectrum; we can hear only a tiny part of the range of sounds. Our sense of touch is useless at extremes of cold and heat, and our senses of taste and smell are relatively crude mechanisms for analyzing chemicals.

So, we, as human beings, live in a very imprecise world. A world where our perceptions of reality are far more important than actual reality. Is it any wonder we don't understand one another? We live in a crazy world and it's *our fault*. The problem isn't that the world doesn't make sense, it's that *we* don't make sense –

... I'm telling the truth. I read once in the paper a story about how psychologists wanted to do a study to discover why people feared murderers – we have a government that, over the last fifteen years, they've spent *five trillion dollars they don't have*, we had those people trying to alter the Constitution to *force* them to do something they *could* do already. You want to balance the budget in this country? We change the salary structure for Congress and the President. Every year they don't balance the budget, we don't pay them. Every year they do balance the budget, we pay them – half a million for the Representatives, a million for the Senators, a million and a half dollars to the President, the budget would be balanced every year.

Where the hell was I?

Reality – reality is bandwidth. Hang on to this idea. We're gonna come back to it.

I WAS A computer salesperson, and then I was a programmer, long before I was a successful science fiction writer.

(Y'all know the difference between a computer salesman and a used car salesman? The used car salesman *knows when he's lying*.)

It's very strange writing science fiction in a world that moves as fast as ours does. In *The Long Run*, published back in 1989, I described a scene where the novel's main character, Trent the Uncatchable, stored information in a ten terabyte infochip. When I wrote this in 1988, 386's with hundred megabyte hard drives were all the rage in small businesses. As file servers. Today, in April of 1995, a gigabyte of hard drive storage can be had for around three hundred dollars – when I wrote my first draft of this speech, by the way, a gigabyte went for four hundred dollars. Assume prices continue to drop as they've been, around 2008 you'll be able to put a terabyte of storage on your desktop for $2,500.

And that's assuming no major breakthroughs ... no nanotechnology, no quantum effect storage technologies, no three-dimensional optical storage. I don't believe any of those assumptions.

That scene I wrote in *The Long Run*? It was set in the year 2069. Today I am convinced I missed the mark on that prediction by at least fifty years. It's happened to me before; once I wrote a short story which made passing reference to a laser printer – I saw my first LaserWriter at a trade show about a week after that story sold.

Alvin Toffler called it future shock. I think it is more accurately *present shock*. Even SF writers are having trouble staying ahead of the curve.

AS A CULTURE we, and probably most of those in the audience with me, are Aristotle's children. This is not a bad thing, but it has its limits.

The parts of us that control the voice boxes, the parts of us that type away at the keyboard and read the words laid down on paper: we are the part that looks at itself. Intellectualism is not generally respected in America, and there's a reason for this: most intellectualism is a conceit, no more complex a thing than the intellect admiring itself. As my friend Steve Barnes has pointed out, there is nothing inherently useful in chess, surely the most intellectual of activities, or there would be fewer chess masters playing games in parks at a couple bucks a game to try and make their rent.

There is, in short, nothing inherently valuable about our intellect, except to the degree that as a tool, it permits us to build better caves. (What do *you* want out of your life? To be warm and well-fed. To be strong and healthy. To love and be loved. These are the basic needs of a human organism, the things that make life worthwhile. It's obvious, but perhaps worth saying, that happiness has virtually nothing to do with the state of your intellect. Some of the brightest people I know are also among the unhappiest.)

In a society that sometimes despises learning, I am reluctant to point out that we who do value it are often crippled in other ways. I've known a lot of computer nerds – I am a computer nerd myself, and I use the phrase with the greatest respect – but as a rule, those of us who get excited when the latest beta software shows up, who chatter lovingly about the latest neat hack, are poorly socialized, out of touch with our emotions, and need desperately to be taught how to stretch, how to breathe, how to eat, and in general, how to use our bodies as something other than a transport mechanism for their brains.

Intellectuals of this sort have existed, no doubt, in every society civilized enough to support them. Aside from the subject we have chosen, there is nothing unique about the computer nerd.

It's the only difference worth mentioning.

The subject.

TAKE A STEP back – and let's look into the future together.

We are reinventing the world. We've set the ball spinning with little concern for where and how it's going to stop. There's no point in talking about the technology, except to note that everything gets bigger and smaller and faster and cheaper and more colorful. Monday's projection is Tuesday's bleeding edge, Wednesday's toaster, and Thursday's Circuit City closeout. All we can talk about meaningfully is the process.

We *can* talk meaningfully about that. About the places we'd like to go, and how we as a culture – we the computer nerds – should plan on getting there. About the places we are strong and the places we are not.

Drexler's 1987 *Engines of Creation* is the seminal work on nanotechnology, a field that is almost by definition computer-driven. The human genetic code is being mapped. AI has been around, depending on how you define it, for several decades now, and is finally starting to show worthwhile results: it would not surprise me to see self-aware machines within twenty-five years. (It would not surprise me *much* to see them within fifteen. Remember where we *were* fifteen years ago.) In the lifetimes of most of the people involved with the computer revolution, we will be able to design a human being, to design a self-aware computer, and to redesign ourselves. Out in Arizona, Alcor is busy freezing corpses in the belief that these dead people can be made to live again. I don't have a time frame, and neither do they, but I don't think they're wrong.

Our species is on the verge of changes that will fundamentally alter what it means to be human ... and *we* are the people driving that change.

We have a quiet moment, right now, to reflect. If we don't, we can *make* a quiet moment. To reflect on ourselves, and on the children we are going to have – flesh and otherwise – and how we would like them to grow up. We *need* to ... because the wheel is spinning faster, and we may not get too many more chances.

FOR YEARS NOW, well over a decade, Steve Jobs has been saying that computers are bicycles for the brain. The hell with that, I want a Ferrari. There's nothing wrong with bicycles if bicycles are all you've got, and today that's all we do have. That's going to change, though. In the forseeably near future we're going to get rid of the damned bicycles and get bionics for the brain, little computers that sit inside our skulls and do the same things our neurons do, only lots faster. Unless we get into the issue of religion, we have to accept that what makes us us is physiology, structure, the patterns of the interconnections between neurons that make up a human computing device. There's nothing inherently holy about neurons – we kill 'em all the time, by drinking, by drug use, or by just simply getting old, and there's so many of them that most of us never notice them going.

The problem a lot of people have when confronted with the idea of personal immortality via a computerization of their thought processes is the idea that they are their brain. We're not – but let's accept that and take a look at what your brain actually is, a collection of ten billion neurons packed into gray jelly and surrounded by bone. As it happens the human brain, in adults anyway, doesn't regenerate neurons once they die. But there's no reason to assume that we can't regenerate neurons, artificially, by regrowth or, more interestingly, by implantation of artificial neurons. I mean that quite exactly – a small computing device that precisely duplicates, via neurochemical transmitters, the behavior of a human neuron. So you have, in place of the dead neuron, an invisibly small piece of doped silicon that behaves *exactly* the same way that neuron would behave if it were still alive. That's called backward compatibility, and it's very important in the computer upgrade industry and will be more important yet in the Brain Upgrade Industry. Your neurons – or million neurons – have been replaced. But you're still you; your brain still works exactly as it always did; with one very minor difference.

You can do things you couldn't do before. Those million extra neurons are *also* an incredibly powerful neural net that turn you into a lightning calculator, that let you run amazingly powerful scientific and statistical analysis software, that let you do anything you can do today with the most powerful computer on the face of the Earth – and then some – in the privacy of your own skull.

You don't have to use that circuitry. You can turn it off, except for the basic features that duplicate the neurons that have died. You can remain 100% human with no changes, be as much *yourself* as you ever were –

Almost nobody is going to. Once you get used to having perfect memory, once you get used to the idea that somebody else's memories, perfectly encoded, can be transmitted to you and allow you to *live* the events they've experienced, once you've tasted the fruit of the tree of good and evil, to live in a world where you and Michelle Pfeiffer can – have dinner together – whenever you want to, you will never go back.

Reality is bandwidth, remember? I'm going to talk politics for a bit now. I'm a liberal where children are concerned, a libertarian where adults are concerned – and thinking very seriously about running for the House of Representatives, for whatever that's worth. One of the worst things about being human is that good people, people of good will – don't live in the same reality you do.

There was a period several years back now, when for the space of several months I went inside Operation Rescue, partially as a spy for the Clinic Defense Alliance of Los Angeles, and partly as research for a book. Operation Rescue is one of the groups that blockades abortion clinics, and undoubtedly some of OpResc's more extreme members do more than that. If there is a political movement in the United States that I more fundamentally disagree with, I've never heard of them. And yet – during my time inside Operation Rescue, I got to know a few of the people pretty well. And they were *good* people. Sincere, dedicated, hard working – they were motivated and brave and tireless – and sometimes they reminded me an awful lot of the people I knew over at the Clinic Defense Alliance.

How does that happen? How can two sets of good people end up in such diametric, unyielding opposition? Different belief systems, based on different experiences. My experiences working with homeless people lead me to believe that our current welfare system, vile as it is in many ways, costs us less than those homeless people cost us, not in the long run but in the short run; that it costs us less than the prisons we will be forced to build to incarcerate the ones who turn to crime because they're hungry and cold and angry. I could be wrong about this – but I'd love the opportunity to take my convictions and experiences and drop them down into Newt Gingrich's mind – to take Speaker Gingrich's experiences and convictions and drop them directly into my mind – and see what the result would be.

I'll tell you what I *think* the result would be. I think the result is that the human race, as sad and funny and occasionally noble as it is, is over. It is the deadliness of our abstractions that makes us what we are as a species – and the time is coming when we will have the option of ceasing to deal in abstractions, when we will be able to deal directly in experience – in understanding, rather than knowledge, or information, or in, thank the Lord, that most useless of all things, data.

A science fiction writer by the name of Vernor Vinge created the idea of the Singularity, the idea that at some point events will become so complex, happen so quickly and with such subtlety, that humans as currently constituted can't understand what's going on. I doubt we're two generations away from that point, myself. Our children, two or three or five generations from now, will be gods – they'll live forever, or close enough to make no difference from where we stand.

Something better than us is coming.

I WANT TO close by talking about what happens between now and the time when the future has arrived – and that means talking about education – and that means talking about money.

Money is power. The most interesting thing about the idea of money is that it makes it possible to measure something in previous ages we couldn't be sure about, and that something is power. There are other types of power, and I won't say otherwise – but with rare exceptions, in a capitalist market society, even those other types of power hinge on the ability to make money from that power, from your looks, or your learning, or your connections.

In 1765, John Adams said, "Liberty cannot be preserved without a genuine knowledge among the people ... the preservation of the means of knowledge among the lowest ranks is of more importance to the public than all the property of all the rich men in the country."

There are people who will tell you today that the Federal Government isn't good for much of anything – except, maybe, providing for the defense. Those people were not sitting in my father's lap in 1969 as Neil Armstrong stepped out onto the surface of the moon, listening to my father tell me how important this event was, how it gave hope for the entire human race. There are things the Federal Government is not competent to do, and other things it should not do – but building infrastructure – that's what the space program was and could be again, it's what the interstate highway system that Al Gore borrowed the name "Information Superhighway" from was – building infrastructure is one of the things the federal government does very well indeed.

If a liberal political philosophy stands for anything, and I am no longer sure it does, then it *must* mean that we are committed to the leveling of the playing field for everyone. Competition is a good thing; virtually any competition helps to grow the pie that we're all eating out of. Fair competition is better, you get a better quality pie when the cooks are chosen on the basis of their skill. The Republican Party has talked of late of an Opportunity Society – and I salute them for that, *if* it means that we intend to work toward a world where a black child has the same opportunities as a white child, where a girl child has the same opportunities as a boy child – and rather more to the point, where the child of poor parents has the same opportunities as the child of wealthy parents. The universe is not fair and it is never going to be fair. But we are human beings and we can *try* to be fair, we can *try* to give everyone the same opportunities, and one of the ways to do that is to see that the Information Superhighway goes into the schools, by seeing, as John Adams put it, to "the preservation of the means of knowledge among the lowest ranks." There is no better use of our dollars; there is no better investment we as a society can make.

One of my favorite writers, Trevanian, wrote, "The Americans seemed to confuse standard of living with quality of life, equal opportunity with institutionalized mediocrity, bravery with courage, machismo with manhood, liberty with freedom, wordiness with articulation, fun with pleasure – in short, all the misconceptions common to those who assume that justice implies equality for all, rather than equality for equals."

We live in a world where there are winners and losers, and I don't think that's ever going to change and I am not sure it should[8]. There are problems that cannot be solved as long as we remain human beings, and the reality that we are people of different skills, drives, and desires, is surely one of them. But fairness, which is in the final analysis almost entirely an issue of education, and of education's flipside, which is poverty – fairness is not among them. We can end ignorance, we can end poverty, the deck is stacked in our favor – and if it doesn't happen, if in the closing days of the 21st Century, our great-grandchildren are sitting together in New York City, or Washington D.C., or Marstown, arguing about what to do over the same problems of fairness and justice that face us today, it will be because we ... as individuals and as a society ... failed ... *when we had no conceivable excuse* ... to fail.

My dad said a thousand times if he said it once, it's money that matters in this world, and Pop, this one was for you.

Ladies and gentlemen, thank you for having me speak.

---

[8]   I am sure it should not. DKM, 2010.

A Faster Darkness (1995)

AS A WRITER I am a fan of the dash.

I used to use ellipses, and I thought in those days that what writers needed was a two-dot ellipse: ..

Four dots means a sentence has been completed and left to trail off, three dots that a thought has been left incomplete; one dot means the sentence is over. You can pause with commas, a small pause, or pause with semi-colons, a larger pause. I used to think that in between a semi-colon and a three-dot ellipse we needed an in-between pause, a two-dot pause, a pause that is..that long.

Perhaps we do need one. Precision is a virtue. But even if we had it, I probably wouldn't use it. I no longer have time for it.

I've grown fond of dashes. A dash is the swiftest of stops. "Zooming to a stop," I told my first wife once – though I was talking about driving my car, a Grand National with a great engine and merely adequate brakes. Dashes zoom. They are very modern and exactly what you require when what you want is to pull the reader through your story without pausing and without letting the reader pause.

Life is fast and writing about it requires strict measures.

Something interesting happened to us all almost without our noticing it. When the world changes fast enough, the world ceases to be the background against which our lives are played out. The *condition of change* becomes the background. Change ceases to be change as we once knew it, and the only change worthy of note would be if the changes were to stop – if things were to revert to being always the same, that would be a change worth noticing. The idea that change will always be with us is in some ways comforting.

WHEN I MOVED to New York there was no sense of discovery, no sense of the strange. I was born in a large city, Los Angeles, and raised there. New York was just another large city – dirtier and with worse weather and the people there have accents.

In March of my first year in New York a girl called my name on the street, Second Avenue around 68th Street, at three in the morning. It was clear and direct: "Danny," which is a name only my sisters and other immediate family call me by, and I thought she spoke in my sister Jodi's voice – that California accent – though Jodi was three thousand miles away. When I looked across the street there was nobody there. I wanted to rush home and call my sister and see that she was all right, for we are taught that such messages are warnings. Instead I went to my coffee shop as I'd planned, and wrote for a few hours. I didn't write this account that you're reading – I worked on a screenplay about a time traveler and the woman he almost falls in love with.

I think it's a good screenplay, though what I think is unimportant. What is certain is that if it were as good as *Terms of Endearment* or *Ordinary People* it would not be as good as *Terms of Endearment* or *Ordinary People* – the audience would not approach it the same way, with the same expectations; they would pay attention to the special effects and the costumes and the sets instead, and the producers would worry about the effects budget instead of the dialogue.

Sometimes I hate writing science fiction.

I called Jodi in the morning. She was fine.

IT'S A CLICHÉ that we are most truly alive in the presence of death. And like many clichés –

One hundred and twenty miles an hour, down the dark freeway. It's three A.M. on the 10 Freeway, East, toward San Bernardino, California. The motorcycle shudders underneath me, low rumbles that crawl up slowly through the frame. I feel them start in the tires, harmonics that work their way through the bike and into me.

At that speed your tires barely touch the road beneath you and the freeway's slow gentle curves, designed for cars moving at seventy miles an hour, come at you with terrifying speed. The inside of my helmet is slightly fogged but I'm afraid to use either of my hands to crack the vent.

You make speed slowly – one hundred and twenty-five, one hundred and thirty – and the bikes shudders up against its limits, speedometer twitching up above 135, twitching up toward 140, falling back –

YOU WALK A lot in New York. It makes no sense to have a car in Manhattan, unless you're extremely well-off, or for some reason *must* have one; it costs $300 or more just to rent a parking space for a month – more than that, to get a good parking space, for a car worth having. The subway is cheap and cabs aren't expensive, and while I was there I learned to enjoy walking. I did a lot of it, hundreds of miles of it in the daylight and the dark, but that girl only called my name once.

Toward the end of his life Philip K. Dick started talking to beams of pink light – God, you know. This has not happened to me yet. I am not convinced that girl was real, or unreal, and probably she was not God – at least there was no beam of pink light in the vicinity either before she called my name, or after. If she *was* God I am not impressed. I would hope God could work up a better effect than that.

I can't shake this unpleasant feeling – and I've tried – that the girl's name is Lita Germain. If it is she came out of one of my stories.

While my first marriage was ending I outlined a story called *Heat and Love*, where I took a good, virtuous man, James Camber, and in a black Irish rage had him kill a woman he loved. I read it in public several times thereafter – at the end of the first section, every time I've read it, one or more of the women in the audience has cried:

Lita stares back at Camber, shaking, and then out of some depth of her own anger slaps Camber once.

Camber is still for just a moment, and then he hits her, hard, the way he would hit a man. It snaps her head straight back and slams it against the wall, and afterward, trying to remember, he is never certain whether he might have killed her with that blow, or with one of the blows that followed; she never makes a sound, never makes a move to defend herself, and he hits her over and over again, holding her upright with the force of the blows, until suddenly something simply stops inside him, the rage vanishing as suddenly as it came, the realization of what he is doing coming home to him. He takes a single step backward and Lita folds to the floor like a rag doll, and Camber stands over her limp form, looking down on her, staring at her with a sudden and immense horror, a horror so profound he literally ceases to breathe. He takes a step toward her, and then kneels next to her, lifts her from the floor and sees that her head is bent over to the side, that her neck is cleanly broken, that Lita is dead. He sinks down on the floor next to her, lifting her up into his lap – as he had once held her in the afternoons when she came home from work. He sits with her, cradling her in his arms. He does not notice when the tears begin, realizing that he is crying only when he cannot see Lita clearly any longer; and then something breaks within him, and he sobs like a child, crying helplessly through the long night. The morning finds him that way, still sobbing with the dead girl as the sun rises over Los Angeles.

IT HELPS, IN all this, to understand that there are two kinds of reality. The first one is trivial and obvious – water is wet, stones are hard, don't step in front of the bus. Call it Engineer Reality, Problem-Solving Reality, they wrote stories about Engineer Reality in *Astounding* in 1955 when they weren't conquering the universe and making it safe for white Americans of a certain social class.

The second kind of reality is internal – our thoughts as influenced by our perceptions. Our perceptions are *bandwidth*. Yes, there is an external reality – but that's not the world you and I live in. We live in a world defined for us by the data we receive over a limited bandwidth, from senses that are terribly crude. We can see only a tiny part of the electromagnetic spectrum; we can hear only a tiny part of the range of sounds. Our sense of touch is useless at extremes of cold and heat, and our senses of taste and smell are crude mechanisms for analyzing chemicals.

So we live in a very imprecise world, a virtual reality of our own making, a world where our perceptions of reality are far more important than our Engineer Reality – the problem isn't that the world doesn't make sense, it's that *we* don't make sense:

I read once in the paper a story about some psychologists who were doing a study to discover why people feared murderers.

WE ALREADY LIVE in a virtual reality, or else "virtual reality" could never be made to work. We're easy to fool – evolved that way.

THE EAST RIVER has a real beauty to it. It's a piece of the wild that's been enclosed by concrete where it runs between Queens and Manhattan. The concrete won't last – maybe two hundred years or a thousand; but the river is old and it will be here when Central Park has grown out to enclose Manhattan again, in two hundred years or a thousand, and the concrete that now encloses it has crumbled and worn away. There is a sense of the river's power, of its capacity for violence, that the concrete does nothing to allay.

Corpses end up in the river in the winter – suicides, murder victims – and the people we used to call bums before we decided that sounded too harsh. Today homeless people end up in the river. In the cold the corpses sink to the bottom of the river, into the dark water. They stay there until spring when it gets warm and the gases of corruption start bubbling up inside them and then they come popping up to the surface like balloons, sometimes carrying concrete blocks up with them. I saw one in early April and it made me wonder, for the first time, what my character Camber had done with Lita's body after killing her. The river patrol came and hauled the body out of the water and I felt an intense surge of nausea. The body was a shapeless gray mass and I couldn't tell if it was a man or a woman. It could have been a woman –

The scene from *Heat and Love* came to me while I watched them pull her up out of the water. It was a waking dream, more vivid than the sight of the body being pulled from the river or the smell of river with its hints of sea salt and sewage, sharper than any real memory I have ever experienced in my life. The world blinked –

and then he hits her, hard, the way he would hit a man. It snaps her head straight back and slams it against the wall

NOTHING LIKE THIS ever happened to me before. I don't have hallucinations and I don't have waking dreams. And I've never hit a woman in my life.

TWO OR THREE years ago I was up late, reading. I don't remember the book, just the phrase – it described someone as the sort of person who would read another person's diary.

Suddenly I was shaking with a rage, a black fury I hadn't known was in me. My father did that. I kept a diary once, when I was a teenager. I didn't do it for long – maybe a month. He found it and he read it and then commented on what he'd read. It did not occur to me until years later that this was not simply a thoughtless piece of rudeness from a man without tact – he had tact when he wanted to use it – but a ruthless attempt at control from a man who had never trusted anyone in his life, not my mother, not his brothers or sisters, not even his own children.

He seemed a big man when I was a boy, and that was not my imagination; he was, as I became. He was handsome as a movie star, black Irish, charming, and I loved and hated him with a terrible passion. He didn't hit me often; he'd have killed me, when I was a child, if he'd ever hit me with his full strength. When he was forty-four and I was eleven he had a heart attack. By the time I was old enough to even think about hitting him back – surely by the time I was old enough to know that I wanted to – he had a heart condition that might kill him if he got angry.

I sat in bed at two in the morning, sixteen or seventeen years later, trembling with an anger that knotted my stomach, dying for someone to hit, while my girlfriend slept at my side.

I LOVE SPEED. *Faster, faster, faster, until the thrill of speed overcomes the fear of death.* It's the best thing about Los Angeles, though nobody ever called out my name as I drove or rode along the darkened freeways late at night, at a hundred or a hundred and twenty miles an hour, with the windows down and the radio up. I had to go to New York for that.

It seems strange with all the science fiction I've written, much of it set in New York, that a dead girl from a story in present-day Los Angeles should have followed me there. Lita Germain seems very real to me; too real, in a way, to be put down on paper. Speech and its extension, writing, are the manipulation of symbols that we pretend have common meaning. But they don't and the subtleties are always different – sometimes the broad strokes, too. We don't mean the same things with the same words, so putting Lita down on paper is just another way of killing her; we won't see the same person when I'm done, you and I.

AUGUST 24, 1996. The 101 freeway, South. Friday afternoon at about 3:30.

It's a bitch of a day. Temperatures hovering around 105. I'm on the bike and not wearing leathers because it's so damned hot I'm afraid I'll have heat stroke. I'm wearing a backpack, jeans, boots, and a long-sleeved pink shirt. Riding through the air is like riding through a furnace – the wind heats you as you cut through it.

Friday afternoon, and people are leaving work early, to get a jump on the weekend. Traffic is bunching up already and speeds are down to a tightly clustered 55 miles an hour.

I've got Bruce Springsteen in my head – *I'm On Fire*. I'm in the far left lane and there's a van about five feet behind me. A car about five feet in front of me, another twenty feet in front of him. A semi back and to the right. I know these things without thinking about them; 350,000 miles of driving L.A. freeways will teach you to map; to know where things are even when you aren't looking at them. It's the same spatial wiring you use on the basketball court, flying down court with teammates you haven't looked at, knowing where they are without seeing – all of that probably comes out of the time we spent in the trees, living in three dimensions. So when the guy in front of me hits his brakes for no apparent reason, I know instantly I'm in bad trouble. I hit back brakes and then front to no avail. My front wheel rides up on the guy's back fender. The bike flips out from under me and I go down doing 55 or close to it.

The memory of the moment is clear. I hit on my back and tumble once and I feel my right leg snap the moment I hit and then I'm sliding down the freeway backward, the backpack shredding beneath me, watching the van and semi come up on me, hitting their brakes and swerving to miss the sliding projectile. The van goes by me first, inches away, and I slap at the pavement exactly as you would do the backstroke in a swimming pool, trying to swim across the pavement and away from first the van and then the semi. (The next day there are bruises on the tips of all ten of my fingers.) I slow and slow, flip once and tumble –

I looked *good.* I slowed and came to my feet almost in one motion, weight up and off the broken leg and lifted my hands, palms outward, to the hundred-odd cars that had just braked to avoid hitting me. Grinning. Alive.

I BELIEVE IN free will.

Isn't that a ridiculous statement? If quantum mechanics is an accurate model of reality, then we are biochemical machines, and underlying the biochemistry is the reality of neurons that fire for no fucking reason other than that an atom chose to jump one way rather than another, because a wave function collapsed in one direction rather than another, all just *because* –

And yet there *appears* to be a connection between what I decide to do, and what I do; between how I plan and the results I achieve.

If free will is anything, it's the mechanism by which we navigate the collapse of the eigenstates.

I GOT MARRIED the second time while I was in New York.

My sister Jodi called me late from California only three days before the wedding, with Heather this time, five years after divorcing Holly after seven years with her –

Jodi mentioned – in passing – that Holly had had a baby, a boy, with that tall guy she's married to now: Baby Donovan, named after that singer from the '60s she always liked.

I hung up and sat that night, rushing into the future, motionless in the dark quiet with the sleeping stranger in my bed, my fiancee, three thousand miles from home.

Driving to San Antonio (1997)

FROM THURSDAY THROUGH Tuesday morning, I drove one and one sixth percent of a light second –

To put it another way, if I'd started driving toward New York from Los Angeles, I'd be somewhere in the middle of the Pacific right now. (Well, more toward the bottom of it. The middle bottom.)

LAST THURSDAY I decided to go to the World Science Fiction Convention in San Antonio, and I decided I would drive. I've driven to San Antonio before; a buddy and I did it when I was about 20, and I remembered the drive as not being all that bad. About 1100 miles, I thought, and I would make it in about 14-16 hours driving.

Thursday night I had an acting class from 7-10. I set off down the 10 freeway, Westbound, at 10 P.M. My sisters have a house a couple miles off the 10 freeway in San Bernardino, and I hadn't seen them in a bit, so I stopped off in San Bernardino to visit for a little while, and to leave them my pager, which doesn't work out of state. We had a nice conversation, played a few games of Boggle, and I got on the road about 1:30 A.M.

I HAD THOUGHT about flying[9], but I like driving, and the distance seemed not too unreasonable. Besides, I've got a story[10] I've been wanting to write for a long time, set on the desert somewhere out in New Mexico/Arizona, about a man on a motorcycle being chased by vampires. I wanted to find a good, really eerie, desolate stretch of road to set the opening scene – the character is on his motorcycle, in the rain, wearing a helmet with a shattered faceplate. The other people he's been riding with have just been slaughtered and he's riding at 100 miles an hour in the rain, the cold rain spraying in

---

[9]   This was probably technically true in the sense of, "Thank God I don't have to get on a plane." I can fly, but I don't like to.

[10]   This became *Hell, Next Five Exits*, and it wasn't even set in this cycle of the universe when I got done with it. It'll be in my next collection, which will have most of my Continuing Time short fiction.

through his smashed helmet – and the vampires following him are gaining on him. (He thinks … .)

GOING THROUGH ARIZONA, I averaged about 90 miles an hour. I lost time the last hour – about sixty miles from the border of New Mexico, I came up over a long curve and at the far end of it a State Trooper was waiting. I was watching for it so I hit the brakes immediately and went from 100 to 70 within seconds – no time for him to get the radar gun on me. I passed him a few seconds after that. He sat and watched me go.

I watched my rear view mirror. About two miles on I saw a white speck come down the road. I set cruise control at 70 and just sat. About 5 minutes later, the State Trooper came roaring on down the highway, lights flashing. I watched him come. He blew by me without slowing.

About ten minutes later I came around another blind curve. He was sitting there waiting for me. I cruised by him without slowing, doing 70. Minutes later he cruised by me doing about 90 … lights off this time. He pulled over in front of me and settled down to 70 himself and rode ahead of me for several minutes … then sped up and moved on down the road until I couldn't see him again.

Twenty minutes later, another blind curve, he was waiting for me again. I hadn't touched the cruise control. I rolled by him at 70. This time he followed me, all the way to the New Mexico border. Just before the border, he pulled up alongside me, and waggled a finger at me. Don't do that again. I nodded at him, crossed into New Mexico, waited until he was out of sight behind me, and pushed it back up to 100.

THE LANDSCAPE AROUND the 10 freeway, through New Mexico, could be modeled with very low geometry, some bump maps, and probably no more than a megabyte worth of texture maps.

About 10 A.M. I pulled off the road and took a nap for half an hour. My eyesight was starting to blur.

I HIT TEXAS about 11 A.M. and cruised into El Paso. This was when I first realized just how badly I'd miscalculated. The sign for San Antonio said 600 miles – 3/4 the distance I'd already traveled.

For the first time I remembered that my friend and I had split time at the wheel, 14 years ago – and that I'd slept when he was driving.

I REMEMBERED WHY I dislike Texas. It's as ugly as San Bernardino. And there's a lot more of it.

I REACHED SAN Antonio at 7:30 P.M. Not counting the rest at my sister's, I'd been on the road for about 19 hours. It was a total of 1400 miles.

THE WORLDCON WAS fun. More fun than the one in Los Angeles last year. Last year in L.A. I was there for one day, Sunday, to appear on a panel I'd agreed to be on. A photo of me from that panel is on the LAcon web page – I wish they would take it off. That photo is two days post-motorcycle accident. I'm still wearing a temporary splint on my broken leg – they wouldn't cast it until Monday. I'm bleeding, road rash, beneath my clothes. I haven't slept much. I'm in fairly substantial pain and the pain medication has caused me to retain liquids –

– that is, I'm saying, the worst photo anyone's ever taken of me. Including DMV photos.

NOT MUCH BUSINESS at WorldCon. I got to visit with Wil McCarthy, who I've never met but knew was going to be a friend, Greg Benford (who invited me to visit with him on Sunday, but I was unable to, and really regret) and, briefly, with my good twin Kevin Anderson. I also got to spend several hours with Amy Stout, which was very nice.

"DAD SAYS TIGERS don't even like ice cream!"

"Tigers don't know if they like ice cream until they've tried every kind."

GOT BACK ON the road Sunday afternoon. Drove through Texas intending to stop in El Paso for the night. Cruising along, I got nailed by Texas's smartest state trooper –

Hot Texas day. Heat waves shimmering along the road. Cruising along at 100 mph. I see a blind curve coming up, so I slow down to 70 to pass it. Nothing there, just more heat shimmers, so I speed up again –

I'm at 85 mph when one of the heat shimmers vanishes, and there, in a depression in the road, is a state trooper waiting for me. I'm completely nailed. I cruise by him at 85, watch him pull out, and I pull over without waiting for the lights to come on. He had me get out of the car and it took him about five minutes to write the ticket. We had a great conversation –

"Where you going?"

"Home. Los Angeles," I said.

"I went to L.A. once," he said. "Great city."

"Not what it used to be. When I was a kid rush hour was half an hour to an hour. Now it's three hours, morning and night both."

He looks at my license. "You live in Sherman Oaks? That near L.A.?"

"Part of it. Sherman Oaks votes for the L.A. mayor."

"You patrolled by the SO?"

I didn't know the phrase. "SO?"

"Sheriff's office."

"No, they patrol the unincorporated county. We have LAPD." He's just looking at me, like he's waiting for something, and I say flatly, "Best police force in the world." Pause. "No offense intended."

He smiles then and nods. "None taken. Where you coming from?"

"San Antonio. World Science Fiction Convention."

He takes his hat off. "Is that so? I used to read that stuff when I was a kid. H.G. Wells – I think I read everything Robert A. Heinlein ever wrote." He smiles at me. "Radar had you going 85, 86. I wrote you at 85."

I said thank you, sincerely enough.

The ticket was almost worth it. I can tell people for years the one about how I got nailed by a Heinlein fan who was hiding in a mirage, for the first speeding ticket I've had in seven years.

I STOPPED OVERNIGHT at a Motel 6 somewhere 200 miles outside of El Paso. I turn on the tv set in the hotel room and see them talking about Princess Di on one channel, and flip past it until I find Janeane Garofolo on HBO. I watch her for a while with the sound off. She plays with her hair a lot, that girl. I'm unconscious within minutes.

THE NEXT MORNING I got started again late – about 9:30 A.M., L.A. time. I've decided to drive up the 10 freeway to the 25, north through Albuquerque, across the 40 to go north on Highway 666, to the 64, to the 160, to Four Corners, where New Mexico, Arizona, Nevada, and Utah all come together. It's the only point contiguous to four states in the U.S.

A.I. War ends there. Years ago I had someone describe the area to me; hadn't been there in years myself, and I wanted to get the details right. She described small mountains, or tall hills, that I didn't remember. This seemed like a good chance to go look at it again and make sure the details in *A.I. War* are right.

I picked up a newspaper to read at breakfast and learned that Princess Di had died in an automobile accident. I drove the next 24 hours straight to get home, with the image of her car accident in my head.

DRIVING THROUGH NEW Mexico, I ran into the same sign a couple of times. "High Winds May Exist." The sign bemused me.

"But Then Again," I think, "They May Not."

This sign was written by either a Zen Master or by a man who was afraid of commitment. Hard to tell[11].

FROM NOW ON, when I want to say "God Willing," I'm going to say, "Quantum willing."

"Boy, it sure looks like the Lakers are going to go all the way this year," a friend will say to me.

"Quantum willing and the river don't rise," I'll agree solemnly.

A YOUNG LADY I know talked to me about why men are such pigs recently. Why we as a group can't keep our dicks in our pants. I explained to her my ice cream theory.

"It's like, you know, vanilla ice cream is good stuff. I eat *lots* of vanilla ice cream. But sometimes you want rocky road. And sometimes, even after you've tried all the 31 flavors, they come out with a *new* flavor. And then you want to try that flavor."

"So you're saying you respect me as a human being –"

---

[11]   And not a big difference, some days ... .

I jumped on it. "But I also respect you as ice cream. Exactly." She's just staring at me and I'm staring at her. "Cookies and cream is *my* guess," I add.

She's a black girl. She blushed visibly and needed to talk about something else then.

I SCREWED UP on distances. Again. On the road at 9:30, thinking I'll be at Four Corners before dark. No go. It starts getting dark at around 7 P.M., Los Angeles time. I'm on the 40 freeway, haven't hit the 666 yet, when it's pitch black. Total screwup, I'm thinking. Can't read a map. Can't figure mileage. Who would believe you've driven 400,000 miles in your life? (Most of it in the last few days, it feels like.)

North on the 666. I'm looking, figuring this is a *great* stretch to put a vampire story. Nothing leaps out at me, though. There's dark, desolate stretches, sure, but nothing that screams evil.

Besides, 666 is probably a little obvious.

I REACH FOUR Corners at about 10:30 P.M., L.A. time. It's pitch black. Four Corners is simply a monument, and the monument's shut down. I lock the car and get out and walk into the monument, but I can't see a goddamn thing, so I turn around and go back to the car and sit for a while, being angry at myself.

After a while I notice that the clouds, which have been ringing the horizon for 360 degrees, are flashing. Lightning. It looks cool –

I look straight up and in the moonless darkness the Milky Way *blazes*. Off on the horizons lightning flashes light up the ground around me, and it occurs to me that if the lightning is bright enough, I can get a feel for the land around me –

Indeed. It's flat. A couple rises off in the distance, but the tall hills, or short mountains, or whatever – no such thing. I'm in the middle of a huge black emptiness, and Greg Benford's Great Sky

River, above me, is so bright I can *see* the glow of the Milky Way. Even out in San Bernardino, at my sister's house, you can't see that. In L.A. you can barely see the brightest of the stars.

I get my notebook out of the car and start typing. In about five minutes I've captured something worth having, the moment, the feel of being completely alone in the middle of nowhere, in a world that's barely aware of the existence of human beings, never mind the idiot with his Dell P133 notebook.

YOU CAN BARELY get the "Four Corners Rock and Roll Oldies Station"at Four Corners. They should change their name.

LEAVING FOUR CORNERS, I go west on the 160. I'm figuring 160 to the 89 north, across the Grand Canyon and into Utah, to the 9, to the 15 South. This will take me through Las Vegas, and I've got $100 I'm going to blow on the dollar slots.

The 160 is a two-lane, long, empty highway. I drive down it for what seems like hours. I'm down to a quarter tank of gas when I finally see civilization again, a little town in the middle of nowhere. Kayenta, I think. I stop to gas up and get a cup of coffee. The thunderstorm is advancing on us now, and the rain has started in, not too bad. The lightning is intense, though. I put the gas nozzle in to start pumping, and stand outside the gas station for a while, watching the lightning. Then I go inside and buy a cup of coffee, come back out and watch the lightning some more.

This is what *could* have happened next. When I drive away, the gas handle sitting in my tank can rip the hose off the tank, flooding gasoline out into the gas island, and then a bolt of lightning can set it on fire, causing the gasoline to explode. Then I could drive away in the confusion, saving me $40, which is apparently what it costs to reattach the head of one of those gas hose devices.

I DRIVE INTO the heart of the thunderstorm.

For the first time *ever* I understand viscerally how primitive people could have made up gods because of stuff like this. The rain comes down so hard I slow to about 30 miles an hour with the wipers on high and I still can't see a goddamn thing. The radio's been wiped out – I can't even get anything on FM through the storm. Lightning crashes down about once every five seconds and it's amazingly bright. All my life I've thought that lightning that turned nighttime to day was just an expression. Now I see it happening all around me. I'm driving through a canyon of sorts, low hills off a mile or two to my right and left, and the closer blasts of lightning light up the hillsides so clearly you can see the blades of grass, the leaves of the stunted trees. Now I think I know why the trees out here are all dwarfs; not because of lack of water, because if they get up to any height, the lightning blows them apart. (This may not be accurate, but at the time it seems convincing.)

Lightning hits *on the road* about a mile ahead of me. The spike is so bright it leaves an afterimage on my retinae, purple, for the next couple of minutes. I don't rattle easily but this is starting to get to me now, the constant rolling thunder and flashing light –

They say you don't hear the bullet that kills you; I don't remember hearing the thunder from the bolt that struck 60 yards ahead of me, just off the road. It was like a bomb had gone off. That bolt *walked* across the road in four or five distinct bars of lightning. I remember the interior of the car lighting up around me, and for some fucking reason I stomped on the brake and the car fishtailed and left me sitting cockeyed on the road when I stopped moving.

I don't think I screamed, but I wouldn't be surprised. I do know that I sat on the road for three or four minutes, until another car came up behind me and honked at me. I pulled over and let him go by and waited another 2-3 minutes after that before I got moving again.

TRAVIS MCGEE SAID once that there are no 100% heroes. I've been shot at and been less rattled than that. All a matter of what you're used to, I suppose –

I DROVE OUT of the storm and at the 89, I went south instead of north. Vegas was going to take me another hour out of my way, and I'd already been warned by Quantum about how my luck was going that night. Besides, I'd already lost $40 of the $100 I'd planned on losing.

MEATLOAF – *BAT OUT* of Hell II – is a very good antidote to having been scared by lightning.

THE 89 SOUTH runs alongside the edge of the Grand Canyon. I was a little rattled yet from the lightning, and the awareness of this Fucking Big Hole in the ground, off to my right, was hovering at the side of my awareness.

I had Melissa on by then. "Brave and Crazy" was playing when I drove by the crosses.

At first I blinked. I really thought I'd imagined it. A little cross, made of white road reflectors, planted at the side of the highway.

The 89 is *dead* at three in the morning. Empty. No traffic to slow me down. I'm running a sensible 90 miles an hour down the flat straight road –

Another cross. Yellow reflectors, this time. Over the next thirty miles, about two dozen crosses, some alone, some in clumps, scattered across both sides of the road. I don't know if any of them faced the other way; I wouldn't have seen them, if so.

I've driven 400,000 miles and I've never seen anything like that[12]. Miles and miles of crosses. It reminded me of the crosses

---

[12] Sure, I've seen individual roadside shrines before. But you really need to drive that road at night to get a feel for the eerie frequency of those things. An awful lot of people died on that road.

leading away from Rome, in Spartacus, after the slaves have all been crucified ... .

I'd found my vampire road.[13]

THE NEXT MORNING, just outside of Los Angeles, I hear that some middle eastern country has re-instituted crucifixion for particularly heinous crimes. Four men have been sentenced to die by crucifixion, so far –

I GOT HOME at 9:30 A.M., Tuesday morning. I drove the last half hour with one eye closed, so that my vision would stop crossing. Got home, crawled into bed, woke up, and wrote this before I forgot any of it.

---

[13]   I hadn't. By the time I finally wrote that story, as I say, it was set in another cycle of the universe entirely. But I'd love to use that stretch of road someday for something.

Infinite Methods (2007)

THE NINE KINDS of words are nouns, pronouns, adjectives, verbs, adverbs, prepositions[14], conjunctions, interjections and articles. My sons didn't know this; nor had I when I was their age.

I dropped out of high school after the tenth grade; the summer I was sixteen I was homeless and sleeping in a park, which put a crimp in further education.

Recently my 8 year old, Richard, wanted to know if I'd played basketball in college. We play together regularly and we have not much in common otherwise outside action movies and being guys. Richard's older brother Bram lives and eats Pokemon, and Richard's almost as bad. My Pokemon knowledge extends to "Ash," "Pikachu," and "training," because you train Pokemon. Aside from this their lengthy discourses on the subject are in Mandarin.

So we talk basketball or movies, which is more than my Dad and I had in common. (To be fair to us, my Dad didn't watch movies much, and football bores me; but I watched University of Miami football games so I could suffer and gloat with him. At the 2 minute mark of Lakers games I'd know Dad was tuning in so he could call and exclaim over Magic or Kobe's brilliance, despite being even more indifferent to the Lakers than I was to Miami. "I love you" can be said lots of ways.)

"Did you play basketball in college" – I sidestepped. "No, honey, I never played organized basketball." My older kids know I didn't go to college (my daughters even know why) – but my kids go to good schools, are doing extremely well in school, and once the habit of good school performance is set, we can talk about why I didn't do well in school.

One of the reasons, though, is that I think analytically and was frequently bored in school because the material wasn't presented in a unifying structure. This analytic tendency has been useful to me as a programmer: decades of hammering away at my craft have sep-

---

[14] A typo in this word had it originally reading "proposition."

arated out what's critical to the process of building scalable, maintainable systems, from what's not.

For example, I used to be a big Hungarian notation guy. Naming conventions are necessary but otherwise largely irrelevant, so long as they're not downright stupid. I've known this for years but still felt that a Hungarian notation-based naming system (iThing for integer data, sThing for string data, and so on) was really the best approach.

For about a year now I've written in, and gotten comfortable with, a non-Hungarian naming standard. And then I returned to a client where my code, three to eight years old, is in production. Working with this code ... I was downright annoyed at how unintuitive the naming convention was. *Obviously* a Hungarian notation-based system is less intuitive than the approach I've been using the last year ... .

I'm never having a naming convention argument again so long as I live. The part of my brain that cares about such things is stupid and fickle.

SO WHAT IS essential? Despite being bright I did badly in school. I was in my teens before I could diagram a sentence. An early story came back from George Scithers, bless him, then editing Isaac Asimov's Science Fiction Magazine, with the suggestion of a book on grammar. I read that book and discovered there were only nine kinds of words. That's it! That's grammar! Or at least the hard core of it ....

If any teacher had ever told me there were only nine kinds of words in the English language, I'd have learned them.

I RECALL ONE class in which I got a rare 'A' – a ten week Geometry class, summer before the tenth grade. The teacher didn't want me: I'd done badly in his Algebra class. But ten weeks was the right speed. It went fast enough to keep my attention, was the sort of material I'm wired for, and across all the years I went to school is my one really outstanding memory for hitting a subject I liked, engaging with the material, and having the class move fast enough. That teacher took me into his tenth grade trigonometry class with high expectations. Bad year – we had the PSATs that year and I got the second highest score at that school, a Catholic boy's school with some very smart kids. I'd skated through the ninth grade without any teachers noticing me; that damned test brought me to their attention and I was miserable the whole tenth grade.

But the person most disappointed in me was my math teacher, because he knew what I was capable of first hand – so halfway through the year he let me study at my own pace, and the second half of that class was better than the first. I was well into a different textbook by year's end.

Aside from a few courses on computers, astronomy, and writing, I've never been back to school. But I've kept learning. I've read over a thousand non-fiction works, learned a variety of useful business and life skills, at my own pace and when I felt like it. And what's come to me through the School of Dan, which I never got straight in real school, is that in all material there are core concepts, peripheral concepts, and chrome. Looking back, most of the schools I went to taught chrome.

What does core look like? In both writing and programming I've come to believe that it boils down to conciseness. I recall, very early in life, reading a book called "Philosophy and Cybernetics." This exposed me, though I didn't realize it at the time, to this idea: *entia non sunt multiplicanda praeter necessitatem.*

IN THE BUSINESS world I work in good database design does not consist of doing more with less: it consists of doing less. Storing less data. Creating less structure. Writing less code.

This is not the way business people think about databases (to the degree they do think about databases.) Business people tend to prefer large to small, more tables to fewer, more data to less. The problem is that data may or may not be meaningful. The following strings contain equal amounts of data:

'ooooooooooo'

'I love you.'

Each string contains eleven characters but the second string contains more information. Plainly, data is useless and information is useful: and the more concisely information can be characterized, the more useful it is.

I approach both writing and programming from the same perspective: do less. Omit words, to quote a smart guy. A sign with the words "Minimize structure – Minimize code" has hung over my desk at several companies.

I've been interviewing DBAs for twenty years. There's a question I ask all prospects, which in twenty years only a few people have ever answered correctly. It's this:

What, in almost all cases, is the difference between a query that performs badly, and one that performs well?

I've interviewed some very bright people over the years, and received interesting answers to this question. Good indexes, I've been told: covering indexes, clustered indexes, high cardinality indexes. Good statistics. A proper execution plan. Proper use of temp tables, or derived tables, or table variables. Proper joins. Correct normalization. Wise denormalization.

None of these answers are necessarily wrong, but they miss the point. Queries run on a computer, a thing in the real world. With rare exceptions they run against magnetic media: and magnetic media is slow. Off a good RAID array at this time, for sequential file transfers, you might pull bursts of 300 megabytes per second. Database queries by nature access media more randomly; 100 megabytes per second throughput is a superb real-world result.

For context, modern high-speed RAM has throughput to the CPU of over 10 gigabytes per second – about two orders of magnitude faster.

The difference between queries that perform well and badly is, almost always, that the query that performs well executes with fewer reads. So the concept that's not peripheral or chrome is this: databases perform well in direct proportion to the degree that they retrieve the correct answer with the fewest reads.

This question will be on the test.[15]

To broaden out from computers, our goal is the correct result with the least effort. Now ... how you get to that goal is peripheral. There's more than one right way to perform most tasks ... but there are an infinite number of ways to perform a task incorrectly. (Moran's Principle of Infinite Methods – "Infinite Methods" is the title of one of the many, many books I'll probably never write.) The first pass in learning any skill is to get out of the Infinite Methods. Once out you're an amateur: you produce functional work, though the work is likely not elegant or scalable or easy to maintain – the criteria vary by field. But the work produces results that match your stated goal.

At some point you're a professional. (I'll define the word for you, ignoring connotations from various fields: a professional gets paid.) By now, one hopes, you know several ways to solve a given problem outside the Infinite Methods ... and so your job grows more complex. If you're honest you'll admit you don't always know which approach is best for a given problem: you haven't solved Problem X often enough to know all the options. (Some people never do solve

---

[15] Things change. Just in the short time since I wrote this, the ubiquity of solid state drives (SSDs) in the database market has altered this equation somewhat.

Problem X more than one way, and they never get past the status of journeyman.) So you flex; curiosity is useful here. Try X, try Y, try Z. You have deadlines and that's life in a capitalist society – so stay late and try the alternate approach. Noodle away at it over the weekend and before bedtime. What's the core of my problem? What's the simplest way to solve it? What approach takes the fewest steps, requires me to build and maintain the fewest objects?

This is one of the places where programming and writing fiction part ways: you don't maintain a production environment in writing. Once a piece is done it works or doesn't, and with some exceptions you're not going to revisit it. This is unfortunate: re-writing an old piece many years later is a good learning experience in both arenas.

If Stephen King and JK Rowling had to come back years later and rewrite their novels, they'd write shorter the first time.

MINIMIZE STRUCTURE. MINIMIZE code. It's a reminder to me to never build something I don't need or that's similar to something I've already built. When in doubt, extend and reuse the similar entity. When in doubt ... don't.

Despite popular misconception, Occam's Razor doesn't say *Pick the simpler solution, all else being equal*; it says entities should not be multiplied needlessly. Which, studying, takes you to reductionism and parsimony. I've written statistical software; if I hadn't been exposed to the idea of parsimony already I'd have written useless statistical software. In business (as opposed to research, or so I'm told) statistical software works best to the degree you can identify the core data required to make successful predictions, and then quitting before you get yourself into trouble...which is parsimony.

What is parsimony? Less is more. Minimize structure, minimize code. And save some thoughts for later.

Fiction

A Day in the Life of a Telephone Pole (1974)
BY DANNY MORAN, AGE 12

MEGATRON I, LEADER of the Delurian colony was listening attentively to his observation and communication officers.

Flyn, his communications officer, was saying excitedly, "Sir, our three other colonies have ceased contact!"

"Furthermore," said Myrn, the observation officer, "all three stations reported that they were being attacked by Terrans, by men, before we lost contact."

The excitement of a moment before was gone. There was now an ominous silence as Megatron realized the implications of their statements.

When he spoke there was an edge to his voice. "How could the humans have detected us?" he asked Flyn. "We have distort shields up, and the size and shape of our colonies so closely approximate that of their telephone poles that detection should have been impossible."

Flyn shrugged, "I don't know sir. We thought Delurian technology was good enough to keep them from detecting us. Their ignorance of our greater technological advancements is apparent, yet, somehow, they have managed to detect us."

The two officers stole a glance at one another.[16]

Myrn spoke. "Sir, thats all we really know of the situation. How the Terrans have detected us is unimportant. What is important is that even if the other three colonies were still in existence, we don't have enough ammunition to ward them off. And, as we cannot return to Deluria because of depleted fuel, there is little choice as to what our dicision must be, as I'm sure our colonies discovered. We must not let these ignorant, backward Terrans[17] get samples of our advanced technology."

"Yes," said the leader after a moment. "Flyn, tell the boys[18] down in defense to prepare for self-destruct."

Silence fell. The whole course of events took 2-1/2 seconds.

Mark and Bill were only two of the hordes of telephone repairmen sweeping the city. Everyone knew what was up, and everyone was enthusiastic about it. The phone company had decided to help beautify the city by running all the telephone wires underground instead of in the air where they had created a massive web of holes and wires.

However, Marks and Bills enthusiasm was reatly dampened, as they speculated on something very strange.

The last three telephone poles they had cut down had vanished ... .without a trace!

"Do you suppose it could have been an accident? You know, spontaneous combustion, or something?" asked Bill.

"Funny sort of accident," growled Mark, "with no fire and ashes." Bill shut up.

---

[16]   A line I might have written today. My characters are always staring and looking and blinking and glancing about ...
[17]   Perceptive bastards.
[18]   Because no girls would be dumb enough to follow this order? Or just generalized twelve-year old 1972ish sexism? I don't know.

They came to their last telephone pole. Mark, who was driving, stopped the truck. Bill and Mark got out of the vehicle, walked around the truck, and got out the power saw. Mark carried the saw, and yelled to Bill, "Turn on the power!" The saw came to life with a thunderous roar. Mark moved forward, and the saw bit deeply into the telephone pole.

MEGATRON I, FLYN and Myrn sat in the observation room. They had viewed the approach of the humans with extensive bitterness. The sound of the roaring saw filled the Delurians with hate and anger toward the Terrans, who were destroying them without giving them a chance to explain what Delurian colonization could mean in terms of technological advancements.[19] There could have been an end to wars, hunger, disease; they could have established weather control, and much, much more.

The leader spoke, "Flyn, do the colonials know that we must commit suicide?"

"No," said Flyn, "Do you think I'm a fool?"

"No comment," said Megatron.

"Thanks a lot," said Flyn drily.

Myrn asked, "Did you get a message off to Deluria Flyn?"

"Yes."

"What was it?"

Flyn crossed the room, picked up a piece of paper and read; " 'To Central Control: Do not colonize Terra. Inhabitants extremely dangerous. All four of our colonies have been detected. We are

---

[19]   OK, now I'm rooting for the humans again. I bet if you'd asked me at 12 I'd have explained how eventually the Delurians were going to build huge domes and make humans wear Caps and start pumping green gas into the atmosphere to kill everyone on the planet eventually ... or maybe that was just a John Christopher plot. But anyway I'm pretty sure we wouldn't really want to be colonized by powerful aliens, so maybe this story turns out for the best after all....

about to put into effect our previously agreed upon plans; we, too, must self-destruct.' "

They all heard the muted roar. It had been going on for some time now. They felt, rather than heard, the colony start to fall.

"Well, this is it," said the leader. He pressed the switch with carefully concealed sadness.

This course of events took exactly three seconds.

MARK AND BILL watched apprehensively as the telephone pole started to fall. They looked at each other, their hopes rising. It was falling! It was falling, but it never reached the ground. It was gone! Gone, without a trace!

Without a word, Mark and Bill picked up the power saw, put it in the back of the truck, and drove back to the city. They did not talk about what had happened. They both stared straight ahead.

That night they both got drunk.

FIFTY-FIVE YEARS later a message arrived at Deluria that had come from a small planet named Terra. This was a planet the De-lurians had been trying to colonize for years. The message was disturbing. It told of the detection and the destruction of the four colonies there.

The Delurian Council discussed the matter in great detail. Their conclusions were: A. The Terrans were deemed uncivilized. B. Many years of research had shown that Terran technology was not advanced enough to detect the colonies. Therefore, it was logical to assume they possessed psychic powers. C. Since the Delurians had not cultivated psychic powers they thought it prudent to avoid further contact with Terra.

The vote to stay away from Terra was unanimous.

*

Clean this up just a bit, flesh it out some, you could have sold this to John W. Campbell with no problem.

In Cool Blood *is set in the same universe as*
Terminal Freedom, *which tells you nothing if you
haven't read that novel, and not much more if you
have. Jodi didn't work on this, but if this had ever
become a book – we outlined one at one point – it
would have been a collaboration.*

*(And yes, I know I'm prone to reusing names. It
amuses me, which is all the reason I usually need.
Doctor Death is not always the same Doctor Death,
depending on the story, and I can live with that. Also,
the Reverend Andy referenced here is not the
Reverend Andy from the Continuing Time stories. As
far as I know.)*

Enjoy.

In Cool Blood

"Satire is death, but parody is life."

– Nabokov

"Choose Life"

– Inscription on a *Wham* t-shirt, circa 1982

Mr. Anthony Bonforte

Professor of Hematology

University of California at Los Angeles

Los Angeles, CA 90025

Dear Tony:

But *no*, the evil bastard said to me, I *cannot* see you this weekend. Busy, you know, very busy, and the weekend after that, and
the weekend after that. Probably forever.

Okay, so it was a mistake, I should never have mentioned the desire to know what goes on inside his head, probably he misunderstood me and thought I wanted to crack his head open and *eat* his brain, the way the Japanese do to monkeys. Oh, I wouldn't do that, he should know.

The other day I was out cruising with my best friends, Loose Lucy LaRouche and Reverend Andy, and Reverend Andy said, "These are evil times we live in, and as Grand Dragon of the Christian Coalition, I report directly to Pat Robertson you know, I sure do see a lot of it."

This was a lie and we knew it; Reverend Robertson had never trusted Reverend Andy, and with good reason since the man was a schizophrenic paranoid. But Reverend Andy wouldn't give up that easy; he shook his head in disgust and Loose Lucy chuckled menacingly. "Wickedness!" screamed Reverend Andy suddenly as we zoomed along with the top down, "vile evil nasty communist ACLU wickedness! Naked, writhing bodies covered in Crisco oil, doing vile evil nasty communist ACLU things to each other!" He shuddered with the overwhelming wickedness of it all and then said to Loose Lucy, "Give me my medicine, bitch, I'm in *need*." And he snorted it back and laughed maniacally, "Oh, oh, that's good medicine, the Lord bless that evil doctor who fucked me over on these!"

Anyhow, that was the final straw because that doctor, he was a good friend of ours, you know? So we stopped the car and heated up some coals, and clamped Reverend Andy down and cut off the top of his head, just like with the monkeys. Then we poured the coal inside his brain, and waited until it had cooked properly, and yes it was a great delicacy, with that fine charcoal flavor.

So anyhow Tony I'm coming to get you now, and we are going to have to do lunch together and settle this misunderstanding once and for all. You promised to get me drunk and I haven't forgotten, you bastard. You can run, but you can't hide. Justice lurks behind the bushes these days. I mean that's what Reverend Andy said before we ate his brain.

Oh and Loose Lucy wants to meet you too.

Ciao.

Sincerely, Thomas

I CAME UP out of the gloom off the San Diego freeway, whipped it onto Sunset Boulevard at sixty-five miles an hour. Playing an old Joe Walsh CD, we were just done with *Theme From Boat Weirdos,* and into *Life's Been Good,* lyrics stomping through my mind in demented counterpoint to the essential eeriness of my life, Walsh snarling at me that he locked his limo door, in case of attack –

Attacked by *what,* you senile old fool? The letter sat beside me on the passenger's seat of the old '69 Sports Satellite. Not a bad letter, no; but even the knowledge that it was going to scare Tony bad, or maybe piss him off, didn't cheer me up much. I zoomed east on Sunset, cut over onto Barrington, and dropped the letter off at the Brentwood Post office; he'd have it in UCLA's Friday morning mail.

Having a bad time of it, you know: Thursday evening in a cold January month, and the chills hitting me bad. I hadn't managed to keep anything down all day, *nothing;* I'd been bitten twice, and she was looking for me.

I *had* to see Tony tomorrow.

The warped son of a bitch thought I was a vampire. There was this false note of hysterical cheerfulness in his voice when I talked to him late Thursday afternoon, you know, "Let's do *lunch,"* someplace sunny he was thinking.

Had the shakes again by the time I retraced Barrington up to Sunset Boulevard; from Brentwood you have to drive through Westwood and Beverly Hills to reach Hollywood, but I didn't mind. Driving down Sunset Boulevard is relaxing, even during rush hour;

Sunset is a particularly civilized piece of road. My best friend Doctor Death says she thinks that Sunset Boulevard was an accident of design that can't, in this degenerate age, be duplicated. It's likely.

I love Sunset.

It's a *good* street; cool and serene in the summer, or splashed with neon on the warm rainy nights of winter, while the people wander around from club to shop to restaurant, to the theaters and comedy houses. My life is here; the Laff Connection and the Comedy Store and the Schtick; south of Hollywood Boulevard, and thank God, north of Wilshire, and the Evil Improv on Melrose.

I do love it. If it wasn't for this one street, I'd go live in Northern California somewhere, on one of those big, four-story tall black rocks that jut up out of the ocean thirty yards from shore. Or maybe I'd just buy the very top of a mountain somewhere, something like that.

East on Sunset, just going with the traffic.

And so I tried to relax and shake off some of the vicious weirdness of the day just past, hunched away inside my apartment with the windows in my bedroom painted black to keep out the light.

And drove.

I LOST IT somewhere around UCLA. I'd been fading in and out ever since I left home.

Hungry.

I sat at a stoplight, waiting for the light to change, and then a sudden horrible flashback gripped me: waves, really *good* waves, crashing against the beach, and riding them are the vampires, a dozen or so, surfing, and for one hideous moment I wasn't sure if this was just some evil dream, or something that really happened, maybe around Malibu, and I came out of it with the sound of the horn from the car behind me, astonishingly loud, reverberating in my skull, and burned rubber pulling away.

I PULLED INTO the parking lot at The Duke's Daughter at 6:20. Somebody, one of Buck's Boys no doubt, had graffitied the west wall: *Peter Buck is God.* The parking lot was still mostly empty; the crowds don't show up at Duke's until after eight o'clock, weeknights. I recognized only two of the cars; the red Porsche belonged to Dreadful Sam, and the big white Caddy meant that the Duke's Daughter himself was there.

Once I closed down *Duke's* with about a dozen friends; I think it was a Wednesday night. About four A.M. Mick "The Duke's Daughter" Cohen was very earnestly explaining his choice of lifestyle to a group of his regulars, myself among them. It was all those old John Wayne movies, he explained in a rare burst of honesty; it was the closest I ever heard him come to admitting that he was *not* John Wayne's illegitimate daughter. "When I was a little girl, I used to watch him on the television, and I tell you, there wasn't ever anything else I ever wanted to do except be a cowboy. And then" – Mick blinked at all of us with an expression of utter woe – "I found out he was just an *actor.*" Nobody laughed. Mick shrugged at length, and took a huge belt straight from the neck of a bottle of dark rum. "We all have problems."

Yeah.

I eased the old Sports Satellite into place next to Dreadful Sam's cherry red Porsche, set the alarm, grabbed my duster out of the passenger's seat, and went inside.

THERE'S A SIGN that greets you upon entering The Duke's Daughter:

If your prejudices cause you to have any problems with your basic redneck Republican homosexual transvestites of Jewish-Irish descent, do yourselves and us a favor and fuck off and stay out. Thanks a lot. Mick.

Duke's is a split-level bar, upstairs and down. There are booths on the bottom half, and large tables for large parties, and a long bar with stools for traditionalists. Upstairs are small tables with big, comfortable chairs you can sink into and hide from the world.

I didn't see Dreadful Sam, but Terminal Sue was tucked away in a corner, talking to a tall guy wearing black leather, a purple vest and a black fedora; she nodded to me as I came in. A big blond guy in white, with a falcon on his shoulder, stood at the bar with a bottle in one hand and a shot glass in the other, pouring into the shot glass, tossing it back, and refilling with metronomic regularity. The bird was a white peregrine and it looked bored. They ignored me and I ignored them and went upstairs, took one of the seats near a window looking out over Sunset Boulevard, and waited for somebody to notice my existence.

The waiter who finally took my order was old and bitchy, your basic aging effeminate gay *crossword puzzle* fanatic. "What'll it be tonight, big boy?" His voice was pitched higher than his throat was really designed for, and his eyes were outlined with pastel blue eyeliner. Aside from that he might have been the waiter at any Jewish delicatessen, say Canter's. He flipped open his order pad and poised a pencil over it.

"Bud Dry. In the bottle. Unopened. Cold."

He held the pencil very still, and finally raised his eyes up from the pad. He looked me over carefully, the midnight black duster coat and the sunglasses. His hands dropped to his hips. "Well, my goodness," he said at last, "cheap black plastic sunglasses. I haven't seen a pair of those since Dirty Harry went out of style."

I stared back at him with my cheap black plastic sunglasses. "Bud Dry. One. In the bottle. In about fifteen minutes if you're not busy you can bring me another."

He shook his head in apparent disgust, and scribbled something on his pad. "Do you really need those trashy things indoors?" he asked rhetorically, since he knew deep in his heart that there was no way that I could possibly have a decent answer.

But you know, I had one for him. It goes, *When you're cool, the sun shines on you twenty-four hours a day*. When you're young, you use those lines whenever the occasion arises. Maturity teaches you not to waste the good lines on the help. I snarled, "Mind your own fucking business," which he seemed to understand.

The bottle of Dry came quickly. Mick doesn't tolerate lazy waiters. Rude, because the regulars seem to like that; but not lazy. I said "Thank you," and he seemed to have forgotten that he disliked me. He was new at *Duke's* and still getting into the swing of it.

I drank the beer and tried to relax. The balcony level is tucked onto *Duke's* northwest corner, giving a view up into the Hollywood Hills, and west, out over Sunset Boulevard. Rush hour traffic had just about finished its crawl down the Boulevard, and the street was nearly fit for decent people to drive on.

About seven, as things were starting to get busy, Mick showed. He dropped himself down in the booth across from me and said in a deep, gravely voice, "People are looking for you, Thomas."

"Oh?"

Mick wore a working cowboy outfit with mascara and false lashes; kind of restrained. If he'd wiped the makeup off you could have cast him in a Western, if they still made the kind Mick liked. "You blew off Connie, over at the *Schtick*. When you didn't show yesterday he had to go up on stage and do one of his old routines, and you know how those go over."

"Yeah, well." I studied my Bud. "Not my fault, man. I've been sick."

"Really?" Mick studied me. "You look like hell," he conceded. "You had the test?"

"Yeah. Twice, negative both times."

"How recently?"

"About four months ago. Terry and I broke up, and I wanted to start dating again … you know."

I saw the relief flicker across his features; the south wall at *Duke's*, lower level, has, in exquisite tiny print, the names of regulars, or the friends and family of regulars, who've died of the virus. When it started Mick had hung photos of the dead; today those photos would have covered five times as much wall space as Mick had available, with some left over. "So what is it, then?"

"Well, I ate the spaghetti at *UnClean Joe's* about a week ago."

Mick blinked, long eyelashes bobbing. "Yeah, that'd do it. I'm glad it's nothing bad, Thomas. But get your shit together, OK? I'm not a Goddam message center."

I'd taken the phone off the hook at home; the ringing was making me crazy. "Who else?"

Mick shrugged. "Terminal Sue was looking for people to go shooting with yesterday, she asked about you, but I don't think it was urgent."

It wouldn't have been. I used to work for Terminal Sue; we're still friends, sort of. She's the best private investigator in Los Angeles – she'll tell you so – and there was a time, a couple of years back, when she thought I had promise. She fired me after about six months. I kept getting beaten up, and she was tired of going to the hospital to visit me.

Naturally I went into stand-up.

I DECIDED TO wait out the evening rush hour before going home. "Rush hour" is the four hours between three in the afternoon and seven in the evening. I sat and nursed my Bud, listening to the music. Terminal Sue came up and said hello, and we talked for a bit, and then she had to go – business with Space Nazis, she said, which I hope was a joke because I fucking hate Nazis.

Around a quarter of eight I was mildly drunk – three longnecks on a stomach that hasn't seen food in two days will do that to you – so the *movement,* down on the bottom level, didn't kick my adrenal gland into action the way it should have.

I felt very calm; without thinking about what I was doing I stood, took off my sunglasses, looked down onto the first level, and the entrance leapt into focus with dazzling clarity: the door swinging shut, nobody near it.

My hands twitched. I knocked the rest of my Bud back in one long pull, and then the music started, jukebox down on the first floor lighting up as it moved into the song, and I scanned around the balcony, down into the bright gloom of the pit near the bar itself.

Nothing.

Bruce Springsteen. It took me that long to hear what she had put on, and then the man's voice just cut through the babble, I mean right down into my soul – something about things dying and things coming back. It gave me the creeps, and baby that's a fact.

She came up the stairs then. I knew it was Lila, had known it since the door had opened, too silently, and the man's voice started wailing that unearthly song. She was just what I remembered: I stood there with the window at my back watching her come toward me, neither nightmare nor dream, the long blond hair and welding-black sunglasses, and the skin, that impossible golden skin. And she *moved,* I can't describe the way she moved except that it made me want her.

She took the sunglasses off –

All of a sudden I couldn't see her any more, I was floating and then the ground touched me. I hit rolling and came to my feet looking up, towards the windows that ran around the balcony at *Duke's.* Glass still fell around me, falling like rain into the parking lot. Something flickered, appeared in the window and after that I do not remember anything until I was on the 405 northbound, my hands clutching the wheel, driving far too fast.

SLOWLY THE FREEWAY came into focus around me. Traffic was still slightly heavy on the 405 northbound coming out of Westwood, up over the hill into the San Fernando Valley. Most everybody was doing sixty-five to seventy miles an hour, standard speed for that time of night; for most of them, coming home late from work, it was the only time of day they were in their cars when they *could* drive that fast. I outpaced them only slightly, maybe eighty-five miles an hour, weaving in and out automatically, brain more or less disengaged; driving, yes, but not dangerously fast, in the cool night air, windows down, and then all of a sudden there were sirens shrieking at me, a bubble machine pulsing a beautiful blue and red. Sucker. I had a lane and I drove it like Worthy in his prime, cut through traffic crossing three lanes, onto the Mulholland Drive off ramp, and went zooming up the ramp into the wealthy gloom.

I read in the newspaper the other day that within the decade the average speed on Los Angeles area freeways will be 17 miles per hour. Suggestions to alleviate this awful mess include double-decking the San Diego freeway.

What brutal nonsense *is* this? Double-deck the freeway?

Here he is and he's driving in the dark, down on the bottom level, on what used to be all there was of the 405. Suddenly cop lights glare behind him, so he pulls over, and the cop comes up and knocks on the window.

Roll down the window, yes; the cop stares into the back seat, which contains every sedative known to humanity and all sorts of weapons, dangerous *shit, Uzis and M-16's, Heckler & Koch 91's and other monster fucking illegal semi – and fully-automatic weapons.*

"My God," whispers the cop, "what is this?" He has his revolver out and is pointing it at the driver.

The driver turns glassy eyes on him, shiny reflective eyes, like he should really be wearing sunglasses. Unfortunately he is not. "Protection, officer, just protection."

"Get out of the car," the cop says unsteadily.

" *... for the bats," the driver is saying earnestly, "it's the damn bats. They* like *these dark gloomy caverns down here. These black, open spaces. And the sound of the horns, echoing away against the top of the freeway, when the drivers snap and start blasting away with the horns because they've driven too deeply into the horror; the sound of the horns drives the bats into wild, bloodsucking fits ... ."*

Shoved beyond his natural limits, the officer opens fire, killing the driver pretty much instantaneously.

Up on Mulholland Drive, parked in my black '69 Sports Satellite, behind a silver Mercedes that shone under the street lamp, I could not help but wonder: *Do they* know *the dangers? Do they* know?

Three Highway Patrol squad cars went zooming down Mulholland while I waited, seat tilted all the way back, staring up at the car's roof. After a quiet hour had passed I sat up again, connected my seat belt and started the engine and eased the black bomb back down onto the freeway, and made my sedate way down the north side of the Big Hill, over to the 101 East, and home to my apartment in North Hollywood.

THE NIGHT IS too long.

I don't know who I am any more.

I don't know *what* I am.

When I was six or seven, and I first learned of vampires, it scared me more than I ever let anyone know. For two solid weeks I went to bed and tied one of my father's big clean white socks securely around my neck. When you're six you can do that, and it helps; pity the poor bloodsucker who tries to take your blood with that sock securely wrapped around your neck. I would wake up in the night, giggling at the thought of the perplexed vampire biting into the sock; as I got better at standup, bits like that became the mainstay of the routine.

The story about the sock to ward off vampire bites never fails to get a laugh.

I spent the rest of the night prowling restlessly through the house. I was viciously hungry but nothing sounded good. A steak shown in the Sizzler ad on the TV looked just good enough to make me violently sick in the kitchen sink. Fortunately, there wasn't anything except beer in my stomach.

About one A.M. I headed out into the January night.

The 7-11 on Laurel Canyon, just down the street from my apartment, is a late-night social spot for half of the brain-dead in North Hollywood, extras from the in-color remake of *Night of the Living Dead* who never forgot that one moment of twisted glory. Some of them doubtless had speaking lines. These are the whites who can't find their way to a club, or would only get themselves kicked out if they did, and the Mexicans and Iranians. There aren't many blacks in North Hollywood, I don't know why[20]. There's a couple million of them south of Wilshire.

I picked up a Los Angeles *Times* and a six-pack of Bud. There were about ten Iranians standing over by the pinball machines, who ignored me, and an amazingly fat white man rummaging through the cold storage section. He had a box of Twinkies and three pint containers of Cookies 'N' Cream Haagen Dazs out already, and he was searching for Number Four ... the *right* ice cream, sir, you understand this is an important decision for me, not one I make every day, no ... .

I walked back home through the cold night air, with my beer and my paper. In the next two hours I drank the six pack and read the *Times* from one end to the other.

Most of the news was the sort of thing you expect. Wars here and bombings there; the President had his foot in his mouth again, and the *Times* editorials seriously questioned his ability to run the country effectively. The comics were only fair; *Doonesbury* made me smile, but only *Calvin and Hobbes* made me laugh out loud. Yes, even while some hideous vampire transformation overtakes me, *Calvin and Hobbes* can make me laugh ... .

I was just stoned enough for the headline to leap up at me:

BLACK DEATH LIVES ON AMONG SQUIRRELS

Meaningless thoughts gibbered in the back of my skull. " ... this ancient scourge, the same disease that ravaged Europe in the Middle Ages as the 'Black Death,' is alive and well and living in ground squirrels in the hills that ring Los Angeles."

Could this be true? They assured me it was. "While ground squirrels stay alive, the fleas will stay on their bodies. But if you get

---

[20]   Until the 1970s landlords usually refused to rent to blacks except south of Wilshire Boulevard. Quite possibly I didn't know this when I wrote *In Cool Blood*, or I knew it and thought my character wouldn't – the phrasing suggests the latter, but I don't recall.

a die-off, then an area can be hopping with infected fleas. When some warm body walks by, they jump on and take a blood meal wherever they can."

I put down the paper and made it to the bathroom before I had to throw up again.

MORNING HIT LIKE a hydrogen bomb, which it was, ninety-three million miles away.

The day dawned cold and clear and gray, terribly overcast. The weather caster on Channel 2, a nice Mexican fellow with more teeth than he needed, said that it was going to rain. He smiled, imparting the news. (This same weather caster once appeared on *Romper Room* as a guest; the children on the show rioted, and he didn't notice because he was busy smiling at the pretty host. Couldn't fault his priorities – she was one of those *hot Romper Room* hosts.)

I got dressed, took my .38 revolver out of its hiding place and dug around in my junk drawer until I found some bullets for it. I loaded the gun with the four that hadn't got stuck together when the Crazy Glue leaked, and put it in the right pocket of my duster. I rubbed SPF 100 sunscreen over my face and hands, and dropped the tube of sunscreen into my other pocket. Sunglasses on ... .

And I sat there for almost two hours getting my nerve up. Staring at the door. Finally I got up and opened and stepped outside, wondering if I would burst into flames –

It was like walking out into a storm of needles. I stood just outside my door until I was sure that if it got no worse, I could take it, and then went down to the parking lot, got into the black bomb, and went to see Doctor Death.

THE FIRST TIME I ever saw Doctor Death, she was drinking beer, telling a story at one of my parties. She was a good looking, tall blond girl with a big chest, wearing a black leather dress with little scarlet zippers and red, silk-lined boots. Her shades were the purest mirrored monochromatic blue I'd ever seen.

"So there we are, off with the goodies," she was saying to a crowd helpless with laughter listening to her, "making our getaway, and all of a sudden this cop comes from nowhere and makes like he's following us, and I mean, I'm pissed, okay? Cause the ice cream in the back seat is *melting,* and I have so much speed in me I wanted to run for it. But Kathy says fuck the ice cream, Christopher is a Pinto, and he won't outrun the ugly Chevy the cop is in." Doctor Death paused in the middle of the story, and looked straight at me, standing on the outskirts of her audience, and said as though the thought had just occurred to her, "And you know, it made sense, cause she was *right.* Anyhow I'm speeding real bad, and I have the twitches, but it's okay cause the freeway's right there, but then there's a roadblock and a sign that says 'Men at Work,' and I can't get on. So I make a quick right hand turn onto Sepulveda thinking I can make a U-turn zip across the street and get on the on-ramp on the north side of Wilshire. And the cop is still following me, and somebody moved the on-ramp on me. I'm in a lane that only turns left and the on-ramp is on the right side of the street. The only way I can get to it would be to turn right from the left turn lane and go east in westbound traffic. And there's a cop in a Chevy behind me.

"So Kathy says, 'There's something wrong here. You better turn, cause the light's not getting any greener and there's a cop in a Chevy right behind you.' So I turn left, and the cop follows me, and I'm like panicking. I pull open my ashtray and dump it out on my lap. There's seven little white ones, two pink ones and one big red-and-white one that I was afraid to take, so Kathy ate it. Then the cop hits us with the lights, and we pull over, and he looks us over and says to Kathy, 'Miss, I think you should drive, since *you're* obviously not intoxicated.'" By this point Doctor Death was laughing so hard she could barely continue with her story, and she had most of the crowd with her. "That set me off, cause I was less stoned than

Kathy was. I start yelling at the cop that the goddamn *ice cream* is melting –"

She talked for, God, an hour. Maybe two, I don't remember. (I do remember how the story ended; the cop asked her for a date.) We ended up having breakfast at Denny's at four in the morning, and talking until noon the next day, when both of us had to go to bed.

We didn't go to bed together. Not that I didn't suggest it.

DOCTOR DEATH HADN'T gone to bed yet – she goes to bed at noon, though not with me – so we sat at her kitchen table and talked while she drank black coffee and ate peanut butter Captain Crunch out of the box.

Kathy came out of her bedroom wearing a t-shirt that was too tight, and a pair of pink panties. She glanced at me on her way to the kitchen, sitting in the living room in duster and sunglasses, and muttered something that might have been *Hi, Thomas* or maybe *Fuck you.* Kathy and I went out back when I was still working as a detective; I don't think she ever forgave me for the four and a half hours we spent in jail that last evening before Terminal Sue bailed us out.

"This chick I met at your party. Lila."

Doctor Death nodded. "Yeah?"

"Where do you know her from?"

"Sears Business Systems," she said promptly.

"What? Where?"

"I sold her a computer."

"You're kidding."

She looked oddly defensive. "No."

"You sold computers for *Sears?*"

She lifted the box of Captain Crunch and held it to her mouth, tilting it back. She looked at me, munching. When she spoke, still eating, I could smell the peanut butter on her breath. "It was a long time ago. Years and years."

"You're a waitress."

She nodded. "Now I'm a waitress. I used to sell computers."

"For Sears."

"For Sears. I sold one to Lila." Doctor Death shook her head. "If you want her phone number, I don't have it." She looked puzzled briefly. "Anyhow, I thought you two left together."

"We went to a hotel. I woke up and she was gone. Two days later she showed up at the Comedy Store while I was working and –"

"– you went to a hotel and you woke up and she was gone." She nodded. "And you don't have her phone number but you do have serious lust."

"No, I have a problem. You sure you don't –"

Doctor Death looked tired. "I could call my friends and see if anyone knows her number, or where she lives. I don't have it, though." Curiosity warred with courtesy, and won. "What'd she give you? Was it – no, wait –"

"*She bit me!*" I yelled at her.

"Oh, Jesus." Doctor Death shook her head in disgust. "I'm sorry, Tommy. I should have *warned* you she was a vampire."

AS I LEFT Doctor Death's apartment, I noticed graffiti on the side of the apartment facing Sunset Boulevard.

On the top it said, *Michael Eisner is Satan.*

Below that, in a different hand, somebody had added, *And Disneyland is Hell.*

CENTURY THRIFT, DOCTOR Death had told me. She'd even, to my amazement, dug up an old business card, for Lila Macauley, Investment Counselor, Century Thrift at 11201 Wilshire Blvd, Suite 500. I knew just by looking at the card that it was old; the phone number listed was a 213 area code, when that stretch of Wilshire had switched over to 310 years ago. Information had no listing for Century Thrift; I drove down to 11201 Wilshire, the World Savings Building, and went up to the fifth floor. Suite 500 was empty; the fellow at the receptionist's desk next door, 510, was extremely effeminate, extremely polite, and didn't seem to find anything unusual in the way I was dressed. He told me that Century Thrift had gone bankrupt over two years ago, right after he'd come to work there. "The fellows who ran it haven't gone to jail yet. Haven't even been charged. I keep waiting, but so far I haven't heard anything about it. Did you lose money?"

"No. Actually I'm looking for someone. Lila Macauley, a blond woman, about 5'6", really great tan. She used to –"

He shook his head. "Sorry, I doubt I'd have noticed her, and I certainly wouldn't have remembered her after all this time." He smiled at me; a nicer smile, I suppose, than most straight men manage to dig up for the women they meet. "Not my type at all."

THERE WAS NO Lila Macauley listed in the 213, 818, 310, 714, 909 or 805 area codes. All of those area codes are within an hour's drive of downtown Los Angeles.

IT STARTED RAINING as I drove to UCLA.

I hate the rain. Nobody in the entire Goddam city knows how to drive in the rain, including me, and I refuse to learn, too, no matter how easy it is. If I wanted to know how to drive in the rain, I'd move to Seattle.

You know, the whole world thinks Los Angeles is shallow. It's not. It's just *warm*. Lord knows, we *could* be deep. And depressed. And wet. I'm sure everyone in Seattle is deep. They can't do anything except read and watch old, meaningful movies of the sort they don't make anymore, since they can't go outside nine months a year.

I made a promise to myself to go see Sly Stallone's next movie the day it opened.

I drove down Wilshire, hating the rain. The rain didn't even stop the needles-on-the-skin effect, which just made me hate it more. I could *feel* my tan fading underneath my SPF 100 sunblock.

Let me tell you something about Los Angeles, anyway. I don't merely live in *Los Angeles. I* live in *La Ciudad de Nuestra Senora la Reina de los Angeles* – the City of Our Lady, the Queen of the Angels. Where do you live? In New York? Fort Worth? *Chicago?* Unless you're very fortunate, *you* don't live in the City of Our Lady, the Queen of the Angels.

For years I used to send the same Christmas card to everyone I knew around the country. It said: "Greetings from L.A.! Things are a bit whiff at the moment, from all the dead fish caused by the radioactive sludge that regularly washes up in Santa Monica Bay, but fortunately, the incense we burn in our Satanic rituals helps mask the odor." It showed a picture of what I suspect was New Jersey, but was certainly not any part of L.A.

You know, the truth of the matter is, Los Angeles really is a lousy place. It rains *all the time.*

Don't visit us. You'd probably enjoy Las Vegas more anyway.

I drove down Wilshire, hating the rain.

TONY TEACHES A one o'clock biology class. I waited for him outside his classroom, and at 1:50 the doors opened and the students began filing out. I stood on the grass in the rain, waiting, and I must have been something to see because they all froze in place as they were leaving, staring, and only moving when the students behind them pushed their way out. I stood there in my wet duster, black jeans and boots, hair soaked down onto my skull, hands deep in the duster's pockets, staring back at them with my sunglasses. I heard Tony's voice, loud and almost cheerful, following his students out to see what they were looking at, and he choked off whatever it was he was saying and went as utterly pale as I have ever seen an adult Los Angelean white man get; it looked like he didn't even have a tan. For a moment I thought he would faint, and then the moment passed. One of his students, a big blond kid, got in my way when I stepped forward, and with one hand I bounced him away from me. He ended up in the grass twenty feet away, moaning slightly.

"Tony," I said softly, "my man." He stood motionless in the doorway to his classroom, and I smiled at him. "Did I get the day wrong? I thought we were supposed to have lunch."

IT TOOK HIM close to two hours to calm down. We spent most of it in his office with the windows shades closed and the door shut.

"How am I?"

"Deathly sick. Or else a vampire."

"I don't mean the obvious stuff."

He spoke precisely. "Your heart is beating very slowly, about twenty beats per minute. Your blood pressure is extremely low. I've had the blood sample you gave me on Tuesday extensively analyzed. You are HIV negative, but your red blood cells are about twice the size they should be and there are only about two thirds as many as there should be, and they do appear to have acquired a nucleus. They're *replicating,* which red blood cells don't do. There are virtually no lymphocytes in your blood; those are the white blood cells primarily concerned with fighting infection. There should be about 1,500 of them per cubic millimeter of blood; you had about 200 per cubic millimeter in Tuesday's sample; a T-cell count below 200 is the working definition of AIDS. And –" He hesitated. "One slide seemed to show a red blood cell – well, one of the things that used to be a red blood cell – eating one of the lymphocytes. We could take another sample, Tom, but I think it would show that your lymphocyte count is, today, zero. Your granulocytes are virtually untouched; those are the white blood cells that eat bacteria."

"Anything else?"

"You're highly sensitized to sunlight, but not to artificial light; we could analyze sunlight until we find whatever it is that's bothering you. But direct sunlight is out –"

"In other words," I interrupted, "my tan is doomed."

"Tans are bad for you," Doctor Bonforte muttered. "They damage your skin and cause wrinkles and, and stuff like that, in old age."

"Great," I sneered. It was the good one, too, my Elvis sneer. "So I'm going to be seventy with good skin, when no one will care."

"How do you feel?"

I let the sneer drop; it was a sincere question. "Odd. I haven't eaten anything in three days, and I'm really hungry – but aside from that, I'm holding up. I've been drinking a lot of beer; it's about all I can keep down."

"Lost any weight?"

"Not much."

He nodded thoughtfully. "That's interesting." He hesitated, and then got this weird smile when he asked it: "Any desire to suck blood?"

I yelled at him. *"I'm a vegetarian!"*

– and then had to wait for the twisted son of a bitch to stop laughing at me.

WE HAD LATE lunch at an Italian restaurant about ten minutes walk from his offices on campus. A little place toward the north end of Westwood, near the Bruin theater. We walked, in the rain, sharing Tony's umbrella.

"How come *she* has a tan?" I demanded.

He shook his head. "I don't know, Tom. Maybe the sensitivity to daylight only happens during the early stages. You seem to be getting by –"

"I've never seen her except at night. I don't think she goes out except at night."

He shrugged. "Maybe the condition –" He paused, and looked at me, and then laughed again. "Oh, come on. You know how she does it! It's *so* obvious!"

I stared at him; we'd reached the entrance to the restaurant, and stood there in the doorway looking at each other through our sunglasses. "Oh, Jesus. Of course."

He nodded and held the door open for me. "Tanning parlor."

I BORROWED HIS cellular phone to call Doctor Death. Her answering machine picked up. I waited until it beeped: "Hi, Doctor Death, this is Thomas. I was just wondering –"

She picked up. She sounded drowsy. "Hey."

"Get the number?" (It wasn't that I didn't *want* to talk to Lila … just that I wanted to do it on *my* terms. Someplace safe. Early in the morning, so if I had to jump in my car to run away, she might think twice about following me.)

Doctor Death said, "Nope. Not yet. You?"

"Nope … I'm eating some spaghetti marinara."

Her voice took on an optimistic note. "And?"

"Haven't thrown it up yet."

"Keep it up," she said encouragingly. "You can do it."

"I've been trying to think up a way to treat you," Tony said as I hung up the phone and handed it back to him. "One of the treatments they tried for AIDS patients was whole body blood replacement. I doubt it'd work, though. Didn't work against the HIV virus, though it showed some temporary improvement in some patients. Your new and improved red blood cells are damned aggressive; I suspect that we couldn't pump the blood through you fast enough to keep them from replicating. Might kill you to try." He took a bite of his chicken parmigiana. "Another possibility would be to do it in two stages – pump you clean with false blood, pure oxygen-transporting plasma. The shit's wickedly expensive, but it's not blood – the stuff in your veins couldn't replicate in it for sure. Once you're clean, we pump you with good blood, and hope your bone marrow remembers how to make its own."

It sounded good to me. "Downside?"

"I doubt that'll work, either. My guess is we'd need to *clean you out* – every artery, every capillary in your body. If we could double it up with a drug that would kill the mutant red blood cells in your veins, without killing *you,* we *might* stand a chance –"

"What you're saying is, the odds suck."

He took another bite of his chicken and didn't look at me. "Big time."

IT WAS ALMOST dark when we left the restaurant; the rain pounded down on us, heavy and brutal, and the sky had grown dark. I felt comfortable, for the first time that day moving around without the needles jabbing into my exposed skin.

We reached Tony's office as his belt phone rang again. He flipped it open. "Doctor Bonforte here. Yes … no, I'm not. What's her name?"

I stood in the doorway of his office, watching him talk. "Who is it?"

He waved a hand at me. "No, send her away. I don't want … she does?" Tony paused just a second, and then said so quietly even I could barely hear him, "Does she have a really great tan?"

The expression on his face was answer enough.

I turned and sprinted for the Sports Satellite.

I ZOOMED EAST down Sunset in the, you know, driving rain, windshield wipers pumping on high, wishing I'd changed the rubber on them last winter like I'd meant to.

She came after me in a Corvette convertible with the top up. I couldn't fault her taste, it was a '77 or '78 white Stingray, gorgeous car. Decent handling, decent pickup, I have no real complaints except they have a plastic body that crumples in accidents.

It was dark enough that I took my sunglasses off. Fifty miles an hour, and then sixty: we tore down the wet streets at suicidal high speed, across the twisting, serpentine surface of Sunset in west-end Beverly Hills, weaving in and out of rush hour Friday-night traffic. She stayed on my tail as I ran a red light, horn blaring, leaving a multi-car pileup in the intersection behind us after we were through it.

Damn that vampire chick could drive. It filled me with lust to watch it, and for just a moment I wondered what I was running from: best oral sex I'd ever had, and she could *drive*.

Neon appeared on the road ahead of me, the outskirts of Hollywood.

I held the horn down with one hand and drove with the other, leaning out the window to scream at people to get out of my way. I side-swiped a squad car, and its bubble lights lit up, but there was no time to worry about *that*, I had serious business going down. The cop pulled out into traffic to follow us, and that was good, maybe Lila would get scared and pull off.

Nope. I could see her in my rear-view mirror, grinning at me as I fought my way through the clogged rush hour traffic –

We hit La Cienega. I took the Sports Satellite up on the sidewalk, ripped a postal box out of the concrete, and went roaring down the big hill, gaining speed, finally going against traffic, everybody else leaving the city and going north up to Sunset. I dropped the accelerator to the floor, the huge 440cc engine kicking in and dragging the big old piece of American steel through the streets at high speed, horn blaring. I could feel my lips pulling back, thinking *even if I die, what a great way to go:* we slammed into the intersection of Santa Monica and La Cienega together, on the yellow, and I hammered the brakes down and fishtailed the car around, through a full three-sixty, and then a one-eighty, hitting three or four cars while I spun, came out of it and stomped the accelerator again. The tires flogged the wet pavement and then grabbed, and the Sports Satellite surged forward, and I went barreling off west down Santa Monica Boulevard, and something was wrong with the car, a high-pitched whine coming from the engine, and steam billowing up off the hood; I looked into my rear view mirror and there she was, in the Corvette, not as pretty as it had been a while ago, but still running, still coming after me –

– and I had no time left. The Excelsior Hotel was up ahead, and on the left; I'd staked someone out there once, a couple years back, and I knew it well, and if I couldn't lose her in the car, maybe I could do it on foot. I pushed the poor beast, and it strained, hit sixty miles an hour for me and then hung there, shaking with pain as we sideswiped one car and then another, the Corvette weaving in and out of the messes I left behind me on the road, going up onto the grass divider once to do it –

We were at the hotel. I gave it until the last possible moment, and then stomped the brakes hard, turning into a slide, and feeding gas to the pedal. A late model Mercedes was trying to turn into the hotel parking lot when I needed to use the entrance, and I slammed broadside into it, the classic American steel in the Sports Satellite shrieking with pain as it tangled with the ugly German. We slid into the parking lot together, twins joined at the hip, and crashed to a stop doing maybe twenty miles an hour, tangling up in a long line of parked cars. The steering wheel came up and smacked me in the face.

I popped the driver's side door open and staggered out into the rain, went to one knee and made it back up again. A hotel employee in a red coat ran to me through the rain, yelling at me, "Oh, my God, are you all right, you're bleeding, you better sit down –"

I made it to my feet and grinned at him with bloody teeth, and yelled at him. "I've never had so much fun in my entire fucking life!" I pointed at the brave wrecked piece of Americana that had brought me there: *"Park that bitch!"*

I pulled my .38 from the duster coat pocket, tucked it into my sleeve, and ran toward the hotel entrance.

Jesus, Mary, and Joseph, *I* wouldn't have tried to stop someone who looked like me.

A kid at the door did. "You must buy a ticket to enter."

I came to a slow stop. At first my mind refused to assimilate what my lying eyes were telling it. A pale, pimply teenager in some kind of odd uniform, with long pointy ears, sat behind a long table, a roll of pre-printed tickets next to him, and a small metal box to keep the receipts. "What?"

"You have to buy a ticket. For the entire convention it is $55. It is $25 for one day." He looked at me. "Hey, you are bleeding."

I looked back at the entrance to the hotel; hotel employees were helping the driver of the Mercedes out of his car –

– and the white Corvette was pulling into the parking lot's entrance.

"We have a first aid station," the kid was saying when I turned back. "I can not let you enter like –"

"Why do you keep talking without contractions?" I screamed at him.

He jumped backward about half a foot. "I ... I ... I am a Vulcan," he stammered.

"And I'm a fucking vampire," I snarled, and headed inside, and he tried to stop me, so I threw him screaming into the bushes at the edge of the parking lot and went in anyway.

THERE WERE MORE Vulcans inside. And blue skinned people, and people with wicked ugly plastic ridges molded all over their heads, most of them wearing some variation on the uniform the kid outside had been wearing. I had a momentary wild idea – knock one of them out, take the uniform and hide out as one of them. I dropped the idea almost instantly, though; apparently the makeup they used caused acne, and they were all either overweight or under-muscled; I didn't see a single one with a costume that would have fit an adult man in decent shape.

I ran toward the south wing; there are half a dozen exits in the south wing, leading into two different parking lots, one leading directly to the street outside. I could hear disturbances behind me, but I was getting used to that. I ran down the corridor leading to the Mezzanine Room, turned right, and ran into Doctor Death and Kathy.

Knocked them right off their feet.

The sign they were attempting to post in the corridor came fluttering to the ground and landed on the ground near them. I stood in the corridor with the gun in my hand, dripping blood down my cheek onto my coat, and looking at Doctor Death and Kathy.

They looked back at me. They were not dressed like the others; a leather mini-skirt, in Doctor Death's case, and a black leather bra with a white silk blouse over it, and wrap-around black sunglasses. Kathy doesn't wear leather; she was dressed in black jeans and Reeboks, and a tight black t-shirt with a purplish tie-died vest over it. They both looked very good, though Doctor Death's panties were blue and didn't match the rest of her ensemble.

My eyes drifted down to the sign on the floor:

Tetracycline is a general treatment for acne, even severe cases. One 150MG tablet ingested twice a day will give most of you a clear skinned complexion. Most dermatologists will prescribe it upon request.

And a little sunlight wouldn't hurt.

I said softly, "Doctor Death?"

She reached up, and I helped her to her feet, and Kathy.

"What are you doing here?"

Kathy thrust her chin out. "We're –"

"It's *missionary work,*" Doctor Death babbled, "yeah, that's it, that's the ticket. We're here doing missionary work among the unwashed, spreading the good news about –"

"Patrick Stewart is here," Kathy said. "He's *really* hot. I want to have his baby."

I stared back and forth between the two of them. "Uhm ... " My brain wouldn't function. My thoughts moved sluggishly, turning over and over in the same rut. "It's just –"

And then in the corridor behind me, I heard Lila Macauley, the vampire, say, "We *really* need to talk, Thomas."

I turned around and pulled the trigger twice.

WE WENT UP to Doctor Death's hotel room together. Why Doctor Death had a hotel room when she lived twenty minutes drive away from this, this whatever-it-was, was beyond me. I wasn't sure I wanted to know, either.

From the window I could see police at the entrance to the parking lot, taking statements. Eventually they'd come inside the hotel and start asking questions –

She sat on the bed behind me, with my gun in her lap, looking at me. I could feel her gaze on the back of my head. "Why do you keep running away?"

I turned away from the window and looked at her, sitting there with my gun in her lap. She hadn't broken my wrist, quite. "I have a better question. Why are you *doing* this to me?"

She shook her head, long blonde hair moving ... I had to drag my attention back to what she was saying. "I'm not. I've bitten two or three hundred people, I've lost track. Men, women, old people, young people – well, mostly young ones," she conceded. "But I don't usually go back, either." She shrugged. "You tasted really good. But even that wasn't it, that second time. I've had a couple dozen that I've gone back to three or four times, and one girl I spent most of a year with. None of them Changed."

"Why me?"

"I don't know, Thomas. All I know for sure is that if you keep calling attention to yourself, someone older and meaner and a lot scarier than I am is going to come and make sure you stop. And I mean permanently."

She sat there watching me with those pale blue eyes. The only thing I could think of to say was, "I don't want this."

"You don't get a choice. None of us did." She stood up and came toward me. "How do you feel?"

"Oh, God," I whispered. "I'm so hungry."

The last thing I remember her saying was, "Let me show you."

SOME TIME AROUND midnight I woke up in the hotel bed. Lila was gone.

I'd never felt so good, so perfectly healthy, in my life.

There are advantages to losing the day. I laid in bed and thought about what Lila had told me.

Never get sick. Never get old. We heal faster and we move faster and we're a *lot* stronger than you are. Our sex drive is no different from yours, and once the real hunger is satisfied, we eat just like everyone else –

I got out of bed and got dressed and headed downstairs, to the back entrance, thinking to myself that I was going to have to do something about the Sports Satellite; they'd trace the registration to me, and charge me with who knows what sort of vehicular insanity. But I could deal with that, as long as I didn't end up in jail. Not that it would be fatal – there's no direct sunlight in jail cells. But it would be bad.

I got down to the main hallway, and found things quieted down slightly, fewer of the strange people in strange uniforms, and most of those apparently making their way from one party to the next. I ignored an invitation to join one party, and headed down the corridor to the south exit, passing, as I left, a sign that must have been Doctor Death's work, a banner twenty feet long, that said, *Some people bathe every day.*

END

STAR WARS: Empire Blues

I DON'T SUPPOSE it took us five minutes that afternoon to execute the Rebels, start to finish.

The Rebellion on Devaron stood no chance. My home world is sparsely settled, even by Devaronians, and politically unimportant; but it is near the Core. Near the Emperor, may he freeze.

I was Kardue sai Malloc, the fifth of the Kardue line to bear that name; a Devish and a captain in the Devaronian Army.

Kardue had served in the Devaronian Army for sixteen generations: through the Clone Wars, back into the days when no one dreamed the old Republic would ever fall. The army lifestyle suited me, and I the army; aside from the stress of dealing with the Imperium, and the detested necessity of placing Devaronian troops under Imperial command during the Rebellion, it was a tolerable life.

Sixteen generations of military service ended the afternoon after we overran the Rebel positions in Montellian Serat. It took me half a year to hang up the armor; but that was the moment.

Montellian Serat is an old city. Well, was; it dated back to the days before my people had star travel. That the Rebels chose to make a stand there was tactically foolish, but not surprising. I spent the night overseeing the shelling of the ancient city walls, and in the first light of morning stopped shelling long enough to offer the Rebels a chance to surrender. They accepted the offer, laid down their arms by the shattered walls at the city's edge, and came out in single file: man and woman they were seven hundred strong.

I herded them into a hastily constructed holding pen, and mounted guards. I had concern for a rescue attempt; half a day's march south, another group of Rebels were still fighting.

After they surrendered, we shelled the city into rubble. The Empire wanted to make sure no one made the mistake of sheltering Rebels again.

Our orders came just after noon. The Rebels were believed to be moving north; I was to take my forces and intercept them. I was not to leave any of my forces behind as guards for the captured Rebels.

The orders were no more specific than that … but they could not be misunderstood.

I had them executed in mid-afternoon: I pulled the guards back into a half circle, and had them open fire on the Rebels inside the holding pen. It took most of five minutes before the screaming stopped and I could be certain all seven hundred were dead.

There was no time to bury them.

We marched south to the next battle.

WITH ONE THING and another it took almost half a year for the Rebellion on Devaron to be put down. Rebellions are drawn-out affairs, even the failures. When it was over, I submitted my resignation. At first my superiors, humans all, could not decide whether to accept it and let my fellow "natives" kill me once I no longer had the protection of the Imperial Army, or to refuse it and execute me for treason for having made the request in the first place.

I recall I did not much care.

They let me go.

I vanished. Neither my Imperial superiors, nor the family or friends left behind, who lusted for my horns, ever saw me, or my music collection, again.

Time passed.

HALFWAY ACROSS THE galaxy from Devaron, on the small desert planet of Tatooine, in the port city of Mos Eisley, in a cantina tucked away near the center of the hot, dusty city, I looked up from my empty drink and smiled at my old friend Wuher.

I gave him the polite one. Devish are more sharply differentiated by sex than most species. Men have sharper teeth than women, designed for hunting; Devish evolved from pack hunters. Women have canines as well, but also have molars and can survive on food that men would starve on. In rare cases, though, about one birth in fifty, a Devish man will be born with both sets of teeth. I'm one of them. In the old days it was a survival trait; Devish men with both sets of teeth were used as solitary scouts by the pack. They could range farther and survive in terrain where most males would starve. It may be cultural and it may be genetic, but there is no question that Devish with doubled teeth are less creatures of the pack than most Devish men.

I doubt most Devish could do what I've done, at that.

My outer row of teeth are female, flat and not threatening. The inner row, composed of sharp, needle-pointed teeth, is for shredding flesh. When I feel threatened or angry, the outer row of teeth retract. In those circumstances it's a reflex; but I can do it on purpose.

Sometimes I do it on purpose. It startles humans ... well, it startles most non-carnivores, but humans are a special case, a whole species of omnivores. There are not many intelligent omnivorous species out there. I have a theory about them: they're food that decided to fight back. In the case of humans, tree munchies. They never quite get over their own audacity, I suspect, and they're a nervous lot because of it.

(A human once tried to tell me that *humans* were carnivores. I did not laugh at him, despite his molars and his pitiful two pair of blunted incisors, and a digestive tract so long that the flesh he ate rotted before it came out the other end. With a body designed like that, *I'd* take up leaf eating.)

Wuher gave me the usual scowl in response to my polite, flat toothed smile. "Let me guess, Labria. The glass is defective."

Wuher is my best friend on Tatooine. He's a squat, ugly human with a bad attitude and none of the human virtues. He hates droids and doesn't care much for anything else. I like him a great deal. There is a purity to his loathing for the universe that is quite spiritually advanced. If I could free him from his love of money, he might well attain Grace. "Yes, my friend. It has ceased functioning. If you would fix it … ."

"With?"

"Oh, the amber liquid, I suppose."

"The Merenzane Gold?"

"The bottle bears that label," I conceded.

"One Merenzane Gold, point five credits."

I dropped the half-credit coin on the bar top, and waited while he refilled my drink. Merenzane Gold is a sweet, subtle concoction, with many thousands of years of brewing tradition behind it. A single bottle goes for well upward of a hundred credits, depending on vintage.

I took a sip of my drink and smiled again. Proper. You could use it to clean thruster tubes, except it might melt the shielding. I wandered over to my favorite booth, as far away from the bandstand as I could get, and settled in with my ear plugs for the day.

I was the first customer in the door that morning. I could barely remember a time when I had not been.

Tatooine is a nasty, useless little planet. The only noteworthy things about it are Jabba, and the pilots it produces year after year. I don't have any idea why Jabba picked Tatooine as a base; maybe because it's so far from the Core that the Empire is less likely to bother him here. Doesn't matter, really.

As for the pilots, well, Tatooine's a desert, filled with moisture farmers north to south. A single farm takes up so much space that to visit with one another they must travel long distance by speedster; their children learn to fly at an early age. On most Tatooine farms it would take you a day to walk from one end to the other, and you'd likely die of thirst first.

I hate Tatooine. I'm still not sure why I stayed here. It was a temporary thing, I recall that. I was following Maxa Jandovar, the great – well, for a human – great vandfillist. I kept *missing* her. She was one of the half dozen surviving artists I hadn't seen live who was worth seeing. I spent half a decade following her around through the outback, hitting planet after planet weeks or days or, in one instance that gave me ample opportunity to demonstrate Grace, a mere half day after she'd left. She didn't leave an agenda; she couldn't, very well. The Empire wouldn't go to the trouble of hunting her, but if she'd announced where she was going next, she'd certainly have found a squad of stormtroopers waiting for her at the spaceport when she arrived.

The Empire doesn't trust artists. Particularly the great ones; they persist in speaking the truth when it is inconvenient.

They arrested Maxa Jandovar on Morvogodine. She died in custody. I was on Tatooine when I got the news, getting ready to head to Morvogodine.

Somehow I ended up staying.

Nightlily, the H'nemthe sitting down at the end of the bar, looked bored and horny. I felt sorry for *someone*. "Hey, Wuher!"

Wuher looked at me from down the length of the bar. "Yeah?"

"Universal Truth Number One: You should never say 'Well, why don't you bite my head off?' to a female H'nemthe who is bigger than you are."

He didn't even smile. Jerk.

In the booth next to mine, two humans were trying to talk a Moorin mere into helping them rob a bar over on the other side of Mos Eisley; I made a note to myself to call the bar's owner and sell him a warning about the men. Not that it looked as if the Moorin were going to help them; only one of the humans spoke the merc's language, his accent was horrific, and his syntax was occasionally hysterical. I could see the merc struggling to take them seriously. At one point the merc, Obron Mettlo, growled at them that he was a soldier, a fighter; he mentioned some of the battles he'd fought in. I'd actually heard of most of them – if he wasn't lying, he was a serious professional.

"Hey, Wuher! "

Wuher looked at me from down the length of the bar. "Yeah?"

"What do you call someone who speaks three languages?"

"Trilingual."

"Someone who speaks two languages?"

"Bilingual."

"Someone who speaks one language?"

He puzzled at it a second. "Monolingual?"

"Human."

He almost smiled before he caught himself.

The day passed slowly. They tend to. I drank enough to keep the world slightly out of focus, and waited for the suns to set. I moved around a bit, sat at the bar a few times, looking for conversation; I even bought two drinks for an off-duty stormtrooper, slumming. Wasted; he was more interested in women than in conversation, and I doubted he knew anything anyway. That is the nature of investments, though; someday he *might* know something, if such a thing were possible for a stormtrooper. And then he *might* think of his old friend and drinking buddy, Labria.

Brokering information is a chancy occupation, at best.

Can't say I'm any good at it.

Long Snoot showed up toward late afternoon. It had been a good day until then; Wuher didn't have musicians that day, and I hadn't had to wear my ear plugs even once.

Long Snoot wanted to sell *me* information.

I smiled at him, in my corner booth as far away from the stage as I could get. The sharp smile. "That's a new one. Pass."

Long Snoot's "name" is Garindan. I had a protocol droid do a search on the word once. In five different languages it meant "Blessed One," "burnt wood," "dust from a windstorm," "ugly," and "toast." None of the five languages were spoken by a species that looked anything like Long Snoot's.

Long Snoot's the most successful spy in Mos Eisley. In a town with as many spies as this city has, that says something. He pays adequately for information; sometimes I give him information of value. Sometimes I even do it on purpose.

"But Labria," he wheedled, voice low, "this is a subject of *particular* interest to you."

"Give me a hint."

He shook his head, trunk waving gently in front of my face. I suppressed an uncivilized urge to swat it with a sharpened nail. (I often have the opportunity to exhibit Grace in dealing with Long Snoot.) "Fifty credits, Labria. You won't regret it."

I thought about it. I took a sip of the acid gold and swished it around my back teeth for a bit. I could feel it helping keep them sharp. "Fifty credits is a lot. Resellable?"

He scratched under his snout, thinking. "I can't think to who."

Something of interest to me, but not resellable ... I could feel my ears straighten. "Who is it?"

"Fift-"

"I'll pay. Who's onplanet?"

"Figri-"

I came up out of my seat. "Fiery Figrin Da'n is on *Tatooine?*"

He made an urk noise. "People ... are ... *looking.*"

I looked around. Some of them were, in fact. Odd, having all those eyes on me. I let go of Long Snoot, and they turned away. "Sorry. Bit excitable."

He rubbed his throat. "Your nails need trimming."

"I expect they do." He sat back down again, but I was too excited. "The band is with him?"

"Fifty credits."

A snarl rose in the back of my throat. I pulled out a fifty-credit note and dropped it into his outstretched hand, and tried to keep the growl out of my voice when I spoke. "Who?"

"They're playing for Jabba."

"All of them?"

"The Modal Nodes."

"That's them," I said, unable to keep the excitement out of my voice. "Doikk Na'ts on the Fizzz, Tedn Dahai and Ikabel G'ont on the Fanfar, Nalan Cheel on Bandfill, Tech Mo'r on the Ommni."

"Yeah. Those are the names."

Oh, my.

The greatest jizz band in the galaxy was in town.

I LEFT EARLIER than usual, as soon as it was dark outside. Wuher nodded at me on my way out. "Tomorrow, Labria."

I nodded at him and went outside into the hot night.

"Labria" is an extremely dirty word in my native tongue. It translates, roughly, as "cold food," though the basic phrase loses the flavor of it.

By my horns, I don't understand humans. I've lived around them close to two decades now. The things they swear by! Sex, excrement, and religion.

I'll never understand them.

THERE ARE FOUR hundred billion stars in the galaxy. Most of them have planets; about half have planets capable of supporting life. About a tenth of those worlds have evolved life of their own, and about one in a thousand of those worlds have evolved intelligent life forms.

These are rough numbers. There are well over twenty million intelligent races in the galaxy, though. No one can keep track of them all, not even the Empire.

I have no idea how many bounty hunters there are in Mos Eisley. Hundreds of professionals, I'm sure. Tens of thousands who would turn bounty hunter without a moment's pause if the bounty were high enough, and if anyone knew of it.

The Butcher of Montellian Serat has five million credits on his horns. But Devaron is halfway across the galaxy, and there may only be a dozen sentients on all of Tatooine who even know for sure what species I belong to. (There are two other Devaronians onplanet, Oxbel and Jubal. I rather like Oxbel; we pretended to be brothers once, during a rather involved scam that didn't work out the way we'd hoped. We don't look *anything* alike – his ancestors evolved at the equator, mine toward the north pole – but the humans we were trying to cheat couldn't tell the difference. I rather like Oxbel, but I don't come close to trusting him. He's been away from Devaron even longer than I have, and it's entirely possible that even *he* hasn't heard of the Butcher of Montellian Serat – but it's best to be safe.

(There are downsides to being safe, though. The closest Devish woman is on the other side of the Core. Just the thought makes my horns ache.)

Most bounty hunters are lazy. If they weren't, they'd be in another line of work.

And research is not their strong point. I took the short way home.

A REASON FOR Living:

I keep a small underground apartment about twelve minutes' brisk walk from the cantina. It's been broken into twice since I've lived there. The first time I came back and found the deed done; the second time I surprised the burglar in the act. A young human. Turns out humans don't taste very good.

The lights come on automatically as I unlock and let myself in. The door leads down a flight of stairs to a cold, sweaty basement that costs an indecent amount to cool. The heat-exchange coils turn on automatically when I enter; I know from long experience I won't be able to sleep until they have been on for quite a while – and at that it will not be properly cold until I am done sleeping, and it's time to turn them off.

There's only one thing of value in the apartment; neither of my two thieves found it, fortunately. From the outer room you go into the sleeping cubicle, and from there into the bathroom. The sanitary facilities are human designed, but they suit me well enough. In the shower, you push back on the tiled wall, and it slides back enough to step through, sideways.

I step through and into a small eight-sided room. The walls are not perfect; they tend to reflect the higher frequencies and absorb the lower ones, so virtually everything ends up sounding brighter than it should. Some of that can be adjusted for; some of it I simply have to live with.

The wall behind me sighs shut. The room is already cool; it's the first part of the apartment to be cooled. Along the walls are the chips.

Some of them are unique, I'm sure. Priceless. Copies of recordings that are preserved by no one else in the galaxy. Some of them are merely rare and very expensive.

I have everyone. Or, to be precise, I have *something* by everyone. I have music the Imperium banned a generation ago ... by musicians executed for singing the wrong lyric, in the wrong way, to the wrong person, by musicians who simply vanished, by musicians who had the good fortune to die before the Empire came to power.

Maxa Jandovar is here, and Orin Mersai, and Telindel and Saerlock, Lord Kavad and the Skaalite Orchestra, M'lar'Nkai'-kambric, Janet Lalasha, and Miracle Meriko, who died in Imperial custody four days after I saw him play *Stardance* for the last time. The ancient masters, Kang and Lubrichs, Ovido Aishara, and the amazing Brullian Dyll.

I have two recordings by Fiery Figrin Da'n and the Modal Nodes. Da'n may be the greatest Klooist the galaxy has ever seen. As for Doikk Na'ts ... there's something about his playing that's always struck me as cautious, careful ... but sometimes, sometimes the fire comes, and he plays the Fizzz as well as Janet Lalasha ever did.

Most of their backup players could play lead, in a lesser band.

I settle down in the seat, set just off center for the room, where the sound comes together most cleanly, open a bottle of twelve-year-old Dorian Quill, and wait for the music to start.

My people believe that to kill something, you must cherish it and love it as it dies. There is no barrier between you and the thing you are killing, and you die as you kill.

Music is the only thing I know that feels the same way.

The music surrounds me until I cease to exist. I die as I kill.

It's what I live for.

I'm glad my fathers are dead.

IN THE MORNING I went to see Jabba.

He had me strand on the trapdoor, and his tail twitched as we spoke. That always bothers me. Part of me was frightened by it; even carnivores get eaten by bigger carnivores. Another part of me wanted to pounce on it.

He regarded me with those slitted ugly eyes, and laughed a rumbling, unpleasant laugh. "So … what information does my least favorite spy have to sell me?"

I made it good. I spoke to him in Hutt, which I normally try to avoid; it hurts my throat, and I have to use both sets of teeth to make some of the sounds. After a long conversation, the front row aches from being pulled up and then dropped down again quickly. "There's a mercenary in town." I'd learned what I could about him before heading over. It hadn't been much, but I'd been rushed. I wanted to move on this quickly – if Jabba didn't like Da'n and the Nodes, I might *never* get to see them play. Nor would anyone else. "Obron Mettlo. A real professional, fought in dozens of battles, often on the winning side, looking for employment. Moorin, has an attitude –"

He made a low, grumbling sound that might have been interpreted as interest. Jabba had plenty of muscle, but not always smart muscle; and Moorin tend to be bright as well as vicious.

I forged ahead. "If you like, I could get in touch with him. Bring him by to meet you … for dinner, perhaps. Possibly some entertainment, some music – music is good with Moorin. Keeps 'em peaceable."

His eyelids drooped slightly; either he was bored or he was thinking. Finally he gave me a slight chuckle, and said, "Send him over."

I bowed and backed away as quickly as was polite, getting off that trapdoor. "As you wish, sir. We'll be by – would first dark be appropriate?"

He smiled at me and it made the fur on the small of my back stand straight up. "Send *him* by," he clarified. "You are not invited."

I stood frozen at the edge of the trapdoor, mind refusing to function. Surely there had to be some way to wangle

Jabba made a sound. A familiar sound; I've heard Devish make it, too – except that it takes a pack of Devish. It straightened my ears and made my front teeth jump out of the way. "You can leave now."

I bowed and got out.

I SPENT THE evening at the cantina, drinking myself into a stupor.

I just *knew* Jabba would feed the Modal Nodes to the rancor. He'd *never* had a decent band before, never, not once. The closest he'd ever come was Max Rebo's bunch, who could carry a melody if you gave them a basket.

But the next morning, I learned that Rebo was out looking for work.

Jabba had a new favorite.

IT CAME *THIS* close to killing me.

For four days I couldn't sleep for thinking about it. There they were, not a half part's speedster trip from Mos Eisley. Playing for *him*. It ate me alive thinking about it. I lost so much Grace in those days that if I had any shame left to me, I'd have to use some of it on that period.

Sometime on the fifth day I drank too much. I awoke lying face down in the alleyway upstairs and behind the cantina, in darkness, with someone nudging my shoulder with his toe. I decided to take a chunk out of his calf –

Wuher knelt next to me. "Can you stand up?"

The cold gravel pressed against my cheek. I had bruises, cuts – the memories came back slowly. Several someones had beaten me – heavy wood or metal staffs, I vaguely recalled. Just a random robbery. My right arm wouldn't move. "I don't think so."

"Come on." M$_y$ body is denser than a human's; he staggered, helping me to my feet. The strain sent a jolt of astonishing pain through my shoulder. "Where do you live?"

He half carried me to my apartment, and stood at the opening while I fumbled with the interlock. "Do you need medical help?"

I don't remember if I answered him or not. It was a stupid question. No doctor on Tatooine knew anything about Devish physiology – or if they did, I didn't want to know *them*.

I made it to the shower before I collapsed. I got the cold water turned on and sat in it until morning, trying to decide how badly I wanted to live.

BY MORNING THE apartment half reminded me of home. I stayed in it and did not go out, kept the heat-exchange coils running all day. Around midday I found the strength to pull a slab of womp rat the length of my arm from the freezer, heat it to blood temperature, and drag it into the shower with me. I sat under the water, nude, eating until my stomach bulged, and when there was nothing left but bones on the floor of the stall; turned the water off and staggered to my bedpit.

IT TOOK ME some time before I felt safe going out in public again. Several times someone came to my door; I didn't open it. Mos Eisley is like a living creature: it eats the sick and weak. I'd survived all these years without having to kill more than a few of my fellow residents, partially by not doing boneheaded things like opening the door just because someone knocked. They'd have heard by now of the attack on me – the humans who'd robbed me might have boasted of it, in which case I'd have them in my freezer, whoever they were, before the month was out.

But in any event I dared not go back to the cantina until my strength was returned.

The arm took longest to heal; weeks later it was still stiff and it hurt when I moved it wrong. But I was almost out of food, so I had no choice. Early one morning I dressed, set my alarms, and headed for the cantina.

Wuher looked up and nodded at me when I entered. First one in the door. He put a glass on the counter and poured a shot of golden liquid. "On the house. Drink it before someone else comes in."

I looked at the drink; and then at Wuher, almost as much at a loss for words as I'd been when Jabba told me to send the merc over by himself. "Many thanks," I finally got out. He nodded and I lifted the glass –

And stopped. Predators have better noses than leaf eaters. There was something wrong with the alcohol. It was –

He poured himself a shot while I was staring at my glass, raised it to me, and knocked it back.

Merenzane Gold. Precious, pure Merenzane Gold.

Wuher corked the unlabeled bottle while I was still staring at him, put it away under the bar, and wandered away from me to finish opening up.

I took the glass to my booth, sat and drank it very slowly. I hadn't known there was a bottle of real Gold on all of Tatooine. I'd almost forgotten what it tasted like.

I wondered how many years he'd had that bottle down there without saying anything about it.

By the Cold, I'm a lousy spy. That's something to be proud of.

I spent the morning listening to the talk throughout the bar. I'd been out of touch … and interesting things had happened while I'd been hidden away from the world. Last night an Imperial battle cruiser had fought in orbit with a Rebel spaceship, and today stormtroopers were looking all over Tatooine for someone, or something, that had escaped them.

And a piece of horrifically bad news: the damn mercenary I'd recommended to Jabba had picked a fight with a pair of Jabba's bodyguards and shot them both up before getting himself fed to the rancor. There was rumor that the merc had been an assassin paid by the Lady Valarian, whose real target had been Jabba himself

Maybe Jabba had forgotten who had recommended him.

And maybe Long Snoot would give me my fifty credits back.

IT CAME TO me in a vision.

Okay, that's not true, but it's close. Long Snoot stopped by and mentioned something interesting: The Lady Valarian was getting married. Max Rebo and band were going to play at the wedding.

I barely noticed when Long Snoot left. I stared straight ahead, through the noonday crowd come to escape the heat, not seeing them, not seeing the cantina. Just thinking.

"Wuher."

He turned away from a conversation with a pair of human females who looked like clones; the Tonnika sisters, they'd introduced themselves as. He did it grudgingly; they were attractive, by human standards. "Yeah?"

"How's business?"

He stared at me suspiciously. "It stinks. It always stinks."

"How would you like entertainment by real musicians?"

"Rebo? Can't afford him, and his bunch don't draw what they cost anyway."

I gave him the polite smile. "Figrin Da'n and the Modal Nodes. They're Bith. They're *good*, Wuher. I mean really, really good."

"What would they cost me?"

"Five hundred a week."

He gave me the suspicious stare again. If something sounds too good to be true, someone's being screwed. "Really. A band better than Rebo's will work here for less than his."

"I think I can arrange it."

"How?"

I told him. When I was done he said in a somber voice, "You are one twisted puppy, Lab."

"Is it a deal?"

He shook his head *no*, said "It's a deal," and wandered away, shaking his head and muttering to himself.

THE LADY VALARIAN is the closest thing to competition that Jabba the Hutt has on Tatooine. That's not saying much; Jabba tolerates her because it keeps all the discontents in one place. She's a Whiphid, which means she's stupid, huge, ugly, has more muscle on her than I do, and smells worse than Jabba. I wouldn't eat her after a long hunt.

I went to see her at her hotel, the Lucky Despot. The Lucky Despot isn't much of a hotel, truth told; just a spaceship that won't ever lift again.

"That's right," I said. "Modal Nodes. Lead is Figrin Da'n. I know you want the best for your wedding, Lady Valarian. This group makes music so glorious, your wedding will be the talk of this corner of the galaxy. People for dozens of light-years will speak with envy and longing of the entertainment provided at the wedding of the great Lady Valarian and her handsome consort, the daring D'Wopp, of the romantic mood set by the finest musicians this poor galaxy has ever seen."

She glared at me – well, I think she glared at me; with those mad little eyes Whiphids have, it's hard to tell – and said skeptically, "Better than Max Rebo? I *love* Max Rebo."

She would. And she deserved to have the ugly little runt play her wedding, for all of me. "Fair mistress, your taste is as that of your tongue, and none would dare say otherwise." I gave her the polite smile. "But the Modal Nodes are currently Jabba the Hutt's favored entertainment. Would you have it said that the entertainment at your wedding was provided by the musicians Jabba deemed too poor to play for him?"

It took her a bit to work through it. I'd gotten a little carried away with my syntax; Whiphids have a working vocabulary of only about eight thousand words. "No! No, I won't have it! I want the Nodal Notes!" She looked briefly uncertain. "Do you think they'll come?"

"They'll be expensive, madam. They'll be braving Jabba's displeasure: to play for you. It might cost ... two, or three thousand credits, perhaps. If I can have the loan of a messenger droid, I would be most happy to begin making the arrangements ... ."

THE MORNING OF the wedding I called Jabba.

He laughed with, I think, real amusement on seeing me. "My least favorite spy!" he boomed. "Perhaps you should come visit me. We can have dinner together, and talk about the mercenary you introduced to me."

"I have information, Jabba."

"Hmmm."

"Do you know your musicians are missing? Figrin Da'n and the Modal Nodes?"

"*Hmmmph!*" He made a bellowing noise and rocked himself off camera. I heard shrieks, steel clanging, things breaking ... I stood patiently in front of my comlink's pickup and waited for him to come back, if he was going to. After a bit he did. "Hoooo," he muttered, shaking his head. "Where are they, least favorite spy?"

"The Lady Valarian is getting married today. She's hired them to play at her wedding at the Lucky Despot Hotel."

The eyes narrowed to slits. "And what does my least favorite spy want for this information?"

I spread my hands. "Let us forget a certain unfortunate introduction ... ."

He looked at me through the slitted eyes for a second, and then gave the booming laugh. "Least favorite spy, call me again sometime."

He broke the connection.

Cold sweat trickled through the fur on the small of my back.

WUHER HAD DRESSED for the wedding. He'd changed his shirt.

The cantina was dark and silent; I'd never seen it like this before, except the first few minutes in the morning. I gave Wuher my invitation; the Lady Valarian had given it to me in gratitude for acquiring the "Nodal Notes" for her wedding, while hinting that, in the future, I might find it better business to share information with her rather than with Jabba.

Someone'll kill Jabba, someday, but it's not going to be Valarian.

"You're sure the wedding's going to be broken up," he repeated.

"I'm sure the Modal Nodes aren't going to want to go back to Jabba after this. All you have to do is offer them a place to lie low for a while, play a few gigs, pick up a few credits. They're going to be broke; Valarian won't pay them after her wedding is broken up."

He shook his head, tucking his shirt in again. "You think they'll go for it?"

"I think they'll jump at it."

Wuher stood there, studying me in the gloom. "Lab … if you put this kind of effort into anything else, you could be a wealthy being."

I shook my head, and said gently, "My friend, this is all that I want."

IT'S HARD TO OUT-THINK Jabba. Also dangerous.

I sat in the shadows of a building down the way from the Lucky Despot, watching the crowd arrive for the wedding. A scummy lot, all around. I recognized several of the "guests" as Jabba's people. I hoped there wasn't any shooting. I didn't see enough of Jabba's troops to make that likely; if he'd decided to wipe out Lady Valarian for her theft of his musicians, he'd have sent more soldiers. That was a good sign.

I could hear, so faintly that my ears twitched, a song that might have been "Tears of Aquanna." It was followed by what was, quite definitely, "Worm Case." Odd choices for a wedding. Maybe they were playing requests.

And then the bad news arrived. Stormtroopers.

Two squads. They set down out of the night, quietly and with running lights doused, in full combat armor. One squad covered the entrance to the hotel, and the second squad went in. From the moment they set down I doubt it took them twenty seconds.

Oh, the noise was *awful*. From where I sat, I could hear it. Screams, blaster bolts, yelling, another round of blaster fire – one of the stormtroopers near the entrance went down. I lifted my mac-robinoculars and watched the building through them. Windows opened and the scum of a dozen different races came squirming out through them. I moved the macrobinoculars up, scanning across the structure of the half-buried ship … . Toward the top of the ship, three stories above the dirty sand, an emergency airlock clanged open. The first head through it was a Bith. I couldn't guess who: All Bith look alike, even when you're not looking through macrobinoculars. More Bith followed, and then the unmistakable squat form of my friend Wuher. They took off across the sand together, Wuher and the Bith, and ran straight by me in the darkness without pausing.

I'd never have guessed that Wuher could move that fast … and a moment later I saw why he was managing it. A pair of stormtroopers came charging after them, weapons at the ready. I shed a little Grace by tripping the one in the lead. The second stormtrooper tripped over him. I bent over them and picked up their rifles. I hadn't handled an assault rifle in a very long time, but they hadn't changed. I pulled the charge cages from them and handed them back to the two stormtroopers as they recovered their feet.

"You appear to have dropped these, gentles."

One of them immediately jumped backward, rifle pointing at me, and shouted, "Don't move!"

The other one looked at me, and then at his rifle, and then at me again.

"Come now," I said gently. "We're reasonable beings. You tripped and I helped you up again. No need for anyone to get upset. If you got injured in the fall, perhaps, I'd be more than happy to compensate you for it … ."

I let my voice trail off and the three of us watched each other for a beat.

The one pointing the useless rifle at me said in a strained voice, "Are you trying to bribe us?"

I drew myself up to my full height and stared down at them, and gave them the sharp smile. "Not," I said, "if you're going to be snotty about it."

IN THE MORNING, when I reached the cantina, I found the Modal Nodes already there, setting up.

Wuher scowled at me. "I got shot at. By a stinking droid."

He didn't seem that angry, though "You heard them play."

He nodded grudgingly. "Yeah. They're pretty good."

"They're the best," I said softly. "And I think you know it."

He just snorted.

"About my fee."

"Yeah?"

"Free drinks for a year."

He snorted again. "Not bloody likely. We won't get a year out of this lot; they'll jump planet as soon as they can find some idiot to run the lines for them."

He had a point. Still … "Their stay might be longer than that," I pointed out. "Jabba will want to keep them from leaving the planet. He might even want them back someday."

He actually smiled at me; I like him better scowling. "Seven free drinks a day as long as they keep, playing. As soon as they sneak out of here, you pay again. You pay for every drink over seven anyway."

I grinned at him before I remembered myself, with the sharp teeth. "Deal." I got up and walked over to where Figrin was setting up with the band, and introduced myself.

I swear, Biths look contemptuous even when they're not trying to. The fellow had obviously heard of my reputation: Labria the drunk. The half bright; half sly, half sober. He barely glanced at me. "Oh, yes. Jabba's least favorite spy."

The fellow was a notorious gambler. "Interested in a few hands of sabacc? The crowd doesn't start showing up here until later afternoon anyhow."

"I don't think so."

"Twenty-credit minimum bid."

His head swiveled as though it belonged to a droid. "Oh? Can you back that up?"

I gave him the sharp smile, on purpose. Bith *know* they're food. "Are you trying to insult me, Figrin Da'n?"

THERE MAY HAVE been a deck somewhere, somewhen in the history of time colder than the one we used, but I wouldn't bet on it. Bith come from a warm, bright world. Devaronians, by the way, see farther into the infrared than practically anyone. It's useful to be able to see heat, when you evolve in the cold.

Buried in the black border along the edges of the cards were markers sensitive to low-spectrum infrared light. I knew every card he held, all that morning.

They were already broke: By the time we were done I owned their instruments, except for Doikk Na'ts's Fizzz.

AND WHAT A day that turned out to be.

For the life of me it seemed the universe had conspired to keep me from enjoying the music. First the band squabbled with each other, and then when they finally got going, with a nice upbeat rendition of "Mad About Me," some old fool chopped up another fool – with a lightsaber, of all frozen things – and interrupted it. That psychotic Solo actually showed his face in the cantina just after that, and then of course had to kill a miserable excuse for a bounty hunter named Greedo. If I'd had a blaster on me I might have shot Solo in the back as he left, but well, opportunities slip by.

Besides, it's best not to draw attention.

AFTERNOON SLID INTO evening, and I nursed my drinks and watched them play. It took them a while to get into it; at first Figrin couldn't stand looking at me, and every time he saw me watching them it threw him out of his game. But it's hard to stay infuriated with someone who is knowledgeable about what you do, and appreciates it as I appreciated them. The music got darker as the day wore on, smokier and more intimate, and Figrin Da'n performed with his eyes closed, moving through the numbers, with Doikk Na'ts at his side; and they played with each other, building through the numbers together, playing off each other, feeding improvisations back upon improvisations, playing, for the first time in who knows how long, for an audience that could, and did, appreciate what they did. An audience of one.

They closed up with "Solitary World," an appropriate choice, I suppose, with the long intertwined sequences of Fizzz and Kloo, ending with one of the most difficult of the Kloo solos, and Doikk finished his piece, bowing out in recognition of genius: And the Bith stood there and played, Fiery Figrin Da'n in the midst of the music: and I watched him wail away; safe, secure, surrounded by the sound, in that place that I would never know.

*

Empire Blues appeared in "Star Wars: Tales From the Mos Eisley Cantina," edited by Kevin J. Anderson. Some of the events in this story won't make a great deal of sense to you unless you've read other stories in that anthology, but there's not much to be done about that. As of 2010 I believe "Tales From the Mos Eisley Cantina" is still in print.

The "About the Authors" in the back of the book has this to say about me:

Daniel Keys Moran claims he has never done anything or been anywhere interesting. He is the author of the wildly popular Tales of the Continuing Time, *and does in fact resemble the character Trent from those books, except that he is handsomer, wittier, and a much better basketball player. The most recent novel in the series,* The Last Dancer, *was published in 1993 from Bantam Books.*

He is extremely pleased to have named, sixteen years after the fact, the Cantina Bar song from Star Wars. It is now called, of course, Mad About Me.

I didn't invent Labria's name, or the "jizz" bands; they came with the material. I think this is an important point to make.

One day I was listening to an online radio service – and the Cantina Band theme came on. And I have to admit, it was a pleasant little moment to notice that the title of the song, as displayed, was Mad About Me.

STAR WARS: A Barve Like That

BY J.D. MONTGOMERY

WITH THE PASSAGE of the years he had learned to recognize certain things.

When he first returned to awareness he knew that he was on the surface of a planet. Artificial gravity shimmers at the boundaries of perception; on a ship under thrust the engines, however well damped, vibrate; and gravity produced by angular momentum causes a Coriolis effect that a human who has trained himself can recognize.

But that was *all* that he knew when the voice out of the darkness said, *You are Boba Fett.*

Fett's head jerked up and he stared into –

Nothing.

He reached for his rifle – and did not move. His arms and legs were firmly restrained. Fett hung in darkness, feet not touching the ground.

He heard a distant crack followed by the same noise again, rather more close. His head was not restrained but the rest of his body felt as though it had been wrapped in –

He stuck out his tongue and flipped the switch that turned on his helmet's macrobinoculars.

You are Boba Fett.

Even with the macrobinoculars, translating up out of the infrared and down from the ultraviolet, there was not much to see. Fett hung against the wall of a tunnel – a tunnel not of stone or any artificial material, but soft and yielding, sponge-like, ridged and corded as though the tunnel had *grown* into its current shape. He could turn his head just enough to see that the tunnel curved sharply out of sight a few meters to his left and right.

Screams in the distance.

A whistling *crack*.

The voice said after a long pause, curiously, *You* are *Boba Fett?*

It came back in a rush – Tatooine, the sail barge, Skywalker and Solo, and with a rush of horror that stilled every other thought fighting for his attention it came to him where he was, in the belly of the Sarlacc –

Being digested.

MOST OF THOSE who dealt with Fett over the course of the decades did not consider him a man of much feeling. This was accurate. He was not.

Leaving Bespin, though, he was filled by a certain fondness for Han Solo. Do not misunderstand – he did not approve of the man – but it was rare to receive two bounties for the same acquisition. But Vader had paid well and the Hutt would pay nearly as well again.

The Hutt had promised a bounty of a hundred thousand credits. A respectable amount, though not as good as some Fett had earned. He had once received a bounty of a hundred and fifty thousand credits for the pirate Feldrall Okor; and on a memorable occasion, half a million credits for the delivery of Nivek'Yppiks, an incautious Ffib heretic who had fled his homeworld of Lorahns, and the religious oligarchy that controlled it.

Fett did not imagine he would ever come to like religious autarchies; they reminded him of his youth. But he had come to appreciate them. They paid exquisitely well and their "criminals" were intellectuals who talked too much and rarely shot back.

Fett's fee for the Solo acquisition was, though the Hutt did not know it yet, about to be increased. Fett did not imagine he would be able to push Jabba to half a million credits – the Hutt was a business creature, not a religious fanatic – but the Hutt was among other things an art collector.

Han Solo, encased in carbonite, *had* to be worth more than Han Solo alive *or* dead.

By the time he got done, counting both his fee from the Empire and his fee from the Hutt, Fett fully intended to better the half million he had received on that Yppiks fool.

FETT SLEPT SITTING up in the pilot's chair, which made a more comfortable bed than some Fett had known, while the Slave I made the last jump to Tatooine.

Hyperspace transit was as a rule the only place Fett felt safe enough to sleep soundly. He did not dream, at least nothing he remembered; his sleep was peaceful and uninterrupted. One might have called it the sleep of a just man.

He awakened not long before hyperspace breakout. No device awakened him; he had decided to awake at the correct time, and he did. He awoke alert, scanning the control board. All seemed well.

Minutes later the hyperspace tunnel fragmented around him. Stars appeared in the viewplate – and a klaxon shrilled through the ship.

Bad news and Fett took it calmly enough, under the circumstances: a beacon had activated itself down in the hold, announcing Fett's arrival insystem to whoever was listening on that frequency. Fett's deduction was instantaneous and correct; another hunter had planted the beacon during his stay on Cloud City. Fett slapped the autopilot control and sprinted below deck.

Another hunter, looking for the Hutt's bounty on Solo. It was the only answer that made sense, and Fett damned himself for a fool for not checking his ship when he had the chance. Basics, *basics,* you ignore the basics and you *deserve* what happens to you. Fett unslung the flame-thrower as he ran, rounded the last corridor before the cargo bay, to the stretch of corridor where the sensors showed the beacon originating, and let loose. He cooked the bulkhead until the metal glowed and the air around him burned hot and stank with ozone, brought the flame tracking upward

The klaxon ceased and Fett left the *Slave I's* maintenance droid to deal with the fire he'd started, and ran back to control.

He slid into his seat. The *Slave I* had continued to head insystem at high speed, Tatooine growing large in the viewscreen. The local shipping did not seem to be taking notice of Fett, which was all to the good, but *somebody* out there knew he'd arrived. Fett fed figures to the autopilot, had it calculate a hyperspace jump back out of the system, started another thread and set a portion of the computer to performing diagnostics on ship functions.

He did not worry about his weapons systems, nor his deflectors; they were either ready, or sabotaged – probably ready. Planting a beacon was one thing, and impressive enough; fooling the ship's on-board diagnostics quite another.

So deep in a planet's gravity well, calculating a new hyperspace jump took *time,* even for a computer as bright as the one Fett had running the *Slave I.* Even so, it had nearly completed the calculations when the subject became moot:

A needle of a ship came up over Tatooine's horizon. The *IG-2000.* It was instantly recognizable, and it told Fett just how very bad the problem was. The ship belonged to the assassin droid IG-88, the second-best bounty hunter in the galaxy, and studying hard to be number one. Fett's fingers danced across the controls and the *Slave I* braked savagely, dropping into a lower orbit. Fett focused and fired his fore blasters as the two ships closed

The *IG2000* exploded instantly, went up in a burst of superheated metal and expanding plasma.

Fett thought instantly, *Bad decoy. That assassin droid would never make a mistake like –*

The *Slave I*'s sensors went wild – a ship was leaving hyperspace only a few klicks away – and then the *Slave* I shuddered all about Fett as blaster fire struck it aft. The aft holocams showed it all clearly. The *IG2000*, the real one, no decoy, breaking out of hyperspace with blasters lit, coming up above and behind Fett, pinning the *Slave I* between the *IG2000* and Tatooine. It was a brilliant maneuver that only the assassin droid, with its droid's reflexes, could have planned and carried out.

The *Slave I* dove for atmosphere, the *IG2000* following at high speed, as the comm unit came alive. IG88's voice lacked intonation: "Surrender your prisoner and you have a thirty percent probability of surviving this encounter."

Fett ignored the droid, fingers flying across his control panel. The droid said something else then, that Boba Fett never heard. He routed what power he could spare to the rear deflectors, sent another round of blaster fire aft to keep IG88 occupied, and then ruined his own ship –

He turned the inertial damper on.

For most of a second the *Slave I* went dark as the inertial damper drew current, shields dropping, weapons going dead for that second, when a single blaster bolt would have destroyed the entire ship – and then the inertial damper came online.

Dual explosions came from below deck, the inertial damper destroying itself as it did its job, and probably taking the hyperdrive with it. Half the indicators on the main board went red, the ship's superstructure *screamed* with the sound of tearing metal, as the ship lost ninety percent of its velocity in the quantum instant it took an electron to descend from one atomic orbital shell to another.

Power returned to what was left of the *Slave I* as the *IG2000* hurtled past Fett at high speed. Fett calmly did all the obvious things, using the ion cannon to destroy the *IG2000*'s rear deflector array before IG88 could bring it online, followed by taking out the fore deflector array. He clamped a tractor beam onto the *IG2000* long enough to keep it from fleeing, and sent a missile down to finish the business off.

INSIDE THE SARLACC, Fett said aloud, "Shouldn't have named it that."

The voice said politely, *Indeed?*

"The *Slave I*. It was a mistake, that. It gave away information, told people I owned more … " Fett's voice trailed off. He hung against a wall, in darkness, his extremities numbed. He could not feel his hands or his feet, and his skin was burning, and worst of all he was *not* aboard the *Slave I,* not at all.

He whispered, "How did you do that to me?"

He had the brief impression of amusement. *It was easy. No —* you *were easy. You live strongly.*

A chill descended upon Fett, and he shivered fiercely, there in the darkness, with the near and distant popping sounds. "Who *are* you?"

A fair enough question, it said, and the dark amusement was unmistakable this time. *As you are my past, Boba Fett … I am your destiny.*

"THE GRIMACE IS quite wonderful," said the Hutt. "We are impressed with your efforts, and we are pleased to pay seventy-five thousand credits for the person of Han Solo."

Fett shook his head. "Jabba" – and he heard the stir that went through the room at the familiarity – "we're not dealing here with the person of Captain Solo – who I recall had a bounty on him of one hundred thousand credits."

Jabba's tail twitched and his voice deepened into a dangerous near-growl. "This is *not* Solo?"

"This?" said Fett, as courteously as he was able – it was not his strong suit. He had not been raised speaking Basic, and his voice and diction tended toward a certain harshness when he used it. "This finely rendered carbonite sculpture, the person of Han Solo? No. What I brought you today is art. Art created by the Dark Lord that happened to use Han Solo as material, like another artist might shape clay." He shrugged. "I tell you what, I've gotten attached to it during my journey here. It has a presence to it, don't you think?"

The Hutt said slowly, "The grimace is … quite wonderful."

"And the hands," said Fett, pushing it. "Let's us two admire the hands together. I like them, they show the *quality* of the Dark Lord's work –"

"Rather," the Hutt murmured in a bass rumble, "rather. One sees Solo's final moments of fear in them." He examined Boba Fett, standing beside the carbonite-encased Han Solo; both Fett and the piece of art under discussion were well back from the trapdoor before Jabba's throne. "There is news," Jabba continued, "that Vader failed to capture Skywalker, that Organa and Calrissian escaped him as well … and that Chewbacca is likewise free. Their combined bounties are … impressive." Heavy-lidded eyes examined Fett. "Impressive."

And Chewbacca, at the very *least, will be coming for Solo.* Fett nodded. "We might discuss my staying," he conceded. "As to the art, an original piece from the hand of the Dark Lord"–Fett could feel himself warming to the subject; the faintest breath of disappointment touched him when Jabba interrupted, with something so close to enthusiasm that Fett found it notable.

"There is further work here, for a brave bounty hunter." The Hutt's tongue flicked out to lick his lips and he leaned forward. "A hundred thousand credits for the capture and delivery of a krayt dragon to do battle with my rancor."

Fett said dryly, "That seems a lot. As much for the delivery of a krayt dragon as for Solo?"

The Hutt waved a negligent hand in dismissal. "We will find a fair price for Solo. For the art. But now –"

Fett raised his head slightly. "A quarter million."

A hush fell over the watching crowd. Those nearest Fett edged slowly backward.

Jabba leaned forward. His voice emerged from his chest as a rumbling threat. "So ... that seems quite a lot. Even for Vader's art."

Fett shrugged. And waited.

Jabba's lips twitched. Fett did not mistake it for anything approaching amusement. "So, a quarter million credits for ... the art." His eyes narrowed to slits. "And we will enjoy your efforts toward acquisition of a krayt, and we will enjoy your company among us. For some time."

"A quarter million." Boba Fett actually bowed slightly. "For some time."

VERY EXPRESSIVE ... YES.

Fett shook his head to clear it. Jabba's throne room faded into nothingness; he hung on the wall himself, deep inside the Sarlacc, the air around him growing dank. A foul taste had begun to develop in his mouth; he sipped at the water tube in his helmet before replying. "Don't do that to me again."

There was a pause. I *won't,* the voice said finally, if *you keep me amused.*

"Who the blazes *are you?*"

I am the inferno, you are quite accurate. I am the Sarlacc. I am the distilled essence of –

"You're not the Sarlacc," Fett said grimly. "Sarlacci aren't intelligent, they don't have a brain worthy of the name –"

The voice chuckled and said softly, *I am Susejo.* The wall Fett hung on shivered. An emotion that could have been delight emanated from the creature. *It's been a long time since I had one like you, all bright and sharp around the edges. You are nearly a work of art, Fett, there is a clarity to you that is –* chuckle *– quite beautiful. A purity to your intent.*

Fett fought back the useless rage that threatened to overwhelm him; it was something he'd had practice at. "I'm a hunter. I bring those who do evil to justice, and there is little room to be unclear on the subject."

You remind me of someone – ah. I have it. You remind me of the Jedi.

Keeping his voice expressionless was an accomplishment. "The Jedi."

Yes. A Jedi we ate a few thousand years ago. We've kept her; would you like to meet her?

"No." Fett closed his eyes and floated senselessly in the darkness. *A Jedi we ate,* it had said. "No. Keep your Jedi to yourself."

Impression of a shrug. *As you wish. You'll look forward to a break in the tedium ... soon enough.*

Fett opened his eyes and stared ahead into the emptiness, listening to the silence. The screams he had heard at first, those of the men who had fallen into the Great Pit with him, had ceased. He had not heard one in some time. The fury built in Fett, self-contained, black and bone-deep. Another crack nearby, sounding very like a whip; Fett took a shuddering breath and when he spoke his voice shook slightly. "I don't understand this. Why is this being prolonged? Is there a purpose? The Sarlacc can eat me when I'm dead, can't it? I've killed, I've killed virtually everything that moves, one time or another, a hundred different species, sentient and dumb; if it breathes I've probably killed it or something like it. But I've killed *clean.* I've killed without stretching it out. Where's the grace in a death like this?"

Fett had the impression that his question was being considered. *For you? Why, I suppose there is none. But your life and death belong to me now, not you; and they serve my purpose. Recognize and understand your place in things, Boba Fett, for you are not even a real thing – merely a collection of thoughts that has deluded itself into a belief in its own existence.*

"You're saying that I'm not real, that nothing's real?" Fett's lips twisted in a snarl. "The air stinks too badly for me to believe that."

You, and I, and everything else – we are merely a process, Boba Fett. A process that has named itself "I." Surely the Real exists, and we are an expression of it. But are you and I real? No. We are processes that have grown arrogant and broken apart from the Real. In time we shall be rejoined to it. The voice paused. *You want to know why this is taking so long? You've barely been down here a day, Boba Fett. There are sentients who've been kept alive for hundreds of years while the Sarlacc digested them.* After a long pause it added, with a sense of weariness so profound Fett believed it would have killed him to experience it, *Thousands of years, in some cases.*

Fett did not know what made him so certain, the weariness; he said, "You ... you lie. You're not the Sarlacc – you're down here, with me."

I'm not the Sarlacc? Considering, thinking: *Don't be so sure of that. I am Susejo of Choi, or I was, and I have been here for a very, very long time. Longer than you can imagine ... but who knows? Perhaps you will not have to imagine it. Perhaps you will survive.*

You entertain me, and that which entertains me entertains the Sarlacc. When I am happy, it is happy. I expect you will be with us for some time.

Let me activate even one weapon system – Fett fought the thought down, pushed it back hard, and said aloud, "You are cruel."

There's a joke, said the voice, *that my Jedi told me. A sentient visits a nearby farm and sees a barve in the front yard. The barve is wandering around on five legs – one leg has been amputated. The sentient in question, JoJo, asks the owner why the barve has had a leg amputated. "Well," says the owner, "let me tell you something about that barve. That's the smartest barve you've ever seen in your life, JoJo. That barve talks, he can fly a speeder, and he's great with the kids, keeps an eye on 'em when I'm out in the field – why, just a few weeks ago he rescued my youngest one from drowning. "And JoJo says, "That's amazing! But what happened to the amputated leg?" The owner stares at JoJo. "Well, man, you don't eat a barve like that all at once!"*

Susejo laughed silently in the darkness, and the wall behind Fett rippled again.

Boba Fett thought to himself, *I wish I had a thermal detonator. I'd take you with me.*

You are eternally the Real, Boba Fett ... and there is nothing to desire.

THE CHRONO THAT glowed in the lower right-hand corner of Boba Fett's helmet visor told him when dawn came. It had been dark already when he awakened; when dawn arrived, the tunnel off to Fett's left lightened noticeably. At noon, when the sun was directly overhead, enough light filtered down through the yawning mouth of the Sarlacc that Fett could see his surroundings clearly.

The walls of the small tunnel in which the Sarlacc had stored him were grayish-green; they looked damp, though Fett's gloves prevented him from being certain. Small tendrils grew along the edges of the ridging in the walls; along the floor the tendrils were larger, proper tentacles, a mat of several hundred tentacles, four to six centimeters wide, three and four meters long. They lay motionless most of the time; when the tentacles did move they whipped around at such speed that the tentacle tips broke the sound barrier, very like the tip of a whip. It was the source of the cracking noises Fett had been hearing since he'd awakened ... and once he knew what it was he shivered. The cracking was a steady background sound, yet the tentacles around him did not move often. It made Fett wonder just how large the Sarlacc's interior was and how far from the surface he might be – how many of those tentacles he would have to fight his way through to get out again.

Oh, but you're not going to get out again, Boba Fett. No one ever has, and you won't be the first. Listen:

THE SARLACC ATE my left leg first, love. I hadn't been able to move either my arms or my legs for ... months, I suppose, a very long time. They didn't hurt anymore, though my skin burned, and never has stopped burning the entire time I've been in this blasted pit.

She has me hanging up in the main chamber while she digests me. I suppose that's something; a thing to be grateful for in the grand scheme of things. Mica and I came down together when our speeder got shot down, and Mica got hustled back into one of those little openings along the edge, down into the Sarlacc's guts. This is a bad way to die, but that'd be worse, that'd be a *lot* worse. I'm blind in one of my eyes now, but I can still see the sunlight striking down into the main pit, through the other, and I tell you, it keeps me going. Never thought I'd see the day when a brief glimpse of Tatooine's pale blue sky would be a reason to keep living.

I try not to look down. My left leg's gone beneath the knee. I didn't even notice it going, tell you the truth. One day I looked down and there it was, on the floor of the pit, down in the acid, being dissolved down into nothing.

That annoying Susejo leaves me alone at times. I don't know what he does when he's not talking to me; maybe he's off draining Mica the way he's draining me. I don't know exactly what Susejo's doing to us … but well, some days I'm not even certain sure who I *am* anymore. There's been a lot of us down here; I guess Susejo keeps the ones he and the Sarlacc enjoy, for a while anyway. It's a sort of immortality, I suppose, but love, I could have tolerated actually dying a lot better. I always thought that's how I'd go, you know; fleeing a blaster wedding at the age of ninety-three, something with a *little* style.

(I'm not even sure if you're the girl I remember. Some days you have black hair and skin and you're studying to be a minister, of all things, and other days it's blond hair and green eyes and you pilot a starship, and darn if I can remember which of you I actually fell in love with, or if it was both of you and you were different people … .

(I did love you. I remember that.)

A lot of memories floating around in here with me. The Sarlacc is a soup, and the ingredients are all the people she's taken, over the centuries, over the millennia. Susejo's never admitted it, but I suspect that's all that he is; the oldest of the soup's ingredients.

Kess, Susejo said.

I'll answer to that, I replied. *Why not? One name being as good as another.*

Your name is Kess, he said firmly. *You're a Corellian gambler … the Sarlacc's been eating you a little faster than I'd like, and I'm sorry about that. You're good company, but the Sarlacc's*

*been hungry recently, and I can't control her entirely. Tell me an-
other story?*

I thought about it, and I remembered the story you told me, little one, not long after we met, back in the old days, that one of you that wanted to be a minister, back when you thought there was nothing in me worth saving – too obsessed with the dice and all, you kept saying, too busy looking for the main chance. A *man, I* told Susejo, *being chased by a logra, comes to the edge of a cliff. He sees there is nowhere to flee, but beholds then a root, protrud-ing from the edge of the cliff. He grabs the root and scrambles over the edge of the cliff, hanging high above the ground. He looks down, and beholds then another logra, pacing below him. He hangs there, unable to go down, unable to climb back up; and along come a pair of tiny banda, one black and one white, and they begin nibbling at the root. The root begins to come apart ... and suddenly the man sees a berry growing at the edge of the cliff, and he plucks it and pops it in his mouth.*

How sweet it tasted.

Silence.

Finally Susejo said, *I'm not sure I like that story.*

I hung there on the wall, and with my good eye watched the dust motes dance in the sunlight; and I thought to myself how beautiful it was.

You'd be proud of me, love, whichever one you were.

Sometime later Susejo said, *The Sarlacc is hungry. I think I'll have her eat your arm now.*

FETT *FELT* THE horror that the Corellian gambler, dead these many centuries, fought against as his limbs decayed, as the Sarlacc ate him from the outsides in. Fett floated in a long dreamtime mo-ment, tied to the gambler's last moments of real awareness down in the slime on the floor of the pit, blind, deaf, limbs dissolved, rib cage cracked apart with the tentacles massaging his organs, dreaming of a woman who loved him –

Boba Fett had been born to anger, and rage was his life. He struggled up out of the vision, fought it wildly, carried himself up out of the nightmare on the back of a wave of fury and abruptly *was* back, there in his body with the pain of the burning acid all around him, suffused with a clear, lucid, *thinking* hatred, an emotion so dark and deep and pure the Dark Lord himself might never have felt its equal.

He could hear his own heartbeat thudding in his ears and he said, "I'm going to kill you *very* slowly," and he had never meant anything more in his life.

He hung in the darkness with his hatred.

Sometime later Susejo said, *I suppose I'll let the Sarlacc start on your leg.*

BLASTER RIFLE, WRIST lasers, rocket dart launcher; grappling hook, flame projector, concussion grenade launcher. Unfortunately almost all of them required the use of his hands, and his arms and legs were spread-eagled against the wall, held flat by an interwoven mesh of several hundred tentacles. Straining did no good; the tentacles merely gripped more tightly, and Fett barely moved.

The tentacles probed against him, seeking a way through his Mandalorian combat armor. A pair of large tentacles had taken hold of Fett's right leg, and they tugged at it, pulling back and forth at the knee joint. The armor had held, and would hold; that much did not worry Fett. The digestive acid the Sarlacc used *did* worry him; it had already made its way through to his skin. Most of his body *burned,* chest and back and arms and legs. So far the acid had not made it through his helmet, and had not made it past the blast armor that covered his genitals; thank Providence for small favors.

He had access to the contents of his helmet. The comlink built into it was silent; he had scanned through all frequencies, and all he got was static, which might mean that there was nobody within range of the helmet's comlink, about ninety klicks, or might mean that the bulk of the Sarlacc was blocking the signal, and finally might mean that the comlink itself was broken.

The Sarlacc wrenched violently at Fett's left knee. His armor held and Fett was yanked down the wall, the tentacles holding his upper body losing their grip slightly. He ended up hanging at an angle as the tentacles wrapped themselves about him again ... and there was a pressure against the sole of his right foot. He'd been dragged down far enough that his right foot was now in contact with the ground.

What good that did him – if any – Fett did not know. He flexed the foot to see if lie could get a purchase; perhaps.

He relaxed and considered.

The sensors and computer built into his combat suit had continued to work, even after Fett had lost consciousness. The computer responded to verbal commands; Fett had it play back the entire sequence of events that had landed him in the Great Pit of Carkoon, using the heads-up tac display in his helmet for video. The first time through the playback he had to switch it off after realizing that Solo had – accidentally! – activated his jet pack. The holocam angle was terrible, but there was no question about it; that illegitimate Solo had sent him flying into the pit by *chance*.

It took him several minutes before he was able to try and watch it again.

He lifted up from the sail barge, dropping down onto the skiff, with the Jedi and Solo and Chewbacca. And ... yes. Right there; the butt of Solo's spear had slammed into the emergency access panel, activating the jets.

The on-board computer couldn't access the jet pack; they were not linked together. Fett couldn't run diagnostics on the pack, had no idea whether the thing was working or not. The emergency access panel was behind him, to his right; if he'd been able to get his left hand free, he might have been able to reach –

If I could get my left hand free, thought Fett dryly, *I could do a lot of things.*

Using radar and. sonar, Fett had mapped out a rough picture of the Sarlacc's interior. Leading away from the main chamber were several dozen small tunnels, heading almost straight down into the earth. He was about ten meters away from the main chamber; and about forty meters beneath the ground. Even if the jet could take him out again, if he could move to activate it, even then he'd be stuck in the middle of nowhere, in the midst of a great desert –

The tentacles holding Fett's left leg tightened painfully, just above the knee.

Fett's lips twisted in a snarl. "I swear by the soul I don't have, I *am* going to kill you."

Kill who? Susejo laughed. *The one who's talking to you? Or the one who's eating you?*

"Either. Both."

Ah. You have a very poor attitude, Boba Fett:

I ALMOST MADE it out, early on my second day in the pit.

I lay on my back on the bottom of the pit, in the acid, through the long night. The Sarlacc and I "talked" for a while; it's very young and not very bright, and I feel sorry for it. It's rare for a Sarlacci spore to survive a landing in a desert environment; they're best suited to wet environments, though they *can* survive almost anywhere. I saw pictures once of a Sarlacc that had managed to survive on the surface of an airless moon; it was quite small, its aperture less than a meter in diameter, but the system it had ended up in was young, and heavy in cometary material. Comets are principally made up of carbon, hydrogen, oxygen, and nitrogen; this poor little Sarlacc was making do, out there in the vacuum. It had the most amazing root system; it was far more plant than animal.

This Sarlacc doesn't have it that bad, tucked away out here in the desert. It's not really aware that it exists; it has a neural system, but it's not very well developed, and not likely to become so in the desert. Sarlacci do interesting things with messenger RNA: over the course of millennia, they can attain a sort of group consciousness, built out of the remains of people they've digested. I talked to such a Sarlacc once, a few decades ago. It was a thoroughly asocial creature that wondered, quite wistfully, whether a Jedi would taste better or worse than the other sentients it had eaten. I remember being amused by it, for I knew that I was not such a fool as to come within reach of its outer tentacles.

I walked right over this baby Sarlacc. It lay buried just beneath the sand, tentacles hidden in the drifts. It got me by the ankle and dragged me down into the pit, through a sand plug nearly a meter thick.

The sand plug came down after me, right on top of me. I lay on the bottom of the pit, held in place by surprisingly strong tentacles, with sand all around me, looking up into the night sky. The Sarlacc's digestive acid is weak, and the sand that came down with me has blotted up much of it. Nonetheless my clothing is already dissolving; if I do get out of here I'll be a sight, a naked sixty-year-old Jedi with a rash trying to make it back to her survey ship.

Even diluted, the acid burns.

I do not blame the Sarlacc; it is behaving as its nature dictates. It's not very bright and it is very young – only five meters wide, and perhaps that deep as well. Hard to say quite how deep underground

I am, looking up into the night sky through what used to be the sand plug.

I may only be the second or third sentient it's ever eaten. One of them is hanging, totally cocooned, on a wall in the chamber here with me; a Choi named Susejo who was mostly digested already when I fell into the pit. I can feel his thoughts; he's mildly telepathic. He's very young, for a Choi, barely out of childhood, and very angry – he has not taken being eaten very well, and I feel rather sorry for him, too.

When morning came, the light filtered down around me, and I saw my chance; my only chance. My lightsaber had come down with me. I hadn't been able to tell, there in the darkness; it no longer hung from my belt, and I hadn't known whether I'd lost it up on the surface, or down here in the pit. It lay on its side in the acid a few feet away from me, and I turned my head to look at it.

It leaped across the pit and into my hand. I lit it and bent my hand back at the wrist, bringing the blade down as close to the tentacles holding my arm as I could get it, straining; the Sarlacc made a sound, a high-pitched squeal, and the tentacles holding that arm pulled free. I wrenched the arm free and sliced away at the other tendrils still holding me, cutting for just a few seconds until I was free, rolled off my back into a crouch, and then –

Five meters is a long way up, even for a young Jedi. I raised the Force and *leaped.*

The tentacle caught my ankle in mid-leap. The Sarlacc broke my leg and two of my ribs pulling me back down. I lost the lightsaber again on the way down and by the time I had the presence of mind to look for it, it was gone for good. I don't know what the Sarlacc did with it, but I never saw it again.

For the rest of the day the Sarlacc remained restless, tentacles waving aimlessly, twitching ceaselessly. It held me so tightly that the blood flow to my extremities was impaired. It was very upset by the whole thing. I tried to tell it that I was sorry, that I would not have hurt her had I been able to avoid it.

That got a rise out of the Choi, hanging on the wall facing me *If you* must *chatter,* it snapped, *at least do it for the benefit* of *the one who can listen to you.*

A slow death has a few things to recommend it; time to get your thoughts in order, at any rate. I blocked the pain radiating from my body, and frankly, after a few days I was bored, too.

Susejo, I said, *why don't we pass the time by telling each other stories?*

SWEAT TRICKLED DOWN Fett's form, pooled beneath his armor, mixed with the burning acid that covered him. An impossible kaleidoscope of lights danced in front of him, and for a moment he thought he might vomit into his helmet; that old Jedi woman had been real. Her thoughts still echoed away within him, mixed in with the thoughts of the Corellian gambler, and the quick bright flashes of a dozen other minds, the thoughts and hopes and desires of men and women, dead years and centuries and millennia. They'd all died, every one of them, sunk down into the acid and let go of life.

I miss the Jedi, Susejo said. *She was very kind to me.* Susejo obviously had some level of contact with the Sarlacc; the Sarlacc had *shivered,* earlier, when Susejo felt happiness. Fett made a decision, and let loose the anger that was never very far beneath the surface.

He snarled, "Then you shouldn't have *eaten* her, you miserable wretch."

The hatred in his voice and in his thoughts brought a response from Susejo, a flare of startled anger. The tentacles holding Fett tightened convulsively and Susejo snapped, *I didn't, the* Sarlacc *ate her.*

Fett wished that the wall behind him were not quite so soft. "And you couldn't have stopped it, you couldn't have tried to help her, or anyone else, in *four thousand years?* You're an ingrate, you pathetic excuse for a sentient. You got taken down here as a child and everything that you know and everything that you are you owe to the people you let get eaten" – and the Sarlacc's tentacles spasmed around Fett, digging into him, hauling him back into the wall behind him – "and your feelings are hurt because I've *told you* so? You could have *helped* that Jedi, she'd have come back for you. Instead you spent the next four thousand years playing at philosophy, abusing the people who taught you to be what you are, never even dreaming that you had options, and *why?*" he screamed at Susejo, building up to it, blasting him with the rage and hatred he had spent a lifetime growing, the Sarlacc's straining tentacles shaking against his body. "Because you're *stupid,* a miserable mean wretch of an excuse for a sentient without the imagination or the courage –"

The tentacles slashed around him, the sound of a thousand whips cracking, drowning out Fett's voice. He shoved, got his right foot solidly against the ground and *pushed* upward.

The switch in the jet pack's emergency access panel, digging into the soft wall behind him, was pushed down as Boba Fett pushed up.

Flame erupted in the enclosed space around them. The Sarlacc itself shrieked in pain, a sound that echoed away down the tunnels, the hundreds of tentacles around Fett whipping themselves into a frenzy, those that held Fett constricting so tightly that for an instant he could not breathe –

The jet pack had never been intended to be run in such tight quarters for any length of time.

It exploded.

IT WAS HIS oldest possession; the Mandalorian combat armor that was almost as famous as he was, famous the galaxy wide. It had protected him, down the decades, from blaster fire and slug-throwers, explosions and knives, from all the various insults the universe was apt to throw at a man in his line of work. But not even Mandalorian combat armor, designed by the warriors who had fought, and sometimes defeated, Jedi Knights, had been intended to withstand an exploding jet pack in close quarters.

Fett could not have been unconscious for more than a few seconds; he came back to awareness unable to breathe. The jet pack's fuel had splattered down the length of the corridor, and the corridor was burning, and so was Fett. The flame touched his skin in exposed places, on his arms and legs and stomach, and flames danced on the surface of his combat armor, the armor itself cracked, broken open by the force of the explosion, and everywhere the armor touched him the metal was scaldingly hot –

Fett surged to his feet. The ground beneath him shook, rolling as the Sarlacc's flesh burned, and the Sarlacc fought against it. Fett reached back over his shoulder, unslung the deadliest weapon he carried.

Standing in the fire, burning alive, Fett fired a concussion grenade into the ceiling thirty centimeters above his head, and threw himself down to the surface of the tunnel, into the flaming mixture of acid and fuel –

The explosion tore apart the world. The concussion slammed Fett down into the flames, and his left arm, trapped beneath him at the wrong angle, snapped as he was smashed down atop it. A pain so great it was like a white light surrounded Boba Fett, and he knew that he was dying, that he had failed, like all the others before him; that he had traded a slow death by acid for a fast death by fire –

SAND RAINED DOWN upon him.

A long time later, Boba Fett became aware that he was still alive. He forced himself up into a sitting position, looking around him.

Fires still burned, along the length of the corridor, and in the distance the sound of cracking tentacles was very loud.

It was quiet where he sat.

Fett's left arm hung useless at his side, and he looked away down the tunnel; it was night, but he knew which direction he needed to go, to get back to the main pit, to the shaft that led back to the surface ... to the main pit, where Susejo hung, where the enraged Sarlacc awaited him, tentacles lashing back and forth in anticipation.

Sand trickled down onto Fett's helmet. He looked up.

Darkness.

Without moving from where he sat, Boba Fett made a long arm, and retrieved the grenade launcher. It carried three grenades; and he'd already fired one of them.

He raised the launcher and fired it a second time, into the darkness above him, and then had to dig his way out of the avalanche of sand that came down upon him. He stood at the edge of a small hill of sand, looking upward into the darkness ... and started to undress. The armor was useless at this point – acid-covered and cracked in places, which was an improvement on Fett having cracked in those same places – and his clothing disintegrated as he moved. He almost fainted while removing the upper body armor; his left arm was broken in at least two places, and he was covered with burns that were already starting to form blisters.

It took several minutes, but finally he had worked his way out of the armor, and he fought against his dizziness and weakness and started climbing, halfway up the small hill of sand, and fired his final grenade into the darkness above him. The wave of sand that collapsed on him this time was unbelievable; Fett struggled up through it as it came down upon him, almost swimming upward through the falling sand. The sand covered him, his nude body and the helmet that still protected his head, and he clawed at it frantically, with no air but that trapped in his helmet with him, using both hands, both the broken arm and the good, possessed by a mortal terror that gave him the access to the final strength he would ever be able to call upon –

A hand broke free, he felt it, felt it thrust up into emptiness, and seconds later, Boba Fett dug his way up out of the sand and into the cool nighttime air, in the middle of the Dune Sea, at the edge of the Great Pit of Carkoon, hundreds of kilometers away from anyone or anything.

Alive.

A YEAR LATER:

Boba Fett returned to Tatooine in the *Slave II*.

He came down out of orbit and hovered above the Great Pit of Carkoon, in the midst of the Dune Sea. On the night desert, the glow of his thrusters burned like the daytime sun, lit the sand for kilometers in all directions.

The *Slave II* descended until the flame of its drive played directly down onto the Pit of Carkoon. The wash of pain that rose to greet Boba Fett tasted like wine of an ancient vintage. If he closed his eyes he could *see* it, the main chamber where Susejo hung, shimmering beneath the superheated air.

You.

"Yes, indeed."

Inside the creature's pain, Boba Fett could feel something like relief. *You liberate me from the long Cycle.* The *Slave II* hovered above the pit ... and then drifted off to the side, and came to a landing fifty meters from the edge, well away from the reach of even the longest of the burnt, writhing tentacles. Susejo's pain and confusion touched Fett. *What strange mercy is this?*

Sitting in the *Slave II*, a faint smile hidden beneath a Mandalorian helmet, Boba Fett said, *You don't eat a barve like that all at once.*

I see … I suppose I shall see you again, then.

"You can count on it," said Boba Fett. His hands danced across the instrument panels.

The thrusters caught fire; light washed once more over the Great Pit of Carkoon

A dark spirit rose into the night.

THE END

A Barve Like That appeared in "Star Wars: Tales From Jabba's Palace," edited by Kevin J. Anderson.

This story is the only thing I've ever put a pseudonym on. (It's the pseudonym my sister and I created when we were planning to write "Terminal Freedom" under a pseudonym – the J.D. stands for Jodi and Danny; Montgomery is my maternal grandfather's last name.) I won't go through the blow-by-blow of why I did that, except to note that Lucasfilm owns this story, not me, and they made changes to it I wasn't happy with. The text herein is the Lucasfilm/Kevin J. Anderson-edited version that appeared in the anthology.

My thanks to Kevin, by the way. It was a mistake for me to work in someone else's universe (and more my mistake than theirs) but Kevin made it as tolerable as possible for everyone.

The name "Susejo" is O Jesus, backwards.

STAR WARS: The Last One Standing

THE LAST STATEMENT of the journeyman Protector Jaster Mereel, known later as the Hunter Boba Fett, before exile from the world of Concord Dawn:

Everyone dies.

It's the final and only lasting Justice. Evil exists; it is intelligence in the service of entropy. When the side of a mountain slides down to kill a village, this is not evil, for evil requires intent. Should a sentient being cause that landslide, there is evil; and requires Justice as a consequence, so that civilization can exist.

There is no greater good than Justice; and only if law serves Justice is it good law. It is said correctly that law exists not for the Just but for the unjust, for the Just carry the law in their hearts, and do not need to call it from afar.

I bow to no one and I give service only for cause.

"JASTER MEREEL."

Journeyman Mereel sat in his cell, in chains, with early morning sunshine streaking in through a tall and narrow barred window, high on the cell's wall.

His ankles were chained together so that he could not walk; another chain encircled his waist, and his wrists were linked to that. He was young, and he did not rise when the Pleader entered his cell; he could see that the discourtesy displeased the older man.

The Pleader Iving Creel seated himself on the bench facing Mereel. He wasted no time on courtesies, himself. "How will I plead you?"

Mereel had been stripped of the uniform of the Journeyman Protector. He was an ugly young man who wore his prison grays with dignity, as though they were themselves a uniform, and he took his time answering, looking the Pleader over, examining him—as though, the Pleader thought with a flash of annoyance, it was Iving Creel facing a trial today, and not this arrogant young murderer. "You're Iving Creel," he said finally. "I've heard of you. You're rather famous."

Creel said stiffly, "No one wants it said you were not treated fairly."

An unpleasant grin touched the young man's lips. "You'll plead me unrepentant."

Creel stared at him. "Do you understand the seriousness of this, boy? You killed a man."

"He had it coming."

"They'll exile you, Jaster Mereel. They'll exile you—"

"I could always go join the Imperial Academy," Mereel said, "if I got exiled. I expect I'd make a good storm—"

Creel overrode him: "—and they may execute you, if you anger them sufficiently. Is it such a hard thing to say you're sorry for having taken a life unjustly?"

"I am sorry," said Mereel: "Sorry I didn't kill him a year ago. The galaxy's a better place without him." Pleader Creel studied the boy, and nodded slowly. "You've chosen your plea; well enough. You can change it any time before I make the plea, if you wish ... think on it, I urge you. You'll face prison or exile for the murder of another Protector; for all the man was a disgrace to his uniform, you had no business killing him. But your arrogance is likely to see you executed yourself, Jaster Mereel, before this day is done."

"You can't love life too much, Pleader." The ugly young man smiled, an empty, meaningless movement of the lips, and the Pleader Iving Creel found himself remembering that smile, at odd moments; for the rest of his life. "Everyone dies."

YEARS PASSED.

THE TARGET WAS young, younger than the man who had taken the name of Fett had been led to believe; indeed, tonight's target was not long out of his teens. In itself that was not a problem; Fett had collected children many years younger than that. Among his earliest collections, not long after leaving the stormtroopers, had been a boy of barely fourteen Standard years; the boy had dishonored the daughter of a wealthy businessman who had, even in Fett's wide experience, a rather remarkable vindictive turn. Most fathers, Fett knew, on most planets, would not have killed a boy for such behavior; indeed, most bounty hunters would have turned down such a job.

Fett was not among them. Laws vary, planet to planet; but morality never changes. He had delivered the boy to his executioners and he had never regretted it.

Now, years later, he stood in the shadows at the back of the Victory Forum, in the town of Dying Slowly, on the planet Jubilar, and watched them set up for the main match in Regional Sector Number Four's All-Human Free-For-All extravaganza.

The Victory Forum was a huge place, poorly lit, named by the winning side for a recent battle in one of Jubilar's wars. The Forum had had another name, not too long ago; and would, in Fett's estimation, have another name again sometime soon. The current war was not going well. Jubilar was used as a penal colony by half a dozen worlds in the near stellar neighborhood; which army a convict ended up in depended upon which spaceport he was evicted at.

The Forum's seats sloped down toward the five-sided ring, two hundred rows of rising seats separating Fett from the ring itself, and the fighting. The audience was still arriving, only minutes before the main bout, and the Forum was only half full, an audience of some twenty thousand, mostly men, filling the seats.

Fett was in no hurry; he focused his helmet's macrobinoculars on the ring, and the area immediately about it, and prepared to wait through the fight.

Young Han Solo watched the ring attendant, a Bith, hosing the blood from the previous bout out of the ring, and wondered how he'd gotten himself into such a mess.

Well, not wondering, exactly, that wasn't accurate, since actually he remembered the events with a certain painful clarity. Wondering how he'd been stupid enough to get himself into the current mess was more like it. Han stood in the tunnel with the other three fighters, watching the blood get cleaned off the mat he would shortly be standing on—fighting on—and swore to himself that if he got out of the current mess with his skin still holding his insides inside, he'd learn to deal seconds so well that no one would ever catch him at it.

Anyway, how was a traveling man supposed to know that cheating at cards was a felony in some jerk backwaters? "A felony, "Han muttered aloud. He glanced over … and up … and up some more … at the fighter standing next to him. "What did you get sent to Jubilar for?"

The man looked down a considerable distance at Han and said slowly, "I killed some people."

Han looked away. "Right … me too," he lied after a moment. "I killed lots of people."

The heavily armed ring attendant, standing behind the four of them, growled, "Shut up."

A movement, out of the corner of his eye, caught Han's attention; he leaned forward slightly and looked off to the right. A fellow in … gray. Gray combat armor of some sort; he appeared to be watching the ring.

BOBA FETT WAS not watching the ring. He was watching a young entrepreneur named Hallolar Voors, who sat ringside with a pair of beautiful, immaculately dressed women in the seats to each side of him; a young entrepreneur who was going to be dead before he had the opportunity to sample the charms of either of them.

EVEN AT THAT early age, Han Solo had managed to get some experience on him: "That's Mandalorian combat armor. Who—"

The muted sounds of the crowd rose up in a roar and drowned him out.

The ring attendant yelled over it. "Time to fight, you low trash, you smelly sinful one-eyed egg-sucking sons of slime-devils! *Time to fight!*"

FROM WHERE HE stood, high above the ring, Boba Fett watched as the fighters came up, out of the tunnel, and into the five-sided ring. Four fighters, as Fett had been told was usual for a Free-For-All; the announcer stood in the fifth corner, waiting patiently as the fighters disrobed and took their positions, as the full-throated roar of twenty thousand men reverberated through the Forum.

Pickups, situated around the edge of the ring, would broadcast the fight around the planet.

Three of the fighters were what Fett would have expected, big bruisers for whom the Free-For-All ring had been the obvious alternative to conscription. The fourth surprised him; Fett zoomed in on the man—

The face jumped into focus. For a moment the image startled Fett; the fighter appeared to be staring straight up at Fett. He zoomed the macrobinoculars out to a wider viewing angle—and interestingly enough the impression was accurate; the fellow *was* staring at him. The young fighter disrobed slowly, staring up past the ring lights, into the gloom, at the spot where Fett stood, as the other, fighters limbered up in their corners.

The man was young—no older, in all likelihood, than Fett's target tonight. *Bad night,* thought Fett, *to be young and quick and full of promise.*

The announcer moved out into the center of the ring, and raised his hands, palms out. His voice echoed out across the Forum and the watching audience: "This is the final elimination! These are the rules: no eye gouges. No blows to the throat or groin. No intentional deaths. There ... are ... no ... other ... rules." He paused, and the audience's cheers rose to a frenzied pitch as his voice boomed out: "The last one standing will be the victor!"

The announcer climbed out of the ring, and despite himself, watching the fighters, the youngster in particular, standing there alone and brave and scared, despite himself Fett found his pulse quickening as, with the rest of the crowd, he waited for the dropping flag that would signal the bout's beginning.

There were moments when Fett appreciated life—he was hardly an old man himself, and there were nights, nights like these, when it was good—and behind the helmet, Fett grinned at the thought as it came to him—when it was good to be young, and quick, and full of promise.

The dark blue match flag fluttered down from the rafters, and into the ring.

The three bruisers moved in on the young fighter ... .

BOBA FETT SAID, "Spice."

The target, Hallolar Voors, said "Yes, Gentle Fett. Spice. Eighteen canisters. And if you can handle it, we can deliver the same amount again, twice a quarter."

Fett nodded as though he were paying attention. It was not long after the end of the fights, and he walked with Voors through a huge, dimly lit, apparently deserted warehouse at the edge of Executioner's Row; Executioner's Row was a slum that was itself at the edge of Dying Slowly. Fett wasn't impressed with the imagination they showed on Jubilar, but he had to concede they displayed a certain consistency.

Voors had traded in the two women for a pair of conspicuously armed bodyguards. The bodyguards trailed behind them.

"The spice trade in this sector has been controlled by the Hutts for a long time," Fett observed. "Where did you find an independent source?"

Voors smiled at Fett; Fett, staring straight ahead, watched the smile in the heads-up tactical display in his helmet. The tac display gave him a 360 degree view of his surroundings; Fett wondered whether Voors knew that, or if he was just smiling for the practice of it. It was a handsome smile, Fett had to admit.

The Mandalorian armor itself bothered people, but Fett had found that it bothered people more when he did not look at them while speaking. And if they thought he could not see what was going on around him, so much the better.

Voors did not seem, to Fett, the sort who would know much about the capabilities of Mandalorian battle armor. In fact the man looked much like what he was: the son of a wealthy local businessman, a dark, charming, handsome, young fellow wearing expensive clothes, with a good smile, who was fatally out of his league and did not know it.

"The source is ... private," Voors said. "And desires to stay that way, I'm afraid."

Fett nodded, once; he hardly cared.

Moments later they came to a wide, relatively empty area, lit well enough that Fett's macrobinoculars, adjusted to the darkness they had been walking through, lowered the gain automatically; inside the helmet, the scene still appeared bright as day to Fett.

Three rows of plastic canisters, six to a row, sat out in the middle of the empty area. The canisters were fat, and half the height of a man. Fett pointed at random. "Open that one."

One of the bodyguards standing behind Fett glanced at Voors; Voors nodded quickly. The warehouse lights changed, went dark red; normal white light activated spice. The bodyguard moved forward, knelt, and touched the two clasps that kept the canister sealed; it left Fett with one bodyguard still behind him, slightly to his left.

Fett took a step forward and looked down._ It looked like spice; he reached in and pulled out a handful. "Seal it and turn the white lights back on."

The lights came back up ... and it was spice, all right. Fett scattered it across the top of the canister, and it lay there glowing in the light, twinkling and flickering as, the spice was activated. Fett's left hand, hanging by his belt, touched a stud on the belt, releasing the neural toxin, and continued the motion, up to touch his right hand. He worked free the glove, stood there with his naked right hand held up in the air. "Do you mind if I smell it? Real spice has a sharp, pleasant odor—"

Voors glanced at his bodyguards. "If you insist." Fett reached up, as though to take off his helmet—saw them watching him with plain anticipation. Another of the armor's benefits; taking the helmet off became an act of theater. He paused with his hand on the base of his helmet, and relaxed. "I wanted to ask you a question." The hand dropped slightly. "Does your conscience ever bother you?"

Voors stared at him. "Are you serious? Over spice?"

"Does it ever bother your conscience," Fett said again, in the voice that always sounded so harsh when he spoke Basic, "trafficking in spice?"

Voors said a little hesitantly, "It's not even addictive. And there are valid medical uses for it—"

The bodyguard nearest Fett blinked, shook his head and blinked again. "Substances that are not addictive," said Fett, "frequently lead to the misuse of substances that are. Doesn't that bother you?"

Voors took a deep breath and exploded. "*No,* it doesn't bother me! My conscience is just—" His mouth shut ... and then opened again as though he intended to continue speaking.

The bodyguard behind Fett was farthest away from the neural toxin; Fett spun, pulling his blaster free left-handed, and shot the man as he went for his weapon. The jolt took the bodyguard in the stomach; he staggered backward, still clutching his blaster, and Fett moved forward as the guard backpedaled, took aim and shot him a second time in the throat for good measure.

He swung back to the spice, to Voors and the other bodyguard. They weren't dead just yet, of course. They fell and Fett stood watching them; the pickups buried in his helmet were busy recording their death throes. Jabba would want to see the recording—this was one of the first times Fett had taken the Hutt's commission, but Fett understood Hutts; Jabba would pay a bonus for the actual images of his enemies' deaths.

He worked the glove back over his right hand; it was numb already, to the wrist, from exposure to the nerve gas he'd released.

After their thrashing had ceased, Fett walked in closer, to get better pickups of them. He bent slightly to give his pickups the best angle. The pale-skinned bodyguard had turned blue; Voors, darker-skinned, had turned purple. His swollen tongue stuck out between his teeth; Fett imagined Jabba would enjoy that touch.

After a bit Fett straightened and stepped backward, getting a good dozen paces between himself and the eighteen canisters of spice.

He unslung his flame thrower, lit the flame, and played it over the plastic drums for what seemed to him a long time.

The Hutt had not paid him to burn the spice; but Jabba had not paid him *not* to, either; and there were things worth doing for free. When all that remained was a smoldering melted mess in the middle of the warehouse, Boba Fett, who thought himself a fair and a just man, slung the flamethrower back over his shoulder, turned about, and walked quietly out of the warehouse, into the dark, silent night, into a future filled with promise.

FIFTEEN YEARS PASSED.

IN THE *SLAVE I*, with engines and shields powered down to almost nothing, only a trickle of power feeding the instruments and the lifeplant, Boba Fett hung up high above Hoth System's ecliptic, high above the system's potentially lethal asteroid belt. He looked down on Hoth System and was gratified to see that he'd beaten the Imperials.

Somewhere down there, on Hoth itself, was, if Fett had guessed right, the current headquarters of the Rebellion. Fett didn't care about the Rebellion one way or another; the Rebels were plainly doomed, and the day and manner of their passing from the universe did not fill him with much interest. The Empire would take care of them; Fett had smaller and more profitable prey in mind.

Where the Rebels were, Han Solo could be found. The hyperspace message from the Imperials had been short and to the point; it had announced a crushing assault on Rebel headquarters, and offered a bounty of fifteen thousand credits to any Hunters who helped chase down Rebels fleeing the site of the battle. Fifteen thousand credits wouldn't have paid Fett's operating expenses for half a year. But where the Rebels were ... .

Not too long ago, Jabba the Hutt's standing bounty on Han Solo had reached one hundred thousand credits. It was one of the half dozen largest extant bounties Fett knew of; and if it didn't exactly put Solo into the company of the Butcher of Montellian Serat, and the Butcher's five million credit bounty, it was getting up there, getting up there.

He trained his sensors on Hoth at highest resolution, and keyed the computer to wake him if it saw the *Millennium Falcon*.

Sitting in the pilot's seat, in his armor, helmet in his lap, Fett closed his eyes and went to sleep.

The hyperwave warning awoke him.

Fett opened his eyes and scanned his instruments. Weak, flickering signals from Hoth, that might have been no more than background noise (except that they weren't); that wasn't what had set off his alarm, though.

Ships, the instruments said, were coming out of hyperspace. *Big* ships, which meant Star Destroyers, which meant the Empire. Fett triangulated—and swore in his native language. Hoth was *between* him and the ships leaving hyperspace. Oh, you fools, you fools, Fett thought. If they'd set off his instruments, as far away as the *Slave I* was from their breakout point, then the Rebels, down on Hoth, must have been jolted out of their beds by the shrill of alarms going off.

Somebody had fouled up bad; and knowing Vader, Fett imagined that that particular somebody was not long for the galaxy.

The *Slave I* sat up above the ecliptic, and Fett did what he could while the inevitable battle played itself out. He lit the engines. and moved in closer to Hoth; when the *Falcon* left the planet, if it did, it would be moving fast; Fett would have time for only a single run at it.

He took up position, still well above the ecliptic, floating above Hoth, above the battle; and prepared to wait. There was nothing else for it; if Fett had learned anything in his time as a Hunter, it was that patience paid. Certainly there was no profit to involving himself in the fighting. Ion cannon blasted up off the surface of Hoth; beneath their cover, Rebel transport ships lifted off, accelerated away from Hoth, and made the jump to hyperspace. At this distance, even with image enhancement, Fett's sensors could do no more than eke out the barest details of ship size and shape; but that little was enough. None of the ships leaving Hoth were the *Millennium Falcon*; the shape of that ship was burned into Fett's brain.

A wave of transport ships. A wave of fighters. Another wave of transport ships ... another. Another.

The ion cannon on the planet's surface were firing more infrequently now; the Imperials must be having some success at taking the emplacements out. Fett waited, fighting back his impatience. The transports were away, occasional fighters still slipping the Imperial line and jumping to hyperspace. But still, no *Falcon*—

There.

That was the *Falcon*, or it was an hallucination. Fett's fingers danced across the controls and the *Slave I* lit its engines to give chase. The computer calculated trajectories, and Fett did half a dozen things at once, readied the tractor beam, fed power to the fore deflectors, threw up the *Falcon*'s projected trajectory and ran an intersect for the *Slave I*; he needed to grapple them just before they hit hyperspace, ideally while avoiding death at the hands of trigger-happy Imperials

Fett swore aloud for the second time in a single day. He wasn't going to catch them.

The *Slave I* streaked through space, high above Hoth System, at the ship's greatest acceleration, but there was no time, and the trajectories showed it plainly. Hoth was a cold world, far from its sun;

the gravity gradient this far out was smaller than usual for a world habitable by humans—the *Falcon* was going to jump to hyperspace practically any moment.

Any moment, now; she was being chased by a Star Destroyer and what looked like its entire complement of TIE fighters. And—remember the basics, and Basic Number One was: *no bounty is worth dying for*. The Star Destroyer and the TIE fighters were directing a withering fire upon the *Millennium Falcon,* laser light washing over the ship again and again; and if Fett got close enough to grapple, he would be close enough to take the brunt of that fire.

Any moment now—

And something was wrong. The *Falcon* wasn't jumping.

Fett doubled-checked the trajectory his computer had run for the *Falcon,* and the trajectory was correct; the gravimetrics were correct, the vectors were correct, the *Falcon* should have jumped by now.

Something wrong with their hyperdrive, Fett thought, and a moment later knew himself correct; the *Falcon* veered off—

—heading straight into the Hoth System asteroid belt.

Fett cut his engines, and simply watched as the *Millennium Falcon* dove into the belt. Solo was desperate; Fett wasn't, not nearly desperate enough to take the *Slave I* in among those tumbling mountains of stone and iron.

The hundred thousand credits could wait for another day; you can't spend money when you're dead—

Fett leaned forward slightly in his seat, thinking to himself that it had, really, been quite a remarkable day for Imperial stupidity:

The TIE fighters were going in after them.

Fett sat back in his seat, shaking his head. Plainly none of those people knew the first thing about cost analysis.

After a long blank moment he turned his sensors back in-system, and picked out the unmistakable shape of Darth Vader's Super Star Destroyer *Executor*.

He hailed it, received confirmation, and charted a course.

THEY TOOK HIM to see Lord Vader.

Vader stood on the bridge, watching the remnants of the battle. Stars glittered and asteroids tumbled across the black sky beyond him. Vader did not look at Fett and wasted no words in greeting, and as always the deep voice seemed more the work of a machine than a man. "How did you know?"

Fett glanced around before replying; the bridge crew was so busy at its duties, or busy appearing to be busy at its duties, that none of them had even looked at him as he was brought in; and as usual Fett found himself touched by a certain grudging admiration for Vader's leadership.

"Your people told me," Fett said after a moment. "In essence. They gave us a meeting point in interstellar space. I knew you wouldn't be jumping the fleet far, from that point; I ran the coordinates against my charts for this area." He shrugged. "One planet too hot, another too cold, a third just right, but already inhabited by Lando Calrissian's mining colony. That left Hoth."

"You know the area well, then." Fett did not think Vader expected a response; he offered none. Vader, still without looking at him, nodded as though he had. "The other Hunters will be here shortly. I'll brief you all when they arrive."

Fett took a step forward. "How much?"

Vader was silent a long moment. "I don't care about the others who escaped. For Solo ... one hundred and fifty thousand credits. The same again for Leia Organa. She will be with him." He turned his head slightly. "No disintegrations."

Fett's escort gestured; Fett shrugged and turned and followed the escort from the bridge: Vader was a difficult client; he wanted living captives, not corpses or pictures of corpses. No disintegrations; he'd said that every time he'd hired Fett, after that first incident.

After the briefing, Fett and his competition were separated and escorted back to their ships.

Fett's escort was visibly uncomfortable in his presence; that suited him. Vader's ship was the largest vessel Fett had ever seen, never mind actually been inside; it took almost five minutes for them to be shuttled from the bridge to the docking bay where the *Slave I* waited for him, and Fett was, by general policy, in no mood to talk. Particularly not to an Imperial officer of low rank.

They walked from the shuttle station to Fett's ship. Halfway there, the Imperial said, "They say you're Lord Vader's favorite bounty hunter."

Fett stopped in his tracks, stood still, and stared at the man long enough to intensify the fellow's discomfort. "Yes." He turned and continued walking, and the Imperial had to hurry after him.

But the man was stupid even for an officer of the Imperial Navy, or his curiosity surpassed his temerity; he didn't take the hint. "They say you know the target. This fellow Solo, the one who helped Skywalker blow up the Death Star. They say that you know him."

Fett walked along without replying for a good bit. Finally he said, reluctantly enough, "I saw him fight once."

"Fight where?"

For some reason Fett answered him. "A long time ago. He got into the All-Human Free-For-All competition, out on Jubilar." With real surprise Fett heard himself adding, "He was young, and he was outmatched: He made the finals round, though. Have you ever seen the Jubilar Free-For-All?"

The escort shook his head. "I've never even heard of the planet it takes place on."

It was like listening to someone else talk; the words simply flowed out of Fett. "They put four fighters together in a ring, usually of the same species. To make it fairer." A quick smile touched Fett's features, as he thought about those fights; it was the first time Boba Fett had smiled in years, and he did not notice it happening. "Fairer," he repeated. "Usually three of them start by ganging up on the one they think weakest, which in this case would have been Solo. He was young, I told you that. They beat the weakest fighter into unconsciousness before turning on each other; and the last one standing is the victor."

"They beat him unconscious? Han Solo?"

Fett stopped walking—and looked sideways at the man. A small motion, but—the Imperial found himself staring into the bounty hunter's darkened visor.

Fett's harsh voice sounded like an attack. "He won. It was one of the bravest things I ever saw." He paused. "I'll enjoy collecting him."

The Imperial made a visible effort to collect himself. "Yes ... I expect you will."

Fett shook his head as though to clear it, turned and headed down the corridor once again, perhaps at a slightly quicker pace.

It was the longest conversation he'd had in years about anything except business.

THE MONTHS PASSED in a rush; and when it was over Boba Fett found himself perhaps the best known bounty hunter in the galaxy.

It was a crowded time, and in Fett's memory the events blurred into one another. Solo had hidden the *Falcon* among the Imperials' garbage, released immediately before the jump into hyperspace, and so escaped from the Imperials at Hoth. A good trick, and one that might have worked against most Hunters; it had worked against Fett's competition.

But Boba Fett had been fooled by that trick before, once. By now he had been in his line of work longer than most, and there were few enough ploys he *hadn't* seen, once or twice or a dozen times. There was only one place they could be going; one place close enough for them to reach with their main hyperdrive disabled; Fett jumped for Cloud City, and there Lando Calrissian made the deal that delivered Solo to Fett.

With Han Solo as cargo, frozen in carbonite, Fett started for Tatooine. There, for the sculpture of Han Solo, and a few months of Fett's time, not to mention a number of inconveniences on the way, Jabba the Hutt paid, not 100,000 credits, but a quarter of a million—

And not too long after that, the rescuers started arriving. Leia Organa, pretending to be a bounty hunter, arrived with Chewbacca in tow. She succeeded in releasing Solo from the carbonite. For the very death of him Fett could not imagine what she'd had in mind; whatever it was, it did not work. The Hutt put Solo down in the dungeon, with Chewbacca, and intended to execute them in the near future; and Leia Organa spent her days in chains at the foot of Jabba's throne.

FETT LAY ON the bed in his darkened quarters deep inside Jabba's Palace, wearing his armor, staring up into the darkness. His helmet was balanced on his stomach and cool air from the ventilators washed across him in rhythmic gusts.

A heavy pounding sounded at his door.

Fett sat up, donning his helmet and lifting his assault rifle; the movements were so automatic he did not even have to think about them. He threw the bolt on the door, took several steps backward and aimed the rifle. He did not turn on the room lights. "Come in."

The door swung open with a reluctant creak. A pair of Gamorrean guards stood out in the passageway; Fett leveled his rifle at them. "What do you want?"

One of the guards stepped to the side; and a form—a human—was shoved into the room. Fett's finger tightened reflexively on the trigger, but he held his fire.

"From Jabba," the near guard grunted. "Enjoy her."

Fett reached back with one hand and touched the control for the light fixtures; and under the cool white light that washed over the room, looked down on Leia Organa, Princess of Alderaan.

She scrambled to her feet and backed up into a corner of the room, breathing heavily. Fett imagined she had fought with the guards as they brought her down to him. "You touch me—" Her voice failed her, and she stood there, shivering, and finally said, "Touch me and one of us is going to die."

He lowered the rifle slowly, and looked around the room. He had few enough possessions here with him in the palace; everything he owned, which was little enough, was aboard the *Slave I*. Finally he pointed at the thin sheet that covered the bed. "Cover yourself. I'm not going to touch you."

Organa moved slightly to the side, leaned over and grabbed the sheet and wrapped it around herself and the brief costume Jabba had allowed her, and backed up again into the corner of the room that left her farthest away from Fett. "You're not?"

Fett shook his head. He sat down in the corner facing hers, moving carefully, and propped his rifle across his knees. He *had* to move carefully; his knees had been getting worse in recent years. "Sex between those not married," said Fett, "is immoral."

"Yeah," said Organa. "So's rape."

Fett nodded. "So is rape." He sat in what was, for, him, a comfortable silence, watching her. She settled down in the opposite corner, being careful of her covering; Fett approved of her modesty, but it did not prevent him from continuing to look at her. He had never so much as held a woman in his arms, Boba Fett, and the desire for a woman came to him less frequently, with the passage of the years; but in Fett's mind his chastity made him no less a man, and she was worth looking at, still flushed from her struggles, with her dark hair cascading down over the pale sheet.

She adjusted the sheet around herself, pushing herself back into the corner for warmth. "You're not going to call the guards to take me back to Jabba?"

"And insult Jabba? I don't think so. He'd feed you to the Rancor, and hold a grudge against me. You can go back in the morning."

Her breathing was quieting. "So we just sit here. All night."

"The stones are cold. If you want to use the bed, you're welcome to it."

Organa's skepticism was obvious. "And you'll just sit there. All night."

"I won't hurt you. I won't touch you. Sleep if you will. Or not; I do not care."

Silence descended. Fett watched the woman as she leaned back against the stone wall; watched her as she collected herself; watched her as she watched him.

Time passed. Both of his eyes were open, but he was only half awake when she burst out, "Why are you doing this? Why are you fighting for them?"

Fett stirred, stretching slightly. The rifle across his knees was steady as a rock. "Over half a million credits," he informed her. "That's what Vader and the Hutt have paid for my work."

"Is it just money? *We'll* pay you. Help us get out of here and we'll pay you—"

"How much?"

"More than you can imagine."

Fett was amused by the audacity she showed, trying to bribe him, here deep inside the Hutt's castle. "I can imagine an awful lot."

"You'll get it."

It was cruel to let the woman hope. "No. What you're doing is morally wrong. The Rebels are in the wrong, and the Rebellion will fail—and it should."

Leia Organa could not keep the outrage out of her voice. "Morally wrong? *Us?* We're fighting for homes and our families and our loved ones, the ones who are still alive and the ones we've lost. The Empire destroyed my *entire world,* virtually everyone I ever knew as a child—"

Fett actually leaned forward slightly. "Those worlds rose in rebellion against the authority legally in place over them. The Emperor was within his rights to destroy them; they threatened the system of social justice that permits civilization to exist." He paused. "I am sorry for the deaths of the innocent. But that happens in war, Leia Organa. The innocent die in wars, and your side should not have started this one."

He shut up abruptly; all the talking was making his throat sore.

His comments appeared to render Organa speechless anyway; she looked off to the side, away from Fett, staring at the blank stone wall, for several minutes. When she finally spoke her voice was quiet and she still did not look at him. "It's hard for me to believe that you can really think like this. I've heard Luke—Luke Skywalker, I know you've heard of him—I've heard him talk about the dark side—"

Fett was amazed to hear himself laugh. "*That* Jedi superstition? Gentlelady Organa, if the Force exists I have seen no proof of it, and I doubt it does."

Now she did look at him. "You remind me of Han Solo, a little. He didn't believe—"

Fett heard his voice rise dangerously. "I am nothing like Solo *and don't you compare me to him.*"

Leia took a slow, deep breath. "Okay. Why does that offend you so?"

Fett leaned forward again. "Do you know what that man has done in his life? Never mind the loyal citizens of the Empire that he, and you, have killed during your Rebellion; war is war and perhaps you, at least, think you are fighting for Justice. But *Solo?* He's a brave man, yes; he's also a mercenary who's never done a decent thing in his life, who's never done a *difficult* thing that somebody wasn't paying him for. He's smuggled banned substances—"

"He ran spice!"

Fett found himself on his feet and yelling. *"Spice is illegal!* It's a euphoric, it alters moods, and the use of it leads to the use of worse substances, and a man who will run spice," he snarled, "will run *anything!*" He stood tense and motionless, holding his rifle in a quivering grip, staring down at Leia. "And if I had been using spice tonight, Leia Organa, perhaps you would *not* be safe with me in this room."

"Han has smuggled spice," Leia said steadily, "which is illegal and does not please me; and he's smuggled alcohol too, which is legal but the tariffs are high enough to make it worth smuggling in various worlds. No, he's not perfect and he's broken laws you've never even *heard* of. But I know Han Solo, and I've seen him take risks for things he believes in, risks that I doubt *you* would have the courage to take—and what *are* you doing working for Jabba the Hutt anyway?"

Fett exhaled, loosened his grip on the rifle. He forced himself down to the ground once more, ignoring the spikes of pain that flared in his knees. "He's paying me. A lot. Once Skywalker comes, I will take him to Vader, and then I will spend no more time here."

"That's not what I mean. Jabba the Hutt has sold mountains of spice, and of far worse than that—"

"Necessity makes allies. Once the Rebellion is over, I expect the Empire will deal with Jabba. But he is less a threat than the Rebels." Fett reversed the assault rifle, touched the butt against the pad that controlled the lights. His macrobinoculars compensated almost immediately as darkness fell on them; she sprang into his vision by the light of her body heat. "I'm going to sleep. My throat is sore."

There was a moment of silence.

"Luke Skywalker," Leia said out of the darkness, "is going to come and kill you."

"Everyone dies," Fett agreed. "But since nobody's paid me to kill you ... sleep well."

HE SLEPT WITH his eyes open, inside the helmet.

THE JEDI, IF he was one, came a day later. Luke Skywalker was his name, and he killed Jabba's Rancor; and Jabba put him down in the dungeon, in a cell near Solo and Chewbacca.

The following morning dawned bright and clear and hot, and Boba Fett was in a vile mood.

It was Tatooine, of course. *All* the mornings were bright and clear and hot.

But the Hutt was going to kill Skywalker. And Solo, and Chewbacca, though that was hardly the point.

Skywalker. *That* was the source of Fett's vile mood. He'd tried to talk Jabba out of killing Skywalker—not that he cared whether Skywalker lived or died; Fett expected the galaxy would be a better place with that fool subtracted from it. He'd seen a lot of remarkably stupid things in his day, but the spectacle of a beardless young man trying to face down Jabba the Hutt in his own throne room was near the top of the list.

But, though Fett had argued with him more than was perhaps wise, Jabba was not behaving like the Jabba whom Fett had known all these years. The point was that Darth Vader would *pay* for the fool—the *Emperor* would pay for him. The largest posted bounty Fett knew of in the galaxy was five million credits; but Fett was certain that Luke Skywalker would bring more.

Jabba didn't want to hear about it. He wasn't willing to share the bounty; he wasn't willing to take the bounty himself, and pay Fett as go-between with Vader.

His pet Rancor had died; and Skywalker was going to die for it.

Some days Fett was convinced he was the only sane businessperson left in the entire galaxy.

It galled him. He planned out scenario after scenario; none of them tempted him. He thought about kidnapping Skywalker out of Jabba's hands, but time was short and Jabba's security was good; even for millions of credits the risk was too high.

And so he walked around on the sail barge's upper deck, with uncharacteristic nervous energy, the morning after Skywalker's arrival, the morning that Skywalker and Solo and Chewbacca were to be executed, trying to decide what he was going to do next, as the sail barge. headed out to the Great Pit of Carkoon, taking the condemned to their deaths.

It came to him as something of a surprise that he hoped Solo died well. Years previously Fett had seen Jabba drop half a dozen of his own guards into the Great Pit of Carkoon, allegedly for conspiring against him; he'd offered them all a chance to grovel for their lives. Two of them had, and Jabba, of course, had fed them to the Sarlacc anyway.

He knew Chewbacca wouldn't beg; he hoped Solo wouldn't.

Maybe Skywalker would beg for his life. That wouldn't be so bad.

Fett stood in the bow and watched the sand disappear beneath them. This far out into the desert, there was nothing *but* desert, all around them. Sand, drifts and dunes as far as the eye could see.

Fett wondered, in passing, who had killed more people, himself or, the Hutt. Probably the Hutt, if you counted his spice trade; probably, himself, Fett thought, if you only counted deaths by your own hand.

Eventually the Great Pit of Carkoon came into view. Boba Fett, his mood improved not in the slightest, abandoned the upper deck and went down to the viewing area, to watch with the others as justice was rendered —

—and who knew how many millions of credits were wasted.

THE DAY HAD started badly; it got worse. Before it was over the sail barge was a flaming wreck, Jabba the Hutt was dead, and Boba Fett was down in the Great Pit of Carkoon, being digested by the Sarlacc.

Oh, he got out; as far as Fett knew he was the only person who ever had escaped the Sarlacc.

But by the time he got out and was healed again, or as healed of that experience as he ever did get, great events had transpired; and the galaxy had become something Fett would never have believed possible.

FIFTEEN YEARS PASSED.

Or, to put it another way:

Darth Vader died; so did the Emperor. The Empire fell and was succeeded by the New Republic. On the human scale fifteen years is long enough for babies to be born and grow into teenagers; human children across the galaxy became adults and bore children of their own. For some long-lived species the period passed without significant change; for others, shorter lived than humans, entire generations were born, grew old, and died.

In a sector of the galaxy Boba Fett had never heard of, a star went nova; it murdered a world and an entire sentient species. It aroused less comment than had the destruction of Alderaan, only a decade prior; the galaxy at large barely noticed the tragedy, and Fett never heard about it. In a galaxy with over four hundred billion stars, over twenty million intelligent species, such things are bound to happen.

The remnant of the Empire rose up against the New Republic, and was defeated; Luke Skywalker fell to the dark side of the Force—and returned, as few Jedi ever had in all the thousands of generations preceding him.

Leia Organa married Han Solo; and together they had three children.

On Tatooine, a drunk Devaronian named Labria killed four mercenaries, and vanished.

Boba Fett grew older.

ON THE PLANET Coruscant, the world that had been the capitol of the Old Republic, the capitol of the Empire, and was now the capitol of the New Republic, in the Imperial Palace, in the quarters he shared with his wife, Han Solo sat on the edge of their bed with his mouth set in an obstinate line.   .

"No. I won't go. Treaty signings bore me, and besides that worthless son of a slorth Gareth tried to cheat me at Laro last time we were there."

Leia stood with her arms folded, her exasperation showing plainly. "You cheated him back!"

"I cheated him *better*. Anyway that fool should feel lucky all he had to deal with was *me,*" Han pointed out. "When I was a kid, getting caught dealing seconds was a felony and they hung you for it."

"That's not true," Leia said—but a touch doubtfully, Han thought; he had known her long enough to know that cheating at cards, and the consequences of it, wasn't among the things they taught princesses.

"It is too true," said Han righteously. "Anyway King Gareth was lucky nothing worse happened to him than losing to me, that's the point here. So I don't know what you expect me to do, go up to the fellow, and say, 'I'm sorry, your. scummy Royal Highlessness, that I cheat better than you do'?"

Leia sighed. "I wish you wouldn't use the word 'royal' as though it were an insult. *I'm—*"

"You're *adopted,*" Han said quickly.

It brought a reluctant smile to her. "You're not going to come, are you?"

"You'd wish two weeks of diplomatic boredom on me?"

"You're sure you'd *be* bored?"

"I was bored last time, except that one night."

"I don't think Gareth will play cards with you again."

"So I'll be bored *every* night."

Leia sighed. "You're not coming."

"I'm not going."

"I was thinking of taking the children with me. They're old enough and it would give them some useful experience in dealing with—"

"It's certainly safe enough," Han conceded. "They won't die of excitement."

"I could leave Threepio with you to keep—"

"You'd leave me here with Threepio? What did I do to deserve *that?*"

Leia Organa worked hard at keeping the smile off her face. "All right, I'll take him with me, too."

Han Solo looked up at her and grinned. "Deal." She leaned in on him and whispered, "You better not be in jail when I come back."

"Hey, hey," he objected. "This is *me.*"

HE CALLED LUKE.

When Luke's image appeared in the hologram, Han said, "Hey, buddy. You busy tonight?"

A smile lit Luke's features. "Han! How are you?"

"Fine. Look, Chewie's gone home and won't be back for another few weeks, my wife and kids are off —"

"—the Shalamite trip," Luke nodded. "Right. Why didn't you go?"

"—and I was thinking," said Han doggedly, refusing to get sidetracked, "we might go and see if we could dig up some trouble tonight."

Luke shook his head. "I can't, Han. I've invited a group of the Senators to dinner ... you are welcome to join us, though."

"Trouble sounds more attractive," Han growled.

Luke grinned. "C'mon, Han. You know I can't cancel my own dinner. Besides, this is Coruscant. We're two of the best known people on the whole planet. Where are we going to find trouble?"

"I've managed it before."

"And you sat in jail for two days before you convinced them you were really you. Leia was worried sick."

"Yeah," Han pointed out, "but Leia's off-planet right now. By the time she gets back, *this* stay in jail will be nothing but a pleasant memory."

Luke laughed. "Han, come to dinner with me. You'll enjoy yourself."

"With half a dozen Senators? I'd rather have a tooth pulled."

"You know," said Luke quietly, "you might think about *joining* the Senate."

"Without *anesthetic* I'd rather—"

"They'd elect you in a heartbeat."

"And impeach me in a month."

"Why?"

Han thought about it. "Bribe taking," he said finally.

"You wouldn't take bribes," said Luke calmly.

"Well, I admit it would depend on the bribe."

"Han, what's bothering you?"

The question startled Han. "Nothing."

The steadiness of Luke's gaze was unsettling. "You're not telling me the truth, Han. Or you're not telling yourself the truth, I'm not sure which—"

That look was making Han uncomfortable. "I don't know. Maybe it's just Chewie being gone—"

"That's not it."

Han stared at Luke. "No ... not really. You know ... I don't know where I'm *going* anymore, kid. I have a wife and children who love me, and who I love. But that's the problem. I'm Daddy. I'm Leia's consort. I tell amusing stories at state dinners—"

"You're very good at it," Luke said gently. "There's a place for those sorts of—"

"—and somebody asked me at one of those blasted dinners a while back what it was like, smuggling I mean, back in the old days. I started to answer and suddenly I couldn't remember. I couldn't remember the last time I'd run an Imperial barricade, or what the cargo was, or how it felt."

Luke grinned at him. "It was me and Ben and the droids."

Han looked startled. "You're right—it was, wasn't it?" He smiled almost unwillingly. "Yeah. All right, let's say I couldn't remember the last time I made any *money* at it—"

Luke turned his head, looked off-pickup, and turned back. "Han, my guests are arriving. Are you sure you won't join us?"

Despite himself Han felt tempted. " ... nah. Not tonight."

Luke nodded. "I'll come by tomorrow. All right?"

"All right. I'll talk to you later, kid."

Luke's lips quirked in a small smile. "Han—"

"Yeah?"

"Han, I'm older than you were when we met." The smile did not fade, but it changed quality subtly, in a way Han Solo did not quite understand. "The world *changes,* Han. You can't stop it and you can't fight it, and you can't ever, ever turn it back." Han had the oddest impression Luke was studying him; and then Luke nodded and said, "I'll talk to you tomorrow. Hang in there."

His image vanished.

Han Solo thought, *The kid's turning into Obi-Wan right in front of my eyes.*

HE GOT A recording when he tried to reach Calrissian. "I'm sorry, but I can't be reached right now. Business has taken me on an extended trip; I'll respond to any messages if I return.

"If this is Han, buddy, you owe me four hundred credits if I get back."

Well, blast it, Han thought. *Lando* had found some trouble.

Late that evening he found himself down at the launching bay where he kept the *Falcon.*

It was dark, except for the bay lights high above him, and quiet except for the distant sounds of cargo being unloaded, in the commercial bays a good ways down.

Nobody questioned Han when he arrived; nobody asked him what he was doing there; he walked through the darkened bay as though he owned the place.

He very nearly did.

Han Solo stood at the edge of the bay, and laid one hand against the control for the overheads; and four banks of floods came to life.

Beneath the wash of light, the *Millennium Falcon* glowed white. She had never been so clean, in all the years Han had owned her; she had never been so carefully painted and beautifully detailed. Her engines had been rebuilt the new hyperdrive engines never so much as blinked. The weapons emplacements were almost all new equipment.

There were even spare parts for everything.

Han had ceased to wonder about how much it had all cost; the New Republic had paid for it all. He'd never even seen a bill.

Sitting in the pilot's seat, in the cockpit, he initiated a launch sequence. He didn't intend to take the ship up; he just wanted to look at the sky.

The dome above the *Falcon* split in two, slid slowly apart as the platform the *Falcon* rested on raised itself up, and the sky came out.

Han Solo stared out at the world.

It was amazing how much better it made him feel, just to be sitting here, in the closest thing to a home that he'd ever had. The seat next to him was empty, and that wasn't right—but it wasn't entirely wrong, either. He hadn't met Chewbacca until well into his adult years; and there'd been a time, before that—before Chewie, after the death of his parents—when there had been nobody.

No one except himself.

Han wondered sometimes—rarely, to be sure—what his family would have thought about him, if they could have seen what he had grown into. He'd never had to wonder about it, when he was younger; his family had loved him, but he knew he had been a disappointment to them, and they had not lived to see him grow into anything better.

You can pinpoint moments when change occurs. Not always; some changes are like the tide, slow and barely perceptible until they have come, or gone. Sometimes, though—

Han *did* think about this, and with, oddly, increasing frequency, as the event itself grew more distant in time: the Death Star was coming; and it was going to destroy the Rebel base, the Rebels themselves, and their plainly doomed Rebellion. Han had taken Chewie and the *Falcon*, and had gotten out with time to spare—

Chewie was furious; Han could tell. Chewie wanted to fight. They'd sat here, together, in the *Falcon*'s control room, with Chewie not talking to him. Han had made not one, but two errors, calculating the jump to hyperspace. Finally he had his trajectory—and he hadn't been able to run it.

"All right, all *right,* let's go fight," he'd yelled at Chewie finally, almost twenty years ago, convinced they were both heading to their deaths—

He sat in the cockpit of the *Falcon,* almost twenty years later, and wondered what might have been: Leia would have been dead; and so would Luke. His children would never have been born. The Empire would still rule the Galaxy, and he and Chewie would be traveling from world to world, one step ahead of the Imperials, one step ahead of the bounty hunters.

No, thought Han. *Not 'one step'. Someone would have caught me. Boba Fett, IG-88—someone—and I'd have had no friends to come and rescue me from Jabba.*

Twenty years.

To this day Han could remember with perfect clarity ... how close he had come to punching in that trajectory, and leaving Leia and Luke behind. He woke up at night, sometimes, in cold sweats, thinking about it.

How very close.

If his parents were still alive, Han thought, they'd be impressed by the man he'd grown into—and not the least bit surprised at how close it had come to not happening.

MARI'HA ANDONA TAPPED a stud when the hail came. "This is Control."

"This is General Solo." Mari'ha grimaced at the use of the title; Solo was certainly entitled to it, but Mari'ha had been running flight control over this sector of Coruscant long enough that she knew Solo only used it when he was going to be pushy about something.

"I'm going to take the Falcon *up for a bit. Any chance I could get you to pipe me a flight path?"*

"Yes, sir. What's your destination?"

"Haven't got one."

Mari'ha said calmly, "Excuse me? Sir?"

"I don't have one. I don't know where I'm going yet." Mari'ha sighed, looking across the screens that showed all the flights in her sector. There were so many of them that it was hard for a human to pick out any single blip as belonging to an individual ship.

She thought, *The flight droid is going to pitch a fit.* Of course the flight droid always pitched a fit; it had acquired a dislike for General Solo many years ago now, when—

"Which part of this are you having difficulty with, Control?"

"I'm going to need a couple minutes," she muttered into the comm unit. "The flight droid doesn't like you."

"You need," said Solo, *"to clear a corridor and give me a flight path and do it right now before I have to go down to the tower personally and* charm *you to death. Do you copy* that?"

"I copy you, General." She finished composing his request for clearance, punched it in, and then sat there punching Override, over and over again, at the flight droid's objections. "And ... here you go. Have a nice trip, General. Don't hurry back."

"Try not to miss me too much, sweetheart. A pleasure as usual. Solo out."

Not long after that, her supervisor's holo sprung into existence, one-sixth sized, in the viewing area off to her right. "This is most ir-regular," he said severely. "Did General Solo give you a flight plan?"

"Nope."

"Estimated time of return?"

"Nope."

It was almost a shriek. *"Destination?"*

"Couldn't tell you. Nowhere in-system, though. He entered hyperspace about twenty minutes ago."

STRANGE THINGS HAPPEN in the course of a lifetime:

When he had started out in his career as a bounty hunter, Boba Fett had never even heard of the place: *Tatooine.* But that small and meaningless desert planet, as it turned out, became a part of Fett's life, and over the course of the years kept intruding back into it. Jabba the Hutt had established headquarters there; Luke Skywalker, Fett learned many years later, had actually grown up on Tatooine.

The worst disaster of his life had taken place there, his fall into the Great Pit of Carkoon, into the maw of the Sarlacc.

Two years ago, Tatooine had intruded into Fett's life again. Four mercs, two of them Devaronian, had walked into a bar in Mos Eisley. One of the Devaronian mercs recognized, or thought he had recognized, the Butcher of Montellian Serat. The identification might not have been accurate; the old Devaronian he pointed to had promptly killed all four of the mercs, and no one was able to question him about it.

The old Devaronian had vanished, clean off Tatooine ... and Fett had tracked him. Here, to Peppel, a world almost as far away from Coruscant as Tatooine.

The target was Kardue'sai'Malloc, the Butcher of Montellian Serat. There was a five million credit bounty on the Butcher, five million credits of retirement money.

Boba Fett was not the man he had once been. His right leg, from the knee down, was artificial. Only constant medical treatment kept him from developing any of a variety of cancers. The days he'd spent in the belly of the Sarlacc had altered his metabolism permanently, had damaged him genetically to such a degree that he could not have had children had he wanted them; his cellular structures did not always regenerate the way they were meant to.

To say nothing of the memories he had carried away from the Sarlacc and the Sarlacc's genetic soup, memories that were not always his own.

Fett waited, on his belly in the cold, in the mud, nude except for the shorts that kept his privates decently covered, with arrows in a quiver slung across his back, and a bow in one hand, and a crystal knife inside a leather sheath. Malloc—or Labria, the name he'd been going by for the last couple of decades now—was trickier and more dangerous than anyone had ever dreamed. He'd had a reputation in Mos Eisley, Fett had learned: Labria, the worst spy in the city. He was a drunk, and nobody had respected him, or feared him, until the day he had killed four mercs in the primes of their lives.

Darkness gathered. Fett waited; shivering, worrying. Artificial light of some sort glimmered in the hut's sole window. The metal content of his artificial leg was low, but Fett did not know how good the Butcher's security system was; all he knew was that it was there. He'd slipped tripwires, light traps; had crawled, centimeter by centimeter, past blinking motion sensors.

If there were not some sort of sensor sweeping the clearing, Fett would have been surprised. It was the reason he had not worn his armor, nor brought more modern weapons.

The lights in the hut went out. The hut had no plumbing; the previous night at this time Malloc had waited for several minutes after the extinguishing of his light, letting his eyes acclimate to the darkness, Fett assumed, before coming outside.

Fett reached over his back, pulled an arrow free, and strung the bow. It was a compound bow, that required the least exertion *after* it had been pulled back; Fett pulled it and waited.

Last night at this time Malloc had come outside to relieve himself. Fett didn't know as much about Devaronians as he might have. (Though he had studied an anatomy chart for Devaronians; he didn't want to shoot the fellow in the wrong place). Conceivably they only relieved themselves once a week. If so, he was going to have to think of some other approach—

The door swung open, and the bounty stood in the doorway, assault rifle cradled in both hands, took a quick step outside, onto the porch, and then stepped off the porch and walked around to the side of the house nearer Fett's hiding place. Fett tracked Malloc as he moved over to the open-air toilet the Devaronian had dug for himself, ten meters outside the hut. He waited for Malloc to disrobe and relieve himself—and then waited until he was done, and pulling his clothing back together again.

He needed to keep this one alive, and Fett had shot too many individuals, of all, species, to shoot anyone before he, she, or it, had emptied itself. Someone usually had to clean up after it, and usually that was the person who wasn't in chains.

Fett let the fellow stand up from his toilet, turning away from Fett, and shot Malloc high in the back. He was on his feet and running, in a half stagger himself, running on legs that shrieked with pain, as Malloc stumbled forward, giving voice to something that managed to mix a scream and roar. Fett closed on Malloc and Fett rolled to get down low, and with the knife slashed Malloc across the hamstring of his right leg. Malloc fell forward, to his knees, still reaching up to try to pull the arrow free from his shoulder.

Fett pushed him forward, up against the hut's wall, grabbed Malloc by one of his horns and pulled his head back, and got the knife against his throat. "Move and you die," he whispered harshly.

THE HUT REEKED.

The Butcher of Montellian Serat, Kardue'sai'Malloc, sat propped up against the wall, the arrow pulled from his back, but the wound still bleeding, and strained against the bonds that kept his hands pulled behind his back.

The hut was spacious; the hut's size was one of the things that had given Fett pause. He'd wondered. what the Butcher was hiding inside it—mostly, wondered what weapons might be tucked away inside there, waiting for the wrong person.

There were no weapons, though, except for the rifle the Butcher had carried with him.

Fett had known the Devaronians were carnivores; had he not known it, the contents of the hut would have told him. The slaughtered carcasses of half a dozen animals hung along the far wall. A corner of the room had a pile of bones and shells in it, stripped almost clean of flesh. Dozens of empty bottles were scattered among them.

In the opposite corner was the pit where Malloc had slept; and another several dozen bottles, still full of Merenzane Gold, lined up along the floorboards next to the pit.

Fett had not bothered to look at anything yet except the controls for the security system. As far as he could tell it was all passive se-curity, nothing that would shoot at the *Slave IV* if he brought it down to a landing in the clearing a few kilometers back along his trail. Finally satisfied, he turned back to the bounty.

"On your feet. We're going to walk a bit. I had to leave the call-back outside range of your sensors." Malloc grimaced, showing sharp teeth. He was large for a Devaronian, which made him very large for a human. He spoke in Basic with less accent than Fett's own. "No. I don't think I will."

Fett hefted the man's own assault rifle. He shrugged. "Devaroni-ans are tough; I know that about you. You do not go into shock and you do not die easily. You'll walk—or I'll burn off your arms and your legs to make you lighter, and then I'll *drag* you where we are going." Fett paused. "Your choice."

The bounty said wearily, "Kill me. I'm not walking."

"I'll do worse than kill you," said Fett patiently—his left knee was paining him, his entire right leg was on fire from the prosthesis upward, and he really didn't want to drag this very large Devaronian two kilometers, not even after lightening him.

Malloc let his head fall back, to the wall behind him. "Do you know what you're doing, bounty hunter? Do you even know who I *am?*"

Fett fired a quick burst into the wall near Malloc's head, to get his attention; it did no more than singe the damp wooden wallboards. "Listen. I am Boba Fett." It had been a generation since one of his bounties had failed to recognize the name; it brought this fellow's eyes alive. Fear, Fett assumed. "And you are Kardue'sai'Malloc, the Butcher of Montellian Serat, and you're worth five million credits. Alive. And *nothing* dead, so you will *not* annoy me into killing you."

"Boba Fett," he whispered. He stared up into Fett's face. "You're an ugly piece of prey … I heard you were after me."

Fett couldn't believe how much talking he was having to do to keep from dragging this fellow two klicks. "Yes. Now do I burn your—"

"They say you're honest."

That was an opening to a negotiation, if Fett had ever heard one. "What do you have? Something worth trading five million credits for?"

Malloc stared at Fett, searching his features for—Fett could not imagine what. He took a breath, winced, and then nodded. "Yes. By the Cold, I do. Something worth five million credits easy. Maybe more. Something *priceless*, Fett—"

Fett said impatiently, "What?"

"Kang," Malloc whispered. "Maxa Jandovar, Janet Lalasha. Miracle Meriko—"

The last name Fett recognized, and knew the idiot was lying to him. "Meriko died in Imperial custody twenty-five years ago, you lying fool, and the bounty on him was twenty thousand credits, not any five mil—"

"Music!" Malloc yelled. He glared at Fett. "You uncivilized barbarian! Music! I have the music of Maxa Jandovar, and Orin Mersai. M'lar'Nkai'kambric," he took a deep breath, yelled again, *"Lubrics, Aishara, Dyll—"*

Fett shook his head wearily. "No. No, I don't care about your music. Now will you get up? Or must I carve you up and drag you?"

The Butcher leaned his head back and stared up at the roof. The light caught his predator's eyes and glimmered back out of them. "By the Cold," he whispered, "but you're ignorant. Even for a human you're ignorant. There are people who will *pay* for that music, Fett. I have the only recordings left of half a dozen of the galaxy's finest musicians. The Empire killed the musicians, destroyed their music—"

"Five million credits?" said Fett politely.

The Butcher hesitated a second too long. "More than that—"

Fett pointed the rifle at the Butcher's legs. "Negotiation is over. I will drag you if you make me," and he was not joking.

Malloc closed his eyes, and spoke a bare moment before Fett had decided to start cutting. "I'll walk. But you have to make me three promises. You dig up my music chips, they're buried in a holding case under a few centimeters of dirt, out back. After you deliver me to Devaron, you take those chips to the person I tell you to take them to, and you sell them to her for whatever she can offer. And finally—" He nodded toward the bottles of golden liquor. "We take six of those with us. I'm going to need them." He saw Fett shaking his head, and said sharply, "This is not a negotiation, ignorant human. You start shooting if you think it is, but I warn you, I'll do my level best to die on you between here and Devaron. I have a mean streak in me, bounty hunter."

Bounty hunting, thought Boba Fett wearily, *is not what it used to be.* He waved the rifle at Malloc. "Fine. Agreed. Get up ... and show me where your blasted music is buried."

"WELCOME TO DEATH, Gentleman Morgavi. What do you have to declare?"

As was so frequently the case anymore, at least when dealing with other humans, the customs agent standing before Han Solo, in the bright Jubilar sunshine, seemed ... well, he struck Han as younger than Luke Skywalker had seemed the first time Han had seen him.

A grin touched Han; he couldn't help it. "No. Nothing to declare."

The boy looked at the *Falcon,* and then back at Han. Suspicion worked its way across his face like a baby negotiating its first steps. "Nothing?" he asked finally.

Despite his best instincts Han's grin grew larger. "Sorry, no. I just came to Jubilar for a visit." The kid thought he was a smuggler. "I'll just head on over to the port bar," he said. "I expect you want to search the ship right about now."

The grin appeared to be offending the customs man. "Yes, sir. Why don't you just ... wait in the bar. While we search. Of course, if you're in a hurry—" The man paused.

Han Solo tried to remember the last time he had bribed a customs official, and couldn't.

"I haven't smuggled anything since, well, practically before the Rebellion," Han told the fellow. He headed off toward the main terminal, turned back for a moment. "There are cargo holds right underneath the main deck. I left them unlocked, though. Don't break anything trying to get into them, okay?" The customs agent stared after him.

"I'LL HAVE A beer," said Han. "Corellian, if you've got it."

The port bar was nearly empty; only a few elderly Gamorreans sat together in a booth in back, playing some game that involved throwing bones; a creature of some race Han had never seen before sat at the far end of the bartop, inhaling something that, even from here, reeked of ammonia.

The bartender looked Han over, nodded, and turned toward the bar. A long mirror hung on the wall behind the bar; Han stared at himself in it. He thought that the gray in his hair gave him a distinguished look.

"I thought this city was called 'Dying Slowly,'" Han said as a dark beer was laid down in front of him. "When did the name change?"

The bartender shrugged. "It's always been called just 'Death,' far as I know."

"How long you been on-planet?"

"Eight years."

"What for?"

The bartender stared at him. "Take some advice—you don't ask that sort of question around here." He shook his head and turned away.

Han nodded, and sat drinking his beer; he'd known that, once. A thought struck him. "Hey, buddy." The bartender looked over at him.

"Just out of curiosity," said Han—

He paused and looked around at the nearly empty mid-afternoon bar.

He leaned back in toward the bartender. "Now that spice is legal ... what sorts of things get smuggled around here, these days?"

THE TRIP TO Devaron took long enough that Malloc's shoulder wound was nearly healed by the time they neared hyperspace breakout, though the leg was starting to fester, and none of the drugs Fett had seemed to be helping—Fett hoped sincerely that the injury wouldn't kill the fellow before they reached Devaron.

Fett had sent a communication ahead to the Bounty Hunter's Guild. Normally he would not have bothered to involve the Guild; but normally he did not have a five million credit bounty. A Guild representative should be waiting at Devaron when they reached it.

Fett kept the Butcher down in the *Slave IV*'s holding room through most of the trip.

In the remaining minutes left before their exit from hyperspace, Fett dressed himself. The Mandalorian combat armor he dressed in was not the armor he had worn in years past; that armor, burned and cracked, was still somewhere deep inside the Great Pit of Carkoon, back on Tatooine. But Mandalorian combat armor, though rare, could still be acquired if you went about it right. For years Fett had been hearing about another bounty hunter who wore Mandalorian combat armor, a fellow named Jodo Kast. It had annoyed him terribly. With some frequency, during those years, Fett had found himself being blamed for, and credited with, things Kast had done.

Less than a year after his escape from the Sarlacc, Fett had hunted Jodo Kast down, via the Bounty Hunter's Guild; he'd pretended to be a client, disguised in bandages; his own Guild had not known him. He'd requested the services of Kast, and Kast had come; and Fett had taken away the impostor's armor, and also his life.

Before the ship left hyperspace Fett brought the Butcher up to the control room and put him in the chair nearest the airlock. Malloc was sweating heavily, fighting with his fear. He'd drunk his first five bottles early in the trip; Fett had held back the sixth bottle for this moment. Fett restrained Malloc at the ankles; and by his right hand; he left the Devaronian's left hand unchained, so that Malloc might drink. Once he was satisfied with Malloc's bonds Fett unsealed and handed Malloc the last bottle of Merenzane Gold. It wasn't a matter of kindness on Fett's part; if it kept Malloc from struggling during the transfer to the Devaronian authorities, better to let him drink.

They'd barely spoken to one another the entire trip. Malloc lifted the bottle to his lips and swallowed three, four times, before speaking. "How much longer?"

Fett glanced at his controls. "Six minutes until breakout. At least twenty before we dock with the shuttle that'll take you downside." He paused. "Time enough for you to finish the bottle, if you work at it."

"Do you know what they're going to do to me?"

"They will feed you, still alive, to a pack of starved quarra." Fett paused. "Domesticated hunting animals—this practice is one of the things that's kept Devaron out of the New Republic, I've heard."

Malloc nodded a little convulsively and took another drink. "It's a bad way to die. I saw it done once, when I was a boy. You were right, Fett, we Devaronians don't die easy. The quarra go at the belly first, the soft flesh. But the condemned doesn't die of that. They may nibble on your ears, or your eyes or horns, but that won't kill you, either. If you're lucky the quarra tear your throat out quickly. You arch your head back and expose your throat, and if you're lucky —"

"The time you saw it done," said Fett curiously, "What had the condemned done?"

Malloc stared at the golden liquid in his free hand, and took another quick drink. "I don't think there's a word for it, exactly, in Basic. He went hunting, during famine, and caught his prey—and fed himself, and his quarra. He didn't bring it back to the tribe." He looked up at Fett. "Do you know what I did?"

Fett glanced over at his instruments. Several minutes left until breakout; best let him talk. He looked back at Malloc. "Yes."

"I was a good servant to the Empire," the Butcher said. "My own people rose in rebellion. They sent my command out to Hunt them down. And I did it, Fett. I Hunted them across the northlands, and I caught them in the city of Montellian Serat. We shelled them until they surrendered—"

Fett nodded. "And after taking their surrender, you executed them. Seven hundred of them."

"The Empire ordered us to move on. To reinforce loyal troops, fighting just south of us. We were not to leave any troops behind as guards for the prisoners ... and certainly we were not to leave any of them living."

"They didn't tell you to execute the prisoners."

"They didn't have to." Malloc drank again, a huge belt, lowering the level of the bottle noticeably. "It took almost five minutes, Fett. We put them in a holding pen and started shooting at them. They screamed and screamed and screamed. We just kept shooting until the screaming had stopped." He said almost pleadingly, "I was following orders."

"I know."

"They say you were Darth Vader's favorite bounty hunter."

"Yes."

"Don't you have any loyalty to what you were?" A touch of real anger glittered through Malloc's despair. "I did the Empire's work, man! Doesn't that count for *anything?*"

Fett thought about it. "I wish," he said finally, "that the Empire had not fallen." He nodded, remembering, and then said softly, "Yes. I used to enjoy my work more."

Hopelessness settled on the Butcher—he sagged, looking as though someone had just doubled the artificial gravity in the *Slave IV*. They always thought they could bargain, or plead, right up to the last moment. Malloc hadn't had a chance to ask the next question; he asked it now. Virtually all of Fett's bounties, given the chance, did.

"How did you catch me?"

A minute left to breakout. Fett nodded toward the bottle Malloc held. "I traced sales of Merenzane Gold across the entire sector Tatooine is in. They said, at the bar you frequented on Tatooine, that it was your favorite drink."

Malloc stared at him. "That crap I drank on Tatooine? That wasn't Merenzane Gold, you idiot, they don't serve Merenzane Gold in bars like that, they just pour it out of bottles that once, eons ago, were looked at hard by a man who heard of Merenzane! Don't you know anything about liquor?" he asked in despair. "Haven't you a single civilized vice?"

Fett shook his head. "No. I do not drink, nor indulge in other drugs. They are an insult to the flesh."

"So you hunted me down because you thought I was drinking Merenzane Gold, all those years on Tatooine. Fett, I had one glass of real Gold the entire time I was on that miserable excuse for a world." Malloc shook his head in disbelief, took another swig from the bottle. "By the Cold. I can't believe I got caught by a nerf herder like you."

The hyperspace tunnel fragmented around them; Fett turned away from Malloc, to his controls. "Reality," said Fett, "doesn't care if you believe it."

Malloc threw the bottle, of course. The security system shot it out of the air with a single blaster bolt. The bottle blew apart into shards that rattled against the back of Fett's helmet; the liquid splashed against Fett's armor.

"You should have drunk it," Fett said. He did not have to look at Malloc to know the despair that crossed his features. He'd seen it before, a thousand times.

FETT DOCKED WITH the shuttle, in orbit about Devaron. The Guild representative came across first. Fett stood in the main entryway, rifle in hand, pointing it at the representative as he entered.

The representative was Bilman Dowd, a human, tall and thin and elderly, with a severe bearing and no discernible sense of humor; he had been in the Guild even longer than Fett, which was a remarkable accomplishment in this day and age. "Hunter Fett," he said, courteously enough.

"Dowd."

Dowd looked the Butcher over. Kardue'sai'Malloc sat motionlessly, staring straight ahead. He did not seem to be aware of Dowd's presence. "This is the Butcher, is it?"

"I believe so."

Dowd nodded. He carried with him a small slate, with various controls on it; he touched one now, and spoke. "Come across."

The *Slave IV*'s lock cycled again; four Devaronians entered, two of them in military dress, bearing rifles that they carried pointed at the *Slave IV*'s deck. The third was a female Devaronian, young, in gold robes and a gold headdress; the fourth, wearing robes of a cut similar to the woman's, except in black, was an older Devaronian, perhaps the Butcher's age.

All four hesitated at the sight of Fett, aiming his rifle at them—

Dowd gestured to the woman and said something in Devaronian. Fett had never actually heard the language spoken before; it was low and guttural and full of snarling consonants. It sounded like an invitation to a fight.

The woman's expression did not change. She crossed to the spot where Malloc sat—Fett had restrained his left hand prior to allowing anyone else on board. She knelt in front of Malloc, looking the shivering prisoner over as though she were inspecting a carcass in the marketplace. Malloc's skin had acquired a blue tinge; Fett supposed it was something that happened to Devaronians when they were deathly afraid.

The woman stood up and nodded abruptly. She spoke in Devaronian—

Dowd said, "She says it's her father."

Fett nodded; it was the reason the bounty had been "Alive," rather than "Dead or Alive." It had only changed a few years back; the Devaronians had no longer been certain that the Butcher would be recognizable, dead.

The older Devaronian said grimly, in rather poor Basic, "We pay him now."

Dowd handed his tablet over to the Devaronian. The Devaronian laid his hand flat against the tablet, and spoke several words in Devaronian. Dowd took the panel back, tapped two of the controls in succession, and turned to Fett.

"You've been paid."

It was not the sort of thing Fett took anyone's word for; he took several steps backward, rifle still pointed at the group, and glanced slightly to the side. In a holofield at the edge of the control panel, a live link to the Guild Bank showed the current balance in Fett's numbered account:

C:4,507,303.

Five million credits, less the Guild's handling fee of 10%, plus the seven thousand, three hundred and three credits Fett had had in the account—business had been bad, recent years.

The relief that washed over Fett at the sight was the strongest emotion other than anger that he'd felt in at least a decade. He could afford to have a replacement clone for his lower right leg; he could afford the cancer treatments that had been bankrupting him. Fett barely heard himself say, "Take him. He's yours."

They hauled the Butcher up out of the chair he was restrained in, being none too gentle with him. As they pulled him to his feet, he yelled at Fett, in Basic: "You do what you promised!" The glare in his eyes was perfectly mad, as they dragged him toward the airlock. *"You take care of my music!"*

After the Devaronians had gone, Dowd stood with his tablet, looking at Fett with plain curiosity. Fett sat in the pilot's seat, still holding his rifle, pointed rather generally in Dowd's direction.

Dowd said, "You'll be retiring, I presume."

Fett shrugged. "I haven't thought about it."

Dowd nodded. "What did he mean—about the music?"

"He had a music collection. Music the Empire suppressed, apparently. He asked me to deliver it to a woman who would see that the music was published."

Dowd lifted an eyebrow. "Are you going to?"

"I said I would."

Dowd nodded. "You're a strange one." The comment didn't offend Fett; Dowd had made the observation before, and more than once, over the course of the decades they had known one another.

Dowd reached into the pocket of his coat, and Fett stirred, bringing the rifle up slightly.

Dowd's smile was thin. "I've a message chip for you. Message that arrived at Guild headquarters. Do you want it?"

"Leave it on the deck," said Fett, "and leave. I'm very tired."

THE MESSAGE WAS amazing.

The encryption code was so old that Fett had to dig into his computer's archives to find the key for it. He'd made the practice, over the years, of giving his informants encryption codes in a numbered sequence; the first five digits of this message were 00802, which made it at least twenty-five years old—Fett's current encryption identification numbers started well upwards of 12,000.

He unarchived the encryption key for the 802 protocol, and decoded the message.

It was short. It said:

Han Solo is on Jubilar—Incavi Larado.

In a lifetime of bounty hunting, Boba Fett had rarely, in conversation with others, said two words when one would do. He didn't talk to himself, not *ever*—

Boba Fett said out loud, "One from the vaults."

ON HIS WAY to Jubilar, Boba Fett played the music that the Butcher of Montellian Serat had thought more important than his own life.

There were over five hundred infochips in the carrying case the Butcher had buried; each chip had the capacity to hold almost a day's worth of music. Fett opened the case, pulled one free at random, and plugged it in.

The sounds that surrounded him were—different, he had to admit. Atonal, crashing, and thoroughly unpleasant to the ear. He shook his head, pulled the chip free, and decided to try one more.

A long silence after the chip was inserted. Fett waited, and finally, impatiently, reached for it—

The sound tugged at the limits of audibility. Fett froze in the motion of reaching for the chip, straining to hear. The whisper grew into the faintest sound of a woodwind, and then a high horn joined it, playing counterpoint—

Fett's hand dropped, and he leaned back in his chair, listening.

A voice that sounded female to Fett, but might have been a human male or an alien of any of a dozen sexes, for all Fett would have sworn to, joined in, weaving in and among the instruments, singing beautifully in a language that meant nothing to Fett, a language he had never heard before.

After a bit he reached up and pulled his helmet off.

"Lights off," he said a while later.

He sat there in the cool cabin, on his way to Jubilar to kill Han Solo, listening in the darkness to the only copy, anywhere in the galaxy, of the legendary Brullian Dyll's last concert.

IN THE ICY Devaronian northlands, beneath the dark blue skies that had haunted Kardue'sai'Malloc's dreams for over two decades, some ten thousand Devaronians had converged in the judgment Field outside the ruins of the ancient holy city of Montellian Serat, the city Malloc had shelled into its current state.

It was a beautiful day late in the cold season, with a chill breeze out of the north, and high pale clouds skidding across the darkened skies. The suns hung low on the southern horizon; the Blue Mountains lifted away up to the north. Malloc barely noticed the Devaronians surrounding him, the members of his family dressed in their robes of mourning, as they pushed him through the crowds; to the pit where the quarra waited.

He heard the quarra growl, heard the growl rising as he grew closer to the pit.

His daughter and brother walked a bare few steps behind him. Malloc recalled he had once had a wife; he wondered why she was not there.

Perhaps she had died.

A dozen quarra in the pit, lean and hungry, leaping up toward the spot where Malloc's guards brought him to a halt.

Devaronians are not creatures of ceremony; a herald cried out, "The Butcher of Montellian Serat"—and the screams of the crowd raised up and surrounded Malloc, an immense roar that drowned out the noise of the snarling quarra; the bonds that held him were released and strong young hands shoved him forward, and into the pit where the starving quarra waited.

The quarra leapt, and had their teeth in him before he reached the ground.

He could see the Blue Mountains from where he fell. He had almost forgotten the mountains, the forests, all those years on that desert world.

Oh, but the trees were beautiful.

Arch your head back.

THEY MADE HAN buy the speeder. Jubilar wasn't big on rentals. Too frequently the rentals, and/or the renters, didn't come back.

In early twilight Han pulled the speeder to a stop at the address they'd given him, and got out to look around.

Almost thirty years.

He felt so odd: everything had *changed*. Places that he remembered as well-kept buildings had grown rundown, places that used to be run-down had been torn down and new buildings built in their steads. Slums had spread everywhere—the planet's never-ending battles had razed entire neighborhoods.

The neighborhood surrounding the Victory Forum, where Han had fought in Regional Sector Number Four's All-Human Free-For-All extravaganza, was a blasted ruin. It looked like the remains of some ancient civilization, worn down by the eons. The small buildings surrounding the Forum had their windows broken out and boarded up; flame and shells and blaster fire had scored them.

All that remained of the Forum itself was broken rubble strewn across a huge empty lot. Han stepped off the sidewalk, into the lot. Glass and gravel crunched beneath his feet as he walked across it, toward the main entrance.

He stood in the empty lot, staring at the desolation, with a cool wind tugging at him—and suddenly it struck him as though he were *there*, that moment, all those years ago:

... standing in the ring. Facing the opponents, with the screams and cheers and taunts of the crowd in his ears. His heart pounding and his breath coming short, as the match flag fluttered down toward the ground, and the other three fighters came at him.

Han took a running leap at the nearest. He got up two meters off the ground and landed a flying kick into the face of the onrushing first fighter. The man's nose broke, his head snapped back—

To this day Han had no clear memory of the next several minutes. They'd recorded the fights, and he'd seen the recording; but the knowledge of what had happened did not connect to his blurred memories of the events themselves. The boy had been hurt badly, walking off the mat with a broken arm and a broken jaw, two broken ribs and a concussion and bruises across half his body; the bruises turned purple the next day. The woman who'd cared for

Han the next several days, he couldn't even remember what she'd looked like, she was a strange one and he did remember her running her fingers over the bruises, plainly fascinated.

Here. Here. Right about ... here.

Han stood on the spot. This empty place ... this was the spot. The ring. And when all was done, he'd been the last one left on his feet—

Thirty years. Over half his life had passed since that day.

Han took a slow step ... stopped and took one last look around at the devastation, a ruin stretching to the horizon; and turned away and walked back to the speeder, and sat motionlessly in the speeder, leaning back with his hands clasped behind his head, staring up at the sky as darkness fell around him, remembering.

"MAYOR BAKER," HAN said. "A real pleasure."

He'd met her in a brightly lit hydroponics warehouse, in a complex of warehouses at the edge of Death, in the part of Death they had used to call Executioner's Row. He'd come prepared; he was visibly armed with a blaster, had a couple of holdout blasters tucked inside his coat, and a third down in his boot.

Not that he expected any trouble; this was business, a business he'd been in for a long time before the Rebellion, and he knew what he was doing. But no point in taking chances, on a planet like Jubilar, in a city like Death.

They wanted him to smuggle Jandarra, to Shalam—Han had almost laughed aloud when the Mayor's representative had approached him; Jandarra was one of Leia's favorite treats. He expected that even she would be amused when he showed up on Shalam with a cargo hold full of it; and certainly the Shalamites wouldn't dare prosecute him for it.

The Mayor smiled at Solo. She was a tall, obese woman with features that did not take to a smile very easily. Four bodyguards were present; two at the entrance to the warehouse, two a few steps behind the Mayor, all armed with assault rifles. "Gentleman Morgavi—Luke, isn't it?"

Han smiled at her. "That's right. Luke Morgavi. As I told your aide, ma'am, I'm an independent trader out of Boranda."

She nodded. "A pleasure, Luke. Please, follow me." She led him down through rows of hydroponics tanks, to a row toward the back where the growing lights were both brighter and of a different wavelength. Inside the tanks, small purple and green tubular vegetables grew. "Jandarra," she said. "They're native to Jubilar; they're a great delicacy, and they usually only grow in the desert after relatively rare rainstorms. After almost two years of work we managed to cultivate them—"

Han nodded. "And the Shalamite slapped a 100% tariff on you."

Anger touched her voice. "We have *eighty* thousand credits' worth of Jandarra here that are only worth *forty* thousand after the Shalamite tariff."

"Those Shalamite," Han commiserated. "Can't trust 'em. They cheat at cards, too—did you know that?"

She stopped and studied Han. "No ... Gentleman Morgavi. I did not." You *cheat at cards,* she thought, and kept the pleasant smile on her face—it was hard work. He really *didn't* recognize her—well, thirty years was a long time, after all, and she'd put on sixty kilos; and her last name, back then, before her marriage to the unfortunate Miagi Baker, had been Incavi Larado.

He'd said he'd come back, and here he was, the New Republic's infamous General Solo—and only thirty years late.

"Eighty thousand credits' worth," she said again. "Delivered to Shalamite. That's a forty thousand upside, and we'd be willing to go—"

"Fifty percent," said Han politely. "Which would be twenty thousand credits, and I'd be happy to make the run for that amount."

Her eyes narrowed. "You think you can get past the Shalamite Navy?"

Han said, "Lady, I used to run the *Imperial* lines. I'm talking about the old Star Destroyers—let me tell you a story—"

OUT IN THE darkness, Boba Fett lay on his stomach, carefully adjusting his aim—he had to shoot in through the main entrance to the hydroponics warehouse, which wouldn't have been difficult except that some of the tanks were in his way—he was going to have to wait for Solo to come back out toward the warehouse's entrance.

Fett waited patiently. He was surprised by his good fortune; who would have thought that a trap he had set three decades ago would come to fruition now?

Good fortune indeed—even today, with the Empire fallen, Han Solo had lots of enemies: Jabba's relatives, loyal officers of the Empire who had managed to maintain small fiefdoms on a thousand planets across the galaxy; and the various bounties on Solo, Dead or Alive, were still impressive, even with Vader and Jabba and the Empire long gone; still worth making an effort for, even with four and half million credits in the bank.

Oddly enough, the sight of Solo—looking at him through the rifle scope—filled Fett with a nostalgia that surprised him. There was no question in Fett's mind that Solo was a bad man, worse in every way that counted than the Butcher of Montellian Serat; and if that bounty had brought Fett no joy, he had handed the Butcher over to his executioners with little enough in the way of regret.

Solo, though—it came to Fett as a revelation that Solo's presence, over the course of the decades, had in a way been oddly comforting. He had been a part, however peripherally, of Fett's life for so long that Fett had difficulty picturing a world without him. The world had changed, and changed, and only Solo had remained a constant.

He'd hunted Solo for various clients, various bounties. Fett had difficulty picturing a world without Solo—he leaned in and touched the scope's focusing ring. Solo's image, and that of the woman Fett assumed was Incavi Larado, though he did not recognize her, leapt into sharp relief; and Fett's finger tightened on the trigger.

He wouldn't make the mistake of trying to take Solo alive, not again.

And he would learn to picture a world without him.

THEY HEADED TOWARD the entrance together, Mayor Incavi Baker smiling patiently, and with a certain effort that Han did not miss. He stayed a half step behind her as she walked, keeping part of her bulk between him and the loading docks outside, where the lights had gone out not long after they had all entered the warehouse together. The loading docks outside were pitch black; they might have assembled an army for all Han knew

"—so this kid," said Han, "his name was—uh, Maris, and this old guy with delusions, Jocko, yeah, anyway this guy Jocko, he thinks he's a *Jedi Knight*—and let me tell you, that old guy with his delusions, he was a pain in the butt—anyway they tell me they have to get past the Imperial lines—"

What did they have waiting for him out there? What had he walked into?

HE KNOWS SOMETHING *is wrong,* Fett thought. *He's—*

THE MAIN POWER line entered the warehouse at the northeast, and split, one bundle running up to the ceiling and the overhead lights, and another bundle running back toward the hydroponics tanks.

Han cocked his wrist a certain way, and the holdout blaster in his left sleeve dropped down into his hand.

BOBA FETT HAD the crosshairs hovering just to the left of Incavi Baker's approaching form; the cross-hair found Solo's breast, lost it, found it again.

Fett squeezed the trigger—

—the warehouse lights died—

The blaster bolt tore through the darkness like a flash of lightning.

HAN HIT THE ground rolling, sparks still trailing away from the spot where his first shot had struck the power cable, rolled away firing left-handed at the locations where he remembered the two closer bodyguards standing, pulling his blaster free right-handed. Screams, the woman was screaming, and he got off four shots with the holdout before it malfunctioned, burning out, the power supply flashing hot and terribly bright as it went, lighting Han as a target to the world, and Han came up out of his roll and made it to his feet and ran backward through the darkness, through the rows of hydroponics tanks, spots dancing in his eyes, using his scalded left hand on the sides of the tanks, to guide himself, as blaster bolts rained around him.

In that single flash as the holdout blaster had arced out, he had seen a shape running toward the warehouse entrance, a shape out of Han Solo's nightmares, a shape out of the galaxy's darkest history—a man in Mandalorian combat armor.

INCAVI BAKER LAY on her back, staring up into infinity. There was a terrible pain in her side, and she knew she was dying.

She wished it weren't so dark. Bright lights flashed around her, blaster bolts that lit the world up briefly, but even the blaster bolts were fading now.

A figure loomed up out of the darkness, knelt beside her. A man in gray armor. Incavi opened her mouth—but nothing came, and the man reached for her. Something sharp and cold touched her neck. Gradually, the pain went away.

A RINGING IN his ears.

The four bodyguards were dead; Solo must have killed the one off to the side, Fett thought, curled up around whatever wound Solo had left in him—Fett knew he had only killed the three who were still standing when he entered the warehouse, and that had been as much reflex as anything.

But—

He knelt beside the woman, holding her hand, until her thrashing stopped.

In all his years as a bounty hunter he had never killed the wrong target before; and there was a tightness in his throat he hadn't felt since the day of his exile from Concord Dawn. He felt an absurd desire to apologize to the woman, which was ridiculous, she was as guilty of sin as any human being had ever been in the history of time, Fett had known her in her earlier days and there was nothing worthwhile in her or in her life, and certainly the galaxy would not miss her presence—

But he had not meant to kill her.

She shuddered slightly and her hand, holding his, went limp.

The macrobinoculars buried in his helmet didn't help much, not in this darkness; they showed the still warm forms of four bodyguards, and the bulk of this dead old woman; they showed the heat still emanating from the lamp fixtures that were now without power.

Toward the back of the warehouse, a heat source moved.

Fett came to his feet, rifle in hand, and went hunting.

MANDALORIAN COMBAT ARMOR.

I didn't come prepared far this, Han thought. He had an assault rifle, taken from the bodyguard he'd kicked in the groin, but that wasn't going to help so much, unless he got in close to Fett, and that was going to be hard, with the macrobinoculars in Fett's helmet.

He had to get out of this darkened warehouse, out into the night, where there were places to run, and places to hide, and try to reach the speeder he'd come here in.

Han couldn't believe this was happening to him. He gathered his legs up beneath him, checked the safety on the assault rifle—he heard movement, out toward the front of the warehouse. Careful and quick—he kept his head down and ran in a crouch toward the warehouse's rear entrance.

Lando would be jealous, if Han made it back to tell him about it, and Lando made it back to be told.

Leia was going to be furious.

FETT DUCKED DOWN behind one of the growing tanks, unlimbered his flare gun and fired a shot toward the warehouse's roof.

Actinic orange light flared; it would give Solo some light to work with. The interior of the warehouse became bright as day, and huge wavering shadows struck away from the warehouse's supporting beams, as the flare hit the ceiling, crawled along it for several seconds, and started to descend.

Something rattled, off at the eastern end of the warehouse; Fett held his position, held his fire. Solo had thrown something—the sound came again. *Patience, patience—*

A single shot, the sound of broken glass, that was Solo making an exit for himself through one of the windows, before the flare faded, while he could still see to run, and Fett surged to his feet to shoot Solo down as he made for the broken window.

He had time to see Han Solo, standing fifty meters away, pointing one of the bodyguards' assault rifles at him. The shot took Fett in his breastplate and blew him off his feet.

Han Solo turned and ran, hit the shattered window and dove through it like a young man in his prime. Boba Fett rolled over, staggered back to his feet only a second later, the breastplate of his combat armor so hot it burned everywhere it touched him, and in a murderous rage charged after Solo, as unaware of the pain that throbbed in his legs and chest as if it belonged to someone else.

HAN RAN TOWARD his speeder under the dim light from the planet's only moon. He was slightly disoriented; he couldn't remember whether the downlot where he'd left the speeder was south and west, or south and east; he ran south down one of the long alleyways between the warehouses, breath coming short, and came up to the last building, the last cover before the downlot, and hesitated before rounding the corner, the downlot was either immediately to his left or immediately to his right. He tried to envision the layout of the warehouse park in his mind—he thought he'd come the quick way around, but maybe not, and if he hadn't, then Fett might have reached the downlot before him.

A scraping sound, metal on stone –

Before he even realized what he was doing Han found himself rounding the corner, rifle up and finger tightening on the trigger as Boba Fett was turning toward him, bringing up his own rifle—

They stood there in the middle of nowhere, on a planet the rest of the galaxy had more than half forgotten, pointing assault rifles at one another, from a distance of less than a meter.

Han didn't fire. Fett didn't fire.

Bizarre details piled in on Han. The aperture of Fett's assault rifle was huge, as big as the first Death Star had seemed at first sight. The barrel wasn't perfectly steady, it wavered slightly, moving around in almost invisibly tiny circles. The moonlight glinted off Fett's scarred armor; Han could see the moon, reflected darkly on the black visor.

He was still out of breath from the running. His voice caught when he spoke. "I guess we're going to ... die together."

Fett's voice—as harsh and raw as ever. "Evidently." Han stared over the sight at him. "Your armor won't save you. Not at this range."

"No."

"I doubt you can kill me quick enough to keep me from firing."

Fett's helmet moved, slightly—a nod. "I doubt it too."

Han did not dare take his eye away from his rifle's sight, aiming at the base of Fett's throat. "You killed those people back there. The woman."

Han could have sworn he saw a shiver run up the bounty hunter's frame. "I'm sorry about that. They—she—was not the target."

Han almost pulled the trigger on him. He could hear the rage in his own voice. "*You're* going to die and *I'm* going to die and maybe we both of us deserve it. That woman didn't do any—"

"She's the one who *called* me!"

Han took a step forward and screamed, *"I don't care!"* He found to his amazement that he was standing with the barrel of his rifle jammed up against Fett's armor, that the barrel of Fett's rifle was digging into his own breastbone. "I don't know what made you like you are, you think you get to decide who lives and dies, I don't care, come on, pull the trigger and we'll die together!" He stared into the black visor. "Last decision you'll *ever* get to make."

Boba Fett said in a voice so soft Han would have sworn it could not have been Fett's, "You first." His voice got even softer, amazingly. "You're married, aren't you? You have children who need you. What were you doing out here, Solo, pretending to be young? This is no place for a man like you."

The fury that touched Han was bone deep. "Don't you talk about my children, I'll kill you so fast—"

"Do you *want* to die?"

Han took a deep breath. "Do you?"

Fett shook his head, the tiniest possible movement of the visor. "No. But I do not see a way out."

The faintest breath of hope touched Han. "All right. You put down your rifle. I won't kill you if you put down your rifle."

Fett whispered it. "No. I won't kill you if you put down yours. I'll let you go back to your family, unharmed. Put down your weapons—"

"I don't trust you."

"Nor I," said Fett, "you."

A cool wind blew across the downlot; Han felt it drying his sweat, chilling him. "We take five steps back," Han said finally. "You drop your rifle and you run like a gundark on fire. Even if I do shoot at you that armor would protect you."

"I have bad legs. I don't think I can outrun you."

Han could not stop thinking of his children, of Leia. "Just walk away, put the rifle down and walk away. I'm an honest man. I won't kill you."

"You're a liar," said Fett, "by all the evidence. I think you would." Fett paused. "When I was a young man," he said finally, "I think I would have pulled the trigger by now. But I find that I do not hate you, and I am not ready to die to remove you from the world."

"I made a mistake, coming here to Jubilar. I *do* hate you, I hate everything you've done—but my wife and children need me."

"I don't see a way out of this," said Fett, "that does not involve trying to trust one another."

"This rifle is getting heavy," said Han, which it was; he watched Fett over the sight. "What are we going to do?"

"Everyone dies," said Fett.

"Yeah. Eventually. But it doesn't have to be today, not for either of us."

Fett shook his head; the helmet barely moved, and Han did not imagine that Fett's attention had shifted even slightly. "I do not know," Fett said softly. "Trust is hard, among enemies. Perhaps we should return to the battle; perhaps, Han Solo, we should let fly, and once more let fate decide who will survive, as we did when we were young."

THE END

The preceding three stories appeared in various "Tales Of" from the Star Wars Extended Universe, short fiction collections edited by Kevin J. Anderson. I'm indebted to KJ for both the opportunity and the care he took with these stories. If you're interested in some more background, there's more detail at:

http://danielkeysmoran.blogspot.com/2007/06/protect-innocent-star-wars-lawrence.html and

http://www.bobafettfanclub.com/news/spotlight/daniel-keys-moran_jaster-mereel/ and

http://www.bobafettfanclub.com/news/spotlight/daniel-keys-moran_jaster-mereel-2/

This piece is from "War of the Worlds: Global Dispatches," which was conceived and edited by Kevin J. Anderson. I do owe the man.

Roughing It During the Martian Invasion
WITH JODI MORAN

... THIS IS A matter for thought, and for serious thought. And it is full of a grim suggestion; that we are not as important, perhaps, as we had all along supposed we were.

– Mark Twain, "Man's Place in the Animal World."

WE WERE ON the open sea, returning from Britain; and despite the odd shower of meteorites we had seen over the previous week, nothing in our prior experience had led us to anticipate Martians.

"By God," the dwarf exclaimed, in an accent I had not heard him use before. "Would you look at that!"

I looked only at the dwarf, my eyebrows pulling together in a frown. We stood side by side at the forward bow of the *Minnehaha*; and we had been gazing, previously, at the dark smudge that would become New York City.

This is, I suppose, what comes of traveling in a ship called the *Minnehaha*. There had been nothing humorous about the trip and the only small thing I had encountered had been the dwarf.

"Ah." The dwarf resumed his phony accent. "You missed it. It is gone."

"You, sir, are a low-down dirty Cajun liar."

The dwarf, who went by the name of Francois Maitrot, turned to me. "And you are not a liar?"

"I'm a storyteller." I added quickly, lest the dwarf, a tricky fellow, tried to equate 'storyteller' with liar. "I get *paid* for my stories."

Francois Maitroit's eyes twinkled. "To tell the truth, Monsieur, I usually get paid for mine, too."

When the dwarf said "the truth," it came out as a flatly Louisiana Cajun "de trut," as opposed to the lisping Parisian "ze tooth" he had been using over the course of our two week voyage from England.`

I shook my head. "I'm baffled, Mr. Maitroit. Why would any man of worth choose to pass himself off as a bloody Frenchman?" I had, through much of the long ocean journey, suspected that the small man was some kind of con man – but by God, what was wrong with being an American con man?

"It's the British." The dwarf shrugged. "One makes far more money, dealing with the British, presenting oneself as a gentleman of noble French extraction, than one makes as a banjo-playing Louisianan dwarf – I've tried both routes."

From behind us, Livy asked, "You play the banjo?"

It was typical of my wife that she had ignored every other aspect of the conversation she had overheard; Francois and I turned from the railing. "All Louisianans play the banjo," Francois assured her.

"Of course they do." Livy smiled at the small man.

I did not much approve of the friendship that had sprung up between the Cajun and my wife. Other men's wives made friends with other men's wives, but not Livy. We were traveling together, we Clemenses, Olivia and myself and our daughters, the lights of my life, Clara and Jean – and still Livy, in a spare two weeks, despite the attentions and company of our daughters, had arranged to take a liking to a four-foot tall lying card sharp of French descent.

Livy said to me, "*Did* you see that?"

"See what, my dear?"

"Well, it was like a spider, with very long legs, but made of metal, and it was skating across the top of the water."

"No," Francois answered for me. "He missed it. I told him to look, but he didn't."

"He's a willful man," Livy conceded. "Pity – it was skating quite well. Quite quickly."

I sighed. "I did not see it, dear."

"Oh, well." She smiled at me. "It was headed toward New York. Perhaps we'll get another chance to see it there."

WE DID NOT get another chance to see it there; in fact we never got to New York. A week later we were in New Orleans, and –

But I am getting a large step ahead of myself. I should explain; it is what I do, and I fancy I am good at it – explaining, that is.

Doubtless you know what awaited us. In the waters off New York we were privileged, if that is the word, to witness the final battle between the United States Navy and the invading Martians. It was short, it was awful, it was to the point. When it was over one surviving battleship steamed away into deep water – and there the Martians did not follow. (We did not know at that time, of course, that they were Martians.) Once the fight was done, and only the sinking hulks of the American ships were left around them, the walkers turned back to shore –

The moment still grips me with a chill, when I think back upon it. We had thought them vessels, you see, sea-going constructs of one sort or another, though unfamiliar to us –

As they approached the shore, the walkers rose up out of the water – ten feet, twenty, forty – a hundred. They towered up over the skyline of New York City, and stood before it as though they owned it. Then one of the walkers swung back out toward us –

"About!" Captain Davis cried. "Hard about!"

The *Minnehaha* steamed south.

ABOARD THE *MINNEHAHA* a tremendous argument raged. We had gathered in the main dining room – many of the sailors, Captain Davis and his First Officer, and most of the male passengers.

"We are at war," Francois said. "We must learn more of the situation, and to do that we must go ashore!"

Captain Davis seemed personally affronted by the whole affair – he commented that we ought to have stayed in England, where we would have been safe. Then talk turned to the issue of assigning guilt. "The Spanish, do you think?"

"No." I lit myself a cigar, to give myself something to do – the Captain edged away slightly. I shook my head. "If you live long enough, Captain Davis, perhaps your taste in cigars will improve – why, these are forty cent cigars!" I drew on the cigar.

"Forty cents a barrel," said Francois. "I think it's the Germans –"

"The French," I said around my cigar. "And they're thirty-three cents a barrel, to come clean – that includes the barrel. I second the dwarf's plan – let's find a safe dock somewhere and go ashore, and find someone who knows something of these walkers."

"Did you see the damage those walkers caused half a dozen of the Navy's best? How can you ask me to take a commercial vessel into that? I can't ask one of my men to go into that."

"I'll go," I said. "Have some courage, man! Let's go ashore and learn the facts."

"Mr. Clemens, you're sixty-five –"

"Sixty-four," I said dryly, "and not in my dotage yet; and I daresay this dwarf has the courage to brave the shore with me –"

The First Officer, a strapping fellow name of Stephen Bradshaw, spoke up. "I'll go ashore with them, Cap'n. We'll get the lay of the land and report back promptly."

"If we're going to send anyone it ought to be some of the seamen –"

"No," I said, shaking my head, "that will not do; for when it comes to learning the truth, and reporting it flawlessly, they have not had my training."

DOWN AROUND SOUTH Carolina we closed in on the shore again.

Walkers patrolled along the length of the beach. One of them turned toward us and strode out into the ocean, making a hooting noise that was eerie, indeed unearthly. Though we saw no weapon discharged toward us, the sea about us began to flash into steam, and then to bubble and simmer –

Captain Davis turned ship again and ran, with the boilers in the red.

AT FLORIDA WE saw more of the Walkers, as we were now calling them, with the word audibly capitalized. One of the Walkers waded out into the water after us – and did not stop when its hood was at the level of the water. The hood dropped below the sea, and Captain Davis turned the ship and ran at full steam, a day and a night, into the Gulf of Mexico, before conceding we had outrun the beast.

TWO DAYS LATER we made port at New Orleans, at the mouth of the great Mississippi river.

It was plain, entering the harbor, that things were not well; the mouth of the river was choked by some terrible red growth, a growth that gave off a vile and somewhat decayed odor; the air above the city was smoky with burning buildings. Captain Davis sent the other passengers back to their cabins – I, trading shamelessly on my fame and age, convinced the Captain to allow me to stay up top, though I sent Livy below with our daughters. Francois Maitroit simply took up position next to me, assuming, I imagine, that nobody would hustle him back to his cabin – no one did.

The harbor was empty of traffic; an astonishing sight. "I am of a mind to put back to sea," Captain Davis muttered to me. "But we are low of fuel, and will soon be low on food."

I watched the city. Buildings of wood were mostly burned down; the brick buildings were mostly still standing, though here and there the brick buildings looked as though they had been smashed to bits with cannon fire.

We saw no Walkers. The ship held motionless, at the mouth of the Mississippi, boilers stoked, for half a day before Captain Davis had the temerity to make shore.

OVER LIVY'S OBJECTIONS and the Captain's dithering, Francois and Stephen Bradshaw and I went ashore in the French Quarter – in its original incarnation the Spanish part of the city. Bradshaw carried a rifle, and Francois a revolver; I declined a weapon.

"We'll be back shortly," I told the Captain. "If you see signs of trouble, cast off; you're to take no chances with the lives of my wife and daughters." The Captain assented – a little readily, I thought, but just as well, in the circumstances; I could not much object to a coward of a Captain, when that cowardice would protect my girls.

It was a hot day and sweltering, as sultry as only Louisiana gets at the height of summer, before we set foot on land. Our plans were not distinct; they involved finding someone still alive, and then questioning that person before he, or she, could be made otherwise by one of the Walkers.

The French Quarter stank. It always stinks, to give it its due justice, but this was a new stink, a different stink and highly improved; of decay and death, rather than the stench of perfume and rotting food. We walked down the center of the road. The wrecks of carriages were scattered here and there; the decaying bodies of dead horses were still yoked to a couple of them. The horses looked as though they had been burned –

"Fire," said Francois. "Fire everywhere. All the wood has burned, the brick is scorched and in some places melted – the city has been attacked by fire."

"The Germans," I conceded finally, "I think you are right. Not that the French would be above this; it is precisely the sort of crime those malignant little soldiers delight in; but the science behind this – the skill – it reeks of German engineering." We neared a cross street, and I slowed as we entered the intersection. For the first time we saw human corpses – fresh ones, dead no more than a day or so. Two adult men lay sprawled in the center of the intersection, one face down, the other face up. Both had been burned hideously –

The motion caught my eye, off to the north, and I turned to look.

It was the first Walker – the first Martian war machine, as we shortly learned – that we had seen up close. It walked on three metallic legs, and it was a hundred feet tall, with a hood-shaped platter atop it. It was a mile or more distant, I reckoned, and even at that distance looked huge. It hesitated briefly, then seemed to catch sight of us and turned swiftly and began lumbering down the street toward us at an amazing speed, faster than land-bound creature I had ever seen –

It gave me an energy that would have astounded and delighted me, under other circumstances; it is impressive, the things a man can do with appropriate encouragement, even an old man such as myself.

We ran like the wind.

THE DWARF RAN remarkably well; he kept up with me easily enough. We ran south, and then cut east, out of the monster's immediate line of sight, looking for a place to hide; I knew that Francois and I could not possibly outrun that monstrosity; and Bradshaw was no longer an issue.

Bradshaw had left us, back at the intersection where we had first sighted the Walker; taken up his stance, and aimed his rifle at the approaching Walker. I glanced back over my shoulder, slowed to a halt and yelled, "Bradshaw! Don't be –"

Something reached out and touched Stephen Bradshaw. It tore him apart and his blood sprayed twenty feet to splatter against my coat. In retrospect, sitting in the cellar with time to think about it, the moment seemed dim and blurred – the First Officer coming apart like a mouse struck by the edge of a hoe. Even today, all these years later, I can but barely remember the next few moments – I could hear the clang of the monster's metal feet moving down the cross-street toward us, could see the flames dancing over what was left of Stephen Bradshaw, could smell Bradshaw's blood where it had spattered me –

"Here! In here!" Hands grabbed me and pulled us down into darkness.

IN THE DARKNESS of the cellar I said, "Damn fool." I was so shaken I could not think up anything witty to say, could not even manage a witticism stolen from someone else. I have seen men die before, some quantity, but not like that, not torn apart by an invisible beam.

"Shhhh!" – came a fierce whisper in my ear. "Not a sound until it passes!" In the abrupt stillness I heard the clinking steps of the Walker – louder and louder, until each step sounded like sledgehammer blows against the surface of the cobbled city street. There came a huge sound then, an explosion that rocked the cellar and sent dust sifting down from the cellar's ceiling. An Irish-sounding voice whispered from somewhere off to my right, "Blew up the house next door, I bet," followed by the sound of flesh smacking flesh, and another "Shhhh!"

Some interminable time later, a candle was lit. I looked about the cellar and found myself in the company of a well-dressed Negro; a barrel of a man of perhaps fifty, Irish at a guess; a boy I guessed to be that man's son, and the source of the earlier whisper; and a beautiful dark-haired girl dressed in what I took to be Gypsy clothing.

A motley lot – I was extraordinarily grateful that I had left Livy aboard the *Minnehaha* – I know her, having been married all those long decades, and though she is a good woman, she would have taken to these people.

In short order the crowd had filled me in on the events of the last several weeks. The Gypsy girl started off. "First they came shooting out of the sky, crashing to the ground – one of them smashed the old St. Louis Hotel, and killed everyone in it, including a priest and a gray mare. Martians, we were told, not long after that. Then they opened up and got up on their legs and started killing people. They had set fire to the remains of the hotel, and the firemen came to put out the fire; they slaughtered the firemen first –"

"Dreadful!" I exclaimed.

"Then the police came and they slaughtered the police."

"Indeed, indeed."

"Then the Army came and they slaughtered the soldiers –"

"I see a drift here," I said, "a trend."

"Then the city government collapsed –"

"Fled," said the Irish boy – Paddy, a redhead of about fifteen.

The elderly Negro – well, about my age, which is elderly, in most men, those lacking my energy and charm – I do not mean to sound boastful, but my reputation on these counts is well known – this Negro said with a pronounced and attractive Southern accent, "Gone, sir, the police, the soldiers, dead or gone; indeed, most of the city has fled the city; I doubt there are five hundred humans left alive in all of New Orleans."

"The psychic pinhead," the gypsy girl said in a profound voice, "predicted this. Back in early 1894."

I glanced at her sourly. "What psychic pinhead?"

"Oh, it doesn't matter." The girl waved an arm airily. "She's dead. Died in late '94."

Francois and I exchanged a look – we each recognized a liar when we were speaking to one.

"This pinhead," Francois asked. "Was she a Gypsy?"

"Oh, no, no, indeed not, Gypsies don't have pinheaded children. We're all especially good-looking."

I declined to comment on that – it was true enough, in this young lady's case; though I had known more than one ugly Gypsy, over the years. "So in 1894, this pinhead predicted that metallic monsters would take over the world at the turn of the century?"

"Well, no, she said Martians would *invade* at the turn of the century. The metallic monsters won't really take over for another few decades. And they'll come from Detroit, not Mars."

"They'll be rollers, not walkers." That was Paddy again.

"I told him that," the Gypsy girl informed us.

"Talia thinks she's the source of all knowledge." Paddy sneered at the girl – she was probably only a few years older than Paddy, but was acting as if she were in charge of the whole cellar.

I tried valiantly to drag the conversation back on track. "Have you any kind of plan to deal with these beasts? Or are we merely hiding out until we're found and killed?"

"Don't be silly, man." The Irish father, one Mister Connor Turley, offered me a fierce look, augmented by a grandly fierce mustache – he would never have my hair or my brow, but one had to admire the facial hair. "This cellar is a hotbed of resistance," Mr. Turley continued. "We've brought down three of the devils already. In Ireland I fought the English; and here in this grand city of New Orleans, I'll fight the Martians to the death."

As the denizens of the cellar took a moment to appreciate this declaration, Paddy added, "*Their* death, he means" – evidently he didn't want anyone to think his father was contemplating either martyrdom or defeat.

"I hate the English," Mr. Turley added.

"They're a cheap lot," Francois concurred.

"I despise the French," I offered, and added, for Francois's benefit, "Though Americans of French descent are rarely scoundrels. It's principally a cultural villainy." In another effort to stay on course, and to return to Livy and my daughters before some Martian fire-beamed them out of existence, I asked, "How exactly did you bring three of them down?"

"Well," said Paddy, "the first one we had help with – this Englishman, Christopher, decent sort for an English, he come up with the idea of digging a pit to catch one of them – then we painted a man and a horse, both of them, bright green, and when the Walker caught sight of him, off it went after him and ran across the hole we dug and fell in."

"And then a dozen more Walkers come along and slaughtered everyone was involved with that," said the father. "We just barely got away."

"Since then," said the elderly Negro, in his deep, distinguished voice, "we've been using dynamite buried at the intersections, set off by percussion caps when the Walkers step on them – New Orleans is a dangerous place for tourists."

I eyed him. "I don't believe we've been introduced yet, sir – though you sound a native of these parts, unlike the others."

"Not quite – I was born a slave in the land of Georgia. Freed by Mr. Lincoln and given a job in the offices of this fine city."

"You're a clerk," I guessed, from the man's suit.

"I am a civil servant – Peter Grayson, at your service." The man's dark eyes gazed at me neutrally. "And you, sir, are Mark Twain."

"Samuel Clemens." I held out his hand and after a moment the other man took it. "And my companion is Francois Maitroit. We arrived by boat this morning, having crossed the Atlantic, and traveled down the coast and around Florida. Aboard the *Minnehaha*."

"Ah." Grayson smiled slightly. "Thus explaining the amusing small man."

"There's fewer than there was," said Connor Turley, speaking swiftly to cut off Francois's response. "Of the Martians, I mean. Must be some others been knocking them down as well – there was dozens of them roaming the city at one point, and now there's only just the few."

"I think they're sick," said Talia. "We've seen a couple staggering around, shooting at nothing –"

Francois glowered at Grayson, still smarting from the man's joke – he made a small gesture with the revolver. "I'm liable to shoot at something."

"I think," I said quickly, "we should go back to the ship."

"No! If –"

"No! We –"

"No!" said Grayson. "Not until dark, sir. Not until dark."

WE WAITED IN the cellar until dark fell.

I sat quietly for the most part, sick with worry – to be sure, I had faith in Captain Davis's cowardice, but not his competence; if one of the Martians attacked, who knew if the man would manage to get under steam in time? The *Minnehaha* had a pair of Gatling guns, and rifles and revolvers, but she was hardly a military ship, and I knew she wouldn't last long in a duel with one of the Walkers.

Only Francois managed to distract me from his worrying. He took me off in a corner and spoke in a low voice:

"The Walkers aren't the Martians themselves," Francois said. "So Paddy tells me – the Martians are inside them; the Walkers are just transportation."

"Of course," I said, "plainly the Walkers are mechanisms. So?"

"So," said Francois persuasively, "the Martians are ugly. Terribly, terribly ugly – tentacles and such –"

"Pretty bad."

"– green skin –"

"Indeed?"

Francois hesitated. "So Paddy tells me."

"He's Irish," I warned Francois. "They're known to improve their statistics some."

"I adjusted for that – he says Martians are more frightening than a Christian Scientist working his theology –"

"I've had the honor of that sight – Paddy is wrong."

"– and uglier than a Capitalist."

"It seems extreme," I admitted. "Uglier than 'Jo-Jo The Dog-Faced Boy;' that sounds plausible, that sounds about right. You could put in on a poster. But uglier than a Capitalist ... there would be skepticism, Francois, healthy skepticism."

"You know what we need?" demanded Francois. "Live specimens. If they are falling sick, if the invasion is failing – well, there's opportunity here, if we grab it."

"Grab a Martian, you mean. For display?" I asked doubtfully. "I doubt it would pay, Francois. We might make a million, selling it to Barnum and Bailey perhaps, and that assumes no one else has had any luck getting himself a Martian to show, and that some circus, somewhere, will pay us what a Martian is worth." I shook his head. "The low level which commercial morality has reached in America is deplorable. We have humble God fearing Christian men among us who will stoop to do things for a million dollars that they ought not to be willing to do for less than two millions. In fact –"

"No," hissed Francois, cutting me off, keeping his own voice low so that we would not be overheard. "Not one Martian for display – two Martians . . . a breeding pair." Even in the dimness of the candle-lit cellar, I could detect the gleam in Francois's eyes. "A breeding pair."

I stared at him, a slow smile appearing below my mustache. *A dwarf after my own heart,* I thought.

I COULD NOT help thinking that it sounded like the setup for a joke, probably a poor one – what do you get when a Negro, two Irish, a Gypsy, a dwarf, and a world-famous writer go out for a nighttime stroll?

We did not stroll, in fact. We scurried. From place to place, cover to cover. My suit, my very good white suit, had been darkened with coal dust, and my long white hair blackened also. We made our way back to the docks without encountering another Martian, and my heart leapt at the sight of the *Minnehaha,* apparently unharmed, still tied up at the dock –

We ran down the dock, and arrived at the ship – I was out of breath from all the running and hiding, and had had about enough of it.

Only Captain Davis was up top when we arrived – the ship was darkened.

"Cast off!" I called as we crossed the boarding planks. "Cast off!"

Captain Davis sat on one of the deck chairs – he leaned forward. "Mr. Clem – Clem – Twain? Is that you, Twain?"

"Cast off, man! We're back!"

Davis shook his head gloomily, settling back into his chair. "I can't, sir. Can't do it, can't."

I could tell from the sound of the man's speech that he was roaring drunk, four or maybe five sheets to the wind. I looked about –

"Where are the passengers? Where are the crew?"

"Oh, the passagers," said Davis dismissively. "They're b'low, they're alive, more or less." He raised a small flask to his lips, drank from it. "The crew, now, that's another story. Another story –"

"Where are they?"

"They fled! – the dogs."

"You impugn the dogs" – I said automatically – "noble creatures, dogs – and perhaps the men, too. To where did they flee?"

"They headed off 'long the coast, sir. For Alabama. They took the boats."

"You *do* impugn them," I said severely. "Their flaw was merely one of judgment, not character – they assumed Alabama was preferable to death. Promptly they learn of their mistake, they'll be back. In the meantime, we must sober you up, we've a project –"

BY JUST THE next day it was plain that the Martians had indeed fallen sick. The Walkers were seen less frequently – late that afternoon one of them staggered out onto the Mississippi, waded a ways into it, and then fell, and apparently drowned; at least it sank beneath the water and did not surface again.

The crew, having learned the truth about Alabama, returned to face the Martians the following day. Captain Davis seemed more relieved than angry, at the sight of them returning in the lifeboats. He lined them up for a speech:

"You have abandoned ship once or twice before this, most of you men. It is all right – up to now. I would have done it myself in my common-seaman days, I reckon, if I'd returned to the States to find Martians invading and the cities in flames. Now then, can you stand up to the facts? Are we rational men, manly men, men who can stand up and face hard luck and a big difficulty that has been brought about by nobody's fault, and say live or die, survive or perish, we are in for it, for good or bad, and we'll stand by the ship if she goes to Hell!"

The men gave up a tolerably decent cheer then, and the Captain seemed to gain a little stature again with that; and added, "And there's a profit, too, men, Mr. Clemens swears it –"

There was a larger cheer at *that*.

THE NEXT MORNING we went out and captured a Walker.

That night was spent in planning – plotting and considering and devising, laying out tactics and strategies; schemes were proposed and modified and perfected, resources counted and estimated – no group of soldiers had ever gone about taking a city with more clarity of purpose than I and Francois and the Captain and Peter Grayson and the two Irishmen and the Gypsy woman went about planning for the capture and care of a Martian breeding pair. We had plenty of dynamite, we had the ship's Gatling guns; we had twenty stout seamen who had been chastised by their failures in Alabama and were prepared to follow orders once more. The plans evolved and developed until it was clear that there were two plans with good support behind them; mine, which I supported, and Francois's plan, which everyone else supported. I proposed they dig a pit, and lead a Walker over it – with a green man aboard a green horse, as the Englishman Christopher had done earlier; I conceded I was not above appropriating someone else's good idea, though perhaps for variety's sake it would be better to paint the man, or the horse, or both, red or blue rather than green, the Martians having seen a green horse at this point. Francois accused me of plagiarism and suggested that we try lassoing one of the Walkers, using one of the *Minnehaha's* two anchor-chains – how the lasso was to be thrown or made tight about the Walker was a minor detail, and not worked out yet. Finally Peter Grayson proposed we put the matter to a vote, and I pointed out that it was nearly daylight, and we had lost an entire night's pit digging; it wasn't safe to go digging in the daytime, I said severely, it wasn't fair to the seamen, brave fellows if a little unclear on their geography, to force them out to do hard manual labor on a sweltering Louisiana summer day – and with the threat of immolation from fire-beams on top of that, I added as it occurred to me.

The sky to the east was lightening with the first hint of morning when Francois suggested we put it to a vote. I lit a cigar to gain time – I knew a losing hand when I saw one; certainly the seamen weren't going to vote in favor of pit digging –

About twenty minutes after dawn a Walker fell over at the West End, not far from Lake Pontchartrain.

BY MID-AFTERNOON, scouring the city, we had found three fallen Walkers. There appeared to be none still moving. Whatever illness had struck them down had done likewise to the red weed that had so choked the Mississippi; the river was cleansing itself; clumps of the red weed were being torn free and deposited, as the river has always cleansed itself of that which it is not pleased with, in the the depths of the Gulf of Mexico.

By evening we had cleared out a hotel on the banks of the Mississippi, and had eight living Martians behind bars – the sailors pulled them from their fallen Walkers, picked them up in canvass lifts, and transported them to the hotel in a sailor-drawn carriage, there being no horses alive that we had yet found.

It was my first sight of the Martians themselves – a thing no human who saw them, while they were still alive, is likely to forget. They were as ugly as their reputations – ugly as a Capitalist, and a sight uglier than Jo-Jo the Dog-Faced Boy had ever been. They have been described frequently enough since then, by a variety of word scribblers; I shall not waste time on it here, except in brief; grayish-green, with two sets of tentacles beneath the mouth; each of them was somewhat larger than a man.

I will mention their eyes at somewhat greater length. They were large and expressive; they seemed somehow both mournful and calculating, as though figuring the probabilities on their situation. They were not human eyes, but there was no doubt in me that they were the eyes of sapient creatures, of creatures as intelligent as any man, including perhaps myself. When I met the eyes of the first of our captured Martians, I had the sense that I was meeting the gaze of a being wiser, and older, and colder, than any Bishop who had ever lived.

Two of the sailors returned from their searching, near evening, with a story that caused us some concern. They claimed to have seen a pair of Walkers, their walking-legs bent double beneath them, kneeling at the edge of the Mississippi; and a vessel of some sort, half-submerged beneath the river's flow, taking on half a dozen Martians, or more, all apparently healthy – they were not specific on this subject, due to the difficulty they had had, trying to observe while fleeing in the other direction.

BY NIGHTFALL WE had seven living Martians behind bars – by midnight it was down to six.

"It's the gravity killing them," Francois insisted. "I've read on this subject, Clemens, I tell you it's the gravity. Their world is colder than ours, and lighter."

I shook his head. "I grant you, the heat's not fit for man or Martian – but there's no electricity, Francois; I doubt there's a working ice-maker within a hundred miles of here."

"We could put one of the Martians in the river," Francois suggested. "Perhaps it would float, relieving the weight upon it?"

It drowned. We were down to five.

TWO MORE DIED the following day. It left us with three.

I SPENT THAT night with the Martians.

The three of them looked listless.

They had trouble moving, and nothing I had arranged for them seemed to suit their appetites – they hadn't touched the beef, or the greens, or the beer, or the fruits or vegetables or eggs. I suspected that at least one of them had drunk some of the water – I'd drowsed, sitting in the padded chair the sailors had brought from the ship, and when I awoke, the water bowl was lower than it had been.

Watching them, I knew I had been a fool to think they could be bred; my optimism had gotten the better of me. I had no more idea if any two of them could make up a breeding pair than I'd have had dealing with snails, or sharks. "For all we know," I told Francois when Francois came by, near three that morning, "they are all three men, or women, or another sex entirely; perhaps they reproduce by division, or require ten mates –"

Francois nodded, and seated himself in the chair beside mine. We sat in a companionable silence, in the cool night air, watching the cage the three Martians had been imprisoned in. The Martians stirred occasionally, moving slowly and with evident pain.

"The sailors have ranged up the river a ways," Francois said at length. "They've found a steamship, run aground about six miles upriver. It's damaged some –"

It perked my interest. "Badly?"

"The texas deck is scarred by that weapon, they say, that heat beam, but otherwise it looks river-worthy." Francois looked at me sideways. "That bunch of Martians that headed upriver, Sam, they were healthy. So the men said."

"They did say that." I withdrew a cigar from its case, offered it to Francois – the small man shuddered and refused politely. I lit it slowly, turning it for a smooth draw. I had the distinct impression that the largest of the three Martians was watching me.

"It seems a long way to come, to die in a cage," said Francois.

I found myself gazing into the eyes of the large Martian, watching it as it died. "I would not feel too sorry for them – they are God's creatures, no doubt, as we are; and therefore doomed and without hope. If there is a Hell, and if they have the Moral Sense humans are blessed with, they will doubtless go there for their sins here on the Earth; if there is no Hell, then death is nothing but release, and they go into a great dark." I shrugged. "Hardly a thing to fear."

The large Martian crept forward a bit, and drank from the water bowl as I watched.

"Man is the Reasoning Animal," I said. "Such is the claim – I find it open to dispute, though. Any cursory reading of history will show that he is the Unreasoning Animal. It seems plain to me that whatever Man is he is not a reasoning animal. His record is the fantastic record of a maniac. These poor monsters had no chance –

if the gravity and heat and disease had not killed them, we would have done it ourselves, I think."

"A river-boat, Sam," the dwarf said persuasively. "An empty river-boat."

"Fifty-five or -six years ago," I said softly, "it was my greatest ambition, as it was of all the boys in my village, to travel down the Mississippi – the majestic, the magnificent Mississippi, to escape Hannibal and ride down that miles-wide ribbon of water to the sea, to New Orleans."

"I've read your work," said Francois. "Most of it, I think, at one time or another."

I took a good drag, letting the smoke settle in my lungs. I spoke as I exhaled, and watched as the Martian drank again. "I expect they'll be dead before morning."

"I expect," said Francois, not taking his eyes from me.

I turned to examine him. "You want to go up the river."

"Yes, yes, I do," he said in that low, intense voice. "Let's take the guns from the *Minnehaha*, fix whatever's wrong with that riverboat the men found, and go after the Martians who fled. For profit, for revenge –"

"The river is beautiful in the summer," I said. "It's harder going upriver than down, though; you must hug the banks to avoid the current. You'd need a pilot, a good one, navigating those shallows, and I confess, I'm a bit rusty." I let the smoke trickle through my nostrils – though I did not like to confess it, the idea appealed to me; there was a symmetry in it. That young boy had wanted to go down the river, had wanted it more than anything; and with the world as it was, unsettled and dangerous, and I an old man, I might never have another chance to navigate its waters –

"I'll do it," I said finally. "Let's follow them up the river."

THE LAST MARTIAN died just after dawn.

On Sequoia Time

JOHN MUIR CALLED the sequoia the "king of all the conifers of the world, the noblest of a noble race." The trees were named for the Cherokee chief Sequoyah, the man who invented the Cherokee alphabet.

They are the largest and very nearly the oldest of all living things.

$-1-$

WHEN MY GRANDFATHER Charles was seven years old he first saw the box canyon where he would spend most of his adult life, the canyon where he would plant the tree.

It was late afternoon on Wednesday, July 2, 1924, that Charles saw the entrance, and a little bit inside. They were driving a two-lane, poorly paved road through northern Arizona. (They were moving from Idaho to California. After twelve years of trying to make the same sixteen acres of Idaho farmland feed his family, with a little left over to sell, my great-grandfather had seen the writing on the wall, and packed it in.) Charles suspected they were lost, but from the way the muscles in his father's neck were standing out he knew better than to say anything about it.

Charles had very good eyes in those days, and when he pointed the canyon's entrance out to his older sister she could not see it.

They sat in the back seat of a battered old Model T, a car that had probably come off the assembly line looking old. It wouldn't go faster than forty miles an hour and it complained above thirty. Aside from their clothes and some boxes of kitchen utensils tied on top of the car it was the only thing their family owned.

His sister Abby peered out the dirty window at the place where two mesas came together, about four or five miles off. "Right *there*,"

Charles insisted. "There's a opening in there and you could go in-side, maybe."

"I don't see it," said Abby crossly, and that was the end of the matter.

WHEN HE WAS twenty-nine my grandfather came back looking for the canyon. It was the summer of 1946; World War II was over, and Charles had just gotten out of the Marine Corps.

His eyesight wasn't as good as it had been as a child. Four years of constant studying in college had damaged his vision, and it had gotten worse during the campaign to take Okinawa from the Japan-ese. He'd broken his glasses early on and had to work and fight without them for several months; it had nearly cost him his life.

He went hunting for the canyon with binoculars and a brand new pair of glasses, a parting gift from Uncle Sam.

It took him a good part of the summer just to find the road on which his family had come to California. He drove a black pre-war Packard that reminded him sometimes of the Model T in which his family had moved to California. It ran a bit faster but it was just as ugly and beat up.

The hunt for the road took up most of his time. There were a dozen roads his father might have come by, including several that were not even listed on the map he had. His father had died during the war (at home, of a heart attack) and his mother had verified, when Charles asked, that they had indeed been lost much of the time while driving through northern Arizona.

On a hot, dusty day in early August he finally found it.

The entrance was just as he remembered it across the span of twenty-two years; a small gap between two mesas, not quite five miles off the road. In 1924 the road had been about as good as roads in those parts got; by 1946 it was rutted and worn away in places.

By the time I first visited my grandfather's ranch in the mid-70's it was almost entirely gone.

Charles drove the Packard slowly off the road. The spare in back held air, but the tread was mostly gone and Charles did not want to take a chance on it. So he drove carefully, and made three miles before the terrain got so rough that he decided to hike the rest of the way. Driving across the desert floor like that raised up a cloud of dust that hung in the dry still air behind him like a long rope; when he got out of the car the dust trail was still visible all the way back out to the road.

He walked the last mile and stood at the entrance to the box canyon. The entrance was not wide, only about forty yards across. The way Grandpa told it to me years later, the instant he first stood there he knew he was home. A spring just inside poured up and over its borders, turning into a slow-moving thread of a creek that ran westward down the length of the canyon. Charles walked the canyon from end to end that first day, even though it was afternoon when he found it and after dark when he left. It ran over a mile and a half wide, and four miles long. Because of the spring, there were bushes and shrubs growing inside, and even a pair of small trees. He saw one rabbit that hid from him quickly.

He was a city boy, then, but he figured that if he saw one rabbit, there were probably twenty he didn't see, and he was right about that.

As he was hiking back up out of the canyon the wind hit him. It came up slow and gentle, a breeze that moved the warm, still desert air pleasantly. Then it got both stiffer and colder, and by the time Charles reached the entrance to the canyon he was leaning into it, shivering, pushing for each step he took.

When he left the canyon it stopped with remarkable abruptness.

After he looked at the lay of the land he realized what was happening. What was no more than a gentle breeze outside the canyon was being channeled and tightened by the converging walls of the two mesas, until the breeze, moving across several dozens of square miles, turned into a small hurricane at the entrance to the canyon.

That was why he planted the trees, of course – as a windbreak.

HE NEVER COULD tell me, or anyone, why he'd come looking for the canyon in the first place. The one time I asked him why he'd spent an entire summer looking for something he'd seen just once, when he was only seven years old, Grandpa looked at me with those wise blue eyes, scratched his bald, leathery skull, and grinned at me. "Danny, damn if I know."

Charles came back to the canyon permanently in 1951, with his wife Laurinda and their three children. One of them was my mother.

I FIRST SPENT the summer with my grandfather in 1975, when I was twelve years old.

Grandpa was fifty-seven then, and Grandma was fifty-two. I don't believe I knew their first names then.

The only people at the ranch were my grandfather and grandmother; all the children had left long ago. The ranch, the desert surrounding it, the mountains rising up above it, were both fascinating and very foreign to a boy from Los Angeles.

There are two kinds of sequoias; I don't specifically remember having seen one of either kind before then, though surely I must have. The tree was not impressive, the first time I saw it; just about my height, and struggling.

Over the course of the years Grandpa had planted several rows of trees at the entrance to the box canyon, staggered to muffle the wind. It worked; the trees at the entrance to the canyon got shaken up every afternoon when it got cold and the wind came up, but the trees away from the entrance were barely stirred, and back at the ranch house the wind was never worse than a gentle breeze.

Five rows of trees had been planted when I stayed that first summer. Lots of them were fruit trees – apple trees mostly, because Grandpa liked apples and apple pie. There were a couple of citrus trees too, though because of the cold they never did so well. (It gets very cold in northern Arizona at night, and during the winter you get snow and ice.)

Grandpa ended up planting seven rows of trees before he died. There were orange trees and apple trees, oaks and a couple varieties of evergreen. There was even, for a while, a cherry tree, but as I recall it died the second or third summer I spent at the ranch.

The sequoia stood in the fifth row of trees, with scraggly orange trees on both sides of it, well back from the wind. Grandpa had just planted it that summer, and it was still small and thin, about five feet tall, but you could already tell it was going to do better than the citrus we had planted around it.

I spent three summers at the ranch. When I was fifteen I stopped going, not because I wanted to, but because my parents got divorced and life spun out of control for a while.

The sequoia was nine feet tall then, in the summer of 1977.

MY GRANDFATHER DIED almost twenty years later, in '96, of pancreatic cancer. It is one of the more unpleasant ways to die. Grandma lasted three more years, but after Grandpa died she was never really the same. She died in June of '99, and that summer was the last time I ever visited the ranch.

We flew to Arizona for Grandma's funeral. It was a small funeral; myself and my older sister Janet, my mother and her sister Beth, and half a dozen of my grandmother's friends, old folks of her generation who made the rounds at the funerals, waiting patiently and with not much fear for their turn to come.

After the funeral my mother and aunt and sister and I drove out to the ranch together. Janet had never been there before; we wandered around and looked at things while my mother and aunt went through my grandmother's few possessions.

The ranch had gone to seed. I'd done the work that had to be done on my visits, but no more, and it showed. The wood needed painting, and the pens where the cows and the one pig had been kept were falling apart.

A small colony of coyotes who didn't know they were supposed to be afraid of humans had taken up residence in the abandoned horse shed, about sixty yards from the main house. I suppose Grandma had never gone out to the shed after the horses were sold. The coyotes stared at us and we stared at them, and we all agreed to leave each other alone.

The creek kept along as it had since that day in '46 when my grandfather had first seen it. It was small enough a that a grown man could step entirely across it. Janet had to take a slight hop.

You could barely see where the garden had once been. It was a slightly empty spot, with a couple fewer weeds, in the midst of the general desolation.

The trees were gorgeous: a small forest, shady and cool in late afternoon. The evergreens were all doing well, and the oaks, and the walnut tree. Only half of the citrus trees had survived, though, and none of the tropicals my grandfather had tried to plant. The corpse of a palm tree, about nine feet tall and virtually mummified, had managed to avoid falling over. I guessed it had been dead at least as long as Grandpa.

The sequoia was eighteen feet tall.

My sister and I stood together and admired it. It was worth admiring: the tallest tree in the small forest by a good bit, the thick bark was a healthy deep brown and the needles glistened a lustrous dark green in the late afternoon sunlight.

When we were done admiring it we left it alone and went back to the ranch house to pick up Mom and Aunt Beth. Aunt Beth was worried about Grandma's cats; she'd had four and they weren't in the house, and Aunt Beth couldn't find them. We looked briefly but it was getting late and I didn't want to drive back in the dark. We drove away from that canyon and I don't recall looking back.

No human ever saw that canyon again.

THE TREE GREW.

In 1972, when my grandfather planted the sequoia, humans had wiped out most of a population of trees that had existed since before the coming of humans to the American continents. The only remaining native populations of Great Sequoias were found in an area about 280 miles long, and less than twenty wide, in California on the western slopes of the Sierra Nevada. They were almost never found at heights of less than a mile above sea level.

The summer I was thirteen I took two books on trees with me to visit my grandparents' ranch. I knew that the small tree was a redwood, but what type of redwood neither I nor my grandfather knew.

The books told me. It was a California big-tree, a Sequoiadendron Giganteum. Of the two kinds of sequoias, the giant sequoia is the one likeliest to survive in the cold, at high altitudes. My grandfather had planted wisely, at least this once. The Sequoia Sempervirens can grow taller than the sequoiadendron, but it's thinner and it handles the cold more poorly; and that canyon got cold.

The tree found itself in an environment that suited it. The other trees, particularly the thick-sapped pines, helped protect it from the wind; and it was closer to the water than most of the other trees, too.

By the time the tree had reached thirty-five feet the United States was fighting a "police action" in Brazil to preserve what was left of the rain forests. Without euphemisms it was a war, and a losing one. Too many people had a vested interest in the slash-and-burn beef-growing economy that was consuming the rain forests, starting with the desperately poor South American Indians who had no other way to survive, and working step by step up the economic ladder to McDonald's corporation stockholders.

While the rain forests died, life in the canyon flourished. The rabbit population, without my grandfather's .22 rifle to keep it in check, exploded. My grandmother's cats – tough farm cats, pushing twenty pounds – did well even without Grandma to take care of them. Shortly there were eight cats, and then eleven, and the cat population leveled off at around twenty. There would have been more except that the coyotes wanted the same food, the desert mice and squirrels and rabbits, and were tougher about going after it. The coyotes rarely hunted the cats; it happened at times, but it was always a fierce fight. For five years one tom, a big orange glandular monster who weighed thirty-three pounds, made it a riskier proposition than usual; he killed and ate two young coyotes before a rattler finally got him one night.

The rattlesnakes my grandfather had spent nearly four decades warring against outlasted him; they killed more of the cats than the coyotes ever did.

About the time the sequoia was nearing forty-eight feet, a couple of owls nested in its lower branches. The owls fed off the snakes, including the rattlers; baby owls were born the next summer.

THE SEQUOIA BROKE fifty feet the year the last of the rain forests went up in flames.

Life in the canyon continued quietly. Water came up from the ground. The sun warmed the canyon during the day, and during the night the mammals retreated to their burrows, the owls tucked their wings beneath their heads, and the snakes and lizards and insects grew still. Tree sap turned sluggish; it would stay liquid, and keep the trees alive, well below the freezing point of water.

The sequoia's bark grew thicker as the tree grew taller. It was still very young, for a sequoia. Giant sequoias can live a very long time; nobody really knows how long. Humans had found giant sequoias as much as thirty-five hundred years old, and there was no reason to believe that they might not live longer.

The sequoia in my grandfather's canyon might have been expected to live a long time, even by sequoia standards. Though it had competition for soil and water, it grew fast, and got up into the sunlight, putting most of the other trees into its shade. By the time it was tall enough to take the brunt of the canyon's wind itself, there was no danger that the wind would kill it.

The giant sequoia was not the only thing that thrived in that canyon. So did the pines surrounding it, and the animals that lived among them, the owls and the snakes and the lizards, the coyotes and the rabbits and bees. There was water and there was sunlight and there was food enough for everything; and the wild creatures flourished.

Some days, when the sun came slanting down into the canyon just right, it was so beautiful that seeing it would have made you glad to be alive.

Fortunately the human race had forgotten about the place, and as a result no one came to admire the beauty, and incidentally to destroy it.

The cats, living in the wild where size was important, got bigger and bigger with the passage of the years, until most of them approached the size of the glandular monster who had once been such a freak. These were not mutants; the genes for size had been floating around in the cat population, but they had not been selected for. Now they were selected for and the cats got big, quickly, and gave the coyotes and owls some real competition for the rabbits and desert mice, snakes and lizards.

Quickly is a relative word: the sequoia continued to grow, too, at its own pace. It was young and beautiful, with dark brown branches laden with dusky green leaves, the branches radiating outward from its trunk in a conical pattern, all the way from the ground to the top of the tree. In later life the branches near the ground would wither away, leaving the tree with a smooth trunk reaching up as much as two hundred feet; but for now the tree was young, and its growth was everywhere. The tree drank the water, and dug down into the soil, and reached for the sun.

As adults, giant sequoias can reach heights of three hundred and fifty feet; by this time the sequoia in my grandfather's canyon had nearly reached a hundred.

– I was dead by then, of course, and so were you, and your grandchildren, and everyone your grandchildren had ever known or loved.

And still the tree grew.

– 2 –

WHEN THE TREE was a hundred and sixty-one feet tall the skies above it turned scarlet at midnight.

Two warring groups of humans had tossed nukes at each other, and everyone else.

(Who were these humans? I doubt it matters, but for what it's worth they were a group of people in what used to be India, and another group in what was once South America. Why did North America get nuked? The United States was gone a long time by then, and its remnants were of no threat to anyone – but everybody had extra nukes they didn't need, and there was not a continent on the planet that didn't receive a few dozen.)

The bombs fell, in a nuclear rain that lasted for days, through a peremptory first strike and a retaliatory second strike, through retaliatory second and third strikes, until only submarines and spaceships remained to launch weapons at one another. Through all of this, the bombs fell, and fell. The nuclear explosions were bad enough in and of themselves, and were succeeded by firestorms of epic size that burned to the ground every sequoia on the west coast of North America.

Worse was to follow. Vast clouds of dust and earth were blasted into the sky. Whole continents disappeared beneath them; and temperatures began to drop.

In the canyon, the sky was an angry orange color for two or three days, and then it got dark and started to get cold.

In the war, and the small Ice Age that followed, most of the living things on the planet's surface died, and a lot of those beneath the ocean. The canyon I had spent three months in, during the days when I was alive, survived better than most places. The canyon was not near any military targets, and most of the species living between its walls made it through. The rabbits had a very hard time of it, and as a result the coyotes died out. But six of the cats survived, four of them females, and in time kittens appeared, and the cats and rabbits struggled on.

It was worse almost everywhere else in the world; and worse in ways the world had never seen before. There had been die-offs before, to be sure. The great majority of the species that had ever existed on the surface of the planet were extinct by the time the last sequoia was planted by my grandfather.

Sixty-five million years ago an asteroid crashed into the Earth, near what is now Mexico. It blasted so much soot and smoke and dust into the sky that years passed in which the planet received no sunlight. Every species of land animal larger than a turtle died off.

This die-off was different, though. It was an orderly catastrophe, planned for and carried out by our children, twenty-five generations removed. This disaster is what finally killed the whales, who had hung on through the slaughter of humans who wanted to slice them up and use their fat as a lubricant or a fuel; who had hung on while those same humans bred new humans, billions upon billions upon billions, and with sheer numbers poisoned the water the whales lived in and the air they breathed. They had hung on through the rise and fall of empires, but they were the largest of all the animals and the ones most damaged when the radioactive debris was inevitably washed down to the sea. The Earth tried to cleanse itself, to wash away the poisons; and the water ended up where it always did. It destroyed the food chain the whales depended upon; and it is a good question whether the last whales died of radiation poisoning or starvation.

The tree was not a complex thing, but it had a sort of awareness, a knowledge of when things were well and when they were not. For a very long time after that things were not well. Many of the trees that had provided it with a windbreak died off as the cold got worse. The spring that fed the stream slowed for several decades, and when it eventually resumed its flow, it was contaminated by radioactive isotopes that might have killed the tree, had it been younger or smaller. It did kill some of the other trees, among those that had survived the cold.

Slowly though, slowly even by the tree's standards, things began to get better. The winds that had nearly killed it, winter after brutal winter, stopped being so severe. The winters themselves grew warmer, as did the summers; and the radiation levels, still lethal elsewhere in the world, declined in the area around the canyon to the point where plants and animals stopped dying of it, much, and started mutating instead. Most of the mutants died too, of course; that's what mutants do.

Things were a little simpler in the canyon, a little less complex; here as everywhere else the great war had knocked out some of the links in the elaborate chain that made life on Earth a viable affair.

But life in the canyon hung on. The tree pushed ahead with the serious business of growing. It broke two hundred feet just weeks before a human being staggered into the canyon to die.

The man came in off the desert, from the east where the fireball sun hung in the morning sky. He was half dead already. He was six generations removed from the men and women who had pulled the trigger and launched the nukes; but in six generations the fighting had not stopped. Instead it had spread, though with less dangerous weapons now, north and south and east and west. He wore combat armor that was supposed to protect him from incidental radiation, still high six generations after the great war, and it did that. What it did not do was protect him from the artillery that had destroyed the rest of his squad. I've said that my sister and I were the last human beings to see the canyon, and this is true. The soldier was flash-blinded and deafened. His right arm was shattered from the elbow down, and a stress fracture in his right leg slowed but did not stop him. Occasionally he called out, in a high cracked voice, words that may have meant something to someone who spoke his language.

He climbed up into the canyon, walked a few hundred yards and then sat down in the shade of an apple tree that was almost as bad off as he was.

It took two days before the lack of water killed him. He was only a dozen yards from the slow small stream that now curled its way around the sequoia's wide base, but he could neither hear nor see it, and so he suffered, screaming out occasionally to an audience of cats who were trying to decide what he was, and whether he was edible.

The tree took little enough notice of it. The man's dying was not affecting its sunlight or its water. Indirectly, after the cats ate him, he would end up fertilizing the ground in the great tree's vicinity, which was all to the good.

We might dwell upon that man, that soldier dying in pain in the desert beneath the harsh sun. We might, but we will not. He was only one man; and worse was coming.

NOT ALL HUMANS died in that great war. Some of those who did not decided that, if the human race was to survive, the race itself needed to change. (Perhaps they were right about that. I don't know. The old design hadn't worked out very well, but then the new one didn't do much better –)

They remade themselves. With genetic engineering they created children who were stronger and faster, who thought more clearly and more quickly than you or I. They reinvented themselves from the ground up, generation after generation, to be the greatest warriors the world had ever seen. Before the tree had reached two hundred and twenty-five feet, the new humans had killed off the remnants of the old humans, the ones who looked more or less like you and me, and were therefore forced to turn their attentions to one another.

You might wonder if these humans were really human. They were. They were people, at least, more so than you and I in all the ways that count. They did not always look like us, but that doesn't matter. I do not know if you could say that they were better than us; but they were more than us.

When I was a boy I used to read sci-fi stories, or watch episodes of *Star Trek,* about how as humans evolved we would turn into something that was all brains and no hormones, all intellect and no emotions.

That isn't what happened. These people who were descended from us were capable of a range of experience that would have destroyed any of us, our best or our worst. They were more dangerous and more generous than us; they grew angrier and happier, grieved harder and rejoiced with more abandon. Love was an emotion so deep they could not lie about it, hatred a passion so black it was almost always lethal to someone.

THE TREE WAS three hundred and fourteen feet tall when the human race finally killed itself, and everything else too. They did it with nanotechnology. One group of humans, who were good people – they would tell you so – created a molecule-sized nanomachine that fed on living creatures, and that reproduced itself, using common materials, to make more such nanomachines. They intended to use the nanomachine on other humans, who were bad people they hated.

Unfortunately something went wrong.

It was humanity's last mistake in a very long line – the Big One. The nanomachines got loose before the good humans who had created them completed the controls that would have let them protect themselves from their creation.

The nanomachines ate them and their children first. Poetic justice, you might say, if that sort of thing amuses you. The nanomachines did not stop after eating their creators; they were not designed to. They drifted out on the winds, to the oceans, to the furthest reaches of the planet. And where they found biomass, they ate it. They swarmed over living creatures, reproducing and eating. They ate indiscriminately, people and pets and leather and wood and rubber and plastic; and when they were done nothing remained but a gray sludge of dead nanomachines with nothing left to eat.

The tree was – well, I do not know if fortunate is the word. It was all the way around the planet from the spot where the world ended; and years passed before the first spores of the gray sludge came drifting in across the desert, born on the back of the wind.

The tree was, in a sense, the last representative of the human race, the last thing that might have said to an uncaring universe, *they were not so bad.* My grandfather planted that tree, and he cared for it while it was young and needed the care. He planted that windbreak for himself, for his own reasons; but any orchard of trees might have served as a windbreak, and more effectively than the trees he planted and labored over. And he loved that sequoia. It was the first tree he showed me, the first summer I visited him; it was the only one I ever heard him mention, or worry over. He worried that it would survive the winters, worried that he had planted it in a location that would stunt its growth, or kill it. And partially because he worried about it, it did survive; and because of the location he picked, it lasted longer than anything.

There were other things created by the human race that stood in monument, despite the nanomachines that were busy turning the world, from the depths of the Mariana Trench to the heights of Everest, into a vast gray sludge. Between its wars and its building humanity had inflicted scars upon the planet that would be erased only in the course of geologic time. The nanomachines did not eat metal or stone or cement or glass; weapons and vehicles and buildings littered the surface of the planet when the nanomachines were done.

But of the good things the human race did, there was one thing that still survived; and that one thing was the tree.

Perhaps it's foolish to talk this way, for the tree was just a tree. So far as I know it had no emotions. It could not think or reason. And yet it could feel, and had a sort of awareness of itself, and it knew that something was wrong. The nanomachines first entered the canyon on the wind; and they made short work of almost everything. All the animals, the lizards and bees and snakes and cats and rabbits and owls and crows, died within hours. The smaller trees took days to die, and even the oaks, large though some of them had grown, were gone within a week.

But an adult California big-tree, a giant sequoia, is *huge*. The gray sludge ate away at the tree, stripped it of its leaves, but the tree was made of more than two million pounds of living hardwood. Its bark alone was two to three feet thick, and the bark served to slow the attack of the nanomachines. The bark protected the tree, as evolution had designed it to, significantly slowed the nanomachine attack.

Months passed while the tree struggled for life. It was the last living thing on the surface of the planet that humanity had killed.

HERE ARE SOME of the things we killed:

Hawks and seaweed. Horses. Puppies and kittens and parrots. Lions and lizards, lobsters and clams. Sharks. Grass and crabgrass and all the flowers, every last one of them; a rose by any other name was just as dead. Bats and vultures and pigeons and bluebirds, boa constrictors and garden snakes and earthworms. Elephants and marijuana plants. Milkweed and tumbleweed and all the other plants humans named "weeds" and tried to destroy because they couldn't figure out a way to make use of them. Snails and frogs and raccoons and bears. We killed the dolphins and the seals and the squid and the starfish, jellyfish and sea anemones and sea horses and all the animals that made the beautiful shells humans treas-ured.

We killed *everything* – the air and the ground and the water, and everything that lived in those places.

THE LAST THING we killed was the tree.

Half a year had passed since the gray sludge's arrival. The tree's leaves had gone first, and then its branches. The nanomachines ate inward, chewing away at the hardwood. They worked quickly enough, under the circumstances. The tree was twenty-five feet around, and it took the nanomachines a long time to eat their way through it. They got started at the base first, about ten feet above the ground. Other nanomachines attacked the tree along its length, but the invasion at the tree's base was the worst one.

If by some quirk of fate my grandfather had been able to see the canyon at that moment, he would not have recognized it as the place where he'd grown old and died. Every tree, except the great sequoia itself, had toppled to the ground and sunk into the gray dust. Where grass and shrubs had sprouted, bare rock stood forth. The wind that had always gathered at the mouth of the canyon once again had nothing to stop it, and each evening it blew the dirt and dust back into the canyon, leaving nothing but the exposed rock behind.

Only the one tree still stood above the expanse of pale rock, covered in a gray blanket of molecule-sized machines.

Only the one tree, in all the world, still maintained a flicker of life. Sap flowed sluggishly within the tree's core, even at the end. The gray sludge ate inexorably away at the tree's base, until the day the wind came up, the wind that had tried to knock my grandfather over almost two thousand years before –

And the tree my grandfather planted, fell.

The fall took quite a while, at least on the human scale. On sequoia time it was faster than the downstroke of a hummingbird's wings.

The fall lasted either a long time or an instant; it doesn't matter. When the tree's thousand tons of hardwood struck the bare stone surface of the canyon the tree shattered, and the sound of its death echoed up and down the length of the canyon for almost thirty seconds before it faded, and the canyon grew quiet again except for the wind.

On Sequoia Time was dedicated to my grandfather, R.D. Montgomery. He died in 2000, four years after this story was published, but he had been senile for several years prior to that, and never knew I'd written this. I wish I'd written faster.

Spiderman Kevin Stout Moran

A LONG TIME ago, when Richard was three, there was a little boy who said his name was Spiderman Kevin Stout Moran.

This is not a story about Spiderman™ – we must be clear about that. Spiderman is a registered trademark of Time Warner, one of the largest corporations in the known universe. They employ 30 billion people – 29 billion of them are lawyers who will sue you into the dirt for violating their trademarks or their copyrights. It's as much as your life is worth to observe, for example, that Superman is an illegal alien who prances around in colored underwear. So we won't say that even though it's true.

No, Spiderman Kevin Stout Moran was not really Spiderman, even though he had a Spiderman outfit and a Spiderman mask and Spiderman sandals and Spiderman underpants. He was just a little boy, and really his name was Richard, though he wouldn't always answer to Richard, and he would always answer if you called him Spiderman Kevin Stout Moran.

Everywhere You Want To Go

IT WAS DARK already when they pulled into the drive-through lane a McDonald's. Sam ordered for them while Kevin fidgeted beside him. As soon as Sam was done ordering Kevin laughed – before telling his joke, because Kevin was four.

After he stopped laughing he said, "Knock knock."

Sam said, "Who's there?"

"The chicken who wanted to go across the street! Get it? Get it?"

Sam laughed for him. "That's pretty funny."

After their food came and Sam pulled out onto the street toward home, Kevin asked, "Can I eat my french fries in the car?"

"It's past your bedtime, so when we get home you're going straight to bed. So I guess this time you can eat in the car."

"Mama and Auntie let me eat in the car."

"Mama and Auntie drive Fords. Uncle Sam drives what?"

In a singsong voice Kevin said, "A Jaguar and we keep it clean."

"When you turn eighteen, this is going to be your car. Then you can make messes in it."

"When I grow up, I'm going to have a car that flies."

"Really?"

"A big car. As big as ... McDonalds."

"There aren't any cars that big, Kevin."

"Yes there are. The Power Rangers have one. And it flies and it turns into things. I'm going to have that."

"Really?"

"Uh-huh. And I'm going to <u>be</u> a Power Ranger too."

"I thought you were going to be a Laker."

"Uh-huh. And I'm going to play for the Super-Globetrotters!"

"Who?"

"You know, Uncle Sam, on YouTube tv. They play basketball, but then they fly and they fight the bad guys."

"Kevin, the Lakers fight the bad guys 82 times a year during the regular season."

Kevin thought about it for a while. "But they don't always win?"

"No, sometimes they lose."

Kevin said definitely, "Super-Globetrotters *never* lose."

Their food came then, and Sam put the bag down between them and fished Kevin's French fries out. They pulled out onto the street and it was briefly quiet while Kevin worked on his fries. Halfway through the bag he stopped and looked over at Sam.

"Uncle Sam, how old are you?"

"34, sweetie. I'm the same age you are, plus 30. You're my birthday present: you came home from the hospital on my birthday."

Kevin considered it. "You're going to be pretty old when I grow up."

"That's true."

"Is Mama going to die? I don't want her to."

Sam thought about how to answer him. "Kevin, Mama's not even as old as I am, and I'm not very old. You know how long Mama's going to live? When you grow up to be my age, I'm still going to be alive. Then you're going to have children of your own, and those will be Mama's grandchildren. And Mama will be alive like your grandma and grandpa are now. And that's a long, long, *long* time from now."

Kevin went back to his French fries, thinking about it. The Jaguar turned a last corner and pulled into the driveway of Kevin's mother's house, a nice two-story house Kevin's grandfather had bought for Kevin's aunt and mother to make sure they had a place to raise Kevin after Kevin's father – the sperm donor, as Sam thought of him – had taken off.

Sam watched ESPN as his sister Jo, Kevin's aunt, gave Kevin his bath. Sam drove two hundred miles round trip every Saturday, to spend the day with Kevin – a long drive, but worth it.

After Kevin got into bed Sam came into his bedroom and sat down next to him.

"I'll see you next weekend."

Kevin smiled at him. "OK. Can we go to the slip-n-slide?"

"Sure. Did you have a good time today?"

"Yeah. I like going for rides with you."

"Good. Whose boy are you?"

The sweet smile got just a little wider. "I'm your boy."

"That's right. Good night, sweetheart."

Sam gave Kevin a kiss and Kevin rolled over in bed, closing his eyes. Sam sat at the side of the bed, watching him – and after a moment Kevin sat back up again.

"Uncle Sam?"

"Yeah?"

"When you get old, I'll drive you everywhere you want to go."

Scripts

5-Minute Brick

INT. A BEAT UP, DIRTY, DARK ROOM

An unusually handsome man enters. His fierce intelligence and unwavering sense of purpose are evident in his demeanor. For the sake of this story, we'll call him DAN.

> DAN
>
> Can you believe that son of a bitch? A hundred dollars, five measly minutes -- and no famous people. Has to be someone I knew -- Christ, this is bait and switch, if I'd known I couldn't talk to Elvis, I wouldn't have come down here in the first place. Hey, buddy! How about bringing him in! Time is money, you capitalist pig bastard!

A door is thrown open and a 6'2" black man, played ably by a white student[21], is shoved into the room. Dan turns to look at his long-dead buddy, MARK --

> DAN
>
> Mark! Buddy!

---

[21] Pepperdine is a Christian college in Malibu. It's an exaggeration to say that the only black students there are on the basketball team ... but not a big exaggeration.

       MARK
Dan! Man, you're looking -- older.

       DAN
    (touches bald spot)
Well. You look -- you know, okay, for
being dead and all. How you been?

       MARK
   (are you fucking *stupid?*)
Dead.

       DAN
Right. I mean, you know, besides that.

       MARK
In Hell.

       DAN
Faux pas, huh?

      GERROLD
Four minutes left!

       DAN
Come The Revolution *that* son of a bitch
is going to be one of the first ones up
against the wall.

       MARK
Man, you haven't changed. Well, except
for the hair -- how long have I been
dead?

       DAN
Six, seven years.

                    MARK
          I don't remember ... dying. What
          happened to me? What was my funeral
          like?

                    DAN
          You didn't have one. Your mom didn't
          want your body back so the County
          incinerated your ass.

Mark stares at Dan.

                    MARK
          My mom didn't --

                    DAN
          Buddy, do you remember how you died? On
          your knees in an alleyway in Pomona.
          Bullet in the back of the head? Bullet
          came out didn't leave much left on the
          front, sort of --
               (gestures face blooming out)
          -- I mean, I just heard that. I didn't
          see the body. Nobody did, your mom had
          you incinerated.

                    MARK
          Why are you doing this to me? Why did
          you bring me back to tell me this shit?

                    DAN
          Elvis wasn't available.

                    GERROLD
          Three minutes!

Dan makes a gesture like he's going to go for
Gerrold and then refrains, simmering.

```
                    DAN
Why you? Why bring you back? Let me
tell you, buddy, I felt like sneering
at someone and you were the logical
choice. Remember our friends? Remember
Ellen?


                    MARK
The chick you used to date ...


                    DAN
Died while you were in prison the first
time. Smacked her car into a pylon on
the 405 at 90 miles an hour.
     (smacks hands together)
Remember David Quan? Lost track of him.
Promiscuous gay man, moved to San
Francisco in 1980, I figure he's
probably dead. Jeff's still alive, I
think, I saw him on the tv doing a
commercial for some cocaine recovery
service. "Hi, I'm Jeff and I'm a
cocaine addict." Like that was a news
flash.


                    MARK
Bobby?


                    DAN
Heroin overdose.


                    MARK
Modesto?


                    DAN
Bullet.
```

                         MARK
          Jim?

                         DAN
          Good news there -- he gets out around
          the year 2000. I promised we'd do lunch.

                         GERROLD
          Two minutes!

                         DAN
          Remember? You and me were supposed to
          have lunch. Your mom had to call me and
          tell me you weren't going to be able to
          make it. Permanently delayed, so to
          speak.
                    (turns to audience)
          This is a cool story --

                         MARK
          Who are you talking to?

                       DAN

The audience -- look, never mind about
that. Detail. The point is, Mark was
pretty light-skinned for a black dude.
In real life, not just when he's being
played by a white actor. One day --
this is like fifteen years ago now,
Mark hadn't gone to prison the first
time yet -- we're at the beach together
and this woman walks up and wants to
take a photograph of us. And we look at
each other, cause this stuff doesn't
happen often, not even to guys as good
looking as us, and the woman says,
"You're darker than he is." And I was.
It was the end of summer and we were
down there on Venice beach together,
and I was darker than the black man I
was hanging out with -- I wish I had a
copy of that photo. I miss you, man.

                   GERROLD

One minute!

                       DAN

I miss all of you -- all the people I
was young with. Cause I'm the last one
standing. I'm the one who got out. And
I brought you back from the dead, you
worthless son of a bitch, so that I
could sneer at you. Bill and Tanya and
Modesto and Bobby were weak. The world
damaged them and took them out. Jim
wasn't weak, but he was stupid and it
caught up with him. I feel sorry for
all of them. You, though -- _you_ were
strong. _You_ were smart. You don't get
any slack.

> (to audience)
> Two trips to prison. Once in the U.S.,
> once in Mexico. The boy sold heroin.
> Crack. Amphetamines. Cocaine. Uppers
> downers floaters buzz ecstasy weed and
> those big pink motherfuckers that
> stretch you in eight directions at the
> same time.
> (back to Mark)
> So anyway I brought you back because I
> wanted to tell you something. I was
> <u>better</u> than you. I was better than all
> of you but you're the <u>one</u> I never felt
> sorry for. Your mother called me up and
> told me you got shot and I thought to
> myself, play with fire, you get burned.
> So this is it -- you were a failure ...
> and it was <u>you</u>. You coulda been here
> with me right now, living nice, living
> large. Instead it's just me and I
> deserve everything I have because <u>I
> fucking worked for it!</u>

                    GERROLD
> Time!

                    MARK
> I'll keep a place warm for you.

                    DAN
>   (kisses Mark on the cheek and
>   whispers)
> Burn, baby.

They turn and exit through opposite doors.

                    GERROLD
> Next!

The door opens and a man enters wearing dark
glasses. A woman enters, looking hesitant -- they
see one another and he yells:

                    MAN
        Priscilla, darlin'!

                  PRISCILLA
        Elvis!

They clinch and we fade out.

I always thought that if I'd been a rapper I'd have gone by Pasty D.

Pasty D

INT. NIGHTCLUB DRESSING ROOM -- NIGHT

The Interviewer, a punk in his early 20s, stands before the camera.

                    INTERVIEWER
          Pasty D. The Man. The Rapper.

CLOSER

                    INTERVIEWER (CONT.)
          One week from tonight, the Original
          White Boy will retire.

CLOSEUP -- SHOT OF A BABY

                    INTERVIEWER (CONT, VO)
          Born Daniel Sipowicz in 1954 --

TWO SHOT -- PASTY D AND THE INTERVIEWER

Pasty D is a middle-aged white dude dressed like a rapper. He's wearing a ridiculous amount of jewelry. Pasty D interrupts the interviewer.

                    PASTY D
          Aw, man. Why you do me like this? '64,
          man. Say '64.

THE INTERVIEWER LOOKS GENUINELY PUZZLED.

                    INTERVIEWER
          I've <u>seen</u> your birth certificate.

> PASTY D
> Check it out, you know Grandmaster
> Flash was born in '58? That dude is <u>old</u>.

The interviewer stares at Pasty.

NEW ANGLE -- SHOT OF BABY

> INTERVIEWER (V.O.)
> Born Daniel Sipowicz, in 1964, Pasty D
> was the first white rapper. In 1981, at
> the age of --

SHOT OF A 30-ISH PASTY D

> PASTY (V.O.)
> Say 22.

TWO SHOT PASTY AND INTERVIEWER.

The interviewer bursts out. He's genuinely pissed off.

> INTERVIEWER
> That doesn't even make sense! If you
> were born in 1964 then in 1981 you
> would have been 17!

> PASTY D
> (waves a hand dismissively)
> Don't bug. I ain't arguin' the math,
> the math is cool. Just say 22.

EXT. HOUSE --

A small house somewhere in the San Fernando Valley.

INT. HOUSE -- PANNING SHOT OF KITCHEN/LIVING ROOM

There are four small children, boys 2 and 5,
girls 9 and 10. The girls are watching television.

MEDIUM SHOT -- 2 YEAR OLD BOY, "RICHARD"

Richard is dressed like a small rapper himself --
backwards cap, chains, baggy pants.

                    INTERVIEWER (V.O.)
          Is Daddy cool?

                    RICHARD
          Daddy is pasty.

                    INTERVIEWER
          Daddy is Pasty D?

                    RICHARD
          Pasty pasty pasty.

                    INTERVIEWER (V.O.)
          Let's try the older boy.

MEDIUM SHOT -- 5 YEAR OLD BOY, JOE.

                    INTERVIEWER
          Did you know your Daddy is famous?

                    JOE
              (impressed)
          Really?

                    INTERVIEWER
          He had a hit called --

NEW ANGLE -- FAVORING MOTHER

A disapproving look. She shakes her head.

                    JOE
          It had butts in it.

                    INTERVIEWER
               (hastily)
          Well, never mind that.

                    JOE
               (confidentially)
          I'm not supposed to know that part.
          Does your car fly?

                    INTERVIEWER
          What?

                    JOE
          When I grow up, Im going to have a car
          that flies.

                    INTERVIEWER
          OK.

                    JOE
          A big car. As big as ... <u>McDonalds</u>.

                    INTERVIEWER
          There aren't any cars that big.

                    JOE
          Yes there are. The Power Rangers have
          one. And it flies and it turns into
          things. Im going to have that car. Uh-
          huh. And I'm going to <u>be</u> a Power Ranger
          too.

                    (pause; sadly)
          Daddy's not a Power Ranger. He's just a
          rapper.

TWO SHOT -- THE TWO GIRLS

The older girl, LAUREN, has a paper grocery bag
in one hand. She's arguing with her sister, SARAH.

                         LAUREN
          I'm going to be so embarrassed --

                         SARAH
          You're going to look so silly --

The Interviewer comes into frame.

                       INTERVIEWER
          Yeah, you know, the bag thing, it's
          been done. It's not funny.
                    (turns away, muttering)
          Her <u>wanting</u> to wear it is funny ...

TWO SHOT THE GIRLS

The girls are stone cold.

                    INTERVIEWER (V.O.)
          What's it been like, having Pasty D for
          a father?

                         LAUREN
          He's embarrassing.

                         SARAH
          None of the other dads dress like that.

EXT. DRIVEWAY -- PASTY D DRIVING A BEATUP VAN

The four kids are all in their seats. Pasty waves
at the camera as he drives by.

                    INTERVIEWER (V.O.)
          Pasty D drives you guys to school every
          morning.

INT. KITCHEN -- TWO SHOT THE GIRLS

                    LAUREN
          His name is Mr. Sipowicz.

                    SARAH
          And we wish he wouldn't.

INT. LIVING ROOM -- ON PASTY D

He's been watching the interviews with his kids.
He's not happy -- his body language is very
defensive.

                    PASTY
          Ya'know, my bizzo --

                    WIFE
          That better not mean --

                    PASTY
          Nah, don't trip. My girl here has to
          leave for work at 7:30. So I drive 'em,
          I pick 'em up. Ya'know.

                    WIFE
              (a little embarrassed)
          He's very reliable.

ON INTERVIEWER

                    INTERVIEWER
               (mutters)
          Maybe I should do the two-year old
          again.

ON RICHARD

                      RICHARD
          <u>My</u> Pasty.

INT. -- DRESSING ROOM -- INTERCUT PASTY AND
INTERVIEWER

                    INTERVIEWER
          Why are you retiring?

                       PASTY
          I've had a good run. Ya'know, I've
          performed -- "All around the world,
          from London to Madrid" --
               (grin fades)
          I can get a crowd anywhere. Even today.
          I get 40, 50 people everywhere I go,
          New York, LA, Chicago, they know, they
          remember. But ...
               (very flat)
          That's $10, $12 at the door. I walk
          with $200, maybe $150. After travel,
          pay for a room ... ya'know ... it pays
          for itself.
               (looks around room, avoiding
               camera, almost mumbling)
          My oldest girl goes to college in eight
          years. My next girl goes year after
          that, my oldest boy four years
          later ... youngest boy boy goes to
          college in sixteen years.

              (looks up)
     I got nothin' set aside for any of
     them. Not even the baby.

DIFFERENT ANGLE

The stage manager pokes his head inside. He's an
elderly black man, JAMES.

                         JAMES
     On in five, Pasty.

QUICK SERIES OF SHOTS -- INTERVIEWS

                    BLACK RAPPER #1
     Pasty always kept it real. I'm sorry to
     see him leave the life.

                    BLACK RAPPER #2
     He didnt swear much. I always liked he
     didn't use too many curse words.

                    BLACK RAPPER #3
     Another goddamn white man stealing the
     black man's art form. SCREW Pasty.

                    WHITE RAPPER #1
     Pasty made it possible for me to rap,
     man. We wouldn't have Eminem without
     Pasty, wouldn't have Kid Rock ...

                    BLACK RAPPER #3
     Him and freakin' Vanilla Ice. SCREW
     Pasty, screw Vanilla Ice, screw Eminem,
     screw Elvis!

INT. BACKSTAGE -- JAMES AND INTERVIEWER, WATCHING
PASTY

The Interviewer is taping Pasty while they talk.

                    JAMES
     Pasty is a <u>what</u>?

                    INTERVIEWER
     Pasty is a genius.

                    JAMES
          (considering)
     Well ... he rhymes good. I give him he
     rhymes good.

                    INTERVIEWER
     Not a fan, huh.

                    JAMES
     Hey, hey ... Pasty is my nigger.
          (Interviewer lowers camera
          and looks at him)
     Don't get fresh, you ain't allowed to
     use that word. Neither's he. But he's
     still my nigger.

                    INTERVIEWER
     He's quitting, he's abandoning his
     career to ... to take a <u>day job</u>.

                    JAMES
     The fuck you want, flowers? Man's got a
     family.

                    INTERVIEWER
          (heated)
     Pasty D is the most influential white
     rapper of the 1980s, he's --

                    JAMES
          That ain't sayin' a lot. Look, boy,
          chill. I like Pasty. I've always liked
          him. I've seen worse talent than him
          get rich and famous. It's mostly luck
          past a certain point.
                    (pause)
          But I've seen better than Pasty never
          even got the one little hit Pasty got.
          He's got him a nice little crowd out
          there to see him off. Let's don't make
          this more than it is.

MEDIUM SHOT INTERVIEWER

                    INTERVIEWER
          Ladies and gentlemen ... the last
          performance of Pasty D.

INT. NIGHTCLUB -- STAGE

The Last Performance of Pasty D.

                    PASTY D
          And I know what y'all wanna finish up
          with tonight --

                    CROWD
          "Smack That Ass!"

                    PASTY D
          Smack that Ass, baby
          Back it right up!
          Show me what you got
          And we'll smack it til it's hot!

INT. DRESSING ROOM -- TWO SHOT PASTY AND
INTERVIEWER -- LATER

Pasty is sweaty and worn out, but he looks happy.
The Interviewer is somber.

                    INTERVIEWER
          That was a good exit.

                    PASTY
               (still high)
          Good, bad, fuck. I got the applause ...
          ya'know, that's what it's all about.
          Give them the love, get it back ... .

While he's talking, Pasty is taking off his
rapper clothes and hat, toweling the sweat off,
and getting dressed in a long-sleeved dress shirt.

                    PASTY
          I tell you my first jingle ran the
          other day?

                    INTERVIEWER
          No.

                    PASTY
               (smiles)
          Yeah. Rap jingle for Cocoa Puffs.
               (raps)
          "We got the Cocoa, We got the Puff" ...
          I was going to make a joke about Puff
          Daddy, but the studio guys didn't get
          it. Didn't know who Puffy was, if you
          can get that.

INT. DARKENED LIVING ROOM --

Four barely visible kids, only their faces
visible, watching TV.

                    JOE
          Wow, that's so cool.

                    PASTY (V.O.)
          Next day at school, I dropped my girls
          off, they walked off telling their
          friends about the Cocoa Puffs jingle I
          wrote.

INT. DRESSING ROOM --

Pasty's coat, jewelry, and hat are all sitting on
a counter. The only piece of jewelry he's still
wearing is his wedding ring. Pasty scoops the
jewelry into a carry bag, folds his coat
carefully and puts it into the bag. He stands
looking at his hat.

TRACKING SHOT

Pasty walks out onto the stage. A microphone on a
stand is still set up. Pasty looks at it a
moment, then hangs the hat on the microphone.
James watches him.

                    JAMES
          That for anybody in particular?

Pasty steps down off the stage, into the
audience, and walks away without looking back.

                    PASTY
          The right person.

                    JAMES
          When I see him, I'll give it to him.

INT HOUSE -- PASTY WALKS IN FRONT DOOR

                         WIFE
          Kids are all asleep. Except Richard.

Richard runs up in his pajamas and Pasty picks
him up.

                         PASTY
          Am I _your_ Pasty?

                        RICHARD
          My Daddy. _My_ Daddy.

                         PASTY
          Boy, I'm doing my best.

This was an unsold spec script that Jodi and I wrote for our then-favorite tv show, Dream On. *If you watched the show, enjoy. If you didn't, it's probable that a lot of the humor in this isn't going to work for you. If you still want to read it, you should know this: Martin Topper is an editor at a New York publishing house. His ex-wife Judith, who he's still a little in love with, is married to the official World's Greatest Guy, Richard Stone. His boss, Gibby, is a slightly less evil version of Rupert Murdoch, and his secretary, Toby, is a snarling bundle of aggression. His best friend, Eddie Charles, is a talk show host.*

One of the gags in Dream On *was that Martin had watched too much television as a child, and that he'd frequently flash on (usually humorous) moments from old tv shows and movies. The bits marked "Clip" are those moments ... .*

Dream On: Another One Bites The Dust

FADE IN:

INT. MARTIN TUPPER'S OFFICE

MARTIN is reading at his desk -- the New York Times Book Review.

INSERT -- NEW YORK TIMES BESTSELLER LIST

The Number One entry for nonfiction is <u>The Last Dancer</u>, by Richard Stone. The Number One entry for fiction is <u>Devlin's Razor,</u> also by Richard Stone.

INT. MARTIN'S OFFICE -- CONTINUING

                         MARTIN
                    (muttering)
               He's at the top of <u>both</u> charts.

TOBY calls from the outer office.

                         TOBY
               Did you say something?

Martin comes out to her desk, waving the <u>Times</u>
angrily.

                         MARTIN
               The Pulitzers weren't enough. The Emmys
               weren't enough. The awards and the
               honors and the appearances on <u>Nightline!</u>
               They weren't enough for him! Now he's
               intruding in <u>my</u> field!

                         TOBY
                    (figuring it out)
               Your ex's husband, Richard, his novel
               is doing well.

                         MARTIN
               Number One! His non-fiction's been at
               the top of the list for three months.
               For three months I haven't been able to
               <u>look</u> at that list! Now he's at Number
               One on the fiction list. How many
               Mondays am I going to have to come in
               here and look at this?

CLIP: FOREVER AND EVER AND EVER

TOBY'S DESK -- CONTINUING

                    MARTIN
          (shakes paper wildly)
     It's not fair! He didn't <u>need</u> this!

                    TOBY
     You know, Martin, you're not dealing
     with this well.

                    MARTIN
     What do you know about this, Toby? All
     your ex's are dead!

                    TOBY
     It's neater that way.

                    MARTIN
          (breathing heavily)
     I'm going home for the day. If anybody
     asks, I'm <u>gone</u>.

Martin goes back inside his office. We HEAR the
sound of things crashing and breaking. JUDITH
enters.

                    JUDITH
     Hi, Toby. Is Martin in?

                    TOBY
     Ah -- no, no. He's not here.
          (crashing sound)
     He left. You should leave too.
          (breaking sound; Toby speaks
          urgently)
     Maybe <u>right now</u>.

                    JUDITH
     Is that Martin?

                         TOBY
          No, that's -- that's the <u>cleaning
          people.</u> They're <u>cleaning</u>. Martin's not
          here.

Martin comes out. Judith looks at Toby in
bewilderment.

                         JUDITH
          Cleaning people?

                         MARTIN
          Judith! How wonderful.

CLIP: MAN SHOOTING SELF IN HEAD

TOBY'S DESK -- CONTINUING

                         JUDITH
          I thought I'd come take you to lunch.
          Sort of a celebration. Richard's novel
          debuted at --

                         MARTIN
               (breathing heavily)
          You don't say.

                         JUDITH
          -- number one. Isn't that wonderful?

CLIP: MAN HANGING SELF

TOBY'S DESK -- CONTINUING

                         TOBY
          He's thrilled.
               (to Martin)
          Neater. Remember that.

                         MARTIN
                    (hyperventilating)
               Thrilled.

                         JUDITH
               ... Can we talk in your office?

                         MARTIN
               No. The cleaning people haven't come.
               It's a mess.

                         JUDITH
               Martin, are you okay? You're
               hyperventilating.

Martin opens his mouth to say something. His
mouth works but nothing comes out and he abruptly
grabs his coat, turns and leaves. Judith looks at
Toby.

                         TOBY
               He's so happy for both of you.

INT. EDDIE CHARLES' STUDIO

They are taping the EDDIE CHARLES show. Eddie's
guest is a Very Famous Horror Writer -- you know,
Steven Prince. Him. Martin stands, watching,
crumpled newspaper in his hand.

                         EDDIE
               -- guest today is the best selling
               writer in the world, a writer who has
               scared more readers than anyone else
               alive today.

CLIP: DROOLING MANIAC

INT. EDDIE'S STUDIO -- CONTINUING

                    PRINCE
          I never really wanted to be a horror
          writer. (Bug eyes.) I wanted to be a
          lumberjack! (Eyes normal.) That's a
          joke. Monty Python. But I always wanted
          to write romances. So I did.

                    EDDIE
             (professional veneer slips)
          You did not.

                    PRINCE
          I've finished the book already. It's
          really good. Hot stuff, cross my heart.
          Unfortunately, my current publisher
          doesn't want to put it out. They think
          it'll damage my image.

                    EDDIE
          Is that possible?

CLIP: VANDALS AT WORK

INT. STUDIO -- CONTINUING

                    PRINCE
          It really is a romance novel. About
          lonely, desperate girl ... named Agony
          Chilblains.

Eddie is at a loss for words.

                    EDDIE
          Romance. Well, romance is -- romance is
          good.

Martin's insane gloom lightens; he has an idea.

CLIP: VAST RICHES SHALL BE YOURS

INT. STUDIO -- CONTINUING

The studio audience is applauding; the show is
over. Martin comes back from his dream, tags
Eddie on his way offstage.

> EDDIE
> Martin! Hey, buddy. You know, I met
> this girl --

> MARTIN
> No kidding.

> EDDIE
> Big horror fan. You'd be _amazed_ at what
> women will do to meet this man.

> MARTIN
> (waving crumpled, sweaty
> _Times_)
> Never mind that. Have you _seen_ this?

> EDDIE
> (taking it gingerly)
> It's damp.

> MARTIN
> He's at Number One, Eddie! Both lists!

> EDDIE
> (hands it back)
> Yeah, I heard.

                    MARTIN
          What am I going to do?

                    EDDIE
          You could hire someone to kill Richard
          Stone.

CLIP: THAT'S AN IDEA!

INT. STUDIO -- CONTINUING.

                    MARTIN
          No -- no, then I'd have to console
          Judith. And I'd feel guilty and she'd
          know. She <u>always</u> knows about things
          like that.

                    EDDIE
          Jeez, Martin, I was kidding.

                    MARTIN
          Look, Eddie, introduce me to Mr. Prince.

                    EDDIE
          Sure.

Prince stands a ways off, chatting with the
show's staff, signing autographs. Eddie and
Martin go over to him.

                    PRINCE
          -- and his head came right off!
          Funniest damn thing I ever saw!

                    EDDIE
          Mr. Prince, I wanted to introduce my
          friend, Martin Tupper. Martin's an
          editor with Whitestone Publishing.

                    PRINCE
You're the guys who publish all those
sleazy exploitation bios, aren't you?

                    MARTIN
That's us!

                    PRINCE
        (suspiciously)
What do you think about romances?

                    MARTIN
        (unconvincingly)
Romances are fine -- fine, really.
Listen, Mr. Prince --

                    PRINCE
Call me Steve. Big Steve.

                    MARTIN
Listen, Steve -- Big Steve -- sleazy
exploitational bios aren't all we do.
We do children's books too! And we want
to branch out, into romances!

                    PRINCE
Really.

                    MARTIN
We'd love to publish your romance.

                    PRINCE
Have you ever published a romance
before?

                    MARTIN
        (thinking quickly)
"The Dame with the Two-Fisted Legs."

                    PRINCE
          That was a romance?

                    MARTIN
          Sort of.

                    PRINCE
          Great! I like to work with people who
          have experience. And conviction! Most
          editors are spineless, gutless, little
          wormlike creatures.

CLIP: SPINELESS, GUTLESS, WORMLIKE CREATURES

INT. STUDIO -- CONTINUING.

                    MARTIN
          Not me!

                    PRINCE
          Well. I'll send the book over. If you
          like it and can pay five million, I'll
          be over on Monday to sign the contract.

                    MARTIN
          But -- you -- five _million?_ You want us
          to publish your book for five million
          dollars?

                    PRINCE
          It's what I get per book. (to Eddie:) I
          thought everyone knew that.

Eddie looks embarrassed; he thought everyone knew
that too.

CLIP: FISHERMAN/THE ONE THAT GOT AWAY

STUDIO -- CONTINUING

                    MARTIN
          We'll publish it! We'll publish it!
          Five million -- no problem.
               (holds hand out to shake)
          I'll see you Monday.

Prince shakes hands, exits. Martin and Eddie are
left together.

                    EDDIE
          So, you figure this book will knock
          Richard out of Number One.

                    MARTIN
          On the fiction list, anyway! Isn't this
          great?

CLIP: YOU'RE BEING PROMOTED, SON!

STUDIO -- CONTINUING

                    EDDIE
          You should call Judith up, really get
          in her face with this.

                    MARTIN
          I am too good a person to do something
          like that to someone I still care about.

Eddie nods, grinning. Sure you are.

INT. GIBBY'S OFFICE

                    GIBBY
          The man gets five million per book,
          Martin. You know that?

        MARTIN
  He's worth it.

        GIBBY
  Oh, I know he's worth it. We'll make
  our money back and then some. But we're
  a small company; to raise this kind of
  money we're going to have to cut at
  least twenty of the books in the
  pipeline. Most of them your writers; it
  only seems fair.

        MARTIN
   (swallowing)
  I can handle that.

        GIBBY
  We'll have to cut back on staff, too.
  Starting with, uhm --

CLIP: YOU'RE FIRED!

INT. GIBBY'S OFFICE -- CONTINUING

        GIBBY
  -- your secretary, what's-her-name.

CLIP: RELIEF/BETTER HER THAN ME

INT. GIBBY'S OFFICE -- CONTINUING

        MARTIN
  Toby.

        GIBBY
  Can't afford her. And you won't have
  that many writers to deal with, you
  won't need her now.

Martin is wavering.

CLIP: YOU'LL NEVER AMOUNT TO ANYTHING!

INT. GIBBY'S OFFICE -- CONTINUING.

                    MARTIN
              (desperately)
     We have to publish this!

                    GIBBY
     That's my boy! You've got a Steve
     Prince novel. Fuck the rest of the
     world, eh?
              (smiling; friendly)
     Knew you had it in you. You should call
     your ex-wife up and throw it in her
     face.

                    MARTIN
     I'm not the kind of person who would do
     that.

                    GIBBY
     Pity. It's great fun.

TOBY'S DESK

                    MARTIN
     Toby, I need to talk to you --

                    TOBY
     Martin! We're really publishing Steven
     Prince?

                    MARTIN
     Well, yes. But --

>   TOBY
> Have you called up Judith yet, to gloat?

>   MARTIN
> No! Toby, this is very difficult --

>   TOBY
> What is it?

>   MARTIN
> Well, this book is very expensive. It's
> costing the firm a lot.

>   TOBY
> Gibby's not taking our bonuses away
> again!

CLIP: KILL HER QUICKLY

TOBY'S DESK -- CONTINUING

>   MARTIN
> We're going to have to let you go.
> We'll give you two weeks and then a
> month's severance pay.

>   TOBY
>   (slowly)
> Is this a joke? Gibby put you up to
> this, right?

>   MARTIN
>   (swallows)
> No. I'm sorry. It's not a joke. Uh,
> where are you going?

                         TOBY
              (clearly shaken; picking up
              her purse)
         Lunch. For the rest of the day. Maybe
         longer.

INT. MARTIN'S OFFICE -- INTERCUT W/JUDITH

Martin sits at his desk a moment, then shakes
himself. This is getting tough. Suddenly he
smiles.

                        MARTIN
         I'm not too good a person to gloat.

Martin picks up the phone and calls Judith.

                        MARTIN
         Hey, Jude!

                        JUDITH
         Martin. Look, I'm glad you called. I'm
         really sorry about this morning, I
         wasn't thinking.

                        MARTIN
              (doesn't want apology)
         Yeah, well, guess what? Guess who we're
         publishing?

                        JUDITH
         Oh, Martin, you didn't buy another one
         of those exploitation bios?

                        MARTIN
         No, no, that's not it.
              (dramatic pause)
         <u>Steven Prince</u>.

                    JUDITH
Oh, Martin, that's wonderful! Uhm, can
your company afford him?

                    MARTIN
Oh, sure. No problem. And get this;
it's a complete change of subject for
him. We're publishing a romance novel
he wrote! Isn't that wild?

                    JUDITH
Romance?

                    MARTIN
Romance. Remember that book he wrote
about the romance novelist?

                    JUDITH
Certainly. Richard said it was a cry
for help.

                    MARTIN
          (annoyed)
Anyway, he's messengering the book over
later today. We're having lunch Monday;
the book should be at the printers
within a week; in stores within a month.

                    JUDITH
But -- that'll knock Richard's book out
of Number One.

                    MARTIN
          (unconvincingly)
Really?

                         JUDITH
          Martin -- you're not just doing this to
          be petty -- are you?

CLIP: I'M GUILTY! GUILTY, GUILTY, GUILTY!

INT. MARTIN'S OFFICE -- CONTINUING.

                         MARTIN
          No. Of course not. It's just a
          coincidence.

                         JUDITH
          You _are!_

                         MARTIN
          It's just business, Jude.

                         JUDITH
          Speaking as a psychologist, this kind
          of behavior is petty and childish and I
          hope you die.

Judith hangs up. Martin doesn't look happy.

INT. MARTIN'S OFFICE -- LATER

Martin is on the phone.

                    MARTIN
          Look, Mary, you understand that we've
          valued your relationship with
          Whitestone Publishing. But with the
          current financial constraints on the
          company, we're going to have to return
          the manuscript to you and suggest you
          seek a new publisher -- no, no, we're
          not displeased with the work -- really,
          I've always loved your writing -- yes,
          yes, I understand that -- no, we're not
          asking for a rewrite, we just can't
          publish your book -- look, I'm trying
          to make this easy for both of us --

CLIP: COLD BLOODED KILLER AT WORK

INT. MARTIN'S OFFICE -- LATER

Martin is on the phone, tie loosened, sweating.

                    MARTIN
          Well, Jack, your last couple of books
          didn't sell so well. This isn't a
          personal thing, we're just cutting
          costs here and you happened to be one
          of the places we've had to cut. No, no,
          please don't cry, it's not your fault,
          really -- please stop crying.

CLIP: ANOTHER ONE BITES THE DUST

INT. MARTIN'S OFFICE -- LATER

His tie and coat are off; he looks like hell.

                    MARTIN
          You think this is easy for me, Terry?
          Do you? I've been editing your books
          for six years! I don't want to stop
          editing your work, but I don't have any
          choice in the matter! And neither do
          you!

CLIP: AND ANOTHER ONE DOES

INT. MARTIN'S OFFICE -- LATER

                    MARTIN
          Hi, Dorothy. Yeah, this is Martin over
          at Whitestone.
                    (shouts)
          Get a new publisher!

Martin slams the phone down.

CLIP: EVERYONE HATES YOU, BUDDY

INT. MARTIN'S APARTMENT -- LIVING ROOM

MARTIN IS READING A MANUSCRIPT. THE TITLE IS, OF
COURSE, AGONY. EDDIE IS IN THE KITCHEN GETTING A
BEER.

                    EDDIE
          How is it, man?

                    MARTIN
               (dazed)
          This is the worst thing I've ever read.

                    EDDIE
          I thought you liked Prince's stuff.

                    MARTIN
          I do. Did. But this -- I don't even
          understand what's <u>happening</u> in this
          story. Agony keeps getting ravished --
          but she's still a virgin -- so I'm not
          sure what happens when she gets
          ravished. Maybe it's just, like, really
          violent foreplay?

Martin looks at Eddie to see what he thinks of
this idea; Eddie nods, maybe that's it.

                    MARTIN
          And she's got five different men in
          love with her and they're all named
          Burke Smythington-Wellesly-Smith.

                    EDDIE
          All of them?

                    MARTIN
          Except for Ralph. But I think Ralph is
          secretly her mother who had the sex
          change operation.
                    (stares at Eddie wide-eyed)
          I can't publish this.

INT. GIBBY'S OFFICE

                    GIBBY
          What's wrong with it?

                    MARTIN
          It's incoherent, Gibby!

                    GIBBY
          The books you buy usually are. It's
          never bothered you before.

                         MARTIN
          Gibby, we can't publish this! The
          reviewers will savage it. We'll be a
          laughingstock!

CLIP: PEOPLE LAUGHING AND POINTING

INT. GIBBY'S OFFICE -- CONTINUING

                         GIBBY
          Martin, listen, I would publish this
          book if it were a collection of letters
          he'd written to Penthouse Forum.

                         MARTIN
          Don't you have any standards?

                         GIBBY
          I'll do anything for money.

                         MARTIN
               (resigned)
          One standard.

                         GIBBY
          We are going to publish this. Now, I
          understand you two are having lunch. Go
          schmooze the man and stop whining.

Martin, whipped, turns to go.

                         GIBBY
          Oh, Martin.
               (Martin turns back)
          When you talk to him -- ask him if he's
          ever written anything to Penthouse
          Forum. Okay? Just, you know, in passing.

AT TOBY'S DESK

                         MARTIN
          Did you make the reservations I asked
          for?

                         TOBY
          What reservations?

                         MARTIN
          For my lunch. With Prince.

Toby advances on Martin threateningly; Martin
retreats toward his office.

                         TOBY
          You think I've got time to make
          reservations for you to go out to
          lunch? I'm busy looking for a new job!
          I'm pounding the <u>pavement</u>. Reading the
          <u>newspaper</u>. Making <u>telephone</u> calls.
          Sucking up to people in interviews. My
          cheeks ache from smiling.
               (shouts)
          I'm not a natural smiler, Martin!

Martin backs into his office and slams the door.

                    TOBY (Yelling, V.O.)
          And stay in there!

AT LUNCH -- IN A SLEAZY DINER

                         PRINCE
               Nice place.

CLIP: BETTE DAVIS -- "WHAT A DUMP"

SLEAZY DINER -- CONTINUING

                    MARTIN
          Yeah, it's got -- got -- <u>atmosphere</u>.
          And burgers -- burgers, shakes, fries,
          that all-American thing, that thing you
          write about. Brand names.
               (whips up ketchup bottle)
          Look, Heinz!

                    PRINCE
               (nods approvingly)
          Americana. You know, Martin, I don't
          think an editor's ever taken me to a
          place like this before.
               (stares at Martin)
          I think you <u>understand.</u>

                    MARTIN
               (abruptly stomping on floor)
          That wasn't a cockroach.

CLIP: MILLIONS OF BUGS SWARMING

SLEAZY DINER -- CONTINUING

                    PRINCE
          Looked like one. Kind of small, though.
          In Texas they have cockroaches as big
          as your hand. Want to see one?

CLIP: ONE GIANT BUG

SLEAZY DINER -- CONTINUING

                    MARTIN
          Have you got it with you?

                    PRINCE
          In the car. His name's Dennis.

                    MARTIN
          I'd love to!

                    PRINCE
          He didn't want to come in.

                    MARTIN
          Oh.

                    PRINCE
          Wasn't hungry.

                    MARTIN
               (starting to lose it)
          Boy, I just love your work! May I ask
          you a question?

                    PRINCE
          Shoot.

                    MARTIN
          What prompted you to give up horror for
          romance writing?

                    PRINCE
          Love! No, fear.

                    MARTIN
          You're afraid of your own writing? I
          can und--

                    PRINCE
               (instant paranoia)
          You're not like the others, are you?

                    MARTIN
          What others?

                    PRINCE
          Lou. Mitch. Marty.

                    MARTIN
          Absolutely not.

                    PRINCE
          Those bastards! You know --
               (ranting, words tumbling out;
               people turn to look)
          -- I can't sleep at night. If you did
          all day what I do all day, you wouldn't
          be able to sleep at night either. Other
          people hear a noise in the night and
          they think the house is settling. Me,
          I'm forty-four years old and I still
          have to check under the bed before I go
          to sleep. My own children are afraid of
          me! I have rats scritching in my walls
          -- giant mutant android rats.
               (leans forward, eyes bug out)
          Playing reggae music.

                    MARTIN
          Really.

                    PRINCE
               (abruptly matter-of-fact:)
          Well, sometimes I think so.

                    MARTIN
          I love romances. I've always kind of
          thought of myself as that romantic
          type. Just ask my ex-wife.

                    PRINCE
          I can trust you, can't I? You're not
          like other editors, are you? You're a
          real person. With emotions; a heart.
          Blood, and intestines.

                    MARTIN
          You bet.

                    PRINCE
          Let's go sign that contract.

                    MARTIN
          You're not hungry?

                    PRINCE
          I ate already. In the car, with Dennis.

INT. MARTIN'S OFFICE

Martin has the contract sitting on the desk in
front of Prince. Prince sits in the guest chair.

                    PRINCE
          This is what I always wanted to do.
          Sometimes, Martin, I just get this urge
          to show my softer side.

                    MARTIN
          Well, you've certainly shown it.

CLIP: SOFT IN THE HEAD!

INT. MARTIN'S OFFICE -- CONTINUING

                    PRINCE
          So what do you like best about the book?

                    MARTIN
                 (looking for a pen)
          Uh -- uh -- Burke Smythington-Wellesly-
          Smith.

                    PRINCE
          Which one?

Martin tries one pen -- it doesn't write.

                    MARTIN
          The second one.

                    PRINCE
          The one that used to be Agony's mother
          before the sex change?

                    MARTIN
               (finding a pen that writes)
          I thought that was Ralph.

                    PRINCE
               (shrugging)
          Could have been.

Prince reaches for the pen Martin is offering
him. He pauses, reaches again; his fingers close
around the pen clumsily, and the pen drops to the
ground. He leans over to reach for it, is unable
to, and slumps back into his chair.

                    PRINCE
               (gasping; clutching chest)
          I need another pen. That one's -- no
          good.

                    MARTIN
               (slow on uptake)
          Are you okay?
               (comes around desk, picks up
               pen)
          It's a perfectly fine pen.

                    PRINCE
               (gasping; turning red)
          It is <u>not</u>.

                         MARTIN
              Look, it writes.

                         PRINCE
                   (spasming)
              I need a new pen!

His head falls forward on his chest and he sits
there limply.

                         MARTIN
                   (grabbing Prince by the
                    shirtfront and shaking him)
              Are you all right? Are you dying?

Prince doesn't answer. He's dead.

                         MARTIN
              You have to sign this contract first!
              You can't die!
                   (shakes Prince violently)
              Thirty seconds! I only need thirty
              seconds!
                   (begins slapping Prince)
              Breathe! Breathe!

CLIP: TAKE THAT! AND THAT!

INT. MARTIN'S OFFICE -- CONTINUING

Toby enters as Martin is slapping Prince around.

                         TOBY
              What are you doing?

                         MARTIN
                   (dropping Prince abruptly)
              Nothing.

                         TOBY
                (peering at Prince closely)
           Is he -- is he -- dead?

                         MARTIN
                (guilty)
           No.

                         TOBY
           Did you kill him?

                         MARTIN
           Of course not!

                         TOBY
                (screaming loudly)
           Oh my God! He's killed the best-selling
           writer in the world!

Gibby enters.

                         GIBBY
           Do I hear screaming?

                         TOBY
           Martin <u>killed</u> Steven Prince!

                         MARTIN
           I did not!

Toby runs outside to her desk. We HEAR HER on the
phone in the background.

                         GIBBY
           You killed him?

                    (pause)
This is wonderful! We couldn't buy this
kind of publicity! I can see it now:
EDITOR OFFS BELOVED HORROR WRITER; GETS
ELECTRIC CHAIR! We'll make money hand
over foot. Or do I mean fist?
                    (looks at Martin
                    consideringly)
And while you're on death row, you can
write your memoirs: WHY I KILLED STEVEN
PRINCE. We'll make money together,
Martin. You and I.

                    MARTIN
          (screaming)
I didn't kill him!

                    GIBBY
Can you prove that?

                    MARTIN
He had a heart attack! Or a stroke, I
don't know. Call an ambulance!

Toby enters.

                    TOBY
I've already called the police.
          (gives Martin the evil eye)
Fire me, will you?

                    GIBBY
Look at the opportunity, Martin. Even
if you didn't do it, I think it would
be in our best interests if you were to
admit to it.

                    MARTIN
He didn't sign the contract, Gibby.

                    GIBBY
I'll send women on visiting days.
Whoever you ask for. I'll send -- he
didn't what?

                    MARTIN
Sign the contract.

                    GIBBY
        (screaming)
How could you kill him before he signed
the contract? You've ruined us. You
bastard -- you --

Judith enters.

                    JUDITH
Do I hear screaming?

                    MARTIN
No.

                    GIBBY
Wait. Wait. We can forge his signature.
        (He knocks Prince from the
        chair, begins rifling his
        pockets.)
Look, his wallet! His driver's license
has his signature!
        (thrusting license at Martin)
Take care of it, Martin.
        (turning to Judith & Toby)
Could you both step outside for a
moment?

                         TOBY
          I'm sorry, Gibby, but I don't feel
          comfortable leaving you alone with the
          murderer.

                         JUDITH
               (a flash of normalcy)
          He's -- dead? Oh, my God, he's <u>dead</u>.

                         MARTIN
          I didn't kill him!

At this point, two police officers enter the
room. Over the general babble, one cop shouts.

                          COP
          All right, all right! Let's have some
          quiet here! Now, who's the victim, and
          who's the killer?

Gibby waves a disgusted hand at the body; Toby
points at Martin.

INT. MARTIN'S OFFICE -- LATER

Paramedics are rolling Prince's body out on a
gurney. In the BG, a cop is speaking to Toby.

                          COP
          Look, we can't arrest him for giving
          the guy a heart attack. It's jerky, but
          it's not a crime.

In the FG, Martin and Judith are sitting
together, ignoring everyone else.

                    JUDITH
I'm so sorry, Martin. I know how much
this book meant to you. And I'm sorry
for what I said the other day.

                    MARTIN
It's okay. You were right, I was being
petty. I only wanted Prince to knock
Richard out of the #1 spot. It's just
-- really <u>hard</u>, having to deal with the
constant reminders of his perfection.

                    JUDITH
He knows. He said to tell you he
forgives you.

TOBY'S DESK -- LATER

Martin is pleading with Toby.

                    MARTIN
Toby, I'd really like you to stay on.

                    TOBY
Hah.

                    MARTIN
Please?

                    TOBY
You fired me!

                    MARTIN
You tried to get me arrested for murder.

                    TOBY
I was upset. My feet hurt. All that
hitting the pavement.

                         MARTIN
          So you'll stay?

                         TOBY
          My eyes hurt, too. Those ads are
          printed in really small type.

                         MARTIN
          Does this mean you're staying?

                         TOBY
          Aw, I guess so.

                         MARTIN
          Great! Look, Toby, would you get me a
          list of my writers?

                         TOBY
             (snarling)
          Get it yourself.

INT. MARTIN'S OFFICE -- LATER

Martin is on the phone.

INSERT -- A LIST OF NAMES, ABOUT TWENTY OF THEM.

Half the names have checkmarks next to them.
Midway down the list, the name <u>Dorothy Fortuna</u>
lacks a checkmark.

INT. MARTIN'S OFFICE

                         MARTIN
          Dorothy -- I understand some maniac has
          been calling -- ha ha -- claiming to be
          me, screaming at you about your needing
          to get a new publisher.

          (listens)
No, we don't know who it was, but we've
notified the police. Yes, yes, the
police are looking into it.

                                            END

A Moment in Time

EXT. DESERT -- LONG SHOT -- BLACK AND WHITE

In TOTAL SILENCE a man walk out of the desert.
Dust swirls BEFORE THE CAMERA, and when we see
the man again a terrible scar has appeared where
his left eye was. We FADE TO BLACK as a female
voice sings <u>a capella</u>:

A million young voices, screaming out their words
Maybe someday those words will be heard
By future generations riding on highways that we built
Maybe they'll have a better understanding
Hope they have a better understanding

So check it out
Where does our time go?[22]

TITLE FADES IN: 96 MINUTES BEFORE THE FIRE

INT. BEDROOM, 2000 A.D. -- NIGHT

SPIDER DEVLIN sits abruptly upright in bed,
startled out of a dead sleep. He clasps one hand
over his left eye and SHOUTS.

FLASH: AN INCREDIBLY QUICK SHOT, BARELY
PERCEPTIBLE

Spider standing at the edge of a bridge in the
middle of nowhere. An arrow pierces him, front to
back --

RETURN TO PREVIOUS SHOT

Spider jerks as though he's been struck by the
arrow, hand falling away, turns toward the phone,
reaching for it, his eyes catching the light as

---

[22] John Mellencamp, *Check It Out*

he turns ... the light in his eyes *ripples* in a
subliminally perceptible fashion. His hand hovers
over the phone, he's confused -- finally the
phone rings.

EXT. LOS ANGELES -- VIEW OF CITY -- NIGHT

Shot of Los Angeles skyline, facing east on the
10 freeway.

EXT. FREEWAY -- ON SPIDER & HARLEY -- EASTBOUND

He zooms to a stop at the side of the 10 Freeway,
heading toward Pasadena. A car has struck the
center divider; Spider gets off his Harley, walks
to the car. We see him clearly for the first
time; a man of perhaps thirty-five, dressed in a
long black duster, black jeans, and cowboy boots
-- no helmet.

EXT. THE CAR AS SPIDER APPROACHES -- FAVORING
SPIDER

A dead man slumps over the steering wheel, a gun
in his left hand, brains all over the passenger
seat. His radio's been left running. We HEAR an
extremely RAPID VOICE:

                    RADIO VOICE (V.O.)
          ... nanovirus outbreaks in D.C.,
          Chicago and Los Angeles. A nuke went
          off in the harbor in New York --

FLASH: A GREEN MEADOW IN BRIGHT SUNSHINE

Spider is vaguely visible in the FG. Two little
girls, six and eight, run toward him.

                    RADIO VOICE (V.O.)
          -- Manhattan ain't there anymore --

RETURN TO PREVIOUS SHOT -- TIGHT ON SPIDER

                    RADIO VOICE (V.O.)
          -- we have unconfirmed reports that the
          Pan Asian coalition has launched
          missiles and that we've struck back ...
          kiss your ass goodbye, people. This is
          the Big One.

Spider shakes his head numbly, takes the man's
gun from his hand, gets back on his Harley and
zooms DIRECTLY TOWARD THE CAMERA, looming to FILL
THE FRAME --

EXT. DESERT, 2100 A.D. -- EXTREME LONG SHOT -- DAY

A continuation of our opening shot, now IN COLOR.
Spider walks out of the desert, walks TOWARD THE
SCREEN in a long, long, long shot, taking our
time, Spider resolving out of a gray desert haze.
He's wearing what we saw him in a moment ago ...
duster, jeans and black t-shirt, and a partially-
buttoned white long-sleeved dress shirt. He's
carrying a black tote bag slung over one
shoulder. The CAMERA STAYS ON HIM as he
approaches, comes into the middle distance ...
and then we DOLLY BACK, pivoting to widen into a
two shot with Spider at the right side of the
shot, and ANGEL at the far left.

She looks like something out of a really good
issue of Heavy Metal -- a wild, dark-haired,
dark-eyed, dark-skinned girl of 20 or so, with
muscles and Post-Holocaust-Chic clothes designed
to show them off, standing guard in front of a

bridge that connects her little island[23] to the rest of the world. She's buff, she's impressive, and she knows it. She stands with a compound bow in her hands, a quiver on her back, an arrow notched and ready to go.

Spider comes to a stop and she raises the point of the arrow at him, a small gesture, and stares at hims.

                    SPIDER
          My time machine broke down.

                    ANGEL
               (politely)
          Really. How did that happen?

                    SPIDER
          There was a black hole in the heart of
          the beast ... it turned me inside out
          and squirted me through the
          singularity. Unfortunately I broke it
          and the black hole fell free. It's
          fallen to the center of the planet
          right now, eating the world alive.

                    ANGEL
          What?

CLOSE SPIDER

                    SPIDER
          You know on mattresses, those little
          tags that say Do Not Remove?

                                        SLAM CUT:

---

[23]   San Pedro harbor.

EXT. LAB PARKING LOT, 2000 A.D. -- NIGHT

Superimposed: <u>84 MINUTES BEFORE THE FIRE.</u>

Spider pulls screeching into the parking lot for
a single story building with a large attached
warehouse beside it. The wide double doors to the
lab explode open. Two men in contamination suits
come charging out as Spider dismounts, descend on
him and pull him toward the lab.

INT. LAB SHOWERS -- TWO SHOT SPIDER AND GENEVIEVE

Spider's showering, naked, standing beneath a
device that's blowing foam down on him, then
rinsing. GENEVIEVE, the Lab Director, is a woman
of 50 or 60. She stands a few feet away, outside
the reach of the spray, wearing a surgical mask.
She doesn't appear to notice that Spider's naked.

                    GENEVIEVE
          You didn't see anyone, you didn't <u>touch</u>
          anyone on your way here?

CU SPIDER, SHOWERING

FLASH: SPIDER PICKING THE GUN UP OUT OF THE CAR

RETURN TO TWO SHOT -- SPIDER FINISHES RINSING

                    SPIDER
          No -- <u>Where the hell are my clothes?</u>

                    GENEVIEVE
          Being irradiated -- to kill any viruses.

A quiet beat. Spider stares at her, dripping wet
and naked.

CLOSE ON SPIDER -- HE LOOKS DEVASTATED

                    SPIDER
          They bombed New York.

WIDE SHOT -- ON CAROLINE

A scientist of about 30 -- she charges into the
room and tosses Spider's clothes to him. She's
wearing jeans and a blouse and a distinctive
silver-turquoise Indian necklace.

                    CAROLINE
          Here, Spider, I nuked these. Nothing
          left alive on any of 'em, I promise.

ON GENEVIEVE

                    GENEVIEVE
          I'm so sorry.

INT. LAB CORRIDOR -- TWO SHOT SPIDER AND GENEVIEVE

As they walk we SEE, in BG, entire families --
small children, husbands and wives. Spider's
dressing as they walk, buckling belt, buttoning
shirt --

                    SPIDER
          Holland still hasn't shown?

                    GENEVIEVE
          We called and called and couldn't get
          through. Then the phones went out.

                    SPIDER
          Just as well, I'd probably kill him
          right now anyway --

                    GENEVIEVE
          Spider!

                     SPIDER
          He's a military asshole and he's better
          off -- wait. Who are we gonna send --
               (realization sinks in)
          -- through? Get real.

INT. LAB -- THE TIME TRAVEL GATE -- TRACKING
SPIDER

They exit the office space and enter the
converted warehouse -- the lab. The Time Gate is
the largest thing in it -- forty feet wide,
twenty high, dwarfing the people who surround it.

                    GENEVIEVE
          Who else am I going to send, Spider?

                     SPIDER
          <u>Anyone</u> would --

He stops and looks around the room -- filled with
elderly scientists, lady scientists, fat
scientists, etc.

NEW ANGLE -- FAVORING JIMBO

JIMBO is a relatively young tech. He's heard
Spider; he speaks without looking up from his
instruments.

                     JIMBO
          Not even in your dreams.

Spider's plainly the only Stud Hero type there.
He turns toward the Time Gate; CAMERA PIVOTS WITH
HIM until Spider is framed in the center of the

shot, with the Gate in BG.

                    SPIDER
     I need my bike.

EXT. BRIDGE, 2100 -- TWO SHOT SPIDER AND ANGEL

A bird hangs upside-down in FG, on an ancient
power line.

                    SPIDER
     You wouldn't believe the day I've
     had ... You know, that bird's either
     dead or it's invented gravity boots.
          (quickly back to Angel)
     What _is_ your name?

Angel looks at the bird as Spider takes a step
toward her--

                 SPIDER (CONT.)
     And what year is --

Angel looks back, sees Spider moving, and lets
fly.

CLOSE SHOT -- SPIDER IN FG, ARROW IN BG FLYING
TOWARD CAMERA

Spider twists aside and _catches_ the arrow, pulls
it out of the air. (Again, almost subliminally,
the arrow should _ripple_ just before he touches
it.) Spider stares at her ... opens his hand to
look at the arrow. The arrowhead sliced his palm
as it went by, and he's bleeding.

INSERT -- ECU SPIDER'S HAND

The blood drips down his hand ... drops to the

dry desert sand. The CAMERA FOLLOWS the blood
down ...

TWO SHOT -- NEW ANGLE

Spider twirls the arrow a couple of times,
casually, like a baton, and grins at Angel.

                    SPIDER
          Ever try to catch a bullet with your
          teeth? Your head rings for <u>weeks</u>
          afterward.

INT. TIME GATE WAREHOUSE, 2000 -- TRACKING SPIDER

SUPERIMPOSED WITH: <u>80 MINUTES BEFORE THE FIRE.</u>
Spider pulls on his duster, stamps into his boots
-- he flexes his right hand, then brings it up
and looks at it.

INSERT -- SPIDER'S RIGHT HAND

It's bleeding -- a faint mirror of the cut he
made/will make catching Angel's arrow.

PULL BACK -- TRACKING SPIDER

He shakes his head, puzzled, dismissing it, and
wipes his hand on his jeans, slings his bag over
his shoulder and mounts the Harley. Despite the
situation Spider is grinning a little, wired and
manic. Lab techs wrestle into position and tie
down the portable Gate -- its about the size of a
small child -- on the seat behind Spider. The
portable Gate has an array of controls and
instruments on its surface.

                    GENEVIEVE
          What's in the bag?

                    SPIDER
          (glances sideways at his bag)
     This? This is my stuff. I don't go
     <u>anywhere</u> without my stuff.

Genevieve looks as though she's going to argue,
then gives it up. Jimbo gets in Spider's face;
they shout at each other, drill-sergeant style,
in what has the feel of an old in-joke, but with
real urgency, stepping on each other's dialog, as
the huge Time Gate starts to WHINE.

                    JIMBO
     Master Programmer!

                    SPIDER
     Master Engineer!

                    JIMBO
     That button right there!

                    SPIDER
     That button right there!

                    JIMBO
          (Spider echoes him)
     Find a flat place, ride however far you
     have to, find flat ground and press
     that button once, <u>only once,</u> when you
     get through to the other side! Don't
     touch anything else, <u>you'll just screw
     it up!</u>

                    SPIDER
     ... I'll just screw it up!

                         GENEVIEVE
                    (Good Citizen alarm)
              Spider, you're not wearing a helmet!

                           SPIDER
              Fuck the helmet ... there's no Highway
              Patrol where I'm going.

NEW ANGLE -- FAVORING CAROLINE AT A CONSOLE

                          CAROLINE
                    (watching equipment)
              Cycling!

PREVIOUS ANGLE -- FAVORING SPIDER ON MOTORCYCLE

                           SPIDER
                         (laughs)
              That's cheap humor --

The WHINE grows VERY LOUD; Jimbo shouts over it --

                           JIMBO
              Go, damn it, go! Go!

                           SPIDER
              Hey! Hey! Where are you sending me?

                          CAROLINE
                    (tension broken; she checks
                    instruments)
              Uh ... Los Angeles ... 2100. Within ...
              twenty miles of the lab?

Spider nods, glances at his watch --

INSERT -- DIGITAL WATCH READS 9:51:32 PM.

ANGLE FROM BEHIND SPIDER -- TIME GATE IN DIRECT BG

Spider hits the clutch and zooms forward, tires
smoking, into the Time Gate --

CLOSE ON JIMBO -- A VERY QUICK SHOT

                    JIMBO
              (half-serious)
          What a total stud.

FLASH: EXT. BEACH -- NIGHT -- IN BLACK AND WHITE

A pair of seagulls flying away, out over the
black ocean.

EXT. THE DESERT 2100, A SHIMMERING RIPPLE -- DAY

Spider rides through a wavering break in reality.
He zooms forward a hundred yards or so, at high
speed, screaming, whooping, making all sorts of
appalling noises. Abruptly he brakes, and the
motorcycle slews to a halt, and Spider leaps off
it, barely taking a moment to see that it's
standing safely, leaping off to the desert sand.
He slips and falls, staggers back to his feet,
laughing.

                    SPIDER
            (at top of his lungs)
          I did it! I traveled through time, me,
          I AM THE MAN! I'm the first time
          traveler in the history of the world,
          the very first one! This is the future,
          this is so amazingly cool --

SHOOTING DOWN FROM ABOVE

-- Spider spins around, looking up at the frozen

gray sky.

                          SPIDER
                 (flings his arms wide)
            HELLO FUTURE!

RETURN TO PREVIOUS ANGLE --

Predictably, the future doesn't answer Spider.
His spin slows, he stares at the dead desert, at
post-Nuclear-Winter Los Angeles -- ruin of
buildings nearby, more ruins in the BG -- arms
falling to his side.

                          SPIDER
            Look what we did.

He completes his turn and circles around again,
much more slowly, just staring in disbelief at
his surroundings. He completes the second
circuit, turning in a growing, insane rage, and
screams, turning on his motorcycle, at the
portable Gate still tied to the passenger support
bar, and kicks the motorcycle, hard, sending it
crashing to the stony ground, sends the Gate
bouncing off the support. He doesn't notice the
Gate, just keeps kicking the bike with his
snakeskin cowboy boots.

                          SPIDER
                 (in rhythm with the kicks)
            You ... dumb ... sons ... of ...
            bitches.

He points out at the dead desert, addressing the
bike he's still kicking, because the world that
created it isn't here to be screamed at.

> SPIDER
> Do you <u>see</u> what you've done? You dumb
> shits, <u>do you see what you did?</u>

He gives the bike a final kick, turns and limps
away from the bike and Gate, with a sore foot.

> SPIDER
> (pulling boot off)
> Oh, <u>man</u> that hurts.

INSERT -- CLOSE ON PORTABLE GATE

The status LED flashes "OFFLINE."

EXT. DESERT, 2100 -- A HILL, LOOKING DOWN ON
SPIDER

WE SHOOT DOWN onto a man wearing dirty, hooded
white robes, lying on his stomach, watching
Spider down in the flats. After a bit he creeps
back away from the edge, and then stands up,
walking downhill. He's a big, strong man -- THE
ARAB, let's call him. We can't see his face,
inside the robes.

> THE ARAB
> Spider Devlin. At last.

INT. LAB -- 2000 -- NIGHT -- ON CAROLINE

At her instruments.

> CAROLINE
> I ... I've lost the remote Gate.
> (rising panic)
> We lost the signal on the Gate!

INT. "TOWN HALL" -- 2100 -- DAY

A big room with an air of disrepair about it --
like virtually everything else hereabouts.
Thirty-odd people are gathered in the room --
most of the surviving human race -- all dressed
in homemade clothes. Gathered about a long table
are JOJO, a big, strong, skeptical fellow of 40
or 50; Angel and MICHAEL, and assorted extras.
Michael's a little older than Angel, maybe late
twenties; she's lighter skinned, a little less
tough, a little more feminine. Angel and Michael
are both armed, knives and bows.

                    ANGEL
          Says his name is Spiderdevlin. He came
          out of the desert, east.

                    JOJO
          Not the north?

                    ANGEL
               (barely pauses for breath)
          No, I asked if he was one of Trader
          Joe's people and he said no, he said he
          was from the past, before the Fire, and
          he'd been walking in the desert all day
          and could I give him some water but I
          wouldn't, and he said that he'd been
          walking because his "Harley" had run
          out of gas, and his time machine had
          broken down.
               (abrupt pause)
          Because he kicked it.

EXT. AN OPEN SQUARE BY THE TOWN HALL

Two guards, armed with compound bows, watch
Spider. Spider's kneeling with his head under a
manual pump, pumping the water over his head. His

bag is on the ground next to him.

INT. TOWN HALL -- ANGLE FAVORING JOJO

We see Spider in BG as JoJo watches him through
the window.

>   JOJO
>   He wants us to go find his "Harley" and
>   his time machine?

THREE SHOT FAVORING ANGEL AND MICHAEL, WATCHING
SPIDER

>   ANGEL
>   Says he's got trade goods.

>   MICHAEL
>   (quietly to Angel)
>   He's not bad looking.

>   ANGEL
>   Hadn't noticed.
>   (to JoJo)
>   Mutants watched him come into town.

>   JOJO
>   (sharply)
>   You saw them?

Angel looks at JoJo long enough to convey her
contempt -- didn't I just say so? -- and turns
back to watching Spider.

EXT. TOWN HALL -- ON SPIDER

He rises from the pump, and looks around.

EXT. TOWN HALL -- WIDE ANGLE -- SPIDER'S POV

A SLOW HALF-CIRCLE PAN -- setup for a later
shot.[24] This pan covers perhaps half the arc of
the town. It's not much -- a few buildings, a
fence with guardposts where guards stand duty,
watching the desert. There's what looks like a
homely, straggly, badly maintained garden, at the
center of town. An ugly "garage" area fills out
the picture, with a couple amazingly dilapidated
trucks sitting in the shade. Far to one side we
see several ancient oil rigs.[25]

EXT. TOWN HALL -- ON SPIDER

                    SPIDER
              (to the guards)
        I gotta tell you guys, this ain't what
        I was hoping for.

He goes inside without waiting for an answer.

WIDE ANGLE -- FAVORING ENTRANCE

Spider walks into the room, water still dripping
from his hair, bag in one hand. His guards follow
him.

                    SPIDER
        I guess you're the Man.

                    JOJO
        The Man?

---

[24]   One of the movie's closing scenes will begin with exactly this pan.
[25]   San Pedro is near one of the largest oil reserves in the U.S.

                    SPIDER
          -- the Man, the Boss, Il Duce, Caesar,
          Kaiser, the President, the King, the
          Big Kahuna ... <u>The Wizard!</u>

                    JOJO
          ... I'm JoJo.

                    SPIDER
          Spider Devlin and I wish I could say
          it's a pleasure to meet you but it's
          not, we'll start this relationship off
          on the right foot with a big ugly dose
          of the Truth, I hope you appreciate
          that. I came from the past, a hundred
          years ago, and I was hoping that in a
          hundred years you'd have built the
          Emerald City and a bunch of munchkins
          or at least Captain Kirk would be
          waiting to greet me. This isn't the
          case and I have to admit I'm
          disappointed. You live in a nasty,
          brutish world that reminds me
          unpleasantly of San Bernardino, so if
          you don't mind I'd like you to haul out
          one of those ugly trucks, give me some
          gasoline for my Harley, and take me to
          go get my damn time machine.
                    (pause)
          I'll pay.

There's a long silence while the crowd attempts
to assimilate this information.

                    JOJO
          What's "pay?"

                    MICHAEL
          Is that like "trade?"

                    SPIDER
               (grins)
          Cool. Let's play Capitalism. I'll be
          the ugly American, and you all can be
          the Russians. It goes like this: you do
          what I want you to do, and I'll give
          you a toaster.

                    ANGEL
          What's a toaster?

                    SPIDER
          That's not important. It's something
          you need, and that's all you need to
          know.

He puts his bag down on the table top.

                    SPIDER (CONT.)
          Unfortunately, I neglected to bring any
          toasters with me. But I did bring my
          stuff here, which is practically as
          good as a toaster and doesn't require
          bread or an electrical outlet, both of
          which I expect are in short supply
          hereabouts.

                    JOJO
          Look, boy, let's you and me get some
          things straight. I don't believe you
          come from some other time. All I know
          is you come out of the desert and you
          want us to go back <u>into</u> the desert.
          That's a lot of work --

                    MICHAEL
          And it's dangerous.

                     JOJO
          (annoyed at interruption)
          -- that too. There's things out there,
          boy, that their grandparents used to be
          human. They catch you, they'll cut your
          balls off and eat 'em while you watch.

                    SPIDER
          Yeah, but you have weapons. Bows, and,
          and arrows, and stuff. And I have my
          stuff here, dollars --

Spider scatters his stuff across the table as he
talks.

                  SPIDER (CONT.)
          -- a hundred and ninety-three of 'em,
          real American dollars, invaluable for
          playing Capitalism. If you're going to
          be Russians, you'll need plenty of this
          stuff. Also we have a notebook
          computer, a CD player with a dozen CDs,
          featuring the rap stylings of Sir Mix-
          A-Lot, two cans of Bud Dry --
          (holds can like Vanna White)
          -- doesn't it just shout "Quality?"

The crowd is playing with the items as Spider
lays them out. Abruptly "Baby Got Back", Sir Mix-
A-Lot's paean to women with big butts, blasts out.

NEW ANGLE -- THREE SHOT, JOJO, ANGEL, MICHAEL

JoJo examines the computer, staring at the screen.

                           JOJO
                   (pointing)
          What are those?

Michael shrugs; Angel peers at it.

                          ANGEL
          Words ... those are words.

NEW ANGLE -- GROUP SHOT FAVORING SPIDER

                   SIR MIX-A-LOT (V.O.)
          Baby got back!

Spider pops a Bud, hands it to JoJo.

                          SPIDER
          Right off the desert, room temperature.
          Exactly how it's drunk, by gentlemen of
          distinction, through much of the
          Southwest. You get me my time machine,
          and I can get you as much of this stuff
          as you want.

JoJo sips at it ... makes a face and tosses it
over his shoulder, to spray against the back wall.

                           JOJO
                   (now openly hostile)
          We make better.

                          SPIDER
                   (producing AmEx card)
          American Express ... it's a Gold Card,
          boys and girls ...
                   (waggles it at them)
          Good throughout the civilized world ...
          not that you really qualify ...

                    (sighs at their lack of
                    response, flips it away)
               Canceled anyway.

Spider stares down into his almost-empty bag.

INSERT -- SHOT INTO BAG

We see a magazine -- and the automatic Spider
took off the dead dude.

RETURN TO PREVIOUS

Spider glances at JoJo, reaches in, and pulls out
... a copy of <u>Penthouse</u>.

                         SPIDER
               Don't need to <u>read</u> to understand this.

There's a brief silence as the men gather around
Spider -- and then JoJo grabs the magazine and
starts leafing through it. The other men try to
touch it and he jerks it away.

                         JOJO
               Keep your filthy hands off. It's <u>mine</u>.

                        MICHAEL
               We are <u>not</u> going out into the desert
               just for those pictures.

JoJo glares at her -- and we learn something
about how things are run around here:

                        MICHAEL
          No.

                         SPIDER
          There's a quantum black hole in the
          center of that time machine.

They don't understand this -- but it gets their
attention.

                         ANGEL
          You said that hole thing fell out.

ON SPIDER -- HE GRINS

                         SPIDER
          I lied. But if you leave the time
          machine out there, the black hole will
          fall out when the power supply fails.
          It'll fall to the center of the Earth,
          eating everything in its path. In a few
          days the earthquakes will start. You
          won't get a lot of warning -- maybe one
          Really Bad Earthquake -- and then the
          black hole will expand logarithmically,
          gamma rays from atoms being torn apart
          will fry you like bacon in the instants
          before tidal effects tear you into
          subatomic particles.

WIDEN SHOT ON CROWD -- DEAD SILENCE -- A BEAT

Nobody knows what this means, but it sure sounds
bad.

                         JOJO
          We'll go get it tomorrow ... if Tommy
          can get the truck to start.

EXT. THE GARAGE -- ON SPIDER -- DAY

He sits on a bench, waiting impatiently, while
TOMMY and TERRY work on an engine together,
ignoring him.

                         SPIDER
            Any day now, guy.

Tommy ignores him. Spider sighs, glances at his
watch, looks up -- startled, he looks back at the
watch --

INSERT WATCH

It shows 10:02:11 PM. The seconds reading is
frozen ... after a very long pause it clicks to
10:02:12 PM.

RETURN TO PREVIOUS ANGLE -- ON SPIDER

A bemused expression. He looks up as Tommy
finally approaches him. Tommy's an old man;
picture Robert Duvall perhaps, an old man with
some air of authority still. He's been babying
these machines since childhood -- of course,
they're all older than he is. He's bright and
sharp and hasn't lost a step. His assistant Terry
is a plump 40ish woman, visible in BG throughout
this scene.

PANNING SHOT OF TOMMY'S TOOLS

The tools, lovingly cared for, are wrapped in oil
cloth. They're wildly out of place; they look new.

RETURN TO PREVIOUS ANGLE

Tommy approaches Spider, wiping his hands as he
talks.

                    TOMMY
Saw them bring ya in. Ya human?

                    SPIDER
Not first thing in the morning. You're
Tommy, right?

                    TOMMY
Ya ever et human flesh?

                    SPIDER
I've had Jack In The Box.

                    TOMMY
        (remembering)
Jack ... Jack ... no, don't remember
anyone named Jack, not in your lifetime
anyway. I suppose I'll fix up the truck
for you.

                    SPIDER
I guess you couldn't fix the truck for
me if I'd eaten someone you knew.

                    TOMMY
        (studies him)
I'd of had to object. Ya can't put up
with that sort of thing, not casual-
like, or next thing winter comes --

                    SPIDER
I get the picture.

                    TOMMY
Ever et anybody <u>except</u> that Jack?

                    SPIDER
No. About the truck --

                    TOMMY
          Mornin', day after tomorrow.

                    SPIDER
          Two <u>days?</u> Look, I have to go in the
          morning, I --

                    TOMMY
          Not a chance. Tomorrow afternoon,
          <u>maybe</u>. But we won't go out in the
          afternoon, we might get caught out in
          the dark.

                    SPIDER
          I spent last night out on the desert. I
          didn't get hurt.

                    TOMMY
          You was lucky, then.

                    SPIDER
          That could be argued. Look, if we get
          some extra people to help you --

                    TOMMY
          Outta my four boys, only JoJo lived.
          Too stubborn to die. He'll argue with
          the world until it shuts up and does
          what he wants. But I can't be argued
          with and I can't be reasoned with --

                    SPIDER
          -- and you absolutely <u>will not stop</u>
          <u>until I am dead</u>.[26]

------

[26] The Terminator.

                          TOMMY
                    (turning away)
              You a strange boy. Truck'll be ready
              day after tomorrow, first light.

WIDE ANGLE -- SHOT OF THE TOWN -- NIGHT

MEDIUM SHOT -- SPIDER

He's sitting up on one of the empty guard posts,
illuminated by torch light, looking down on the
quiet town.

CLOSE SHOT SPIDER

Tears trickle down his cheeks.

INT. BEDROOM -- TWO SHOT -- NIGHT

Michael and Angel lie together in bed, whispering
together.

                          MICHAEL
              He's very strange.

                          ANGEL
              Yes.

                          MICHAEL
              I think I like him.

                          ANGEL
                    (smiles)
              All right.

                    MICHAEL
          He's not as old as JoJo. If we had
          babies with him ... maybe they'd live.
          And maybe he could stay, and take care
          of them with us.

INT. LAB, 2000 -- A CROWD OF FAMILIES --

-- waiting to go through the Gate. Superimposed:
73 MINUTES BEFORE THE FIRE. Jimbo walks among
them, calming them.

                    JIMBO
          Just stay cool! As soon as we get a
          synch on the remote Gate everyone will
          go through! Everyone will go through!

INT. A CONFERENCE ROOM --

Half a dozen staff are standing around watching
CNN. One of them is Caroline, holding a little
girl of about three. A boy of ten or so stands
beside them.

                    CNN ANNOUNCER
          We'll broadcast as long as we can keep
          our satellite uplink ... reports of
          missile launches from the Pan Asian
          coalition are unconfirmed, I repeat,
          unconfirmed. So far as we can
          determine, only New York City and Hong
          Kong have been destroyed ...

ON CAROLINE -- NEW ANGLE

In the BG, we see JACK HOLLAND, still dripping
wet from decontamination, pushing through the
crowds; Caroline catches sight of him and quickly
gives the little girl to her brother, the ten-

year old.

                    CAROLINE
          Watch your sister.

NEW ANGLE -- TRACKING JACK HOLLAND

He pushes his way through the crowds, into the
warehouse with the huge Time Gate, with Caroline,
unnoticed, on his heels. Jack is a decade younger
than Spider; a Navy SEAL -- tough and resourceful
and patriotic. He's not really even a bad guy,
though he plays one in the movies.

Genevieve looks up at his approach.

                    GENEVIEVE
          Where the hell have you <u>been?</u> We've had
          a nanovirus outbreak, reports of
          missiles launches, we can't get a lock
          on the remote Gate --

                    HOLLAND
               (very calmly)
          What?

                    CAROLINE
          We can't get a lock --

                    HOLLAND
          I heard that part. You sent someone
          through with the remote Gate? Sweet
          Jesus, who?

                    GENEVIEVE
          Well ... uh, Spider. We sent Spider.
               (on Holland's angry reaction)
          You weren't <u>here</u>, Jack.

Holland turns away from her.

                    HOLLAND
          How quickly can you power the Gate?

Jimbo glances at Genevieve -- answer him? She
nods.

                    JIMBO
          We've been recharging since Spider went
          through. We'll hit Ready in about
          twelve minutes.

                    CAROLINE
              (reading her instruments)
          We're still locked on Spider's send-
          through, we've been drifting downtime a
          little on it and it would take two
          hours to recalc, two hours we don't
          have. You'll come in about two days
          after he did --
              (pause; she looks at Holland)
          He took a motorcycle with him.

Holland stares at her a beat -- then turns and
runs through the crowd clogging the corridors, to
the parking lot.

                    HOLLAND
          Our of the way! Out of my way!

EXT. BRIDGE, 2100 -- LONG SHOT -- DAY

Angel is standing guard duty. Spider walks toward
her, from town, carrying his bag. Angel watches
him approach.

TWO SHOT

                    SPIDER
          Brought you some lunch.

                    ANGEL
               (politely)
          Why?

                    SPIDER
          You tried to kill me yesterday.

                    ANGEL
          So?

                    SPIDER
          Got my attention. Reminded me a little
          of my ex-wife.

Spider sits on the ground near Angel; Angel
glances around at the bridge, at their empty
surroundings and, a little uncomfortably, joins
him. He speaks while opening his travel bag and
taking out their lunch --

                    SPIDER
          We got water, bread, and dried, salted
          chicken ... next time I time travel,
          I'm bringing some Taco Bell.

Angel doesn't appear to hear him; she's tearing
into the chicken. Spider sighs, staring at her.

                    SPIDER
          The woman who gave me this pointed out
          there weren't any flies on it.

                    ANGEL
          (nods; seriously)
     It's better when there's no flies ...
     does Tommy have the truck running?

                    SPIDER
     Working on a bad axle ... what the hell
     is your name?

Angel studies Spider -- eating, calculating.
Finally:

                    ANGEL
     Angel.

                    SPIDER
     And your girlfriend's name?

                    ANGEL
     Michael.

                    SPIDER
     Really. I think I expected you to be
     the one with the butch name.

                    ANGEL
     The what name?

                    SPIDER
     Never mind. Doesn't matter.

Angel nods; she believes that. She finishes her
bread, sucks back the water, and stands up again,
bow in hand.

                    ANGEL
     I have to get back to work now.

                         SPIDER
          Do I make you uncomfortable?

                         ANGEL
               (considers)
          No.

                         SPIDER
          Why the hurry? You see mutants out
          there somewhere?

                         ANGEL
          I see 'em all the time.

                         SPIDER
          And kill them.

                         ANGEL
          All the time.

                         SPIDER
          Well, I guess I appreciate your not
          killing me.

                         ANGEL
               (unsmiling)
          Could happen.

INT. LAB SHOWERS, 2100 -- NIGHT

A Humvee is being scrubbed down by two men in
decontamination suits[27]. SUPERIMPOSE WITH: <u>69</u>
<u>MINUTES BEFORE THE FIRE.</u>

---

[27]   We cleverly ignore the issue of how they actually got the damned thing
into the showers.

                    SUIT #1 (RADIO VOICE)
          I can't believe we're doing this --
          first a Harley and now a Humvee --

                    SUIT #2 (RADIO VOICE)
          Man, this is the Cadillac of military
          transport vehicles ... you got no
          appreciation for style, that's your
          problem.

                    SUIT #1 (RADIO VOICE)
          Six years in grad school ... so that I
          could spend the last day of my life
          working in a car wash.

Suit #1 scrubs away viciously.

INT. LAB -- TWO SHOT JIMBO AND CAROLINE WATCHING
CNN

Genevieve and Holland are visible talking in the
BG, their BARELY AUDIBLE VOICES blending with CNN.

                    CAROLINE
          What do you think?

                    JIMBO
          If it goes up, everyone will launch at
          once. Us, Pan-Asians, the Russians;
          they'll all have to, or else lose
          first-strike capability. Right now
          everyone's waiting to see how the
          nanovirus strikes went --

                    CAROLINE
          They're going to launch, aren't they?

                         JIMBO
              (beat)
          Oh yeah.

                       CAROLINE
          (voice breaking)
     Jimmy, I am so fucking scared.

Jimbo takes her in his arms and she holds on,
trembling.

                     CAROLINE (CONT.)
     We should have sent _anyone_ except
     Spider.

                         JIMBO
     Hang in there. Spider'll get the Gate
     open. Hang in there, darlin'.

EXT. CATWALK, 2100 -- LONG SHOT OVERLOOKING TOWN
-- NIGHT

Spider's sitting up on the catwalk, watching the
quiet evening. In the BG, we can see the
nighttime desert, glowing with radioactivity.

EXT. CATWALK -- MEDIUM SHOT, SPIDER BY HIMSELF

Angel and Michael enter. Michael's carrying a
tray.

                       MICHAEL
     We brought you dinner.

They sit down across from him, settling in as
though they assume he wants their company.

                    SPIDER
          (quietly)
     No flies on it, right?

This comment visibly ticks Angel off.

                    MICHAEL
          (puzzled)
     It's beans and potatoes. They don't get
     hung up to dry, so the flies don't --

                    SPIDER
          (accepting plate, spoon)
     Right. Thanks.

He picks at the beans and potatoes, takes a bite.

                    ANGEL
     Look, I'm sorry I tried to kill you,
     okay?

                    SPIDER
          (eating)
     Don't mention it.

                    ANGEL
          (pissed she has to)
     I wasn't going to, but you seem to be
     holding it against me.

                    SPIDER
     Why would you care?

                    ANGEL
     I don't. Well, not much. But Michael
     wants you to sleep with us and if
     you're mad at me you might not.

Silence. Spider stares a bit, then takes another
bite.

                         SPIDER
          Been reading my <u>Penthouse</u>, have you?

                         MICHAEL
          Your what?

                         SPIDER
          The magazine I gave JoJo. It concerns
          itself with situations like this.

                         MICHAEL
          Oh. No, we haven't.

                         ANGEL
               (to Michael, quietly)
          I'll read it to you if you want.

                         SPIDER
          Where did this idea come from?

Angel's suggestion has distracted Michael
slightly.

                         MICHAEL
          ... I want to have children. I tried to
          have children with JoJo, but they both
          died.

                         ANGEL
          You look healthy. She thinks if she has
          children with you they might live.

                         MICHAEL
               (to Angel)
          Do you <u>mind?</u>

The subtext being, _I can explain myself._

> ANGEL
>> (in disgust)
> She's all worked up over this.

> SPIDER
> And you're obviously _not_.

This _really_ ticks Angel off.

> ANGEL
> You're talking about my shooting at you
> again, aren't you? _Dangerous things_
> come off the desert --

> SPIDER
> And you thought I might be one.

> MICHAEL
> You have that look.

> SPIDER
> So you tried to kill me.

> ANGEL
>> (sullenly)
> Haven't decided _yet_ it was a bad idea.

> SPIDER
>> (laughs)
> This is lousy seduction technique.

A momentary silence. Angel and Michael glare at
each other briefly; then they all eat for a bit.

> MICHAEL
> ... are you really from the past?

                         SPIDER
     Yep.

The next question obviously has great meaning to
them:

                         ANGEL
     From before the Fire?

                         SPIDER
     If I understand you ... yeah. The world
     was sure as hell on fire when I left it.

                         MICHAEL
     Why did you come here?

                         SPIDER
     That's a long story.

They look at each other and shrug; they have time.

                         SPIDER
                    (practically bursting)
     We built a time machine. I mean,
     Christ, we spent years on it. I was
     working on it when I got married; I was
     still working on it when my wife
     divorced me and took my daughters to
     New York. We'd sent two probes through,
     and we were supposed to send our first
     live subject through early next month.
     This Navy SEAL, Jack Holland. Then ...
     two nights ago, I guess, the PanAsian
     coalition nuked one of our South
     Pacific naval bases. Then the
     nanoviruses hit, then Hong Kong went
     up, and then New York ...

                    (fiddles with his food)
          We had some warning in Los Angeles. Not
          much. We gathered at the lab, and we
          were going to send our trained SEAL
          through with the remote Gate. But he
          hadnt shown yet when I got there, so
          they sent me instead.

                         ANGEL
          Why you?

                         SPIDER
                    (louder, growing angry)
          They looked for somebody who was brave
          and stout of heart ... had an assault
          record. And how many talented, violent
          computer programmers are there out
          there? Not many, by God, and damn few
          as witty and well-dressed as me.

                         MICHAEL
          What are you so <u>angry</u> about?

NEW ANGLE -- THREE SHOT FAVORING ANGEL

During Spider's following monologue, the CAMERA
STAYS ON ANGEL, watching her reactions -- she
flinches as though struck when Spider hits the
phrase "bring them through."

                         SPIDER
     The world _ended_. I saw it die, saw
     nanoviruses eat people alive, saw the
     mushroom clouds on CNN. I look out at
     this hellhole you live in and I _know,_
     nobody made it, nobody survived. No one
     I know or care about. They sent me
     through to save their lives,
     sonsabitches have _no_ style, okay, _Jimbo,_
     sure, but he rides a Ninja, minus two
     big style points, them and their
     families clustered around the Gate when
     I went through, staring at me, waiting
     for me to save their butts, find a new
     Garden of Eden and set up the Gate and
     bring them through before the fires of
     Hell come down on them --
          (pause)
     My ex-wife and daughters were in
     Manhattan ... . They _were._ Now they're
     radioactive dust.

Spider looks away at the nighttime desert, the
distant radioactive glow.

                    SPIDER (CONT.)
     Have been for two days. Or a hundred
     years, whichever comes first.

                      MICHAEL
     Gate? Bring them ... through?

                       ANGEL
          (shakes her head slowly)
     Spiderdevlin, there's no _room_ here.

INT. TOWN HALL -- WIDE ANGLE SHOT -- MORNING

Spider enters. Waiting for him are about half the
town's inhabitants, and JoJo, Angel, Michael, and
Tommy. They're embroiled in an argument when
Spider enters. JoJo stands.

                    JOJO
          What the hell is this about bringing
          people to live here?

The hostility in his voice slows Spider a second.

                    SPIDER
          The time machine ... the Gate. That's
          what it's for.

                    JOJO
          I can't let you do that.

                    SPIDER
          But you don't even believe I'm from the
          past. Remember? So going to go get my
          time machine is no big deal.

When Michael talks she's being as reasonable and
as honest as she can be -- on a difficult subject.

                    MICHAEL
          I had two children and neither one
          survived their first winter. We don't
          have enough in the summers and we
          barely survive the winters. Now you
          want to bring more people --

Mentioning dead children is not the best approach
with Spider. His response is <u>intended</u> to hurt her
--

                    SPIDER
          Didn't _you_ want to work on making
          people, with a little help from me?

                    ANGEL
          Spiderdevlin! That's --

Michael overrides her -- with anger that matches
Spider's.

                    MICHAEL
          That's _not fair!_ We could have left you
          out there in the desert and you'd be
          dead now! We don't have enough food and
          we don't have enough water and -- how
          many people are you talking about?

Spider's been living in his own grief; her anger
takes him by surprise, and he tells the truth.

                    SPIDER
          About two hundred.

The crowd's reaction is shock -- they can't even
imagine two hundred people. That's _five times_ the
size of the human race as they know it. JoJo
speaks numbly:

                    JOJO
          No. No. No ... there's only forty ...
          of us. We can't do it, that's too many,
          Spiderdevlin. We can't --

Spider takes a step forward, eyes glittering --

                    SPIDER
          Couldn't get the truck running, huh?

                    TOMMY
              (blankly)
         The truck is fine.

Spider moves toward them, radiating rage --

                    SPIDER
         The hell you say. I don't know why I
         imagined you people would be of any use
         anyway, you incompetent, illiterate
         barbarians, crouched in the shadows of
         buildings other people raised, using
         machines other people built, staring at
         the women in your copy of Penthouse
         because --
              (voice raising to a shout)
         -- YOU CAN'T READ THE DIRTY LETTERS IN
         IT, CAN YOU?

The moment hangs there, Spider staring in his
rage at the crowd, not knowing what's going to
happen next -- JoJo steps forward, equally angry,
but in control.

                    JOJO
         We're not going to leave your time
         machine out there for the mutants.
         We'll go get it -- but you won't like
         what I'm going to do to it.

NEW ANGLE -- CROWD DISBANDING -- FAVORING SPIDER

The crowd passes Spider like a river around a
boulder.

CLOSE ON ANGEL -- SPIDER'S POV

She glares at him with barely contained fury.

                         ANGEL
            I know how to read.

NEW ANGLE -- TRACKING JOJO

He brushes by Spider, stops, turns and walks
toward Angel --

FLASH: JOJO, FROM SPIDER'S POV

SFX: A raven is perched on JoJo's shoulder,
looking at Spider, at us, its eyes shining with
the ripple effect.

RETURN TO TRACKING SHOT --

                         JOJO
            You better get him armed. We run into
            trouble --
                 (turns to face Spider)
            -- you'll fight -- or die -- with the
            rest of us.

Spider leans in on JoJo, and whispers in his ear
in a harsh, chilling voice:

                         SPIDER
            There's a black bird on your shoulder.

INT. ARMORY -- TWO SHOT ANGEL AND SPIDER -- DAY

A room with rifles, shotguns, machine guns,
pistols, bows and arrows, swords, knives --
Spider is obviously shaken looking at it all.
Spider reaches out to touch a shotgun -- he just
brushes his fingers over it.

                         SPIDER
            God, I hate guns.

                         ANGEL
                    (shrugs)
               These guns are perfectly safe.

                         SPIDER
                    (thinks he understands her)
               Right ... guns don't kill people ...
               people kill people. Right?

Angel stares as if he's the craziest thing she
ever saw.

                         ANGEL
               No. The _bullets,_ Spiderdevlin. The
               bullets kill the people.
                    (shakes her head)
               We've been out of bullets for a really
               long time. You better take a bow and
               some arrows.

EXT. DESERT -- LONG SHOT THE "TRUCK" -- DAY

A '95 Chevy longbed tools through the desert,
making about ten miles an hour. The wheels are
wood and the tires are tightly wound rag cloth.
The steering wheel is a crowbar, welded into
place, and there's no glass, mirrors, or chrome.
Tommy is driving and lecturing Terry in the front
seat. In the flatbed are Spider, Angel, JoJo, and
assorted extras. Michael hasn't come. Spider sits
slightly apart from the others, next to a large
can of gasoline.

NEW ANGLE -- THROUGH EMPTY FRONT WINDSHIELD,
FAVORING TOMMY

                         TOMMY
          ... and that there is the speed gauge
          and it tells you how fast you're going.
          You see it goes up to a hunnerd twenny
          em pee aitch --

CLOSE SHOT -- SPIDER

A compound bow propped at his side. He closes his
eyes and leans back in the rocking flatbed.

                    TOMMY (V.O., CONT.)
          -- that was a joke by those built this
          truck. The human body <u>explodes</u> if it
          goes above sixty em pee aitch, that's a
          scientific fact, I seen it happen once
          when I was a spud.

                         SPIDER
               (muttering, eyes closed)
          Probably just had one too many after-
          dinner mints.[28]

                       ANGEL (V.O.)
          Spiderdevlin?

                         SPIDER
               (eyes closed)
          They're <u>wafer-thin</u>.

                       ANGEL (V.O.)
          I never understand you.

---

[28] Monty Python and the Meaning of Life.

                    SPIDER
              (eyes closed)
     Accessibility is overrated. You have to
     throw in little in-jokes, or else the
     critics don't feel smarter than
     everyone else, and then where are you?
     Off-off-Broadway, or the Santa Monica
     Playhouse, whichever comes first.

TWO-SHOT -- SPIDER AND ANGEL -- DESERT IN BG

Spider opens his eyes to find Angel watching him.
This line should play amusingly, but <u>Spider's</u> not
making a joke when he speaks -- he's <u>depressed</u>:

                    SPIDER
     This is as bad as San Bernardino.

CLOSE SHOT OF MOTORCYCLE -- FROM GROUND --

-- with the time machine tied to the passenger
bar. The truck is approaching in the BG. The
truck pulls to a halt and people come spilling
out of it. The SHOT STAYS ON THE MOTORCYCLE --
people approach the motorcycle, moving out of
frame; all we see are their feet.

                    JOJO (V.O.)
     So this is your "Harley."

                    SPIDER (V.O.)
     You bet.

                    ANGEL (V.O.)
     You put gas in this ... and it goes.

                    SPIDER (V.O.)
     Like the Energizer Rabbit, darlin'.

Hands reach down INTO FRAME --

NEW ANGLE -- GROUP SHOT W/HARLEY IN FG, TRUCK IN
BG --

-- and Spider hauls the machine up and onto its
wheels.

                        JOJO
              The Energizer Rabbit?

Spider stares at them. Angel makes a little
clapping gesture with her hands -- the rabbit
with its cymbals.

                        ANGEL
        It keeps going and going and going.

Spider stares DIRECTLY INTO THE CAMERA for a beat
-- then JoJo steps forward with a knife, slices
the ropes holding the time machine, and lifts the
time machine free.

                        JOJO
          We'll just carry this in the truck.

Spider shakes himself and unlocks the gas tank as
Tommy brings the gas can over -- he speaks loudly
while filling the tank, without looking away.

                        SPIDER
              You be careful. Black hole ... very
              dangerous. Boom. I've seen it a
              thousand times. Massive trauma.
              Horrible. Just horrible.

NEW ANGLE -- FAVORING JOJO W/TIME MACHINE

He lays it carefully on a piece of cloth in the

flatbed.

                              JOJO
                        (to himself)
                  That thing'll fall over before he gets
                  five feet.

WIDE ANGLE -- DESERT -- AFTERNOON

The truck makes its slow way back toward town.
Spider zooms around the truck, at thirty, forty
miles to an hour, making wide, slaloming loops,
sand spraying up into the air --

NEW ANGLE -- FAVORING ANGEL, JOJO IN BG

She watches the bike zooming around. Angel is in
love -- with the bike, of course.

NEW ANGLE -- TRUCK FROM REAR

Spider pulls alongside the truck, which continues
to tool along at 8 or 9 miles an hour. Spider
grins at Angel.

                              SPIDER
                  Want to ride back with me?

                              JOJO
                  No she _doesn't_ --

Too late. Angel's already leaped over the edge of
the flatbed, onto the still-moving motorcycle.

NEW ANGLE -- ANGEL SEATING HERSELF ON THE BIKE
BEHIND SPIDER

With the truck in BG. The sexual angle should not
be underplayed -- she settles herself in, molding

herself against Spider. Spider doesn't seem to
notice her; he's exchanging fuck-you stares with
JoJo.

                    ANGEL
          Come on. Go ... . go fast.

NEW ANGLE -- TRACKING -- SPIDER PEELS OUT --

-- showering sand over the truck. CAMERA FOLLOWS
as they zoom off into the desert --

EXT. DESERT -- LONG SHOT HARLEY -- LATE AFTERNOON

The Harley is parked beside a small rise; Spider
and Angel have found some convenient shade.
Spider's drinking from a water bottle; Angel is
lying back with her hands beneath her head,
totally relaxed.

NEW ANGLE -- TWO SHOT SPIDER AND ANGEL

                    SPIDER
          So ... did you explode when we passed
          sixty em pee aitch?

                    ANGEL
               (drowsily)
          I think it was right about then.

Spider looks off toward the horizon.

                    SPIDER
          I think I see the truck coming.

                    ANGEL
          JoJo's going to be mad at you.

                    SPIDER
          Oh, I expect.

                    ANGEL
          You don't care.

CLOSE ON SPIDER

He's pissed off a lot of people in his time --
and his answer is immediate and automatic, with a
slight smile:

                    SPIDER
          Fuck him if he can't take a joke.

EXT. BRIDGE -- LATE AFTERNOON

Michael's standing guard, with an ugly fellow of
thirty, CLARK. Clark's got a cancerous,
disfiguring skin disease; he is evidently not
long for the world. Michael looks into the
distance -- and then lifts a spyglass to her
right eye. (The spyglass is an ancient pair of
binoculars, sawed in half.)

                    MICHAEL
          People coming.

She passes the spyglass to Clark. He looks --

                    CLARK
          That ain't the truck.

CLOSE SHOT -- MICHAEL

                    MICHAEL
              (start of a smile)
          No ... that's Trader Joe.

EXT. GUARD POST -- TWO SHOT TJ AND MICHAEL --
SUNSET

They're looking out into the darkening desert.

                    MICHAEL
          ... and then he made JoJo take the
          truck out into the desert. It's getting
          dark and they're not back.

NEW ANGLE -- FAVORING TRADER JOE

TRADER JOE is a man of indeterminate age --
forty, fifty. He's clean-shaven and fit, wearing
carefully nondescript clothing: jeans, vest,
white long-sleeved shirt, sandals. A pair of
granny glasses poke up out of his shirt pocket.

                    TRADER JOE
          You say he kicked his time machine.

                    MICHAEL
               (shrugs)
          That's what Angel said he said -- I'm
          afraid that "black hole" got them.

                    TRADER JOE
          Don't worry. He probably lied about the
          black hole.

                    MICHAEL
          What makes you -- what's that?

NEW ANGLE -- WIDE SHOT OF DESERT, MICHAEL AND TJ
IN FG

A firefly appears to be bobbing around in the far
distance.

RETURN TO PREVIOUS ANGLE --

                    TRADER JOE
            (smiles)
        That's a headlight.

                    MICHAEL
        A "head light?"

                    TRADER JOE
        The Harley they went to go get,
        Michael. The motorcycle.

MEDIUM SHOT -- TRUCK, FAVORING SPIDER

He sits on the tailgate of the truck, smiling --

TRACKING SHOT -- ON ANGEL, ON THE HARLEY --

-- zooming around the truck, having the time of
her life.

EXT. TOWN -- THE EMPTY GARAGE -- NIGHT

The truck is parked; the time machine has been
unloaded and put up on a work table in the
garage; the status LED is a vague red light on
its surface. The motorcycle is parked by the
truck. Another vehicle is BARELY VISIBLE at the
side of the shot. We PAN to Trader Joe's vehicle.
Also a truck -- it has four wheels and a flatbed
full of boxes. But the passenger cab is open to
the air, like an old-time buggy. There's no
visible engine --

INT. TOWN HALL -- WIDE ANGLE -- NIGHT

The room is well-lit by firelight. Virtually
everyone who's alive in 2100 appears in this

scene, excepting a couple of people standing
guard duty. Spider sits at the far end of the
table, with Angel standing (by choice) beside
him; JoJo, Michael, Trader Joe, etc., are all
gathered together near the table head.

ANGLE ON SPIDER AND ANGEL

Spider watches TJ with obvious wariness. TJ
barely appears to notice Spider; he's busy laying
out trade goods.

                    ANGEL
        He comes by every two years to trade.
        His people are up north. I don't know
        why he's back so soon; he was just here
        at the end of winter.

                    SPIDER
        How long has he been coming here?

                    ANGEL
            (puzzled by question)
        Always.

                    SPIDER
        Trader Joe ... that's a goofy name.

                    ANGEL
        It is <u>not.</u> Tommy named JoJo for him.

Spider stares at her.

                    SPIDER
        That man can't be more than forty.[29]

____

[29]   Or fifty, or whatever, depending on the actor. But clearly too young for JoJo
       to have been named after him; JoJo and Trader Joe should be about the
       same age.

NEW ANGLE -- FAVORING TRADER JOE, W/SPIDER IN BG

                    JOJO
          We weren't expecting you back so soon.
          We haven't refined hardly any gasoline
          since you left, just enough for
          ourselves.

                    MICHAEL
          Not enough to trade.

                    TRADER JOE
               (keeps laying out goods)
          ... and here we've got antibiotics.
          That's the stuff that cures infections,
          you remember I brought a batch two
          trips ago. It helps during childbirth,
          too.

He finishes and gestures at the tabletop.

                    TRADER JOE (CONT.)
          Tools for Tommy, two new books for
          Angel.
               (to Angel)
          Brought you the dictionary I promised.
               (to JoJo again)
          Also 8 boxes of spark plugs, 20 bags of
          cracked wheat, 5 cases of canned corn,
          and the water distiller I promised ...
          I have a feeling this winter's going to
          be a bad one.

                    JOJO
          I got nothing to trade with.

                         TRADER JOE
          And in return, all I ask is fifty cans
          of gasoline.
                    (pause; quietly)
          You can pay me my next trip.

                           JOJO
                    (breaks into a huge grin)
          Deal.
                    (starts yelling orders)
          You! And you, too! You all get out
          there and get to unloading Trader Joe's
          truck. Tools go to Tommy, the book goes
          to Angel, food and medicine to the
          store room. Move! Move!

People hop to, with a will -- not unlike a crowd
of refugees dealing with a Red Cross delivery.
(Which, of course, is pretty close to the truth.)

CLOSE SHOT -- SPIDER

Motionless, staring across the room at Trader Joe
--

FLASH: TJ, FROM SPIDER'S POV

The ripple effect is crawling all over him --

CLOSE SHOT -- TRADER JOE

He glances at Spider.

FLASH: SPIDER AND ANGEL, FROM TRADER JOE'S POV

Spider stands there, motionless -- except that
its not Spider, exactly; its an older man, with a
terrible scar where his left eye used to be. Hes
looking back at Trader Joe and he looks dire --

dangerous and almost evil. The ripple effect
crawls over him -- and abruptly its just Spider
and Angel, and then an arrow pierces Spider, a
bullet strikes Angel, blood spraying from the
exit wound --

All in the space of a second or so.

RETURN TO PREVIOUS SHOT -- TJ, NO SFX

He shakes his head, plainly disturbed.

TWO SHOT SPIDER AND ANGEL

                    SPIDER
          Bad news.

EXT. GARAGE -- ANGLE UPWARD -- NIGHT

All is still. CAMERA PANS across the empty
garage, over the time machine, by itself with its
blinking red LED. A SINGLE GUARD sits near it,
half awake. WE CONTINUE TO PAN right, to the
empty main street, showing two guards at the
watchtowers, PANNING FURTHER --

The CAMERA CEASES PANNING on Trader Joe. He
strides toward us, his manner grim and severe,
utterly different from the cheerful, almost
professorial fellow we've seen so far.

CLOSE SHOT -- TRACKING TRADER JOE

In his right hand he's holding a hand grenade
with a glowing, non-Arabic numeral on the side of
it.

TWO SHOT -- TJ AND GUARD --

The guard looks up, looks briefly startled --

                    TRADER JOE
          Go to sleep.

The guard does. Trader Joe has barely broken
stride on his way to the Gate.

INSERT -- SHOT OF GRENADE

Trader Joe runs a thumb over a particular
spot ... and the glowing "numerals" start
counting down.

CLOSE SHOT -- TRADER JOE AND TIME MACHINE

He reaches forward to attach the explosive to the
side of Spider's time machine.

                    SPIDER (V.O.)
          I want you to pretend that you have a
          14-shot, 9 millimeter automatic pointed
          at the back of your skull.

Trader Joe turns around, the SHOT WIDENING ...
the hand grenade counting down in his hand.
Spider is of course pointing the automatic at him.

                    TRADER JOE
          I _do_ have a 14-shot, 9 millimeter
          automatic pointed at me.

                    SPIDER
          Power of imagination, man.

Trader Joe thinks it over ... then runs a thumb
over the grenade. The blinking "numerals" freeze.

                    SPIDER
          Good boy. Let's you and me go somewhere
          private.
                    (Glances at sleeping guard)
          And if you even think about trying any
          Jedi mind tricks, I'm going to shoot
          you.

EXT. OTHER END OF TOWN -- TWO SHOT -- NIGHT

Spider and Trader Joe are sitting together
beneath one of the fences. Spider's still
pointing the gun at Trader Joe; the hand grenade
is on the ground between them.

                    SPIDER
          Trader Joe is a goofy damn name.

                    TRADER JOE
          Spider's nothing to write home about.

                    SPIDER
          Where you from?

                    TRADER JOE
          Up north. About two hundred miles.

                    SPIDER
          You know, I've never shot a man before
          -- stabbed one once, that's a real long
          story -- but right now you're tempting
          me to put a cap in your ass. Whatcha
          got against my time machine? <u>Why did
          you show up here two days after me?</u>

                    TRADER JOE
          That's also a long story, Spider.

                         SPIDER
          I'm a little tight on time and --
               (jacks a round in chamber)
          -- patience I am <u>way</u> short on. You
          monitored my stochastic wave. <u>That's</u>
          what brought you here two days after
          me. The wave function collapsed and you
          rode the wave front back to its
          source ... <u>When are you from?</u>

Trader Joe thinks it over and then nods.

                       TRADER JOE
          Most recently ... about fifteen hundred
          years uptime of here. And I wish I knew
          what to do with you.

                         SPIDER
          So what's your real name, Future Boy?

                       TRADER JOE
          That's a difficult question --

                         SPIDER
          I am gonna <u>kill</u> you.

                       TRADER JOE
          Most recently I've been called Maktai
          Shumaktikahn Dekshuperai.

                         SPIDER
          What the hell kind of name is that?

                       TRADER JOE
               (shrugs)
          It means ... "This Guy Joe We Found In
          Pasadena In 1968."

                         SPIDER
                    (flatly)
          1968. Hippies. The Summer of Love.

Trader Joe reaches into his shirt pocket ...
carefully takes out a pair of ancient granny
glasses, and puts them on. He smiles at
Spider ... and makes a peace sign.

                       TRADER JOE
          Peace, little brother.

Spider turns away in disgust, gun dropping to his
side.

INT. TOWN HALL -- WIDE ANGLE -- SPIDER AND TRADER
JOE

They're sitting at the long table, facing one
another across the narrow length, drinking the
flat brown beer the town makes. The "hand
grenade" is next to Spider's mug.

                         SPIDER
          You know they're using the wheat you
          bring them to make this.

                       TRADER JOE
          Man does not live by bread alone. At
          least it's good beer.

                         SPIDER
          I've had lots worse ... in good
          restaurants. You going to try and stop
          me from fixing my time machine, Future
          Boy?

                    TRADER JOE
          Why do you keep calling me that?

                     SPIDER
               (shrugs)
          I feel silly calling you Trader Joe,
          and Captain Galaxy was already taken.[30]
          Answer the question.

                    TRADER JOE
          You can't bring those people through,
          Spider.

                     SPIDER
          I expect I can. I helped program that
          machine out there, Future Boy. It's
          showing <u>offline</u>, which means the
          diagnostic circuitry knows something's
          wrong, and knows what it is -- which
          means I can fix it. I <u>wrote</u> those
          diagnostic routines.

CLOSE SHOT, TRADER JOE AT RIGHT OF SCREEN

Superimpose as he speaks -- the left side of the
screen shows beautiful slow-motion shots of
nuclear weapons exploding.

---

[30]   From an episode of *Quantum Leap*, the best time travel television
       show ever. No one but *Quantum Leap* fans will get this; which is
       enough of a reason. "Doctor Sam Beckett, theorizing that one
       could time travel within his own lifetime, stepped into the quantum
       accelerator ... .and vanished."

                         TRADER JOE
                    (gently)
          The bombs <u>fell,</u> Spider. In a nuclear
          rain that lasted for days, through a
          peremptory first strike and a
          retaliatory second strike, through
          retaliatory second and third strikes,
          until only a few lonely submarines
          cruised through the ocean to fire their
          weapons upon an enemy who no longer
          existed, through all of this the bombs
          fell, and fell. Billions died ... in
          fire and blasting shock waves and
          radiation. Billions more died in
          famine, and in the firestorms caused
          when the bombs went down.

TWO SHOT SPIDER AND TRADER JOE

Spider's expression has slowly gone numb. A pause
--

                         SPIDER
          Why are you telling me this?

                         TRADER JOE
          But that was not the worst. Vast clouds
          of dust and earth were blasted into the
          sky. Whole continents disappeared
          beneath them; and temperatures began to
          drop. As the glaciers traveled south,
          the last crumbling pockets of
          civilization vanished.

> (very gently)
> They died, Spider. They all died, all
> the people you're trying to save have
> been radioactive dust for a century.
> <u>This</u> is the human race, right here in
> this small town. And if you leave them
> alone <u>they'll make it!</u>

Trader Joe comes to his feet, beer in one hand,
pacing.

> TRADER JOE
> The people who picked me up in Pasadena
> in 1968, the ones who sent me here to
> make <u>sure</u> these people make it, I don't
> know if you'd recognize them as human.
> They don't look much like us.
> They've ... moved on. But, oh, Spider;
> they're <u>good</u> people, they healed the
> planet we tried to destroy. I can't let
> you destroy <u>them</u> by bringing through
> two hundred people who are already dead.

> SPIDER
> (numbly)
> Why didn't you try to kill me? Why just
> go after the machine?

                    TRADER JOE
          First ... I don't think you belong
          here. But I'm not sure; we've avoided
          this time, the years Angel has her
          children, for fear of disrupting it.
          Maybe you're a part of this matrix;
          there's no record of you but there's no
          record of most of this era. But your
          two hundred people from the past were
          never a part of this matrix and they
          can't be allowed to enter it.

                    SPIDER
          What else?

                    TRADER JOE
               (surely it's obvious)
          Spider Devlin -- killing is <u>wrong</u>.

                    SPIDER
               (rises, in a growing rage)
          Is it. Killing people is wrong ...
          unless they're innocent men and women
          and children about to have a hydrogen
          bomb dropped on them. Then it's not
          your Goddamn problem.

NEW ANGLE -- SPIDER AT RIGHT OF FRAME, TJ AT LEFT

                    TRADER JOE
          I'm an old man, Spider, a lot older and
          a lot tougher than I look. They took me
          from Pasadena a hundred and forty years
          ago -- and my loyalties are not yours.

The gun appears in Spider's hand and he shoots
Trader Joe. WE TRACK as Trader Joe peddles
backward under the hail of bullets. Spider moves

forward, rants like a speed junkie:

                    SPIDER
        Fuck you (BLAM) and your toughness
        (BLAM) and your loyalties and the
        (BLAM) future you came from.

Trader Joe hits the wall behind him and slumps to
the ground. Spider stands over Trader Joe:

                    SPIDER
        Why should _you_ be any luckier than my
        little girls?

He shoots Trader Joe a fourth time. A pause ...
Trader Joe is obviously in great pain --

                    TRADER JOE
        Oh, _God,_ that hurts.

A slug pushes its way out of Trader Joe's
clothing, and rattles to the floor -- and then
the second, third, and fourth, in quick
succession. Trader Joe takes a deep breath, looks
up at Spider:

                    TRADER JOE
        I've been shot by lots better people
        than _you_.

CLOSE ON SPIDER, IN A COLD FURY --

                    SPIDER
        You stay out of my way -- or I'll kill
        Angel. And won't _that_ fuck things up.

He turns to leave, brushing past a couple of
extras who've come to see what the noise is all
about . . . and sometime during all of this, the

hand grenade has vanished.

INT. ANGEL AND MICHAEL'S QUARTERS

A pretty low tech place, but lived in; an attempt
has been made to pretty it up, and it's the
cleanest place we've seen yet. Spider enters;
Angel is sitting on her bed looking at the CDs
and the CD player. She looks up --

                    ANGEL
          You.

                    SPIDER
          Me. Where's Michael?

                    ANGEL
               (returns to CD)
          Guard duty. She usually works nights,
          she has the best night vision. How do
          you make this go?

Spider looks at the player. He sits down on the
edge of the bed, not too close to Angel; he pops
the CD out, flips it over and puts it back in.

                    SPIDER
          You had it upside down. The side with
          the writing on it goes face up. Then
          here, "POWER?" This button has to be
          pushed in. Then you push the "PLAY"
          button.

Angel looks embarrassed.

                    ANGEL
          Oh. I was afraid to touch the Power
          button.

                         SPIDER
          Why?

                         ANGEL
          I was afraid it would catch on fire.

                         SPIDER
          Why?

                         ANGEL
               (still embarrassed)
          That's what our power machine does when
          you turn it on. Tommy keeps trying to
          fix it but every time he puts gasoline
          in it and turns it on, it catches on
          fire. I thought this might be like that.

                         SPIDER
          Who taught you to read?

                         ANGEL
          My mother, before she died. I don't
          read as good as she did, but I read
          better than anyone else ... Tommy can
          read. Almost as good as me.

                         SPIDER
          What sorts of things do you read?

Angel studies Spider with real distrust, then
gets up and goes to a cupboard in the corner. She
opens it --

INSERT -- PANNING SHOT OF SEVEN OR EIGHT BOOKS

Among them are "The Armageddon Blues;" "The Man
Who Folded Himself;" and "A Canticle for

Leibowitz."[31]

RETURN TO PREVIOUS SHOT

Angel takes down two books; a Harlequin Romance,
and an oversized picture book. She sits down on
the bed again, a little closer this time. She
opens the Harlequin --

CLOSE ON ANGEL

-- as she talks the toughness melts away from
her; she speaks with more animation than we've
yet seen from her.

                    ANGEL
          This one is my favorite. It's about
          this woman, Courtney, and she works in
          "teel-vizzion" saying into a "caim-ra"
          what happened that day so everyone
          knows. And there's a man named Blake,
          and at first she just <u>hates</u> Blake,
          because they're going to give him her
          job just because he's a man, but then
          she finds out he's not so bad, and he
          ends up being her boss but that's okay
          because she gets to stay on the "teel-
          vizzion" and now she likes him, and it
          ends up they fall in love.

---

[31]   A classic time travel story (David Gerrold), classic nuclear war story (Walter
       M. Miller) and one of mine – a time travel nuclear war story.

                (reads aloud)
        "Courtney's heart pounded, the blood
        running like molten metal through her
        veins. Blake's lips brushed against her
        neck and she melted against him; he
        crushed her savagely in his embrace,
        and she whispered his name over and
        over again, 'Oh, Blake.'"
                (pause)
        Then they --

TWO SHOT -- FAVORING ANGEL

                        SPIDER
        I can imagine what they then. And after
        that they get married and live happily
        ever after.

                        ANGEL
        You know this story?

                        SPIDER
        Sort of.

                        ANGEL
        "Happily ever after" -- Well ... until
        the Fire, anyway.

Spider nods. He has the picture book open in his
lap and is flipping through it. Angel leans
forward and stops him on a particular picture --

INSERT -- PICTURE OF LANDSCAPE

A valley, a rolling green landscape, shade trees
in FG, mountains in the BG. A reasonable
facsimile of Paradise ...

TWO SHOT SPIDER AND ANGEL

                    ANGEL
     When I was little my mother read to me.
     This was our favorite picture. She said
     this is where you go when you die, a
     place like this. All green and grassy
     and shady, and it's cool in summer and
     warm in winter ... I guess that's where
     she went.

                    SPIDER
     It's nice.

                    ANGEL
     We had grass here when I was little. My
     mother used to water it. When she died
     nobody else would use their water
     rations to keep it alive. JoJo says you
     can't eat grass. I used to, though. I
     would sit on the grass and chew on it.
     It tasted OK ... it was really pretty.

                    SPIDER
          (closing picture book)
     <u>You're</u> pretty.

                    ANGEL
     You're very nice when you try.

                    SPIDER
     I'm different from other men.

                    ANGEL
     Yes.

                    SPIDER
     Better. <u>Bigger.</u>

                         ANGEL
                 (breath quickening)
          Say some poetry for me, the way Blake
          does in the book.

                         SPIDER
          Laugh and dance and shout
          And you can smile then at the news
          Despite that nuclear depression
          And those Armageddon Blues

                         ANGEL
                  (lust derailed)
          That's not very romantic.

Spider shuffles through the CDs on the bed.

                         SPIDER
          Romantic. No, I guess not.

He pops the top on the CD player, and slides a CD
in.

                      SPIDER (CONT.)
          He was romantic, though. He had a voice
          ... like an angel ... his own father
          shot him to death.
                  (he presses PLAY)
          Oh, Marvin --

Marvin Gaye singing "Mercy Mercy Me (the
ecology)" plays over the following:

TRACKING SHOT --

The CAMERA PULLS BACK -- back through the window
of Angel's quarters, out into the center area. WE
TRACK BY Trader Joe, who's standing out in the
darkness, standing perfectly, inhumanly still,

wind tugging at his clothes, watching the window
to Angel's room, watching Spider inside.

MONTAGE OF DEATH --

As "Mercy Mercy Me" continues:

SHOT OF MICHAEL --

PROFILE SHOT: She's standing guard duty, looking
out over the empty desert. WE TRACK AROUND HER
until our POV is out over her shoulder, looking
at the desert she's watching, the ruined
nighttime emptiness, with a faint radioactive
glow.

SHOT OF GRAVE DIGGERS -- INSIDE CITY

Digging a grave, in what we thought was the
"garden" earlier -- it's actually a cemetery in
the center of town.

SHOT OF CORPSE --

It's Clark, the disfigured fellow we saw earlier
standing guard with Michael. They lower him into
the ground.

PANNING SHOT -- EMPTY DESERT

We're outside the walls of the small town now.
Nothing moves. Nothing stirs.

SHOT OF A SMALL TRIBE --

Further from town. Mutants, down in a ravine,
gathered around a flickering fire, roasting on a
spit something that looks vaguely human -- though
with too many arms.

MEDIUM ANGLE -- FAVORING THE ARAB

He sits cross-legged next to the fire, with a
book propped on his knees, reading. A river runs
through their camp and our POV LIFTS AND SWOOPS
OUT OVER IT --

FOLLOWING THE RIVER --

The eddies glow with a phosphorescent light. The
rare dead fish floats through the water, and
birds that have made the mistake of drinking from
this river are scattered dead at the edges of
still pools along the banks.

PULLING UP FROM THE RIVER -- A CRANE SHOT --

Moving up thirty or forty feet -- WE SEE the
river flowing down to the nighttime ocean. Red
foam covers the surface of the ocean -- the beach
is sterile and rocky.

PANNING DOWN THE LENGTH OF THE BEACH --

Death in all directions. Utter emptiness.

MUSIC:

Following the lyrics, "Mercy Mercy Me" ends with
an extended instrumental section.

SUPERIMPOSE ON OCEAN, AND DISSOLVE TO --

-- Angel and Spider, by candle light, on the bed,
Angel leaning back against Spider. He has his
arms around her, and one hand is moving slowly
across her body, tracing up her legs and across
her stomach; she arches her back, and his hands
move up and under her shirt, stroking her breasts

beneath the thin cloth, and we --

FADE TO BLACK. BLACKNESS --

For the last fifteen seconds or so, blackness as
"Mercy Mercy Me" fades away into nothing.

INT. ANGEL'S QUARTERS -- FIRST LIGHT OF DAWN

They're sitting up together in bed; all is still
and quiet.

                         ANGEL
                   (sleepily)
              Play that again. Make it sing.

                         SPIDER
                   (staring sightlessly)
              Batteries are dead.

EXTERIOR TOWN CENTER -- MORNING

Michael walks through the town, bow slung over
her shoulder; and sees Trader Joe standing
motionless in the square facing her quarters.

                         TRADER JOE
              I wouldn't go in there.

                         MICHAEL
                   (unsurprised)
              Really.

Trader Joe shrugs.

                         MICHAEL (CONT.)
                   (sighs)
              I guess I'll go get some breakfast.

EXT. DESERT -- MORNING -- A SMALL GROUP OF MUTANTS

In dirty white robes; a few of them are visibly deformed. They stand in a ragged line, in the middle of nowhere.

ANGLE FROM SIDE -- THE ARAB

He's carrying a book in one hand. We don't see his face.

INSERT -- CLOSE SHOT OF BOOK:

It's a diary -- one of those bound books of empty pages. The handwritten title is, "In The Days Before the Fire."

EXT. DESERT -- WIDE ANGLE, MUTANTS IN FG

The air shimmers ... and a tear appears in reality and the Humvee comes hauling through with Jack Holland at the wheel. He looks startled when he sees what's awaiting him, and the Humvee slides to a halt bare inches in front of the Arab. The Arab doesnt bother to move; he looks up and sees Jack Holland looking down at him through the windshield.

                         THE ARAB
           You, I think, would be Jack Holland.

INT. ANGEL'S QUARTERS -- MORNING

Angel is getting dressed. Spider lies asleep in the bed. Angel wakes him and he sits up.

                    ANGEL
          I have to go. You should get up.
          Michael won't want to sleep with you
          after standing guard all night.

                    SPIDER
               (groggily)
          No problem. I can understand that.

Angel kisses him, slings a bow across her back,
and leaves. Spider sits up at the side of the
bed, staring blankly into the distance. He turns
slightly --

NEW ANGLE -- TRADER JOE IN DOORWAY, LOOKING
PISSED --

There's real hostility here from TJ; Spider's
mostly just fucking with him. Spider yawns --

                    SPIDER
          You didn't vanish. Maybe I am a part of
          this matrix. That would make your
          bosses ... my great-great-great-
          great ... great ... grandchildren. Is
          that right?

                    TRADER JOE
               (almost a whisper)
          Perhaps. I doubt it fills them with any
          pride.

                    SPIDER
          What, no ancestor worship?

                    TRADER JOE
          Spider Devlin, my "bosses" have never
          <u>heard</u> of ancestor worship. They
          wouldn't know what you mean by that.
          Their <u>ancestors</u> destroyed the planet.
          Killed the forests. Killed the oceans.
          Killed each other. I expect you should
          have started with the last part first.

Trader Joe steps toward Spider, and Spider brings
the gun out from under the blankets to point it
at Trader Joe.

                    TRADER JOE
          If your descendants knew your names
          they would use them as curses.

                    SPIDER
          I think I'll try a head shot.

                    TRADER JOE
              (worst insult he knows)
          You're <u>uncivilized.</u>

Trader Joe turns and stalks out.

INT. HALLWAY -- TRADER JOE IN FG, APPROACHING
CAMERA

Spider jumps out into the corridor behind Trader
Joe, FACING THE CAMERA. Trader Joe looks back and
he strikes a pose --

                    SPIDER
          Male frontal nudity!

Trader Joe shakes his head in disgust, walks on.

                         SPIDER
          Jerk.

He turns around and goes back into the room.

INT. EMPTY ROOM -- DAY

They're storing the time machine here. A single
guard sits, bored, next to it. Spider enters and
the guard stands.

                         GUARD
          JoJo said you couldn't touch this.

                         SPIDER
          No problem.

He kicks the guard in the nuts, whacks him with a
huge undercut as the guard folds, smashing his
nose, and follows up by banging the man's head
against the wall, murderously, three or four
times. The whole things takes only a moment, and
Spider leans over and hoists the time machine,
staggering a little, and walks out with it.

EXT. BRIDGE -- LATER -- DAY

One of the extras is standing guard duty. Spider
goes zooming by on his motorcycle, time machine
strapped to the passenger support rise. He waves
at the guard.

EXT. BRIDGE -- LATER -- ANGEL AT GUARD DUTY -- DAY

Angel stands looking out across the desert.
Michael lounges on the ground beside her, eyes
closed, hands laced behind her head. There's no
real tension in the following scene --

                              ANGEL
                    I wonder where he went.

No response.

                              ANGEL
                    Maybe the mutants got him. Maybe he
                    started the time machine.

No response.

                              ANGEL
                    You're not doing a very good job
                    keeping me company today.

                              MICHAEL
                         (sleepily)
                    I'm _tired._ Somebody was in my bed this
                    morning.

                              ANGEL
                    Yeah, well.

Michael opens her eyes.

                              MICHAEL
                    So?

                              ANGEL
                    So what?

                              MICHAEL
                    How was he?

                              ANGEL
                         (thinks about it)
                    Lots of energy.

                    MICHAEL
          I bet.

                    ANGEL
          A little rough.

                    MICHAEL
          (dryly; a little challenge)
          I bet you liked that.

Angel looks over at Michael, lying in the shade.

                    ANGEL
          Yeah. So?

Michael sighs and closes her eyes again,
accepting it.

                    MICHAEL
          So nothing.

Angel shakes her head in bewilderment.

MEDIUM SHOT SPIDER -- LATER -- DAY

Spider's off in the wasteland on the other side
of the bridge, at work on the time machine. He's
got a panel open, has pulled a small keyboard out
and is typing away, reading the diagnostics on an
active matrix LCD.

CLOSE SHOT -- SPIDER -- NEW ANGLE

Spider stares at the FLASHING RED readout. It
shows a diagram with a part HIGHLIGHTED.

                    SPIDER
             (quietly)
          Well, damn.

EXT. DESERT -- GROUP SHOT MUTANTS -- DAY

A dozen mutants sit around a fire. Some look
nearly human; others are hideous. Holland sits at
the fire; the Arab faces him over it, with the
book open in his lap. The Humvee is visible in
BG. We don't get to see the Arab's face, deep
within his hood. His voice is deep and rough.

                    THE ARAB
          "In The Days Before the Fire." It's our
          record of the end of the world, by one
          of the people who caused it, General
          Gerold Friedman.

                    HOLLAND
          You've been expecting me?

                    THE ARAB
          And Spider Devlin. After the war,
          General Friedman went to a ... labor-
          atory ... in Pa-sa-de-na.

                    HOLLAND
          Laboratory. Pasadena. He ... Friedman
          was in charge of the project, if you
          went far enough up the line.

                    THE ARAB
          The laboratory was destroyed. From the
          notes that remained he learned that two
          men had been sent into the future, one
          after the other. Spider Devlin and then
          you.

                    HOLLAND
          That's Friedman's diary?

                         THE ARAB
          It is.

                         HOLLAND
          He was a good man. What happened to him?

                         THE ARAB
                    (gestures around)
          These are his great-grandchildren.

PAN AROUND AT THE WATCHING MUTANTS

FAVORING HOLLAND

The news rocks Holland; it's obvious that he's
horrified and rattled. He gets to his feet slowly
...

                         HOLLAND
          I've got to go. Which way is this
          island Devlin went to?

Holland literally backs away from them -- and one
of the mutants, unfortunately, is standing behind
him. Jack bumps into him, turns and drives a
knife into the man, kicks the mutant to free his
knife, and shoots the mutant twice before he even
hits the ground.

                         THE ARAB
          Wait! Please! We mean no harm!

Holland points his gun at the Arab; the Arab has
his hands spread wide, a "don't shoot" gesture.

                         HOLLAND
          Where the hell did Devlin go?

                        THE ARAB
            East. He went east ... Go.

NEW ANGLE

Holland climbs up into the Humvee and rolls off
into the desert. A couple of the mutants grab
bows and start after him --

                        THE ARAB
            Let him go.
                (gestures at body)
            Strip that. At least you'll have
            something to eat tonight.

INT. TOWN HALL -- LATE AFTERNOON

Tommy, JoJo, Angel, and Michael sit together at
one table. Extras sit at another table; Trader
Joe sits at the same table with the first four,
but slightly apart. The guard Spider attacked
sits nearby.

                        JOJO
            I think we find that time machine and
            smash it. Wreck it good.

                        ANGEL
            (fucking with him)
            You mean wreck it "bad."

                        JOJO
            I don't _need_ your backtalk --

Angel's already tuned him out.

NEW ANGLE -- FAVORING TRADER JOE

He talks over JoJo until JoJo shuts up.

                    TRADER JOE
          I'm not sure you can afford to wreck
          that time machine.

                    ANGEL
          The black hole thing?

                    TRADER JOE
          No, I think he lied about that. That
          device weighs maybe a hundred fifty
          pounds. Too small; if he's telling the
          truth they'd have had to use a non-
          rotating quantum black hole. I don't
          know where they'd have got one, and
          anyway a hole that small would
          evaporate by quantum tunneling if it
          escaped its enclosure.

                    MICHAEL
          Is that good?

                    ANGEL
          It sounds good.

                    TRADER JOE
          Its medium bad -- but that's not the
          point. I don't think Spider Devlin
          belongs here. I don't think he's part
          of this matrix. So far he hasn't
          changed things much, but if he stays,
          he will. Which means he has to go back
          to the time he came from.

NEW ANGLE FAVORING ANGEL

                    ANGEL
          But -- he'll die if he goes back where
          he came from.

                    GUARD WHO SPIDER STRUCK
          Good.

                         TRADER JOE
          More people will die if he doesn't.

PREVIOUS ANGLE

                           JOJO
          Hell with this. Let's just kill him and
          get it over with.

                           ANGEL
          No. No, you won't.

                         TRADER JOE
                      (real fury)
          Haven't you learned anything?

                           JOJO
          But this is --

Trader Joe comes to his feet and slaps JoJo,
open-handed. It knocks JoJo off his chair and to
the floor.

                         TRADER JOE
          Self-defense? Right? You want to kill
          him because he might be a danger to
          you? Never mind trying to talk to him,
          never mind seeing if there's some
          compromise, let's just kill. Solve the
          problem, quick and easy.

JoJo gets up slowly. He's bleeding and he's
enraged -- but Trader Joe, the man he was named
for, stares him down.

                         JOJO
          Why did you hit me?

                       TRADER JOE
          Well, you <u>might</u> have said something I
          didn't feel like hearing.

They stare at one another -- JoJo's still pissed
--

                         JOJO
          Yeah, well, he <u>might</u> do something that
          endangers us!

NEW ANGLE -- FAVORING ENTRANCE TO TOWN HALL

Spider sweeps in.

                        SPIDER
          Yeah yeah yeah. That's a hell of a
          possibility, except the damn time
          machine's broken so I can't go back and
          can't bring my people forward, the
          containment field on the black hole is
          failing and we're <u>all</u> going to die if
          it does, and I need an escort, someone
          who knows the territory, to take me to
          Los Angeles, or anyway what's left of
          it, to find my lab, or anyway what's
          left of <u>that</u>. For parts. And since life
          is short and the charm of y'all's
          company has worn thin and the
          motorcycle only seats two, I thought
          I'd just take Angel.
                    (to Angel)
          Wanna come?

                          ANGEL
          Uh ... I don't think --

                          JOJO
          No! <u>Hell</u> no!

                          ANGEL
              (instantly)
          Sure.

                          SPIDER
          You guys have a map I can look at?

                          ANGEL
              (looks at JoJo)
          Yeah. Come on --

Spider and Angel head back out together.

NEW ANGLE -- FAVORING TRADER JOE AND TOMMY

                          TRADER JOE
          Tommy, my truck's too slow to follow
          them, I need you to help me make a
          sidecar.

                          TOMMY
          What's that?

                          TRADER JOE
          A little cart on wheels, it's got a
          seat in it, we hook it to the
          motorcycle and it runs alongside.

                          TOMMY
          I 'spect. C'mon, let's take a look.

TWO SHOT JOJO AND MICHAEL, FAVORING MICHAEL

Michael sits with her chin propped on her hands,
staring into the distance. She SPEAKS without
looking at JoJo:

                    MICHAEL
          You are _so_ stupid. Someday before you
          die, _maybe,_ you'll figure out the best
          way to get her to do anything is to
          tell her not to.

EXT. WALKWAY AT EDGE OF TOWN -- NIGHT

ANGLE DOWN INTO TOWN -- WE SEE Tommy and Trader
Joe working on the sidecar, welding lights
flashing, casting an eerie light over the scene.

CLOSE ANGLE -- FAVORING TJ IN A STRONG, HARSH
LIGHT

We get a good look at the "welding" tool he's
using -- simply a beam of light that he holds
like a pen, "writing" to weld. Where he writes
with it, metal runs like water. TJ plainly
doesn't notice the amazing heat, spreading the
molten metal with his thumb to get the joins he
wants.

NEW ANGLE -- SPIDER AND ANGEL, ON WALKWAY,
WATCHING

                    ANGEL
          He says he wants to protect me. From
          you. Are you really going to take him?

                    SPIDER
          Why not? With all the trouble he's
          going to ... he's pretty tough. We run
          into trouble, he might be useful.

                         ANGEL
         He says you shot him. With bullets.

                         SPIDER
         A little. He was cruising for it.

                         ANGEL
         A little?

                         SPIDER
         Four times ...
              (waggles hand, estimating)
         ... five.

                         ANGEL
         He says you threatened to shoot me.

                         SPIDER
         I said that to him, but I was lying. I
         wanted something to scare him with ...
         I would never hurt you.

CLOSE ON ANGEL -- VULNERABLE

                         ANGEL
         Do you love me?

                         SPIDER
         I hardly even know you.

                         ANGEL
         Do you?

                         SPIDER
         A little.

                    ANGEL
            (same vulnerability)
I don't love you.

                    SPIDER
I know.

                    ANGEL
I love Michael. She makes me happy. She
cares about me. After my mother died
she was the only one who did care for
me.

                    SPIDER
You don't have to love me; just come on
this trip. You'll enjoy it, if we don't
get killed.

                    ANGEL
... I'll take lots of arrows.

                    SPIDER
There's wonderful things out there in
the world. <u>Amazing</u> things.

                    ANGEL
Really?

                         SPIDER
Things so wonderful, Brian de Palma
would have to steal from <u>ten</u> Hitchcock
movies to show them to you. Why, on
this very continent there are places
where the winds come down in huge
monster hurricanes, rip the roof off
your house, pull you and your little
dog Toto too shrieking and screaming up
into the air, wetting your panties, not
that you wear any ... Tornadoes,
actually. It's tornadoes that take you
to Oz. Hurricanes are a football team
in Miami. I'm from Los Angeles, I never
do get those two straight.

EXT. TOWN -- DAWN, THE NEXT MORNING

Most of the town has assembled to see them off.
Spider's motorcycle has been fitted out with the
sidecar Trader Joe built. Angel is putting a huge
quiver of arrows into the sidecar where Trader
Joe is already sitting.

                         ANGEL
You hold these.

                       TRADER JOE
          (impressed)
My goodness. How many arrows do you
have here?

                         ANGEL
It's ten tens.

                       TRADER JOE
A hundred.

                    ANGEL
          Yeah, whatever.

WE TRACK as she walks over to where Michael is
watching.

                    MICHAEL
          You be careful. You come back.

                    ANGEL
          The tribes are all south, we're mostly
          going north. And I have lots of arrows.
          "A hundred."

                    MICHAEL
               (smiles)
          Trader Joe tell you that?

                    ANGEL
          I knew it.

                    MICHAEL
          Uh-huh. What comes after twelve?

                    ANGEL
               (off-handed)
          A hundred.

                    MICHAEL
          Your momma should have taught you your
          numbers, too.

NEW ANGLE -- TRACKING SPIDER

He walks INTO THE FRAME with his bag slung across
his back, carrying a mug carefully in one hand.
He walks past Michael and Angel, who are kissing
-- stops to admire them, then moves on and sits

down on the bike. A tank of gasoline is strapped
to the back of the passenger bar.

                    SPIDER
          That's a lot of arrows.

                    TRADER JOE
          A hundred.

                    SPIDER
          Would have been my guess.

He takes a drink from the mug.

                    SPIDER (CONT.)
          A little carbonation, you could sell
          this in Westwood at eight dollars a
          bottle.

                    TRADER JOE
          That's beer?

                    SPIDER
          Better than what I brought with me.

                    TRADER JOE
          You're going to drink and drive?

Spider eyes Trader Joe.

                    SPIDER
          I thought you were from the '60s.

                    TRADER JOE
          That was a <u>long</u> time ago.

                    SPIDER
               (still looking)
          You sure you want to come along? With
          an attitude like that I'm entirely
          liable to shoot you again.

                    TRADER JOE
               (settles back in his seat)
          I wouldn't. You might make me angry.

                    SPIDER
          "You wouldn't like me when I'm angry."[32]

                    TRADER JOE
          What?

                    SPIDER
          You missed <u>so much</u> television.
               (watching Angel & Michael)
          They're a really cute couple.

NEW ANGLE -- TRACKING ANGEL

She breaks away from Michael, turns to where
Spider is waiting, and settles in on the bike
behind him. Spider guns the bike, feeds gas to
the throttle --

TWO SHOT -- SPIDER AND ANGEL

Angel leans in close to Spider.

                    ANGEL
          JoJo's gonna smash your time machine
          while we're gone.

----

[32]   Opening sequence of *The Incredible Hulk*.

                         SPIDER
          He'd have to find it first.

WIDE ANGLE -- HARLEY AND SIDECAR

They drive off through the town gates, out onto
the road leading to the bridge. THE CAMERA TRACKS
THEM -- and CONTINUES TO TRACK after the
motorcycle has vanished from the frame, over to
where JoJo stands, compound bow in his hands,
staring grimly after them as they leave. He
speaks to an EXTRA standing beside him.

                         JOJO
          Take the truck. He was only gone two
          hours yesterday, he couldn't have gone
          far. You find out what he did with that
          box.

EXT. "FREEWAY" -- TRACKING -- LATE AFTERNOON

Once this was a road that went somewhere, but
that was a long, <u>long</u> time ago. Conceivably this
was once part of a major freeway. Spider and
company ride down the center of the highway,
making slow time, over what would once have been
the dividing line. The barely recognizable wrecks
of cars, eaten away by a century's worth of ruin,
dot the surface of the highway.

STILL SHOT -- MEDIUM DISTANCE

Spider and company ride through from right to
left. The CAMERA HOLDS STILL after they are
gone ... and after several seconds have passed we
realize that in the deep BG of the frame is a
tiny patch of dust. WE MOVE IN on the patch of
dust, VERY SLOWLY. The patch of dust RESOLVES
into the image of Navy SEAL Jack Holland, walking

across the desert, unaware of the "road" off to
his right, trudging toward town, back in the
direction Spider has just come from.

INT. LAB CONFERENCE ROOM -- 2000 A.D. -- NIGHT

SUPERIMPOSED WITH: <u>22 MINUTES BEFORE THE FIRE.</u>
People are crowded into the room, pushing out the
door. They're watching the large television set.

                    CNN ANCHOR
          I am sorry to report ... we have
          confirmed the launch of missiles from
          within Russia, and from bases in the
          South Pacific. Evidently ... `in
          response ... the United States has also
          launched. We will continue broadcasting
          until Atlanta is struck in, we
          estimate, fourteen minutes. The
          following are our estimates of impact
          times for other cities, assuming those
          cities are not first destroyed by
          cruise missiles or submarine-based
          missiles: Washington D.C., four
          minutes. Chicago, eleven minutes.
          Detroit --

NEW ANGLE -- STUNNED AND SOBBING CROWD

                    GENEVIEVE
          James, how long do we have?

Jimbo doesn't respond -- just stares at the TV.

                    GENEVIEVE
          James!

                         JIMBO
     If we survive the bombing of downtown
     Los Angeles? There'll be at least one
     submarine sent to take out downtown.
     We're sixteen miles from downtown, with
     the hills between ... we might ride
     that out. Warheads for Pasadena won't
     get here until the ICBMs come in ...
     twenty minutes. Twenty-two.

NEW ANGLE -- FAVORING CAROLINE

She's in the corner, crying, holding her children
to her.

EXT. DESERT -- 2100 -- NIGHT

A fire glows. Angel stands guard at the edge of
the illumination, BARELY VISIBLE in the shot.
Spider and Trader Joe sit beside the fire.

                      TRADER JOE
     You really think you're going to find
     anything at your lab?

                        SPIDER
          (shrugs)
     We had six stories beneath the ground.
     Some of our work was military hardened.
     It would have survived anything short
     of a direct strike.

                      TRADER JOE
     You think there wasn't one? On a
     military research installation?

                        SPIDER
     I dunno.

                    TRADER JOE
You think the part you're looking for
is there? That it survived a nuclear
strike and a hundred years of decay?

                    SPIDER
Maybe.

                    TRADER JOE
This is the part that broke when you
kicked it.

                    SPIDER
You have a nasty attitude, you know
that? You got a better suggestion?

                    TRADER JOE
Let me take Angel back to town. Go out
into the desert and die without
bothering these people any more.

                    SPIDER
        (points a finger at him)
There's no talking to you. <u>I'm bringing
them through.</u> You want to stop me? Kill
me. Otherwise shut up.

                    TRADER JOE
I can't kill you and I won't shut
up ... but I <u>can</u> take you forward.

                    SPIDER
What?

                    TRADER JOE
     Take you forward. Take you to the
     future. Our descendants ... they're not
     like us. They can't go among us, so
     they need people like us, people they
     can trust.

                    SPIDER
     And you think they'd trust me? I_
     wouldn't trust me ... of course I
     wouldn't trust anyone.

                    TRADER JOE
     There's no one in the world you trust,
     or admire?

                    SPIDER
     Trust? No. Admire?
          (mutters)
     Well, Buckaroo Banzai.[33]

TJ doesn't hear this last -- he steps on that
line.

                    TRADER JOE
     Spider, you <u>cannot stay here</u> ... and if
     you go home you'll die. But I can take
     you back to the future with me.

Spider bursts out laughing; TJ's a little ticked.

                    TRADER JOE
     What?

---

[33] *The Adventures of Buckaroo Banzai.* Buckaroo is a brain surgeon,
rock star, race car driver, physicist, and superhero. An all-around
stud; Spider would be a big fan.

                         SPIDER
          "Back to the Future." It was a movie.
          After they took you from 1968, didn't
          you ever come back?

                         TRADER JOE
          The period before the Last War is very
          sensitive. They've never let me go back
          to it -- Hey! What happened after I
          left in '68?

                         SPIDER
          You want me to cover thirty years?

                         TRADER JOE
          We have all night.

                         SPIDER
          That's a year every sixteen minutes ...
          I can do that.

EXT. DESERT -- NIGHT

Jack Holland walks through the darkness. He
trudges, staggering, swaying; then he falls.

EXT. DESERT -- NIGHT

Spider and Trader Joe sit next to the ashes of
the fire. Angel's asleep in a blanket on the
ground. Trader Joe has a happy, bemused
expression on his face. Spider's got the bow and
arrows beside him; theoretically he's on guard
duty.

                         TRADER JOE
          Wow. Apollo landed on the moon. We
          actually made it.

                         SPIDER
          That was in 1969. It's my first memory
          of the outside world, sitting on my
          father's lap when the <u>Eagle</u> landed,
          while my father told me how important
          this was ... I was six.

EXT. DESERT -- LONG SHOT SPIDER AND TJ -- TIME
PASSING

EXT. DESERT -- TWO SHOT SPIDER AND TJ -- LATER

Angel is sleeping at the side of the shot. The
fire has guttered down.

                         SPIDER
          Then we elected Ronald Reagan, and it
          was the beginning of the end.

                       TRADER JOE
          You lying bastard. They did <u>not</u> elect
          Ronald Reagan President --

                         SPIDER
                (Academy Award-Winning Rant)
          Twice, by huge margins. He was the
          Forrest Gump of Presidents, and the
          country just loved him to death. He cut
          income taxes on the rich and raised
          spending and left us four trillion
          dollars in debt. The dollar collapsed
          against Asian currencies, our trade
          deficits with Asia reached billions and
          then tens of billions of dollars every
          <u>month,</u> and we poured money into the
          military while our children went hungry
          and our schools collapsed. We were poor
          and we were ignorant and we paid our
          sports stars millions of dollars a
          year. The rich got richer, lobbyists
          bought the government out from under
          us, and finally, a country full of
          people who couldn't reason and wouldn't
          read, who glorified stupidity and
          despised learning, got the leaders they
          deserved and those leaders dragged us
          into a global war we couldn't and
          didn't win.

NEW ANGLE -- GROUP SHOT FAVORING ANGEL

Angel doesn't open her eyes.

                         ANGEL
                    (sleepily)
          You're the angriest person I ever met.

                         SPIDER
          I have more <u>reason</u> to be angry than
          anyone you ever met.

EXT. NEW YORK CITY -- SFX -- NIGHT

Music cues up: Randy Newman, <u>I Love L.A.</u>

Newman singing about New York, and we see
Manhattan at nighttime, after the Fire has come.
The city has been leveled. Flickering fires burn
here and there.

EXT. CHICAGO -- SFX -- NIGHT

He's on to Chicago: Equally devastated -- just
minutes after the nukes.

EXT. THE IMPERIAL HIGHWAY -- LOS ANGELES -- NIGHT

TRACKING a red convertible. This sequence is shot
as a living HALLUCINATION -- bright, surreal
colors. An improbable redhead is in the passenger
seat of the convertible. Someone who looks a bit
like Randy Newman is driving --

The city stretches away in the background as the
convertible rolls down the street -- missiles arc
through the sky overhead.

On "winds hot from the north," a HUGE MUSHROOM
CLOUD appears over downtown Los Angeles.

AERIAL SHOT -- THE EXPLOSION RACES ACROSS LOS
ANGELES

SHOT DOWN WILSHIRE BOULEVARD AS THE SHOCKWAVE
PASSES

SHOT OF IMPERIAL BOULEVARD AS THE SONG CONCLUDES
--

With the line "We gonna ride it til we just can't
ride it no more" ...

The shockwave washes across the scene. The scene flares white.

AERIAL SHOT -- LOS ANGELES IS DEVASTATED

INT. LAB -- 2000 -- TRACKING JIMBO

Walking quickly down corridor, shouting instructions. People are gathered in little groups, holding on to each other.

>   JIMBO
>   We're going to rock hard when L.A. gets
>   it. Stay in the centers of rooms, or in
>   doorways, don't look out the windows.
>   There's hills between us and the flash,
>   but it's still going to be bright
>   enough to blind you --

SFX: EXT. SKY OVER LAB -- AMAZING SCARLET FLASH

INT LAB. -- ANGLE FAVORING JIMBO, STANDING IN A DOORWAY

The frosted windows light up as though searchlights have been put up against them. The light gets brighter, and brighter, and then the ground rumbles, the walls shake. The SCREAMING almost equals the sound of the nuke --

>   JIMBO
>   (yelling over noise)
>   Hang on! We'll make it through this!

EXT. DESERT -- 2100 -- MORNING

A patrol from the town, led by Michael, are sweeping up along the side of the river. An EXTRA speaks:

EXTRA

> This is a waste of time. He coulda hid
> that time thing anywhere.

MICHAEL

> JoJo said to -- what's that?

EXT. DESERT -- LONG SHOT

Jack Holland lying unconscious on the ground.

INT. ROOM -- THREE SHOT MICHAEL, JOJO, AND TOMMY

Michael and JoJo are looking over Holland's
sidearm, knife, etc. -- all his SEAL toys. WE
HEAR a moan.

NEW ANGLE -- FAVORING JACK HOLLAND

Sitting up in bed. He leans back against the wall
behind him -- he looks terrible. An EXTRA brings
him a jug of water. Holland seizes it and drinks
-- pauses, drinks some more, and then pours some
of the pitcher over himself.

MICHAEL

> You're lucky to be alive.

JOJO

> Who are you?

HOLLAND

> Jack --

                         TOMMY
                    (startled)
          Jack? *Jack Indabox?* That lying bastard
          Spiderdevlin said he ate you!

                         MICHAEL
                    (gestures Tommy to shut up)
          What were you doing out there?

                         HOLLAND
          My --

He stops and clears his throat again. It's
obviously painful for him to talk; his voice is
like sandpaper.

                         HOLLAND
          My Humvee ran out of gas.

Michael bursts out laughing. JoJo is disgusted.

                         JOJO
          Another one.

EXT. DESERT ROAD -- TRACKING MOTORCYCLE -- DAY

They're approaching the spot where the lab was
located, a hundred years ago. There's no sign of
it immediately visible -- just an empty hillside.

EXT. HILLSIDE -- FROM SPIDER'S POV

                         SPIDER (V.O.)
          Here. I think this was the place.

                         ANGEL (V.O.)
          There's nothing here, Spider.

EXT. THE LAB PARKING LOT -- 2000 A.D. -- NIGHT

SUPERIMPOSED WITH: *E.T.A. THIRTEEN MINUTES.*

Genevieve walks out through the wide double
doors, through the contamination guards, steps
out into the empty lot; she looks up at the sky.
It's perfectly QUIET, serene. The LOUDEST THING
WE HEAR is the wind --

WIDE ANGLE -- SHOWING SKY TO THE SOUTH --

The remnants of a mushroom cloud has climbed high
enough to be visible, still glowing with the
light of demolished L.A.

SAME SHOT -- 2100 -- DAY

Only the hill is the same. Spider and Co. are
visible in FG.

CLOSE SHOT -- SPIDER LOOKING DEVASTATED AND LOST

                    SPIDER
          I thought ... I thought the building at
          least would still be here.

                    TRADER JOE
          A hundred years is a long time.

Spider dismounts from the bike.

                    SPIDER
          I'm going to take a look around.

TWO SHOT -- ANGEL AND TRADER JOE

Spider walks out of the frame. Throughout most of
this the two don't look at one another -- Angel's

manner is different, a little more mature, a
little more cynical.

                    ANGEL
          Why did you lie to us?

                    TRADER JOE
          About what?

                    ANGEL
          Who you are. Where you came from. When.
          Spider didn't lie to us.

A longish silence --

                    TRADER JOE
          Trying not to interfere.

                    ANGEL
          Oh, but you did. You interfered every
          time you brought us books, or drugs, or
          tools, or food.

                    TRADER JOE
          We wanted you to make it.

                    ANGEL
          But that's *not* true, is it? Or else
          you'd have done more. Brought us
          ammunition, made sure we all knew how
          to read, and do numbers -- even taken
          us to another time where the world ...
          wouldn't be like it is. You could do
          that, couldn't you? Take us all to a
          place where it was green and warm.

                    TRADER JOE
          Yes. We could.

                    ANGEL
     So what you did ... it wasn't so we
     would make it. It was so *you* would make
     it. So the people from your time would
     make it.

                    TRADER JOE
          (very quietly)
     Yes.

                    ANGEL
     I think I prefer Spider. He's trying to
     save his people, and he's honest.

                    TRADER JOE
     He's demented and he's dangerous -- and
     if I was even halfway human anymore
     he'd be a murderer, too.

Now Angel looks at him.

                    ANGEL
     Nobody's perfect.

TRACKING SHOT -- ON SPIDER

He climbs up through a gorge, moving up and
around the hill, pushing his way through
shrubbery. He climbs up onto a large ridge and
looks up over the stretch of hillside. Something
catches his eye, a depression irregular and
squarish and unnatural, buried into the almost
vertical side of the hill.

CLOSE SHOT -- SPIDER AND IRREGULARITY

Spider brushes at the dirt -- then raps against
it. Clods of dirt cascade down on him. He takes a

step back and kicks hard. A chunk of hillside
slides down around him, and he leaps to the side.
A moment passes and he looks back up -- at a
door. He comes back to it, and kicks again and
again, savagely, losing himself in it --

The door gives way. It splinters, rotten with
age, and Spider kicks the splinters out of the
frame -- and peers into a somewhat-lighted
darkness.

Something GROWLS at Spider, low and rumbling.
Spider screams:

                    SPIDER
        Out! Out! *Out of my goddamn laboratory!*

CRANE SHOT -- AROUND EDGE OF HILL --

We see a wolf come scurrying out of a bolt hole,
on the other side of the hill. CAMERA MOVES INTO
THE BOLT HOLE -- we SEE Spider peering into the
ancient room thus exposed, its two entrances
being the door he's just opened, and the hole dug
by the wolf.

INT. LAB -- TRACKING -- 2100

Spider, Angel, and Trader Joe are working their
way down a long dark corridor; they're lighting
their way with a torch, carried by Angel. In the
view of the torchlight we see the crumbled
remains of chairs, consoles -- but no --

                    SPIDER
        No bones. There's no dead people in
        here.

                         TRADER JOE
                  (knows what he's thinking)
              They may have been outside when the
              bombs hit, Spider. Or down below --

Spider walks off to the side, stops next to one
of the control panels with a chair before it. He
whispers:

                          SPIDER
              I was just here. Just a little while
              ago.

He reaches out, touches the ancient chair --

FLASH: INT. CONTROL ROOM, 2000 -- ANGLE ON JIMBO

Jimbo jerks as though someone has touched him
unexpectedly.

                          JIMBO
                  Spider?

RETURN TO PREVIOUS SHOT -- 2100

The chair collapses as Spider touches it, falls
apart. Spider looks startled --

                          SPIDER
              Maybe they went somewhere.

                         TRADER JOE
              I promise you they didn't.

NEW ANGLE -- FAVORING ANALOG WALL CLOCK

Spider stops, looks at the clock. It's smashed
and motionless, like the Hiroshima clocks -- and
it reads *11:11.*

CLOSE SHOT -- CLOCK AT *11:11*

CLOSE SHOT SPIDER -- HORRIFIED

Spider raises his hand to look at his watch --

INSERT MAGIC WATCH -- IT SHOWS *10:59:05 PM.*

WIDE ANGLE -- FAVORING SPIDER -- A LITTLE DAZED

                    SPIDER
          The stairs are this way.

INT. STAIRWELL -- TRACKING FROM ABOVE

They walk down one flight after another, five in
all. We see them descending into darkness, Spider
carrying the torch, Angel behind him, an arrow
strung in her bow. TJ is last.

INT. LAB BASEMENT -- PITCH BLACK

A door is pushed slowly open, with an amazing
CREAK. TORCH LIGHT FLOODS into the room. Spider
enters, followed by Angel and TJ. On one side of
the otherwise dirty, decayed lab is a large steel
door -- streaked with age, but still standing.

CLOSE SHOT -- LARGE STEEL DOOR

                 TRADER JOE (V.O.)
          Let me guess. Spares are on the other
          side of *that.*

GROUP SHOT -- FEATURING DOOR

                    SPIDER
      Yep.

CLOSE ANGLE ON DOOR -- FAVORING SPIDER

Spider leans in close with the torch. We SEE
THREE LOCKS set flush along the edge of the door
frame.

> TRADER JOE
> You're going to kick it open, right?

Spider produces a key ring from his pocket,
inserts the key -- it enters easily -- and turns
it. The key turns smoothly in the hundred year
old lock and WE HEAR THE TUMBLERS CLICK.

NEW ANGLE -- SPIDER LOOKS AT TRADER JOE

> SPIDER
> I *work* here.

INT. LAB -- 2000 A.D.

SUPERIMPOSED WITH: *E.T.A. ELEVEN MINUTES.*
Genevieve addresses the assembled families,
waiting to take a trip through the Gate. Among
them are Caroline and her kids.

> GENEVIEVE
> I can't promise the Gate is going to
> open in time. We have ten minutes
> before the missiles get here. Anyone
> who wants to take their chances, we're
> opening the basement vault. It's six
> floors down and heavily shielded; it'll
> survive anything short of a direct hit.
> If we get the Gate open, we'll call
> down -- and then you have to try to
> make it up six flights of stairs before
> the Gate closes. Your choice.

REACTION SHOT -- WIDE ANGLE CROWD, FAVORING
CAROLINE

Scared and unsure about what to do.

INT. BASEMENT -- 2100 A.D. -- ON SPIDER

The locks are unlocked, keys still hanging in
lock #3, and Spider is *standing* on the wall
beside the door, feet braced, hauling against the
lever that opens the door. Evidently it's jammed
-- and then it opens with a huge SUCKING NOISE,
as the hundred-year old airtight seal is broken.
Spider tumbles to the ground --

THREE SHOT -- INTERIOR OF VAULT NOT VISIBLE

Spider gets to his feet; Trader Joe looks into
the basement vault, then looks away; Angel winces
visibly, and then moves forward with the torch.

SHOT THROUGH DOORWAY

Angel's POV -- she pushes her way into the vault,
and we see two dozen mummified bodies, gathered
in little groups, in the positions they died in.
There are little families of mummies, parents
sitting clutching their mummified children. The
vault is huge -- racks of equipment, still
standing, extend backward through it.

TRACKING SPIDER

He steps forward, stunned, moving in shock. He
looks at the dead surrounding him, walking with
an eerie steadiness toward the back of the vault
-- and then stops at one of the wire-rack
shelves. He reaches up like a robot --

                         SPIDER
          This is it.

He takes down a half dozen rotting ancient
cardboard boxes, his fingers punching through
them despite his gentleness; he opens one and
takes out a circuit board in a transparent
silvery anti-static package. He opens the anti-
static package.

CLOSE ON CIRCUIT BOARD AS SPIDER TAKES IT OUT --

RETURN TO PREVIOUS SHOT

                         SPIDER
          It looks brand-new.

Angel enters the shot.

                         ANGEL
          Let's go.

Spider looks around, dazed, surprised to see her
there.

                         SPIDER
          Sure. No problem.

He turns and walks back out toward the entrance,
where TJ is still waiting, barely visible,
looking almost sinister at the edge of the shot.
Spider stops -- a glint of genuine madness
touches him, and he smiles.

                         SPIDER
            Hey, that's Caroline! I recognize that
            necklace, her ex gave it to her ...
            those must be her kids.

SHOT OF MUMMIFIED CAROLINE, CLUTCHING HER CHILDREN

RETURN TO PREVIOUS SHOT

Spider turns to Angel, still smiling.

                    SPIDER
          Hey, I know those people.

                    ANGEL
               (horrified)
          Let's go *right now*.

                    SPIDER
               (reasonably)
          Okay.

OUTER ROOM -- FOCUS ON DOOR

Trader Joe exits, followed by Angel with the
torch, followed by Spider. Spider, without
looking, without slowing, takes his keys out of
lock #3 and puts them back in his pocket, absent-
mindedly, leaving the door open behind him.

EXT. HILL -- DAY

Spider is just sitting on a low rock, staring
aimlessly off into the desert, with Trader Joe
nearby. Angel is sitting on the motorcycle,
examining one of the circuit boards.

                    SPIDER
          I've been here six days ... and seventy
          minutes have passed for them.

                    TRADER JOE
          How do you know that?

                    SPIDER
     I have a magic watch. It's running on
     Lakers time.

TJ takes a step forward -- really thrown.

                    TRADER JOE
     You've kept your watch running in a
     different time frame?

                    SPIDER
          (explaining calmly, crazily)
     I didn't do anything. It just does
     it ... Pat Riley used to coach the Los
     Angeles Lakers, and then he coached the
     New York Knicks for four years. In all
     those years he never did reset his
     watch from Los Angeles time. I think
     this is like that.
          (pause)
     The watch says seventy minutes have
     passed, so the time flow differential
     is about 125 to one. For every second
     that passes there, two minutes pass
     here.
          (Looks up at TJ)
     I've got to have that Gate open by
     tomorrow ... by noon.

                    TRADER JOE
     Spider, they *died*.

                         SPIDER
                  (very calm)
          Only some. We had lots more people here
          than that. And they died of the
          nanoviruses, not radiation; that vault
          was hardened. So repeat after me,
          Future Boy --

He comes to his feet and gets in Trader Joe's
face. Suddenly he's shaking with rage --

                         SPIDER (CONT.)
          I've got six circuit boards and they
          are goddamn solid state circuitry,
          silicon, no moving parts, and one or
          all of them is going to be working even
          after all this time and *I am bringing
          my people through.*

EXT. DESERT -- TRACKING THE TRUCK -- DAY

JoJo, and Michael, and Jack Holland are in the
flatbed. Tommy and Terry are in the front seat,
driving. Tommy's usual Training Monolog is going
on in the BG. Two gas cans are in the bed with
them; Holland has a terrain map open over his
knees.

                         HOLLAND
          I left the Humvee here. You say they
          went up this road --

                         MICHAEL
          Yeah.

                         HOLLAND
          Headed for the lab, all right.
          Shouldn't be too hard to catch them.

THREE-SHOT FAVORING JOJO

He's got Holland's automatic stuck in his belt,
Holland's knife hanging at his waist.

                    JOJO
          Nobody's following anybody. We're
          getting your Hummer and taking it back
          to town.

                    HOLLAND
              (a nice smile)
          Humvee. Hummers are cheap ripoffs.
          Anyway, you like it, no problem. Plenty
          more stuff like that where I came from.

ANGLE FAVORING MICHAEL --

She looks at Holland with an exquisitely polite
expression, eyes half-lidded. Right.

WIDE ANGLE -- DESERT

The truck pulls to a stop next to the out-of-gas
Humvee. JoJo grabs one of the gas tanks, walks
over the Humvee; Holland removes the gas cap for
JoJo to pour. JoJo does -- pours the contents of
the first can out, then stops.

NEW ANGLE --

                    JOJO
          That's got it --

Holland grabs his automatic, tucked into JoJo's
belt, and fires several times into JoJo's
stomach, *then* pulls the gun free from the belt to
aim it at Michael --

ANGLE FAVORING MICHAEL

JoJo sags to his knees. Michael never trusted
Holland and she's already moving, running past
the truck, pulling her bow from the flatbed as
she passes; from this angle the bulk of the truck
shields her from Holland's fire.

ANGLE FAVORING HOLLAND

He shrugs and puts a slug into the second gas
can, in the flatbed. It explodes, sends flaming
gasoline into the truck's cab, everywhere. Tommy
makes it out of the truck with remarkable
spryness, tumbling to the sand and squirming
around to the front of the truck, for cover --

SHOOTING IN THROUGH WINDSHIELD --

Terry is burning. She SCREAMS --

ANGLE FAVORING HOLLAND

He gets into the Humvee, hits the ignition and
revs the engine. JoJo, from his knees, topples to
the sand.

ANGLE ON MICHAEL

In a fury she strings her bow and fires as
Holland is bringing the vehicle around. The first
arrow bounces of the vehicle. She strings another
arrow, fires again; it passes in through an open
window, embedding itself into the seat behind
Holland. She strings a third arrow -- takes two
steps back and aims it through the empty
windshield of the truck.

                         MICHAEL
          Terry!

The screaming burning woman turns toward Michael;
Michael fires in through Terry's eye socket,
killing her instantly.

NEW ANGLE -- FAVORING TOMMY

He staggers to the spot where JoJo is lying. WE
HEAR the Humvee's engine fade. Tommy sinks to his
knees, pulls JoJo's head into his lap. JoJo's
head rolls loosely, as though he's already
dead ... and then his eyes open and he says in a
normal voice:

                         JOJO
          Daddy?

His eyes stay open and he does not move again.
Michael walks INTO THE FRAME and stands
motionless, bow hanging from one hand. Tears
trickle down Tommy's cheeks and his mouth moves
soundlessly, as though he's trying to speak.

FLASH: NEW ANGLE -- SLOW MOTION

A raven descends from the sky, to perch on JoJo's
shoulder.

EXT. DESERT -- CAMPSITE -- NIGHT

Spider and Angel sit on a blanket facing one
another. Trader Joe stands a good distance off,
looking into the distance.

CLOSE ON SPIDER AND ANGEL

                    ANGEL
          Don't fix it.

                    SPIDER
          I don't know for sure that I can.

                    ANGEL
          Stay with me. Let the past and future
          take care of themselves. Stay with me
          and we'll have children together, and
          we'll teach our children to do numbers,
          to read --

Spider sits up on the blanket and whispers
fiercely, trying to keep this private; Angel sits
up --

                    SPIDER
          I had children! I had two daughters in
          New York City and they were burned to
          ashes and I don't want to fucking hear
          about having children. *My daughters are
          dead!*

He runs out of anger all at once, stares at her
through his tears. He talks into her ear,
intimate speech from a man who can barely find
reason to live.

                    SPIDER (CONT.)
          My daughters were burned up. Do you
          know what that means? A hydrogen bomb
          was detonated within a few miles of
          them. If they were lucky it killed them
          instantly. If they were lucky ... God,
          I hope they were lucky.

He seems to fold in on himself; Angel leans in to
hold him.

CLOSE SHOT OF TRADER JOE --

Spider and Angel are visible in the BG, next to
the fire, holding on to one another. Trader Joe
speaks in a robotic voice, to no one.

                    TRADER JOE
          JoJo is dead and he wasn't supposed to
          die. The future is changing. The future
          is changing.

EXTREME CLOSE UP OF TRADER JOE

In a normal and very scared voice:

                    TRADER JOE
          Oh God.

LONG SHOT -- LATER -- WIDE ANGLE OVER DESERT --
NIGHT

Trader Joe is visible at the far left. A figure
clad in white slowly makes its way into the shot,
from far right. It strides across the desert --
we dolly in on it as closes in on TJ, and see at
last that it's the Arab. They speak fiercely, in
harsh whispers:

                    TRADER JOE
          Go back.

                    THE ARAB
          I'm scared.

                    TRADER JOE
          You should be. It didn't happen this
          way last time.

                    THE ARAB
          Let me help.

                    TRADER JOE
          You're not ready. Go back *now*.

We hold a beat ... and then the Arab seems to
slide backwards out of the shot, as though he's
not actually walking. TJ closes his eyes.

EXT. DESERT -- AERIAL VIEW TRACKING THE ARAB --
NIGHT

The Arab walks along the desert floor, without
looking around at himself. WE PAN UP ...

JUST A GLIMPSE: TWO FIGURES FLOAT IN MID-AIR

A figure dressed in black, and another in white
armor. They're facing one another, hovering in
the night air above the Arab.

EXT. DESERT -- NIGHT -- LATER

The fire has died down. Spider and Angel are
asleep. Trader Joe is standing motionless. It's
very QUIET --

SFX: The Ripple Effect, Feature Showing. The
scene wavers, ripples, as though we are
underwater, odd highlights glinting off of
improbable surfaces. The effect stops -- Spider
rolls out of bed, to his feet with his gun in
hand.

                    SPIDER
          What the hell was *that?*

Trader Joe looks over at him -- in real surprise.

                    TRADER JOE
          You felt that.

                      SPIDER
          I ... I woke up in Los Angeles that
          night and I knew my daughters were
          dead, I knew it before I heard about it
          on the radio. I knew I was going to see
          Angel and she was going to shoot at me,
          I knew JoJo was going to die and I
          would fight the Angel of Death ...
          what's *happening to me?*

Trader Joe looks away again.

                    TRADER JOE
          JoJo did die, and it's caused a time
          change. I don't know how bad yet ...
               (looks around at the night)
          Bad. The wave front rippled uptime;
          it's possible that the people who
          plucked me out of time in 1968 no
          longer exist, never went back to get
          me. If so I'm lost. Secondary effects
          will ripple downtime, and that event
          will cease to have occurred; third
          order waves will ripple back uptime to
          now ... and I will flicker out as
          though a candle had been snuffed, as
          though I had never happened.

It's plain he's not going to answer Spider's
question; Spider takes a breath and accepts it.

                      SPIDER
          How long for the third order wave?

CLOSE SHOT -- TRADER JOE

                    TRADER JOE
          Eight hours, maybe ten.
               (looks back at Spider)
          I can't believe you felt that.

                    SPIDER
          Let's get on the road.

EXT. DESERT -- A HILL -- NEAR DAWN

Angel is looking down the hill. Spider and TJ are
near her.

                    SPIDER
          You're sure?

                    ANGEL
          Of course I'm sure. Can't you see him?
          His truck is still glowing a little bit.

                    SPIDER
               (automatically)
          Humvee. Better than a truck. Cooler.
               (to Trader Joe)
          She sees heat -- infra-red.

                    TRADER JOE
          The human race is evolving at a savage
          pace. If it survives, it's going to be
          very impressive.

                    SPIDER
          That's Jack Holland. If something
          killed JoJo last night, it was probably
          him. It's what he does.
               (beat)
          I'll be right back.

JACK HOLLAND'S CAMP -- NEAR DAWN

There's no fire in this camp; Holland's tough. He
sleeps sitting up in the passenger seat,
ILLUMINATED BY MOONLIGHT. He and the Humvee are
parked up next the edge of a large overhang,
where nobody can easily sneak up on him.

NEW ANGLE --

Spider has ridden up onto the overhang, on his
bike. From his coat we see him pull free the
"grenade" that Trader Joe had earlier. He zooms
up to the cliff's edge, drops it, and zooms away
again.

INT. HUMVEE -- CLOSE ON HOLLAND

Something has awakened him, some sound perhaps.
He has his gun in hand and opens the door to the
Humvee -- looks up --

He lunges back into the Humvee as the cliff above
him comes crashing down around him.

EXT. DESERT -- BRIGHTER MORNING

Spider rolls up to where TJ and Angel wait with
the sidecar, pulls to a stop. From the rise
they're waiting on, we can see the landslide that
has covered Jack Holland.

                          ANGEL
               Did you kill him?

                          SPIDER
               Close enough. He ain't going to dig out
               from under that.

                         TRADER JOE
              He'll die if we leave him here.

                           ANGEL
       Good.

                          SPIDER
       People like him killed the entire world
       ... never did like that son-of-a-bitch.

INT. HUMVEE -- MORNING

It's almost entirely dark inside the Humvee.
Jack's trying to get the door to open; it won't
budge. He's started the engine and is trying to
get the Humvee to move; *it* won't budge. Suddenly
he HEARS VOICES -- two of them, male and female,
and he kills the engine:

                   UNIDENTIFIED FEMALE
       I must protect this sequence of events.

                    UNIDENTIFIED MALE
       I won't fight you.

Abruptly WE HEAR rocks moving -- huge boulders
shifting position. Abruptly one monstrous chunk
of rock is thrown aside and the Jack Holland can
see through the windshield again. A figure in
white armor passes in front of the windshield --
too quickly to make out any detail. More of the
rocks shift position -- and Jack Holland guns the
engine and pushes his way free of the landslide.
He kicks the door open and comes out with his gun
in hand, looking for the people who belong to the
voices -- and there is, of course, no one there.

EXT. MORNING -- FAR END OF BRIDGE -- DAY

No one's standing guard at the other end. Spider, with Angel and Trader Joe following him, scrambles his way down a steep bank, to the water.

                    TRADER JOE
          You hid it in *salt water?*

                    SPIDER
          I was sure no one would look there.

                    TRADER JOE
     But --

Spider finds an almost invisible string, tied to a rock, and pulls on it. The strings pulls a rope up from beneath the surface of the river, and Spider pulls on the rope hard, hauling it in, and slowly, the Gate comes into sight. He speaks while pulling:

                    SPIDER
          Seals are air and watertight. When we
          sent the first Remote Gates through we
          were worried about bringing back
          contaminants from the future. So we
          designed them to be airtight, and made
          them tough enough to withstand
          sterilization after they came back.
          They're pretty indestructible once
          they're sealed.

ROAD LEADING TO BRIDGE -- LATER -- DAY

This is the area on the other side of the bridge -- the desert side, not the town/island side. It's surrounded by decaying buildings, the shells of dead cars, lots of good-cover stuff like that.

Spider sits in the BG with the Gate, now opened

up again. He's swapping boards in and out. In the
FG, Trader Joe talks to Angel. TJ is sweating and
looks horribly gray.

                    ANGEL
          I keep thinking I should shoot him.

                    TRADER JOE
          That's one solution.

                    ANGEL
          I don't know if I can.

                    TRADER JOE
          There's not enough food. There's not
          enough water. He brings those people
          through with their guns ... JoJo won't
          be the last one who died. Just the
          first.

He smiles at Angel, with an effort.

                    TRADER JOE
          JoJo was a beautiful child.

CLOSE ON SPIDER AND GATE --

He rips one of the circuit boards out, tosses it
toward the water, swearing. He pulls another
board from the wrapping, slides it in and presses
one of the switches ...

INSERT -- SHOT OF CONTROL PANEL

The schematic showing that board goes from red to
yellow.

RETURN TO PREVIOUS SHOT

Spider looks at his watch.

INSERT WATCH -- IT SHOWS *11:10:57 PM.*

As we watch, the second reading advances to *:58.*

RETURN TO PREVIOUS SHOT

                    SPIDER
          (to himself)
     We're gonna make it, we're gonna *make*
     it. Oh, I am *so* handsome. There ought
     to be a law against being this good at
     anything.
          (thinks about it)
     Maybe there is.
          (laughs)
     Fuck 'em.

Spider jumps to his feet, turns toward Angel and
Trader Joe, singing a little song under his
breath --

NEW ANGLE -- GROUP SHOT

                    SPIDER
     I'm too sexy for this song --[34]

We HEAR TWO SHOTS -- Trader Joe staggers and
falls; Angel, standing near the bank above the
water, goes over the edge and we HEAR THE SPLASH.
Spider whirls, gun in hand --

Jack Holland pops up from behind some convenient
piece of cover. He's got the drop on Spider --
Spider sees him, freezes, and without being told,

---

[34]   *I'm Too Sexy*, by *Right Said Fred*. It would be very cool to have the
       actual song sort of echo in on Spider as he sings this, a little sur-
       real reverb ... .

drops the gun.

                    HOLLAND
               (very cool)
          Hello, Spider.

                    SPIDER
               (equally cool)
          Suck my Big American dick, Jack.

                    HOLLAND
               (advancing carefully)
          You're not my type.

                    SPIDER
          I knew I should have just blown you and
          that Goddamn Humvee up.

                    HOLLAND
          What did I ever do to you, Spider?

WIDE SHOT OF WATER --

The sloping bank obscures this spot from Jack's
view -- Angel pulls herself from the water, one-
handed, hanging on to her bow with a death grip.
She tries to stand, collapses. She's been shot in
the leg. Lying on the ground, with the buzz of
Jack and Spider's conversation BARELY AUDIBLE in
the background, she uses her knife to cut a slice
out of her already too-short skirt, to make
herself a tourniquet.

TWO SHOT -- WIDE ANGLE -- SPIDER AND HOLLAND

Jack circles Spider. Jack spreads his hands wide:

                    SPIDER
You dress badly, vote Republican, and
you've never even *heard* of the Church
of the Sub-Genius. And you just shot my
girlfriend.

                    HOLLAND
How's our time machine, Engineer?

                    SPIDER
I'm a Master Programmer, dickhead, and
it's not *our* time machine, it belongs
to me and the dozen other people who
built it. You're just the experiment we
were gonna send through with it.

                    HOLLAND
        (smiles)
So how is *your* time machine?

                    SPIDER
Beats me. I just put a hundred year old
circuit board into it. If it doesn't
work, I have one more.

                    HOLLAND
Turn it on.

                    SPIDER
Diagnostics aren't finished yet, Jack.
See the yellow light? Yellow isn't
green. I turn it on right now and we've
guessed wrong and everything within a
mile of here's going to get sucked into
a nonrotating quantum black hole.

Spider takes several steps toward Jack, speaking
very slowly and clearly, as though to an idiot.

                    SPIDER (CONT.)
          See? Yellow. If your fascist parents
          had let you watch Sesame Street as a
          child, you'd know how important the
          colors are. Red means *stop,* yellow
          means *go slow,* green means --

Spider's within a pace of Jack -- Jack has the .
45 pointed at Spider's face. In BG we see Angel
crawling up over the bank, up onto the roadway, a
tourniquet around her upper leg. She crawls over
Trader Joe, who is staring up into the sky, eyes
all whites, and staggers painfully to her feet,
using her bow as a crutch. She reaches her feet
and stands with blood oozing from her shot thigh,
leg scarlet, and reaches over her back for an
arrow. Jack and Spider SPEAK OVER each other.

                    JACK
          I'll shoot you, Spider.

                    SPIDER
          -- reflex time!

Angel fires. The arrow slices its way through the
air and strikes Jack high on the shoulder as
Spider slaps the gun away and Jack pulls the
trigger; the bullet WHINES AWAY. Spider kicks
Jack in the nuts, kicks him in the face as he
goes down.

                    SPIDER (CONT.)
                  (screaming)
          Reflex time! In the time it takes your
          eyes to see I've slapped the gun --

He kicks Jack some more, keeps kicking him as
Jack rolls across the ground, breaking the arrow
off as he rolls --

                    SPIDER (CONT.)
     -- to send the message across your
     optic nerve to your pitifully slow
     brain --

More kicking. Jack's still got the gun in his
hand.

                    SPIDER (CONT.)
     -- for your brain to interpret the
     message, for the nerve signals to go
     back down your arm to your hand and
     pull the trigger, the gun's not pointed
     at the *target* anymore --

Jack rolls again, comes out of it lying flat on
the ground and shoots Spider in the right knee.
Blood sprays everywhere.

TIGHT SHOT -- SPIDER AND JACK HOLLAND

Spider collapses atop Jack, blood spurting from
his ruined knee, scarlet red in the sunshine.
Spider's SCREAMING, so is Jack; Spider grabs the
wrist of Holland's gun hand; Holland is now lying
on the ground with Spider's back to him, and he
leans in and bites Spider in the neck. Spider
jerks forward, then slams back, butting his head
back against Jack's face, never letting go of
Jack's gun hand.

ON ANGEL -- AS SHE STRINGS ANOTHER ARROW

CLOSE ON SPIDER AND JACK --

Spider head butts Jack again and again, smashing
the back of his head into Jack's nose. In the
fighting, Spider's magical Pat Riley Watch gets
ripped off, drops into the dust. Jack rolls *over*

Spider, gets in front of him, and knees Spider --
not in the groin, but on his shot knee. Spider
screams, an almost WHISTLING NOISE, and lets go
of Jack's gun hand. Jack scrambles up, back to
his feet, hunched over a little, and aims down at
Spider.

CLOSE SHOT TRADER JOE

His eyes roll back, pupils appearing.

WIDE ANGLE SHOT -- SLOW MOTION

Angel is stringing her bow. Jack Holland is
standing over Spider, about to kill him.

INSERT -- SHOT OF GATE'S CONTROL PANEL

It blinks green and says: READY.

NIGHT SKY OVER L.A./PASADENA -- 2000 A.D.

SUPERIMPOSED WITH: *E.T.A. 20 Seconds*. We watch
streaks of light crossing the sky, missiles
incoming.

INT. CONTROL ROOM -- NIGHT

                    JIMBO
              (shouts)
          Lock! We have a lock, we have a lock!

                    GENEVIEVE
          Cycle the Gate.

WIDE SHOT -- SLOW MOTION BY BRIDGE -- DAY

INSERT SPIDER'S POV -- ECU HOLLAND'S GUN HAND --

Staring into the barrel. Holland pulls the
trigger and a spinning, deformed bullet, moving
so slowly we can see it revolve, leaves the
barrel on a cushion of smoky gas.

TWO SHOT -- SPIDER AND JACK HOLLAND

The world seems to have come to a complete halt.
The bullet hangs in mid-air. Spider, moving in
slow motion, rolls out of the path of the bullet,
steps in on the completely motionless Jack
Holland --

RESUME NORMAL MOTION -- TWO SHOT SPIDER AND JACK

Spider jams Jack's gun, still in Jack's hand, up
Jack's nostril. Jack Holland pulls the trigger
and blows his own face off. He falls OUT OF FRAME
-- Spider pulls the gun free from Holland's hand
as he falls, and then staggers toward the time
machine, dragging his ruined leg, bright red
blood still flowing freely down his calf.

WIDEN SHOT

Spider reaches the time machine. Angel stands
with an arrow on her string, the arrow not quite
pointed at Spider, facing him. Trader Joe sits up
slowly and uses a conveniently placed rock, or
girder, or something, to get to his feet.

NEW ANGLE -- TRADER JOE AND ANGEL IN FG

Spider's in BG; Trader Joe's got his back to the
CAMERA and we see that the bullet blew a hole in
him the size of a man's fist. It's not bleeding
-- there's no bone or muscle there -- it looks
vaguely like the inside of a tree, blown open,
the "fibers" moving slightly as we watch.

RETURN TO PREVIOUS ANGLE

                         SPIDER
                  (bleeding to death)
            I think you saved my life.

                       TRADER JOE
            I probably ... shouldn't have.

Spider reaches toward the time machine --

NEW ANGLE -- FAVORING ANGEL

She brings her bow up slightly.

CLOSE ON SPIDER

With his left hand Spider pulls free a small
control pad, connected to the rest of the time
machine by a 10-foot coiled cord. The LED on it
glows green; there's a single button on it --
Spider looks up at Trader Joe and Angel.

WIDE ANGLE SHOT -- PULLING BACK

The shot pulls back to reveal that every extra
we've seen yet, all the townspeople, have
surrounded the site. They're standing beside and
behind the available cover, pointing their bows
-- at Spider.

SHOT OF MICHAEL -- WITH A STANDARD BOW

Not far from Angel; arrow pulled all the way
back; she's shaking, fighting to hold the bow
steady.

RETURN TO WIDE ANGLE SHOT

Angel is still not quite pointing her arrow at
Spider.

                         ANGEL
     Please don't.

CLOSE ON TRADER JOE

                       TRADER JOE
               (whispers)
     Your time is over. This is their time
     -- let them have it.

WIDE ANGLE SHOT -- FAVORING SPIDER AND TJ

Michael is visible in the shot; Spider is not
quite pointing the automatic at Trader Joe. He's
shaking too, with pain, with rage and fear.

                         SPIDER
     There isn't one person on the other
     side of that Gate who I care about as
     much as I care about Angel. But they're
     innocent. They have children. They
     don't *deserve* this!

                         ANGEL
     They're not innocent, Spider. *They
     started the Fire!*

                         SPIDER
     No they didn't, they were victims,
     that's all, they were in the wrong
     time, good people in the wrong time.
     You have to let them come through.

                    MICHAEL
              (shouts)
         We'll *all* die if they do. There's no
         water for them. There's no food!

                    SPIDER
         They're *scientists!* They built this
         machine! They can clean the water, they
         can teach you to plant crops that'll
         grow year round, they can --

                    TRADER JOE
         -- teach them how start the Fire again?

                    ANGEL
         We don't need that. We don't need
         them ... or you.

CLOSE SHOT -- SPIDER

His expression is purely that of a man who feels
betrayed, again, the final betrayal in a life
that's been full of them. He stares at Angel --

                    SPIDER
         Fuck you all.

He pulls the trigger and toggles the switch for
the Gate.

WIDE ANGLE --

Spider's shot strikes Trader Joe between the eyes.

MEDIUM SHOT --

Spider is at the far left of the frame; Trader
Joe is in the middle; Angel is at the far right.
Angel lets fly, lets loose an arrow driven by a

compound bow at full extension. TJ staggers into
its path and it passes *through* him, strikes
Spider and drives him back up against the Gate,
which has begun shimmering, glowing.

WIDE SHOT -- EVERYONE FIRING ARROWS --

ANGLE FAVORING SPIDER

Another arrow strikes Spider, and another, and a
fourth, he staggers around, gets the gun pointed
at Angel --

SPIDER'S POV -- POINTING GUN AT ANGEL

A beat.

RETURN TO PREVIOUS ANGLE

Spider *fires,* strikes Angel dead on, killing her,
blowing her back like a rag doll, as another
round of arrows arc in on him, fifth and sixth
and seventh arrows striking him --

SFX: SLOW FLARE TO WHITE

A ROCKY BEACH -- THREE SHOT -- IN BLACK AND WHITE

Spider, Angel, and Trader Joe walk along a rocky
shore together. There is an eerie, otherworldly
sense to the shot, foggy and dark, but not grim,
not cold. They are the only visible things in the
world; the beach trails off into UTTER DARKNESS
in both directions. The sea itself seems to
vanish, twenty yards out.

They walk along for a good distance, Trader Joe a
few steps ahead of Spider and Angel. They're all
clean, nicely dressed, uninjured. Trader Joe is

wearing clothes that are almost robes, nothing
like what we've seen him in before; Spider and
Angel are both dressed in clean, appropriate
clothes.

TWO SHOT -- SPIDER AND ANGEL

Walking beside each other. They barely seem aware
of themselves, and not of each other. Spider
shakes his head, as though to clear it, and Angel
glances over at him.

TRACKING SHOT -- FOLLOWING ALONG AS THEY WALK

                    TRADER JOE
          If someone had ever told me I'd end my
          life here, with you two, I think I'd
          have called him a liar.

Trader Joe comes to a stop, glances back at them.

                    TRADER JOE (CONT.)
          Do you know who you are?

                    SPIDER
          I'm Joseph Devlin ... Spider.

                    ANGEL
          My mother ... named me Angel.

                    TRADER JOE
          Do you remember why you're here?

                    ANGEL
          Where are we?

                    TRADER JOE
          It's just another place. Some people
          think it's where you go when you die. I
          don't know about that ...
                    (looking around)
          Though I think I'm going to find out,
          soon enough.

                    SPIDER
          Are we dead?

Trader Joe examines Spider, *looks* at him --

                    TRADER JOE
          That would make it so much easier,
          wouldn't it? No more decisions. No more
          fear, no more rage ... no. You're not
          dead, Spider Devlin. Not yet. Do you
          want to be?

                    ANGEL
          No!

                    SPIDER
          I don't know.

                    TRADER JOE
          I brought us here. I stopped the moment
          we were just in. And I can undo it. I
          can take us back through the moment,
          and let you try again.

                    SPIDER
          How the hell can you do that? *What are
          you?*

                    TRADER JOE
              (smiles)
     I'm a dead man who knows how to do
     things you don't: in fifteen hundred
     years the human race has learned some
     things.
              (smile fades)
     Think about it, Spider. You didn't mean
     to kill this girl, I know that, but you
     did. You don't mean to hurt those
     people back there, but if the Gate is
     activated, two hundred people from your
     time are going to come charging through
     with guns --

                    SPIDER
              (whispers)
     Yes.

                    TRADER JOE
     People on both sides will die. And the
     survivors ... *won't* survive. Not after
     combat, not in the fragile ecosystem
     they're trapped in. You're dead, and so
     is Angel, and so are her children,
     which is the entire human race. Do you
     want the human race to survive?

                    SPIDER
     I don't know.

                    ANGEL
     I want children. I want to teach them
     to read and watch them grow up. Is that
     so much to want?

                    TRADER JOE
          She led a hard life. She bore seven
          children, two of them died at birth,
          and another two died young. But she
          raised the three children who *did* live,
          the children the whole human race is
          descended from, a thousand years from
          now.
               (voice grows harsher)
          She raised them well, and they loved
          her, and when they were raised she
          walked into the desert and died there.
          A hard life and a hard death. But she
          deserves the chance.

                       SPIDER
          I don't know that the human race is
          worth saving.

                    TRADER JOE
               (a terrible severity)
          You hate yourself, and perhaps you
          should. *But better things than you are
          coming.*

It strikes Spider as nothing else has --

                    TRADER JOE
          Better things than you are coming. Let
          them live.

                       SPIDER
          Undo the moment.

WIDE ANGLE -- THREE SHOT

In BG we see a pair of white seagulls fly over

the ocean together[35], mirroring the shot at the movie's beginning.

SAME SHOT, NEW ANGLE -- FAVORING TJ

Trader Joe begins to glow. A brilliant light washes outward from him, until he glows like an angel --

EXT. ROAD BY BRIDGE -- A MOMENT IN TIME

Spider stands by the time machine, gun in one hand, switch in the other. The scene IS FROZEN -- black and white.

CLOSE SHOT MAGIC WATCH -- BLACK AND WHITE

Showing *11:11:11 PM* ... .and then we RESUME NORMAL MOTION, SOUND AND COLOR flood back in -- and the watch starts moving normally. *11:11:12, 11:11:13, 11:11:14 --*

NEW ANGLE FAVORING SPIDER

Spider drops the gun, drops the switch that controls the Gate. The moment holds, and holds --

ANGLE FAVORING TRADER JOE

-- Trader Joe smiles at Spider, and his eyes roll straight up into his skull. He collapses as though boneless.

---

[35] *Jonathan Livingston Seagull* – there's a scene where Fletcher Seagull flies into a granite cliff, and "dies," as Spider and Angel and TJ just have. I always envisioned the world Fletcher found himself in – "a strange, strange sky," we're told – as looking something like this. The two seagulls flying away over the ocean are Jonathan and Fletcher, of course.

ANGLE FAVORING MICHAEL -- STARTLED BY TJ'S
MOVEMENT

She takes one step forward and lets fly.

SPIDER'S POV -- APPROACHING ARROW -- SLOW MOTION

In extreme slow motion we watch the arrow
approach --

MEDIUM SHOT ON SPIDER -- SLOW MOTION

Spider twists away, turning, one hand moving
forward to close around the shaft of the arrow,
in a replay of the opening scene with Angel ...
and the arrow slides gracefully through his hand,
strikes him in the chest, and pierces him front
to back.

CLOSE SHOT SPIDER -- RETURN TO NORMAL SPEED

He looks down at the arrow that's pierced him.
Slowly, with his right hand he touches the front
of the shaft -- reaches behind himself with the
left hand, and touches the tip of the arrow
protruding from his back.

WIDE ANGLE --

No one else shoots.

CLOSE ON MICHAEL

She can't believe what she's done.

ANGLE ON SPIDER

Blood seeps out around the arrow, front and back,
down the white dress shirt he's been wearing the

whole movie, bright red in the sunshine. He turns slowly toward the time machine, moving like a drunk, trembling with shock.

WIDE ANGLE -- FAVORING SPIDER

The bows come up again to point at Spider ...

                    ANGEL
          Don't.

We're not sure if she's talking to Spider, or to the people pointing arrows at him -- Spider collapses forward, onto the time machine and --

-- the glow touches him *before* he reaches the time machine, and he and the time machine vanish.

EXT. HILL/BUILDING -- WIDE ANGLE -- DAY

Overlooking the sight of the battle we just witnessed. The Arab is looking down on the mess; we see him in a side shot.

                    THE ARAB
          This isn't right, this isn't *fair*. No
          man should have to know so much about
          his own death.

He takes a step forward, throwing back the hood -- and we see that it's a young, long-haired Trader Joe, probably not long after he was taken from the year 1968.

                    TRADE JOE/ARAB
            This isn't *fair*.

EXT. TOWN -- CRANE SHOT SHOOTING FROM ABOVE -- EVENING

We're back at the spot where Clark was buried,
earlier. Three new graves have been dug; the one
in the middle is being filled in as we watch; we
see that it's JoJo. (Terry's in the first grave,
already buried.) Two extras are busy laying
Trader Joe down in the second grave; Tommy stands
nearby, numb with grief. Michael and Angel stand
by the edge of the third grave. Michael is
helping Angel stand; her leg is splinted and
heavily bandaged.

                   ANGEL
     Do you know if we still have any grass
     seeds left?

                MICHAEL
      (shakes her head)
   I don't know.

CRANE SHOT BEGINS CIRCLING TO THE RIGHT[36] --

Angel and Michael (or, more precisely, the
cemetery) are still the focus of the shot, as the
shot begins to track around them.

                  ANGEL
     We should check. I think Trader Joe
     would like grass growing over him.

Michael nods. The two men burying Trader Joe
start shoveling dirt in over him.

                MICHAEL
   Where do you think he went?

---

[36] We build a track around the cemetery, and put the camera on that, tilted
high enough that we don't see the track. Since the cemetery is in the center
of town, as the camera makes loops of the cemetery, we'll also see, in BG, the
rest of the town.

                    ANGEL
          Home. I guess he went home. He wanted
          to die. He hurt so bad.

                    MICHAEL
          I'm sorry.

A shovelful of dirt covers Trader Joe's face.

                    ANGEL
          You probably did the right thing ...
          let's go inside.
                    (she looks around)
          It's going to be cold tonight.

CAMERA HAS LOOPED ENTIRELY AROUND --

-- to the beginning of the previous shot. Angel
and Michael are gone, and the scene darkens into
nightfall. The SHOT CONTINUES TO LOOP --

                    SPIDER DEVLIN (V.O.)
          It *was* cold that night ... and other
          nights. But they survived, and their
          children survived, and humanity
          survived. And outgrew the ignorance and
          the fear that had nearly killed it. And
          in time the race matured, and became a
          thing that humans of another time would
          not have recognized, as it moved on to
          other and greater pursuits ... and put
          away at last the concerns of childhood.

LOOP CONTINUES -- THE TOWN BRIGHTENS.

In daylight. Looking no different -- except that
there's a little patch of green, where Trader Joe
was laid to rest.

PLAY *THE LAST RESORT,* BY THE EAGLES

LOOP CONTINUES -- TOWN AT NIGHT

Lights glow at the guard towers.

LOOP CONTINUES -- RAINING OVER CEMETERY -- DAY

The grass is really growing around Trader Joe's
grave.

LOOP CONTINUES -- BACK TO START -- FAVORING ANGEL
-- DAY

A new grave is being dug in the cemetery. The
grass covers the cemetery. Angel, Michael, and an
extra (a man, the father of the dead child) stand
by the grave. Angel kneels to place the shrouded
form in the grave.

LOOP CONTINUES -- FAVORING MICHAEL

We see that Michael is holding the hand of
another young child, who's watching the
proceedings without comprehension.

LOOP CONTINUES -- BACK TO START -- DAY

The town architecture is visibly different --
there's a new building being raised, off to one
side. The grass has grown to cover much of the
town center. Everything is cleaner.

LOOP CONTINUES -- ANGEL AND CHILD COME INTO SIGHT

The construction is visible in the BG, with
Michael overseeing it. Angel is visibly older,
perhaps thirty. She has a child in her lap, and
is reading to her, while two other children play

together not far away.

LOOP CONTINUES -- FAVORING MICHAEL

Overseeing the building; also older, she looks
happy.

LOOP CONTINUES -- BACK TO START -- DAY

A family shot: Michael is being laid into the
ground. She looks to be perhaps fifty years old,
and Angel looks to be about forty. Most of the
town is out for the burial -- Michael is being
buried next to Trader Joe's grave. Angel has
three children with her -- the oldest of them a
boy of about eighteen, the youngest a girl of
about thirteen.

LOOP CONTINUES -- INTO A CLOSER SHOT OF ANGEL

Tears pour down her cheeks, but otherwise she is
expressionless. She's older ... wrinkles around
her eyes, streaks of gray in her hair. The green
grass has covered every place that used to be
dirt, everywhere in town.

LOOP CONTINUES -- LATE AFTERNOON

Angel's son is in the garage, working on Spider's
Harley, stripping it down. He's about twenty now,
two years older than in the last shot.

LOOP CONTINUES -- ANGEL'S DAUGHTER COMES INTO VIEW

We see his assistant, Angel's daughter, now
fifteen. She's reading to him, aloud, from a
Harley Davidson maintenance manual, turning the
fragile pages with great care; she's plainly
related to him, and to Angel --

LOOP CONTINUES -- ANGEL COMES INTO VIEW

Sitting with a middle-aged man -- the father of
her children, simply one of the extras we saw
throughout. They're sitting together on a porch
outside the "town hall," now rebuilt, repainted
-- Progress. Angel is about 40 and her hair is
completely white. The LOOPING CAMERA slows, slows
... and stops on Angel. WE DOLLY IN:

                         ANGEL
                    (quiet pride)
              Listen to her read.

GRAVEYARD -- CRANE SHOT -- NIGHT

SHOOTING DOWN into the graveyard. It's covered
with grass, end to end. Angel is lying on the
grass, by herself, staring up into the night sky.

CLOSE SHOT -- ANGEL

She's lying with her head resting against a
headstone that says "MICHAEL ALTALOMA." A book
lies facedown on the ground beside her -- the
picture book Angel showed Spider, twenty years
ago.

BRIDGE LEADING OUT OF TOWN -- TRACKING -- NIGHT

Angel walks slowly, without hurry.

LONG SHOT -- DESERT -- NIGHT

Angel walks on and on through the darkness.

YET ANOTHER SHOT OF ANGEL WALKING --

We SEE HER BREATH frosting around her in the

bitter cold.

LONG SHOT -- A ROCKY AREA

Angel sits among the rocks, barely moving.

CLOSE SHOT

Angel stares into the darkness. Waiting for the
end.

EXT. TOWN -- NIGHT

Angel's daughter walks into the street outside
the town hall. She has a flashlight in one hand
-- she speaks to someone OFF-CAMERA:

                    DAUGHTER
          Have you seen Mom?

EXT. DESERT -- NIGHT

Angel looks up, looking into the distance. The
reflection of a light touches her eyes --

LONG SHOT -- DESERT -- ANGEL'S POV

A white light appears in the distance. With
Angel, we watch it approach ... watch it resolve
into Spider Devlin.

("LAST RESORT" BEGINS A LONG INSTRUMENTAL BRIDGE)

TWO SHOT -- SPIDER AND ANGEL

He appears to be perhaps a few years older ...
but quite aside from that, he's *changed*. The
bitterness, the angry set of his features, has
vanished. And he's glowing ... glowing in the

darkness.

                    ANGEL
          Are you an angel, Spider Devlin?

Spider smiles at her.

                    SPIDER
          No. Just a man who knows how to do some
          things I didn't used to.

                    ANGEL
          You went forward. You didn't go back at
          all.

                    SPIDER
          I was *taken* forward -- forward a very
          very long way. Would you like to come
          home with me?

He holds out his hand; she takes it. They step
into --

FRAME FLARES WHITE

LONG SHOT -- EXT. HILLSIDE -- DAY

Spider and Angel step through the Ripple Effect,
and find themselves looking down onto a green
valley, at the foot of a huge chain of mountains,
the western slopes of the Sierras; the valley
beneath them is filled with trees and high grass.
At the far end of the valley, BARELY VISIBLE, are
a small set of buildings.

                    ANGEL
          You went back and got your people.

                    SPIDER
          Some of them. The ones I could. A few
          thousand, in the cities right before
          the bombs hit. They ... the people who
          taught me. That was all they would let
          me take. Where their disappearance
          wouldn't affect the course of events.
          Your children grew up, and their
          children and their children ... and one
          day *their* children didn't need this
          planet any more. This place. They said
          we could have it.

                    ANGEL
               (softly)
          We?

Spider's smile is so filled with joy, with a
wisdom born of loss, that it is almost painful.

                    SPIDER
          My children ...
               (sudden grin)
          And their mother ... come home with me,
          Angel. I'd like you to meet my
          daughters.

SOMEWHAT LATER -- WIDE ANGLE

They've walked halfway down the mountain when two
little girls appear, running toward them.

NEW ANGLE -- FAVORING GIRLS

Spider is vaguely visible in the FG. Two little
girls, six and eight, run toward him.[37] Spider

——————————————

[37] This is the shot we used at the beginning of the movie, when Spider learns
      New York has been nuked, back when we think his girls are dead.

grabs them and lifts them up, spinning around
with them, and Angel and Spider and the children
walk away down the hill together --

ROLL CREDITS --

The sky darkens, and we pick out in the distance
the lights of a small town, nestled in the
foothills of a mountain. OUR POV lifts up, moving
and turning a hundred and eighty degrees, passing
over the small forms of Angel and Spider Devlin
and the children, heading out toward the ocean.
We hit the coast, flying low, crossing pristine
empty stretches of beach, out into the ocean,
across the darkening waters, flying straight into
the scarlet setting Sun --

The Sun expands to fill the frame and all we can
see now is the DEEP SCARLET LIGHT --

SLOW, *SLOW* FADE, SCARLET TO BLACK:

BLACKNESS -- END CREDITS -- "THE LAST RESORT"
ENDS.

In the SILENCE, we hear the faint sound of
CRICKETS CHIRPING, of FOOTSTEPS. The BEAM OF A
FLASHLIGHT strikes down into the darkness --

SHOT OF THE PICTURE BOOK

-- lying on Michael's grave. Angel's daughter
reaches down INTO THE FRAME, picks the book up.

SHOOTING OVER DAUGHTER'S SHOULDER --

Lit by the flashlight, the picture Angel showed
Spider, all those years ago ... it's upside down,
and she ROTATES IT UNDER THE CAMERA --

MOVING IN SLOWLY ON THE PICTURE BOOK AS IT ROTATES

... and now visible, in the picture's distance, are Spider and Angel, with Spider's daughters a little ahead of them, walking into the end of time together.

HOLD SHOT --

THE END